GOETHE
THE SORROWS OF YOUNG WERTHER
ELECTIVE AFFINITIES
NOVELLA

GOETHE

Selected Poems
Faust I & II
Essays on Art and Literature
From My Life: Poetry and Truth (Parts One to Three)
From My Life: Campaign in France 1792 • Siege of Mainz (Part Four)
Italian Journey
Early Verse Drama and Prose Plays
Verse Plays and Epic
Wilhelm Meister's Apprenticeship
Conversations of German Refugees & Wilhelm Meister's
Journeyman Years or The Renunciants
The Sorrows of Young Werther • Elective Affinities • Novella
Scientific Studies

Collected Works in 12 Volumes

Goethe's Collected Works, Volume 11

Johann Wolfgang von
GOETHE

The Sorrows of Young Werther
Elective Affinities
Novella

Edited by David E. Wellbery
Translated by Victor Lange and Judith Ryan

Princeton University Press
Princeton, New Jersey

Published by Princeton University Press, 41 William Street,
Princeton, New Jersey 08540
In the United Kingdom by Princeton University Press, Chichester, West Sussex
Copyright © 1988 Suhrkamp Publishers, New York, Inc.

Reprinted in paperback by arrangement with Suhrkamp Publishers

Library of Congress Cataloging-in-Publication Data
Goethe, Johann Wolfgang von, 1749–1832.
[Selections. English. 1995]
The sorrows of young Werther ; Elective affinities ; Novella /
Johann Wolfgang von Goethe ; edited by David E. Wellbery ;
translated by Victor Lange and Judith Ryan.
p. cm. -- (Princeton paperbacks)
Originally published: New York : Suhrkamp, 1988. (Goethe's
collected works ; v. 11
ISBN 0-691-04346-9 (alk. paper)
1. Goethe, Johann Wolfgang von, 1749–1832. Translations into
English. I. Wellbery, David E. II. Lange, Victor, 1908– .
III. Ryan, Judith, 1943– . IV. Title. V. Title: Elective
affinities. VI. Title: Novella. VII. Series: Goethe, Johann
Wolfgang von, 1749–1832. Works. English. 1994 ; v. 11.
PT2026.A1C94 1994. Vol. 11
[PT2027.A2]
831' .6 s—dc20   95–36759
[833' .6]

First Princeton Paperback printing, 1995

Printed in the United States of America

1 3 5 7 9 10 8 6 4 2

Contents

Prefatory Note

The translations of *The Sorrows of Young Werther* and *Novella* by Victor Lange were first published in 1949 by Rinehart & Co., New York and Toronto. They have been thoroughly revised for the present edition. Judith Ryan's translation of *Elective Affinities* appears here for the first time.

D. E. W.

THE SORROWS OF YOUNG WERTHER

Translated by Victor Lange

I have carefully gathered together, and present to you here, everything I could discover about poor Werther's story. You will thank me for doing so, I'm sure. His mind and character can't but win your admiration and love, his destiny your tears.

And you, good soul, who feels the same urge as he, take comfort from his sufferings and let this book be your friend if, due to fate or personal responsibility, you can find no closer one.

Book One

How glad I am to have got away! My dear friend, what a thing is the heart of man! To leave you, from whom I was inseparable, whom I love so much, and yet be happy! I know you will forgive me. Were not all my other attachments especially designed by fate to torment a heart like mine? Poor Leonore! And yet I was not to blame. Was it my fault, that, while the capricious charms of her sister afforded me agreeable entertainment, a passion for me developed in her poor heart? And yet—am I wholly blameless? Did I not encourage her emotions? Did I not find pleasure in those genuine expressions of Nature, which, though but little amusing in reality, so often made us laugh? Did I not—but oh! what is man, that he dares so to accuse himself? My dear friend, I promise you, I will change; I will no longer, as has always been my habit, continue to ruminate on every petty annoyance which fate may have in store for me; I will enjoy the present, and the past shall be for me the past. No doubt you are right, my best of friends, there would be far less suffering among mankind, if men—and God knows why they are so constituted—did not use their imaginations so assiduously in recalling the memory of past sorrow, instead of bearing an indifferent present.

Will you be so kind as to inform my mother that I shall look after her business to the best of my ability, and shall give her news about it soon. I have seen my aunt, and find that she is very far from being the disagreeable person our friends make her out to be. She is a lively, temperamental woman, with the best of hearts. I explained to her my mother's grievances with regard to that part of the legacy which has been withheld from her. She told me the reasons why she had done it, and the terms on which she would be willing to give up the whole, even to do more than we asked. In short, I don't wish to write further on this subject now; just tell my mother that all will be well. And in this trifling affair I have again found, my dear friend, that misunderstandings and neglect cause more mischief in the world than malice or wickedness. At any rate, the latter are much rarer.

For the rest, I am very well off here. Solitude in this terrestrial para-
dise is a wonderful balm to my emotions, and the early spring warms
with all its fullness my often-shivering heart. Every tree, every bush is a
bouquet of flowers; and one might wish himself transformed into a cock-
chafer, to float about in this ocean of fragrance, and find in it all the food
one needs.

The town itself is disagreeable; but then, all around it, nature is inex-
pressibly beautiful. This induced the late Count M. to lay out a garden
on one of the sloping hills which intersect here and form the most lovely
valleys. The garden is simple and you feel upon entering that the plan
was not designed by a scientific gardener, but by a man who wished to
give himself up here to the enjoyment of his own sensitive heart. I have
already shed many a tear to the memory of its departed master, in a
summer house which is now reduced to ruins, but was his favorite
retreat, and now is mine. I shall soon be master of the garden. The
gardener has become attached to me within the few days I have spent
here, and, I'm sure, it will not be to his disadvantage.

May 10

A wonderful serenity has taken possession of my entire soul, like these
sweet spring mornings which I enjoy with all my heart. I am alone and
feel the joy of life in this spot, which was created for souls like mine. I
am so happy, my dear friend, so absorbed in the exquisite sense of tran-
quil existence, that I neglect my art. I could not draw at all now, not a
single line, and yet I feel that I was never a greater painter than in such
moments as these. When the lovely valley teems with mist around me,
and the high sun strikes the impenetrable foliage of my trees, and but
a few rays steal into the inner sanctuary, I lie in the tall grass by the
trickling stream and notice a thousand familiar things; when I hear the
humming of the little world among the stalks, and am near the countless
indescribable forms of the worms and insects, then I feel the presence of
the Almighty Who created us in His own image, and the breath of that
universal love which sustains us, as we float in an eternity of bliss; and
then, my friend, when the world grows dim before my eyes and earth
and sky seem to dwell in my soul and absorb its power, like the form of a
beloved—then I often think with longing, Oh, if only I could express it,
could breathe onto paper all that lives so full and warm within me, that
it might become the mirror of my soul, as my soul is the mirror of the
infinite God! O my friend—but it will destroy me—I shall perish under
the splendor of these visions!

May 12

I don't know whether some deceiving spirits haunt this spot, or whether it is the ardent, celestial fancy in my own heart which makes everything around me seem like paradise. In front of the house is a spring—a spring to which I am magically bound like Melusine and her sisters. Descending a gentle slope, you come to an arch, where, some twenty steps lower down, the clearest water springs forth from the marble rock. The little wall which encloses it above, the tall trees which surround the spot, and the coolness of the place itself—everything imparts a pleasant and yet chilling sensation. Not a day passes that I do not spend an hour there. The young girls come from the town to fetch water—the most innocent and necessary employment, but formerly the occupation of the daughters of kings. As I sit there, the old patriarchal idea comes to life again. I see them, our old ancestors, forming their friendships and doing their courting at the well; and I feel how fountains and streams were guarded by kindly spirits. Whoever cannot share in these feelings has never enjoyed a cool rest at the side of a spring after the hard walk of a summer's day.

May 13

You ask if you should send my books. My dear friend, for the love of God, keep them away from me! I no longer want to be guided, animated. My feelings are so stormy by themselves! I need a cradlesong to lull me and this I find abundantly in my Homer. How often must I still the burning fever of my blood, for you have never seen anything so unsteady, so restless, as my heart. But need I confess this to you, my dear friend, who have so often witnessed my sudden transitions from sorrow to joy, and from sweet melancholy to violent passion? I treat my heart like a sick child, and gratify its every fancy. Do not repeat this; there are people who would misunderstand it.

May 15

The poor people hereabouts know me already, and love me, particularly the children. When at first I associated with them, and asked them in a friendly way about this and that, some thought that I wanted to ridicule them and treated me quite rudely. I didn't mind this; I only felt keenly what I had often noticed before. People of rank keep themselves coldly aloof from the common people, as though they feared to lose something by the contact; while shallow minds and bad jokers pretend to descend to their level, only to make the poor people feel their impertinence all the more keenly.

I know very well that we are not all equal, nor can we be; but I am convinced that he who avoids the ordinary people in order to keep his respect, is as much to be condemned as a coward who hides from his enemy because he fears defeat.

The other day I went to the spring and found a young servant girl, who had set her pitcher on the lowest step, and looked round to see if one of her companions were near to place it on her head. I went down and looked at her. "Shall I help you?" I said. She blushed deeply. "Oh no, sir!" she exclaimed. "Come now! No ceremony!" I replied. She adjusted her headgear, and I helped her. She thanked me and walked up the steps.

May 17

I have made all sorts of acquaintances, but have as yet found no one I really like. I don't know what attraction I possess for people, so many of them like me, and attach themselves to me; and then I feel sorry when the road we go together takes us only a short distance. If you ask what the people here are like, I have to say: like everywhere else! The human race is a uniform lot. Most people work the greater part of their time just for a living; and the little freedom which remains to them frightens them so that they use every means of getting rid of it. Such is man's high calling!

But they are a good sort of people. If I occasionally forget myself, and take part in the innocent pleasures which are granted us humans and laugh and joke, for instance, round a well-set table with genuine freedom and sincerity, or arrange a walk or dance or suchlike, all this has a really good effect upon me; only I have to forget that there lie dormant within me so many other qualities which wither unused, and which I must carefully conceal. Ah! How this torments my heart!—And yet to be misunderstood is the fate of a man like me.

Oh, that the friend of my youth is gone! Oh, that I ever knew her! I might say to myself, "You're a fool to seek what is not to be found on this earth." But she was mine. I have felt that heart, that noble soul, in whose presence I seemed to be more than I really was, because I was all that I could be. God! Was there a single power in my soul that remained unused? And in her presence could I not develop fully that intense feeling with which my heart embraces Nature? Wasn't our life together a perpetual interplay of the subtlest emotions, of the keenest wit, whose many shades, however extravagant, bore the stamp of genius? Ah! the few years by which she was my senior brought her to the grave before me. I shall never forget her, never forget her steady mind or her heavenly patience.

A few days ago I met a young man named V., a frank, open fellow, with most pleasing features. He has just left the university, does not think himself overwise, but still believes he knows more than other people. He has worked hard, as I can tell from many indications and, in short, is well informed. When he heard that I sketch a good deal, and that I know Greek (two unusual accomplishments for this part of the country), he came to see me and displayed his whole store of learning, from Batteux to Wood, from De Piles to Winckelmann: he assured me he had read all of the first part of Sulzer's "Theory" and possessed a manuscript of Heyne's on the study of antiquity. I let him talk.

I have also become acquainted with a very worthy fellow, the district judge, a straightforward and sincere man. I am told it is a delight to see him in the midst of his nine children. People especially talk about his oldest daughter. He has invited me to visit him, and I will do so soon. He lives at one of the prince's hunting lodges, an hour and a half walk from here, which he received permission to occupy after the death of his wife, since it was too painful for him to live in town at his official residence.

I have also come across a few curious eccentrics who are in every respect annoying and most intolerable in their demonstrations of friendship.

All the best! This letter will please you; it's quite factual.

May 22

That the life of man is but a dream has been sensed by many before; and I too am always haunted by this feeling. When I consider the narrow limits within which our active and our cognitive faculties are confined; when I see how all our energies are directed at little more than providing for mere necessities, which again have no further end than to prolong our wretched existence; and then realize that all our satisfaction concerning certain subjects of investigation amounts to nothing more than passive resignation, in which we paint our prison walls with bright figures and brilliant prospects; all this, Wilhelm, strikes me silent. I turn within myself and find there a world, but one of imagination and dim desires rather than of distinctness and living power. Everything swims before my senses, and I smile and dream my way through the world.

All learned teachers and tutors agree that children do not understand the cause of their desires; but no one likes to think that adults too wander about this earth like children, not knowing where they come from or where they are going, not acting in accord with genuine motives, but ruled like children by biscuits, sugarplums, and the rod—and yet it seems to me so obvious!

I know what you will say in reply, and I am ready to admit it, that those are happiest who, like children, live for the day, amuse themselves with their dolls, dress and undress them, and eagerly watch the cup-board where Mother has locked up her sweets; and when at last they get what they want, eat it greedily and exclaim, "More!" These are cer-tainly happy creatures; and so are those others who dignify their paltry employments, and sometimes even their passions, with high-sounding phrases, representing them to mankind as gigantic achievements per-formed for their welfare and glory. Happy the man who can be like this! But he who humbly realizes what all this means, who sees with what pleasure the cheerful citizen converts his little garden into a paradise, and how patiently even the unhappy people pursue their weary way beneath their burden, and how all alike wish to behold the light of the sun just a minute longer; yes, such a man is at peace, and creates his world out of his own soul—happy, because he is a human being. And then, however confined he may be, he still preserves in his heart the sweet feeling of liberty, and knows that he can quit this prison whenever he likes.

May 26

You know from long ago my way of settling down somewhere, of select-ing a little place of my own in some pleasant spot, and of putting up in it. Here, too, I have discovered such a comfortable spot which delights me.

About an hour from the town is a place called Wahlheim.[1] It is inter-estingly situated on a hill; and by following one of the footpaths out of the village, you can have a view of the whole valley below you. A kindly woman keeps a small inn there, selling wine, beer, and coffee; and she is extremely cheerful and pleasant in spite of her age. The chief charm of this spot consists in two linden trees, spreading their enormous branches over the little green before the church, which is entirely surrounded by peasants' cottages, barns, and homesteads. Seldom have I seen a place so intimate and comfortable, and I often have my small table and chair brought out from the inn, and drink my coffee there, and read my Hom-er. Chance brought me to the spot one fine afternoon, and I found it perfectly deserted. Everybody was in the fields except a little boy about four years of age, who was sitting on the ground, and held between his feet a child about six months old; he pressed it to his breast with both arms, so that he formed a sort of armchair for him; and notwithstanding the liveliness which sparkled in his black eyes, he remained perfectly still. The sight charmed me. I sat down upon a plow opposite them, and sketched with great delight this little picture of brotherly tenderness. I

---

[1] The reader need not take the trouble to look for the place thus designated. We have found it necessary to change the names given in the original letters.

added the neighboring hedge, the barn door, and some broken cart wheels, just as they happened to be there; and after an hour I found that I had made a well-formed and interesting drawing, without adding the slightest thing of my own. This confirmed me in my resolution of adhering in the future entirely to Nature. Nature alone is inexhaustible and can form the great artist. Much may be alleged in favor of rules; about as much as may be said in favor of middle-class society: an artist modeled after them will never produce anything absolutely bad or in poor taste, just as a man who observes the laws of society and obeys decorum can never be a wholly unwelcome neighbor or a real villain. Yet, say what you will of rules, they destroy the genuine feeling of Nature and its true expression. Do not tell me that I am "too severe, that rules only restrain and prune superfluous branches, etc." My good friend, I shall give you an analogy. It is like love. A warmhearted youth becomes strongly attached to a girl: he spends every hour of the day in her company, lavishes all his energies and his fortune to prove that he is wholly devoted to her. Along comes some Philistine, a man of position and respectability, and says to him: "My good young friend, to love is human; but you must love within human bounds. Divide your time: devote a portion to business, and give the hours of recreation to your sweetheart. Calculate your assets; and from what is left after expenses you may buy her a present, only not too often—on her birthday, and such occasions, etc. etc." If he were to follow this advice, he might become a useful member of society, and I should advise every prince to give him a post; but it is all over with his love, and, if he be an artist, with his art. O my friend! why is it that the torrent of genius so seldom bursts forth, so seldom rolls in full-flowing stream, overwhelming your astounded soul? Because, on either side of this stream sedate and respectable fellows have settled down; their arbors and tulip beds and cabbage fields would be destroyed; therefore in good time they have the sense to dig trenches and raise embankments in order to avert the impending danger.

May 27

I notice now that I fell into such raptures, declamations, and parables that I forgot to tell you what became of the meeting with the children. Absorbed in my artistic contemplations, which I described so inadequately in yesterday's letter, I had been sitting on the plow for two hours. Toward evening a young woman, with a basket on her arm, came towards the children, who had not moved all that time. She called out from a distance, "You are a very good boy, Philip!" She greeted me. I thanked her, rose, and went over to her, inquiring if she were the mother of those pretty children. "Yes," she said. And, giving the elder half a roll, she took the little one in her arms and kissed him with a mother's tenderness. "I left my baby in Philip's care," she said, "and went into the town with my eldest boy to buy some bread, some sugar, and an earthen dish for his cereal." I saw these various things in the basket, from which the cover had fallen. "I shall make some broth tonight for my little Hans (which was the name of the youngest): that wild fellow, the big one, broke my dish yesterday while he was scrambling with Philip for what was left of the food." I inquired about the eldest and she had scarcely told me that he was chasing a couple of geese in the field when he came running up and handed Philip a hazel switch. I talked a little longer with the woman and found that she was the daughter of the schoolmaster and that her husband was gone on a journey into Switzerland after some money that had been left to him by a relative. "They tried to cheat him," she said, "and would not answer his letters; so he has gone there himself. I only hope he hasn't had an accident; I haven't heard from him since he went." I left the woman with regret, giving each of the children a penny and one too for the youngest, to buy some wheaten bread for his broth when she went to town next; and so we parted.

I tell you, my dear friend, when my thoughts are all upset, the sight of such a creature as this quiets my disturbed mind. She moves in a tranquil happiness within the confined circle of her existence; she makes the best of it from one day to the next; and when she sees the leaves fall, she has no other thought than that winter is approaching.

Since that time I have often gone out there. The children have become quite used to me; and each gets his bit of sugar when I drink my coffee; and in the evening they share my sour milk and bread and butter. They always get their pennies on Sundays, and if I do not get there after evening service, my landlady has orders to give it to them.

They are quite at home with me, tell me everything; and I am particularly delighted when I can watch their passions and the simple outbursts of their desires when some of the other village children are with them.

It took a good deal of effort to allay the apprehensions of the mother, lest (as she says) "they should inconvenience the gentleman."

May 30

What I said the other day about painting is equally true of poetry. We must only know what is really excellent and dare express it; and that is saying a great deal in a few words. Today I watched a scene which, if I could only convey it, would make the most beautiful idyll in the world. But why talk of poetry and scenes and idylls? Can we never take pleasure in Nature without thinking of improving it?

If, after this introduction, you expect something grand or magnificent, you are sadly mistaken. It was only a peasant lad who aroused this interest. As usual, I shall tell my story badly; and you, as usual, will think me extreme. It is again Wahlheim—always Wahlheim—that produces these unusual things.

There was a coffee party going on outside the house under the linden trees. The people did not exactly please me and, under one pretext or another, I lingered behind.

A peasant lad came from an adjoining house and busied himself with the same plow which I had sketched the other day. I liked his manner, spoke to him, and inquired about his circumstances. We became acquainted, and as is my way with people of that sort, I was soon on fairly familiar terms with him. He told me that he was in the service of a widow and did fairly well. He spoke so much of the woman, and praised her so, that I could soon see he was desperately in love with her. "She is no longer young," he said, "and was treated badly by her former husband; now she does not want to marry again." From his account it was so evident what beauty and charms she possessed for him, and how ardently he wished she would choose him to extinguish the memory of her first husband's faults, that I should have to repeat what he said word for word in order to relate the genuineness of the poor fellow's attachment, love, and devotion. It would require the gifts of a very great poet to convey the expression of his features, the harmony of his voice, and the fire of his eye. No, words cannot portray the tenderness of his every movement and his manner. Whatever I might say would only be clumsy. His fears that I might misunderstand his position with regard to the woman or question the propriety of her conduct especially touched me. How charming it was when he spoke of her figure, her body, which although without the graces of youth, had won and attached him to her! I can only recall it within my innermost soul. Never in my life have I seen or imagined in this purity such intense desire or such ardent affections. Do not scold me if I say that the mere recollection of this innocence and truth burns in my very soul; that this image of fidelity and tenderness haunts me everywhere; and that I consume myself in longing and desire, as though kindled by the flame.

I must try to see her as soon as I can; or perhaps it is better that I should see her through the eyes of her lover. When I actually see her, she might not appear as she now stands before me; and why should I spoil so sweet a picture?

June 16

Why haven't I written? You who pretend to know so much and yet you ask such a question! You should be able to guess that I am well—that is to say—in a word, I have made an acquaintance who has won my heart: I have—I don't know.

To tell you in orderly fashion how I met this most enchanting of

creatures will be a difficult task. I am happy, ecstatic, and therefore not
a very reliable reporter.

An angel! Nonsense! Everybody says that of the girl he loves. And yet
I find it impossible to tell you how perfect she is, or why she is so per-
fect: enough—she has completely captivated my soul.

So much simplicity with so much intelligence—so kind, and yet so
resolute—a mind so calm, and a life so active.

But all this wretched stuff and pale abstraction tells you not a single
concrete thing about her. Some other time—no, not some other time,
now, this very instant, I will tell you all. Now or never. For just between
us, since I began my letter, I have been three times on the point of
putting down my pen, saddling my horse, and riding out there. I swore
this morning that I wouldn't, and yet now I rush to the window every
few minutes to see how high the sun is. . . .

I couldn't help it—I had to go out to her. I've just come back,
Wilhelm; I shall have my supper and write to you. What a delight it is
for my soul to see her in the midst of those dear, happy children—her
eight brothers and sisters!

But if I go on like this you will be no wiser at the end of my letter than
you were at the beginning. Listen, then,—I'll force myself to go into
detail.

I wrote to you the other day that I had become acquainted with the
district judge, and that he had invited me to visit him soon at his her-
mitage, or rather in his little kingdom. But I neglected to do so, and
perhaps might never have gone, if chance had not revealed to me the
treasure concealed in that retired spot.

Some of our young people had arranged a ball in the countryside,
which I agreed to attend. I invited for the evening a pretty and pleasant,
but rather dull sort of girl from the neighborhood. It was agreed that I
should hire a carriage and take my partner and her cousin. On the way
we were to pick up Charlotte S. My companion told me, as we drove
along through the park to the hunting lodge, that I should make the
acquaintance of a very beautiful girl. "Take care," added the cousin,
"that you don't fall in love." "What do you mean?" I said. "She is
already engaged to a very worthy man," she replied, "who is gone to
settle his affairs upon the death of his father and apply for a lucrative
position." All this seemed of little interest to me.

When we arrived at the gate, the sun was about to set behind the hills.
The air was sultry and the ladies expressed their fears of an approaching
storm, as masses of greyish clouds were gathering on the horizon. I re-
lieved their fears by pretending to be weather-wise, although I myself
had a feeling that our party might be interrupted.

I had got out and a maid who came to the gate requested us to wait a moment—Mademoiselle Lottchen would be with us presently. I walked across the yard to the house, and when I had gone up a flight of steps in front and had opened the door, I saw before me the most charming scene I have ever witnessed. Six children, from eleven to two years old, were running about the room, surrounding a lovely girl of medium height, dressed in a simple white frock with pink ribbons. She was holding a loaf of dark bread in her hand, and was cutting slices for the little ones all round, in proportion to their age and appetite. She performed her task with such affection and each child awaited his turn with outstretched hands and artlessly shouted his thanks. Some of them ran off at once to enjoy their supper, while others, of a gentler disposition, walked to the gate to see the strangers and to look at the carriage in which their Charlotte was to drive away. "Forgive me for causing you the trouble of coming for me and for keeping the ladies waiting, but dressing and making arrangements for the house while I'm out made me forget my children's supper. They don't like to take it from anyone but me." I paid her some indifferent compliment, but my whole soul was absorbed by her air, her voice, her manner. I had scarcely recovered from my surprise when she ran into her room to fetch her gloves and fan. The young ones looked at me questioningly from a distance and I approached the youngest, a delicious little creature. He drew back and Charlotte, entering at that moment, said, "Louis, shake hands with your cousin." The little fellow obeyed willingly and I could not resist giving him a hearty kiss, notwithstanding his dirty little face. "Cousin?" I said to Charlotte, as I offered her my hand, "do you think I deserve the happiness of being related to you?" She replied, with a quick smile, "Oh! I have such a number of cousins that I should be sorry if you were the most undeserving of them." In taking leave, she impressed upon her next oldest sister, Sophie, a girl of about eleven, to take good care of the children, and to say hello to Papa for her when he came home from his ride. She enjoined the little ones to obey their sister Sophie as they would herself, and some did promise that they would. But a little fair-haired girl, about six years old, said, "Sophie isn't you, Charlotte, and we like you best." The two eldest boys had climbed up behind the carriage and, at my request, she permitted them to accompany us to the edge of the wood, if they promised to sit still and not to tease.

We were hardly seated, and the ladies had greeted one another, making the usual remarks upon each other's dress, especially their bonnets, and upon the company they expected to meet, when Charlotte asked the coachman to stop and told her brothers to get down. They insisted upon kissing her hand once more, which the eldest did with all the delicacy of a youth of fifteen, but the other in a lighter and more impetuous manner. She asked them again to give her love to the children, and we drove off.

The cousin inquired whether Charlotte had finished the book she had sent her the other day. "No," said Charlotte; "I don't like it; you can have it back. And the one before that wasn't much better." I was surprised, upon asking the title, at her reply.[2] I found so much character in everything she said, every word seemed to brighten her features with new charms, with new rays of intelligence, which appeared to increase gradually, as she felt that I understood her.

"When I was younger," she said, "I loved nothing so much as novels. Nothing could equal my delight when, on Sundays, I could settle down quietly in a corner and enter with my whole heart and soul into the joys or sorrows of some Miss Jenny. I don't deny that they still possess some charms for me. But I read so seldom that I prefer books that suit my taste. And I like those authors best who describe my own situation in life—and the friends who are about me—whose stories touch me with interest because they resemble my own domestic life, which is perhaps not absolutely paradise, but on the whole a source of indescribable happiness."

I tried to conceal the emotion which these words aroused, but it was of slight avail; for when she incidentally expressed her opinion of "The Vicar of Wakefield," and of other works,[3] I could no longer contain myself but said what I thought of it; and it was not until Charlotte had addressed herself to the other two ladies that I remembered their presence, and observed them sitting silent and astonished. The cousin looked at me several times with a mocking air, to which, however, I paid no attention.

We talked of the pleasures of dancing. "If it is a fault to love it," said Charlotte, "I confess that I prize it above all other amusements. Whenever anything worries me, I go to my old squeaky piano, drum out a quadrille, and then everything's all right again."

How I gazed into her rich dark eyes as she spoke; how my own eyes hung on her warm lips and fresh, glowing cheeks, how I became lost in the wonderful sense of what she said—so much so, that I often did not hear her actual words! In short, when we arrived at the dance, I alighted from the carriage as if in a dream and was so lost in the dim world around me that I scarcely heard the music which came from the brightly lit ballroom.

---

[2] We feel obliged to suppress this passage in the letter so as not to offend anyone; although no author need pay much attention to the opinion of one simple girl or that of an unbalanced young man.

[3] Though the names of some of our native authors are omitted, whoever shares Charlotte's approbation will feel in his heart who they are, if he should read this passage. And no one else needs to know.

Two gentlemen, Mr. Audran and a certain N. N. (I can't be bothered with names), who were the cousin's and Charlotte's partners, received us at the carriage door and took charge of their ladies while I followed with mine.

We danced a minuet. I engaged one lady after another, and it seemed to me that precisely the most disagreeable could not bring themselves to change partners and end the figure. Charlotte and her partner began an English quadrille and you can imagine my delight when it was her turn to dance the figure with us. You should see Charlotte dance! She dances with her whole heart and soul: her body is all harmony, elegance, and grace, as if nothing else mattered, as if she had no other thought or feeling; and, doubtless, for the moment, everything else has ceased to exist for her.

She was engaged for the second quadrille, but promised me the third, and assured me, with the most disarming ingenuousness, that she was very fond of the German way of dancing. "It is the custom here," she said, "for the previous partners to dance the German dance together, but my partner is a bad waltzer, and will be grateful if I save him the trouble. Your partner can't waltz, and doesn't like it either. But I noticed during the quadrille that you waltz well, so, if you want to waltz with me, do propose it to my partner, and I will ask yours." We agreed, and it was arranged that while we danced our partners should entertain each other.

We began, and first delighted in joining arms according to the usual variety of patterns. With what charm, what ease she moved! When the waltz started, and the dancers whirled round each other like planets in the sky, there was some confusion, since some of the dancers were fairly clumsy. We kept back, allowing the others to wear themselves out, and when the most awkward dancers had left the floor, we joined in and kept it up with one other couple—Audran and his partner. Never had I danced more lightly. I felt myself more than human, holding this loveliest of creatures in my arms, flying with her like the wind, till I lost sight of everything else; and—Wilhelm, I vowed at that moment that a girl whom I loved, or for whom I felt the slightest attachment, should never waltz with another, even if it should be my end! You understand what I mean.

We took a few turns in the room to recover our breath. Then Charlotte sat down and we ate some oranges that I had secured—the only ones left; but at every slice which she politely offered to a greedy lady sitting next to her, I felt as though a dagger went through my heart.

We were the second couple in the third quadrille. As we were dancing along (and Heaven knows with what ecstasy I gazed at her eyes which shone with the sweetest feeling of enjoyment), we passed a lady whom I had noticed because of her charming expression, although she was no longer young. She looks at Charlotte with a smile, shakes her finger at her, and twice repeats with great significance the name Albert.

"Who's Albert," I asked Charlotte, "if it's not too impertinent?" She was about to answer, when we had to separate, in order to execute the figure of eight, and as we crossed in front of each other, I felt that she looked somewhat pensive. "Why should I conceal it from you?" she said, as she gave me her hand for the promenade. "Albert is a worthy man, to whom I am as good as engaged." Now, there was nothing new to me in this (the girls had told me of it on the way), yet it struck me as new since I had not thought of it in connection with her whom in so short a time I had grown to like so much. At any rate, I became confused, got out of the figure, and caused a general confusion so that it took Charlotte's whole presence of mind to straighten me out by pulling and pushing me into my proper place.

The dance was not yet finished when the lightning which we had for some time seen on the horizon and which I had pretended was only summer lightning, grew more violent and thunder was heard above the music. The women ran in all directions, followed by their partners. The confusion spread and soon the music stopped. When any distress or terror interrupts our amusements, it naturally makes a deeper impression than at other times, partly because the contrast makes us more keenly susceptible, or perhaps because our senses are then more open to impressions, and the shock is consequently stronger. This probably accounts for the looks of fear I saw everywhere on the faces of the ladies. One wisely sat down in a corner with her back to the window, and held her hands over her ears; a second knelt down and hid her face in the other's lap; a third pushed herself between them, and embraced her sisters with a thousand tears. Some insisted on going home; others, unaware of what they were doing, lacked sufficient presence of mind to resist the impertinences of their partners, who had had something to drink and who sought to capture for themselves those sighs which the lips of our distressed beauties had intended for Heaven. Some of the gentlemen had gone downstairs to smoke a quiet pipe, and the rest of the company gladly accepted the wise suggestion of the hostess to retire into another room which had shutters and curtains. We had hardly got there when Charlotte arranged the chairs in a circle; and when the company had sat down at her request, she proposed a game.

I noticed some of the guests purse their lips and stretch themselves at the prospect of some agreeable forfeit. "Let's play at counting," said Charlotte. "Now, pay attention: I shall go round the circle from right to left and each one is to count, one after the other, the number that comes to him. But you must count fast; whoever hesitates or makes a mistake gets a box on the ear, and so on, till we have counted a thousand." It was delightful to see the fun. She went round the circle with upraised arm. "One," said the first; "two," the second; "three," the third; and so on, till Charlotte went faster and faster. One man made a mistake— instantly a box on the ear; and amid the laughter that ensued, another box; and so on, faster and faster. I myself came in for two cuffs, which to my inner delight seemed a little harder than the ones she gave the others. General laughter and commotion put an end to the game long before we had counted to a thousand. The party broke up into little separate groups, the storm was over, and I followed Charlotte into the ballroom. On the way she said, "The boxes on the ear made them forget their fears of the storm." I could make no reply. She continued, "I was as frightened as any of them, but by pretending to be brave, to keep up the spirits of the others, I forgot my own fears." We went to the window. It was still thundering in the distance; a soft rain was pouring down over the countryside and filled the air around us with delicious fragrance. Charlotte leaned on her elbows, her eyes wandered over the scene, she looked up to the sky, and then turned to me, her eyes filled with tears; she put her hand on mine and said, "Klopstock!" I remem- bered at once that magnificent ode of his which was in her thoughts, and felt overcome by the flood of emotion which the mention of his name called forth. It was more than I could bear. I bent over her hand, kissed it in a stream of ecstatic tears, and again looked into her eyes. Divine Klopstock! If only you could have seen your apotheosis in those eyes! And your name, so often profaned, may I never hear it uttered again!

June 19

I no longer remember where I stopped in my story. I only know that it was two in the morning when I went to bed; and if you had been with me and I might have talked instead of writing to you, I should probably have kept you up till daylight.

I think I have not yet told you what happened as we rode home from the ball, nor have I time to tell you now. It was a magnificent sunrise; the whole country was fresh, and the dew fell drop by drop from the trees. Our companions were dozing. Charlotte asked me if I didn't want to join them, and urged me not to stand on ceremony. Looking at her, I answered, "As long as I see those eyes open, there is no danger of my falling asleep." We both kept awake till we reached her gate. The maid opened it quietly and assured her, in answer to her inquiries, that her father and the children were well, and still sleeping. I left, asking her permission to see her that day. She consented, and I kept my promise. And since that time sun, moon, and stars may pursue their course: I know not whether it is day or night; the whole world about me has ceased to be.

June 21

My days are as happy at those God gives to his saints; and whatever be my fate hereafter, I can never say that I haven't tasted joy—the purest joys of life. You know my Wahlheim. I am now completely settled there. It is only half an hour from Charlotte: and there I feel my full self and taste all the happiness which can fall to the lot of man.

Little did I imagine, when I selected Wahlheim as the goal of my walks, that all Heaven lay so near it. How often in my wanderings had I seen, either from the hillside or from the meadows across the river, this hunting lodge, which now holds all the joys of my heart!

I have often reflected, dear Wilhelm, on the eagerness of men to wander about and make new discoveries, and on that secret urge which afterwards makes them return to their narrow circle, conform to the customary path, and pay no attention to the right or the left.

It is so strange how, when I came here first and looked out upon that lovely valley from the hills, I felt charmed with everything around me—the little wood opposite—how delightful to sit in its shade! How fine the view from that summit!—that delightful chain of hills, and the exquisite valleys at their feet!—could I but lose myself amongst them!—I ran off, and returned without finding what I sought. Distance, my friend, is like the future. A dim vastness is spread before our souls; our feelings are as obscure as our vision, and we desire to surrender our whole being, that it may be filled with the perfect bliss of one glorious emotion—but alas! when we rush towards our goal, when the distant *there* becomes the present *here*, all is the same; we are as poor and limited as ever, and our soul still languishes for unattainable happiness.

And so the restless traveler at last longs for his native soil, and finds in his own cottage, in the arms of his wife, in the affection of his children, and the labor necessary for their support, all that happiness which he sought in vain in the wide world.

When I go out to Wahlheim at sunrise, and with my own hands gather in the garden the sugar peas for my own dinner; and when I sit down to string them as I read my Homer, and then, selecting a saucepan from the little kitchen, fetch my own butter, put my peas on the fire, cover the pot, and sit down to stir it occasionally—I vividly recall the illustrious suitors of Penelope, killing, dressing, and roasting their own oxen and swine. Nothing fills me with a more pure and genuine happiness than those traits of patriarchal life which, thank Heaven! I can imitate without affectation.

I am glad that my heart can feel the same simple and innocent pleasure as the peasant whose table is covered with food of his own growing, and who not only enjoys his meal, but remembers with delight the happy days, and the sunny morning when he planted it, the mild evenings when he watered it, and the pleasure he experienced in watching its daily growth.

June 29

The day before yesterday the physician came from the town to pay a visit to the judge. He found me on the floor playing with Charlotte's brothers and sisters. Some of them were scrambling over me, others romped with me, and as I caught and tickled them, they made a great uproar. The doctor is the sort of person who adjusts his stuffy cuffs and continually settles his frill while he's talking; he thought my conduct beneath the dignity of a sensible man. I could see it in his face, but I did not let myself be disturbed and allowed him to continue his wise talk, while I rebuilt the children's card houses as fast as they threw them down. He went about the town afterwards, complaining that the judge's children were spoiled enough, but that now Werther was completely ruining them.

Yes, Wilhelm, nothing on this earth is closer to my heart than children. When I watch their doings; when I see in the little creatures the seeds of all those virtues and qualities, which they will one day find so indispensable; when I see in their obstinacy all the future firmness and constancy of a noble character, in their capriciousness that gaiety of temper which will carry them over the dangers and troubles of life— everything so simple and unspoiled—I always remember the golden words of the Great Teacher of mankind, "Unless ye become even as one of these." And yet, my friend, these children, who are our equals, whom we ought to consider models—we treat them as though they were our inferiors. They're not supposed to have a will of their own! Don't we have one? And why do we privilege ourselves? Because we're older and more experienced! Great God! from the height of Thy Heaven Thou beholdest only children, older and younger ones; and Thy Son has long since declared which of them afford Thee greater pleasure. But they will not believe in Him, and hear Him not—that, too, is an old story; and they train their children after their own image, and—

Adieu, Wilhelm, I must not continue this useless talk.

July 1

What Charlotte can be to an invalid I feel in my own heart, which suffers more than many a poor creature lingering on a bed of sickness. She will spend a few days in the town with a woman, whom the physicians have almost given up, and who wishes to have Charlotte near her in her last moments. I accompanied her last week on a visit to the vicar of St., a village in the mountains, about an hour away. We arrived about four o'clock. Charlotte had taken her little sister with her. When we entered the courtyard of the vicarage, we found the good old man sitting on a bench before the door, in the shade of two large walnut trees. At the sight of Charlotte, he seemed to gain fresh life, rose, forgot his knotty stick, and ventured to walk towards her. She ran to him, and made him sit down; then, placing herself by his side, she gave him her father's greetings, and then caught up his youngest child—a dirty, ugly little thing, but the joy of his old age. I wish you could have seen her attention to this old man—how she raised her voice because of his deafness; how she told him of perfectly healthy young people who had died when it was least expected; praised the virtues of Karlsbad, and commended his decision to spend the next summer there; and assured him that he looked better and stronger than when she saw him last. In the meantime, I paid my respects to his good wife. The old man seemed in excellent spirits and, as I could not help admiring the beauty of the walnut trees which formed such an agreeable shade over us, he began, though with some little difficulty, to tell us their history. "The older," he said, "we do not know who planted it—some say one vicar, and some say another; but the younger one, there behind us, is exactly the age of my wife—fifty years next October. Her father planted it the morning of the day she was born. My wife's father was my predecessor here, and I cannot tell you how fond he was of that tree; and it is quite as dear to me. Under the shade of that very tree, on a log, my wife was seated, knitting, when I came into this courtyard for the first time as a poor student, just twenty-seven years ago." Charlotte inquired after his daughter. He said she had gone with Mr. Schmidt to the workers in the field. The old man then resumed his story, and told us how his predecessor had taken a fancy to him, as had his daughter; and how he had become first his curate, and subsequently his successor. He had scarcely finished his story when his daughter returned through the garden, accompanied by Mr. Schmidt. She welcomed Charlotte affectionately, and I confess I was much taken with her appearance. She was a lively looking, good-humored brunette, good company for a short stay in the country. Her suitor (for such Mr. Schmidt appeared to be) was a polite but reserved person who would not join our conversation, in spite of Charlotte's efforts to draw him out. I was much annoyed to see by his expression that his silence was not due to any dullness or stupidity, but to obstinacy and ill-humor. This became only too evident when we set out to take a walk, with Friederike accompanying Charlotte, and, on occasion, myself. The worthy gentleman's face, which was by nature rather somber, became so dark and angry that Charlotte had to touch my arm and remind me that I was talking too much to Friederike. Nothing distresses me more than to see people torment each other, particularly when young people, in the very season of pleasure, waste their few short days of sunshine in quarrels and trifles, and only perceive their error when it is too late. This thought preoccupied me and in the evening, when we returned to the vicar's and were sitting round the table with our bread and milk, the conversation turned on the joys and sorrows of the world, and I could not resist the temptation to attack bitterly ill-humor. "We are apt," I began, "to complain, but surely with very little reason, that our happy days are few, and our days of sorrow are many. If our hearts were always disposed to receive what God sends us every day, we should have strength enough to bear misery when it comes." "But," observed the vicar's wife, "we cannot always control our tempers, so much depends upon our nature; when the body suffers, the mind is ill at ease." "I admit that," I continued, "but let us regard it as a disease, and ask whether there is no remedy for it." "That sounds plausible," said Charlotte, "at least I think very much depends upon ourselves. I know it is so with me. When anything annoys and disturbs me, I run into the garden, hum a couple of dance tunes, and everything is all right again." "That's what I meant," I replied. "Ill-humor resembles laziness: it's natural to us, but if once we have courage to exert ourselves, our work runs fresh from our hands, and we find real enjoyment in activity." Friederike listened very attentively; the young man objected that we are not masters of ourselves, and still less so of our feelings. "We are talking about a disagreeable emotion," I added, "from which everyone would gladly escape, but none know their own powers without trial. Surely sick people are glad to consult doctors and submit to the most scrupulous regimen, the most nauseous medicines, in order to recover their health." I noticed that the good old man inclined his head, and strained to hear our discourse. I raised my voice and addressed myself directly to him. "They preach against a great many vices," I observed, "but I can't remember a sermon against ill-humor."[4] "That should be done by your town clergymen," he replied; "country people are never ill-humored. Still, it might be useful occasionally—to our wives, for instance, and the judge." We all laughed, and he joined us so vigorously that he was seized by a fit of coughing, which interrupted our conversation for a time. Mr. Schmidt resumed the subject. "You call ill-humor a vice," he remarked, "but I think you exaggerate." "Not at all," I replied, "if a vice is simply that which is pernicious to ourselves and those around us. Isn't it enough that we lack the power to make one another happy, must we deprive each other of the pleasure which each of us can at times feel in his heart? Show me the man who has the courage to hide his ill-humor, who bears the whole burden himself without disturbing the happiness of his companions. No, ill-humor arises from a sense of our own inadequacy— from a discontent with ourselves and an hostility towards others incited by foolish vanity. We see people happy whom we have not made so, and cannot endure the sight." Charlotte looked at me with a smile as

---

[4] We have an excellent sermon on this subject by Lavater, among those on the Book of Jonas.

she observed the emotion with which I spoke; and a tear in Friederike's eye made me proceed. "Woe unto those," I said, "who use their power over another's heart to destroy the simple pleasures it would naturally enjoy! All the gifts, all the attentions in the world cannot compensate for the loss of that happiness which the cruel tyranny within us has destroyed."

My heart was full as I spoke. The memory of past events pressed upon my mind and filled my eyes with tears.

"We should daily repeat to ourselves," I exclaimed, "that we can do little for our friends except leave them their own joys and increase their happiness by sharing it with them! But when souls are tormented by a violent passion, or their hearts rent with grief, is it in your power to offer them the slightest comfort?

"And when the last fatal illness seizes the being whose untimely grave you have prepared, when she lies languid and exhausted before you, her dim eyes raised to heaven, and the damp of death upon her pallid brow, then you stand at her bedside like a condemned criminal, with the bitter feeling that all your strength and will could not save her; and the agonizing thought haunts you that all your efforts cannot impart even a moment's strength to the departing soul, or quicken her with a moment of consolation."

As I spoke these words, the memory of a similar scene at which I had once been present fell with full force upon my heart. I put my handkerchief to my face and left the room; I was recalled to my senses only by Charlotte's voice, reminding me that it was time to go home. With what tenderness she scolded me on the way for the passionate interest I took in everything! It would destroy me, she said, and I ought to spare myself.—O, Angel! I will live for your sake.

July 6

She is still with her dying friend, and is always the same helpful and lovely creature whose presence softens pain, and brings happiness wherever she goes. She went out yesterday with little Marianne and Amalie: I knew of it, went to meet them, and we walked together. After about an hour and a half, we returned to the town. We stopped at the spring I am so fond of, and which is now a thousand times dearer to me than ever: Charlotte sat down by the low wall, and we gathered about her. I looked round, and recalled the time when my heart was all alone. "Beloved spring," I said, "since that time I have not come to enjoy cool repose by your fresh stream; I have passed you with scarcely a glance." I looked down, and observed Amalie coming up the steps with a glass of water. I turned towards Charlotte, and felt deeply how much she means to me. Amalie approached with the glass. Marianne wanted to take it from her. "No!" cried the child with the sweetest expression, "Charlotte must drink first."

The goodness and simplicity with which this was uttered so charmed me that I sought to express my feelings by catching up the child and kissing her heartily. But she was frightened and began to cry. "You shouldn't do that," said Charlotte. I was perplexed. "Come, little one," she continued, taking her hand and leading her down the steps, "wash yourself quickly in the fresh water, and it won't hurt." I stood and watched the little dear rubbing her cheeks with her wet hands, in the fervent belief that all the impurities would be washed off by the miraculous water and that she would surely be spared the disgrace of an ugly beard. Even though Charlotte said it would do, she continued to wash with all her might, as if she thought too much were better than too little—I assure you, Wilhelm, I never attended a baptism with greater reverence; and when Charlotte came up, I could have fallen on my knees as before a prophet who has washed away the sins of his people.

In the evening I could not help telling the story to a man who, I thought, possessed some natural feeling because he was a man of understanding. But what a mistake I made! He maintained it was very wrong of Charlotte—that we should not deceive children, that such fanciful explanations occasion countless mistakes and superstitions from which we should protect the young. It occurred to me, then, that this very man had had his child baptized only a week before. I said nothing, but silently kept my belief that we should deal with children as God deals with us—we are happiest under the influence of innocent delusions.

July 8

What a child I am to be so covetous of a look! What a child I am! We had been to Wahlheim: the ladies took a carriage, but during our walks I thought I saw in Charlotte's black eyes—I am a fool—but forgive me! you should see them, those eyes. However, to be brief (for I can hardly keep my own eyes open), when the ladies stepped into their carriage again, young W., Seldstadt, Audran, and I were standing about the door. They were a merry lot of fellows, all laughing and joking together. I tried to catch Charlotte's eye. Her glance wandered from one to the other, but it didn't light on me—on me, who stood there motionless, on me who alone saw her. My heart bade her a thousand adieus, but she didn't notice me. The carriage drove off, and my eyes filled with tears. I looked after her: suddenly I saw Charlotte's bonnet leaning out of the window, as she turned to look back—was it at me? My dear friend, I don't know. And I am suspended in this uncertainty; but it is also my consolation: perhaps she did turn to look at me. Perhaps! Good night— what a child I am!

July 10

You should see how foolish I look in company when her name is mentioned, and particularly when I am asked how I like her. How I like her!—I detest the phrase. What sort of creature must he be who merely likes Charlotte, whose whole heart and senses are not entirely absorbed by her? Like her! Someone asked me the other day how I liked Ossian.

July 11

Mrs. M. is very ill. I pray for her because I share Charlotte's sufferings. I see Charlotte occasionally at a friend's house, and today she told me the strangest thing. Old Mr. M. is a greedy, miserly fellow who has long nagged his wife and kept her on an unreasonably strict allowance; but she has always been able to manage. A few days ago, when the doctor knew that there was little chance of her recovery, she sent for her husband—Charlotte was present—and said this to him: "I have something to confess which, after my death, may cause trouble and confusion. I have always managed your household as frugally and economically as possible, but you must forgive me for having deceived you for thirty years. At the beginning of our married life you allowed a small sum for the kitchen and other household expenses. When our establishment increased and our property grew larger, I could not persuade you to increase the weekly allowance in proportion. In short, you know that when our household cost most, you expected me to supply everything with seven florins a week. I took the money from you without saying anything, but made up the weekly deficiency from the receipts—as nobody would suspect your wife of robbing the till. I have wasted nothing, and should have been content to meet my eternal Judge without this confession, if I did not know that whoever looks after the house when I am gone will not be able to manage, and that you might insist that your allowance had been quite sufficient for your first wife."

I talked with Charlotte of the incredible blindness of mankind; how anyone could avoid suspecting some deception when seven florins were allowed to defray expenses twice as great. But I have myself known people who would have believed, without any visible astonishment, that their house possessed the prophet's never-failing cruse of oil.

July 13

No, I am not deceived. In her black eyes I read a genuine interest in me and in my life. Yes, I feel it; and I can believe my own heart which tells me—dare I say it?—dare I pronounce the divine words?—that she loves me!

That she loves me! How the idea exalts me in my own eyes! And—since you understand my feelings, I can say this to you—how I worship myself since she loves me!

Is this presumption, or is it an awareness of the truth? I do not know the man able to supplant me in Charlotte's heart; and yet when she speaks of her betrothed with so much warmth and affection, I feel like a soldier who has been stripped of his honors and titles, and deprived of his sword.

July 16

How my heart beats when by accident I touch her finger, or my feet meet hers under the table! I draw back as from a flame, but a secret force impels me forward again, and I begin to feel faint. Oh! Her innocent, pure heart never knows what agony these little familiarities inflict on me. Sometimes when we are talking she lays her hand on mine and in the eagerness of conversation comes closer to me, and her divine breath brushes my lips—I feel as if lightning had struck me, and I could sink into the earth. And yet, Wilhelm, with all this heavenly intimacy—if I should ever dare—you understand. No! my heart is not so depraved; it is weak, weak enough—but isn't that a kind of depravity?

She is sacred to me. All desire is silenced in her presence; I don't know what I feel when I'm near her. It is as if my soul beat in every nerve of my body. There is a melody which she plays on the piano with the touch of an angel—so simple is it, and yet so lofty! It's her favorite song, and when she strikes the first note all my worry and sorrow disappear in a moment.

I believe every word that is said of the ancient magic of music. How her simple song enchants me! And how she knows when to play it! Sometimes, when I feel like shooting a bullet into my head, she begins to sing. The gloom and madness are dispersed, and I breathe freely again.

July 18

Wilhelm, what is the world to our hearts without love? A magic lantern without light. You have but to set up the light within and the brightest pictures are thrown on the white screen. And if that is all there is, fleeting shadows, we are still happy, when, like children, we behold them and are transported with the wonderful sight. I haven't been able to see Charlotte today. I was prevented by company from which I could not disengage myself. What was I to do? I sent my servant to her house, that I might at least see somebody today who had been near her. Oh, the impatience with which I awaited his return, the joy with which I welcomed him! I should have liked to hold him in my arms and kiss him, if I had not been embarrassed.

It is said that the Bologna stone, when it is placed in the sun, absorbs the rays and for a time appears luminous in the dark. So it was with me and this servant. The idea that her eyes had dwelt on his countenance, his cheek, his coat buttons, the collar of his surtout, made them all inestimably dear to me, so that at the moment I would not have parted with him for a thousand crowns. His presence made me so happy! For heaven's sake, Wilhelm, don't laugh at me! Can it be a delusion if it makes us so happy?

July 19

"I shall see her today!" I say to myself with delight when I rise in the morning and happily look out at the bright, beautiful sun. "I shall see her!" And then I have no further wish for the rest of the day; all, all is swallowed up by that one thought.

July 20

I cannot quite agree to your proposal that I should accompany the ambassador to * * *. I don't like subordination, and we all know that he's a disagreeable person. You say my mother wishes me to be employed. I could not help laughing at that. Am I not sufficiently employed? And in the end isn't it the same whether I count peas or lentils? The world runs on from one folly to another; and the man who, purely for the sake of others, and without any passion or inner compulsion of his own, toils after wealth or dignity, or any other phantom, is simply a fool.

July 24

You insist so on my not neglecting my drawing that it would be better for me to say nothing than to confess how little I have done lately.

I never felt happier, I never understood Nature better, even down to the stones or smallest blade of grass. And yet I am unable to express myself; the creative power of my imagination is so weak, everything seems to swim and float before me, so that I cannot make a clear, bold outline. But I imagine I should succeed better if I had clay or wax to model. I shall try, if this state of mind continues much longer, and will take to modeling, even if it's only cakes I make.

I have begun Charlotte's portrait three times, and have as often made a fool of myself. This is the more annoying, since I was formerly very successful in catching likenesses. I have since traced her profile, and must content myself with that.

July 26

Yes, dear Charlotte! I will take care of everything as you wish. Do make me more requests, the more the better. I only ask one favor; use no more writing sand with the little notes you send me. Today I quickly raised your letter to my lips, and it set my teeth on edge.

July 26

I have often resolved not to see her so frequently. But who could keep such a resolution? Every day I succumb to temptation and promise faithfully that tomorrow I will really stay away. But when tomorrow comes, I find some irresistible reason for seeing her; and before I can account for it, I am with her again. Either she said on the previous evening, "Be sure to call tomorrow, won't you?"—and who could stay away?—or she gives me some errand, and I think it proper to take her the answer in person; or the day is lovely, and I walk to Wahlheim; and once I'm there, it's only half an hour to her. I am within the enchanted atmosphere, and suddenly find myself at her side. My grandmother used to tell us a story of a mountain of loadstone. Any ships that came near it were instantly deprived of their ironwork; the nails flew to the mountain and the unhappy crew perished amidst the debris of the planks.

July 30

Albert has arrived, and I must leave. Were he the best and noblest of men, and I in every respect his inferior, I could not endure to see him in possession of such perfection. Possession!—Enough, Wilhelm—her betrothed is here—a fine, worthy fellow, whom one cannot help liking. Fortunately I was not present at their reunion. It would have broken my heart! And he is so considerate, he has not given Charlotte one kiss in my presence. Heaven reward him for it! I must love him for the respect with which he treats her. He shows a regard for me, but I suspect I am more indebted for that to Charlotte than to his own feelings. Women have a delicate tact in such matters, and rightly so. They can't always succeed in keeping two rivals on good terms, but when they do, they are always the ones who benefit.

I cannot help respecting Albert. The calm of his temper contrasts strongly with the impetuosity of mine, which I cannot conceal. He has a great deal of feeling, and knows what he possesses in Charlotte. He is free from ill-humor, which you know is the fault I detest most.

He regards me as a man of sense; and my attachment to Charlotte, and the interest I take in all that concerns her, only augment his triumph and his love. I won't inquire whether he doesn't at times bother her with petty jealousy; I know that in his place I should not be entirely free from such feelings.

But, be that as it may, my joy in being with Charlotte is over. Call it folly or infatuation, what does a name matter? The thing speaks for itself. Before Albert came, I knew all that I know now. I knew I could make no pretensions to her, nor did I make any—that is, as far as it was possible to be without desire in the presence of so much loveliness. And now look at me, the silly creature, staring at the other fellow coming along and taking the girl away.

I grit my teeth and feel infinite scorn for those who tell me to be resigned, because it all can't be helped. Let me get away from these stuffed creatures! I roam through the woods and when I return to Charlotte, and find Albert sitting by her side in the arbor in the garden, I can't bear it. I behave like a fool, and indulge in a thousand absurdities. "For Heaven's sake," Charlotte said today, "no more scenes like the one last night! You frighten me when you're so exuberant." Between us, I merely wait until he's busy elsewhere and then I'm out there in no time, delighted when I find her alone.

August 8

Believe me, Wilhelm, I didn't mean you when I spoke so severely of those who always advise resignation in the face of inevitable fate. I didn't think you would have any such ideas. Of course you're right. Only remember one thing: in this world it is seldom a question of "either ... or." There are as many shadings of conduct and opinion as there are turns of feature between an aquiline nose and a flat one.

Thus, you mustn't think ill of me if I concede your entire argument and still contrive to find a way somewhere between the "either . . . or."

I hear you say: "Either you have hopes of obtaining Charlotte, or you have none. Well, in the one case, pursue your course and press on to the fulfillment of your wishes. In the other, be a man and try to get rid of a miserable passion which will enervate and destroy you." My dear friend, this is well said—and easily said.

But would you ask a wretched being, whose life is slowly wasting under a lingering disease, to do away with himself by the stroke of a dagger? Does not the very disorder which consumes his strength deprive him of the courage to effect his own deliverance?

You may answer me, if you please, with a similar analogy: "Who would not prefer the amputation of an arm to the risk of losing his life by hesitation and procrastination?" I know . . . let's not fence with metaphors.

Enough! There are moments, Wilhelm, when I could rise up and shake it all off, and when, if I only knew where, I think I would go away.

The same evening

Today I found my diary, which I have neglected for some time, and I am amazed how deliberately I have entangled myself step by step. To have recognized my situation so clearly, and yet to have acted like a child! Even now I see it all plainly, and yet seem to have no thought of acting more wisely.

August 10

If I weren't a fool, I could lead the happiest and most delightful life here. So many agreeable circumstances, all designed to please a man's heart, are seldom to be found. Ah! I feel it so clearly—the heart alone makes our happiness! To be admitted into this most wonderful family, to be loved by the father as a son, by the children as a father, and by Charlotte!—then Albert in all his generosity, who never disturbs my happiness by any appearance of ill-humor, receiving me with sincere affection, and loving me, next to Charlotte, better than all the world! Wilhelm, you would be delighted to hear us on our walks, talking about Charlotte. Nothing in the world could be more absurd than our relationship, and yet it often moves me to tears.

He tells me sometimes of her wonderful mother; how, on her death-bed, she entrusted her house and children to Charlotte, and asked him to look after her; how, since that time, a new spirit has taken possession of her; how, in her concern for the children's welfare, she became a real mother to them; how every moment of her time is devoted to some labor of love in their behalf—and yet her gaiety and cheerfulness has never left her. I walk by his side, pluck flowers by the way, arrange them carefully into a nosegay,—and then fling them into the brook and watch them as they float gently downstream. I forget whether I told you that Albert is to remain here. He has received a court appointment, with a very good salary; I understand he is in high favor there. I have met few persons so regular and conscientious as he is in his profession.

August 12

Certainly Albert is the best fellow in the world. I had a strange scene with him yesterday. I went to take leave of him, for I felt the desire to spend a few days in these hills from where I now write to you. As I was walking up and down in his room, my eye fell upon his pistols. "Lend me those pistols," I said, "for my journey." "By all means," he replied, "if you will take the trouble to load them; they only hang there pro forma." I took down one of them, and he continued: "Ever since I nearly paid for my extreme prudence, I will have nothing to do with these things." I was curious to hear the story. "I was staying," he said, "for some three months at a friend's house in the country. I had a brace of pistols with me, unloaded; and I slept without anxiety. One rainy afternoon I was sitting by myself, doing nothing, when it occurred to me—I don't know how—that the house might be attacked, that we might require the pistols, that we might—in short, you know how we sometimes imagine things when we have nothing better to do. I gave the pistols to the servant to clean and load. He was dallying with the maids and trying to frighten them, when the pistol went off—God knows how! The ramrod was still in the barrel and it went straight through the ball of the right thumb of one of the girls and shattered it. I had to endure her lamentations and pay the surgeon's bill; so, since that time, I have kept my weapons unloaded. My dear fellow, what's the use of prudence? We can never guard against all possible dangers. However,"—now you must know I am very fond of him until he says "however"; isn't it self-evident that every general rule must have its exceptions? But he is so exceedingly anxious to justify himself that if he thinks he has said any-thing too precipitate or too general or only half true, he never stops qualifying, modifying, and extenuating till at last he appears to have said nothing at all. On this occasion Albert was deeply immersed in his sub-ject; I finally ceased to listen to him and became lost in reverie. With a sudden motion I pointed the mouth of the pistol to my forehead, over the right eye. "What are you doing?" cried Albert, turning the pistol away. "It's not loaded," I said. "Even so," he asked with impatience, "what is the meaning of this? I can't imagine how a man can be so mad as to shoot himself; the very idea of it shocks me."

"Oh, you people!" I said, "why do you always have to label an action and call it mad or wise, good or bad? What does all that mean? That you have fathomed the motives of these actions? That you can explain with certainty why they happened, why they had to happen? If you could, you would be less hasty with your 'labels.'"

"But you will admit," said Albert, "that some actions are wrong, let them spring from whatever motives they may." I granted it, and shrugged my shoulders.

"Still," I continued, "there are some exceptions here too. Theft is a crime, but the man who commits it from extreme poverty to save his family from starvation, does he deserve pity or punishment? Who shall throw the first stone at a husband who in just rage sacrifices his faith-less wife and her perfidious seducer. Or at the young girl who in an hour of rapture forgets herself in the overwhelming joys of love? Even our laws, cold and pedantic as they are, relent in such cases, and withhold their punishment."

"That is quite another thing," said Albert, "because a man under the influence of violent passion loses all reasoning power and is regarded as drunk or insane."

"Oh, you rationalists," I replied, smiling. "Passion! Drunkenness! Madness! You moral creatures, so calm and so righteous! You abhor the drunken man and detest the eccentric; you pass by, like the Levite, and thank God, like the Pharisee, that you are not one of them. I have been drunk more than once, my passions have always bordered on madness, and I'm not ashamed to confess it. I've learned in my own way that all extraordinary men who have done great and improbable things have ever been decried by the world as drunk or insane. And in ordinary life too, is it not intolerable that no one can undertake anything noble or generous without having everybody shout, 'That fellow is drunk, he is mad'? Shame on you, ye sages!"

"Here you go again," said Albert; "you always exaggerate, and in this matter you are undoubtedly wrong. We were speaking of suicide, which you compare with great actions, when actually it is impossible to regard it as anything but weakness. It is much easier to die than to bear with fortitude a life of misery."

I was on the point of breaking off the conversation, for nothing puts me off so completely as when someone utters a wretched commonplace when I am talking from the depths of my heart. However, I controlled myself, for I had often heard with equal vexation the same observation. I answered him, therefore, with considerable intensity, "You call this a weakness—don't be led astray by appearances. When a nation which has long groaned under the intolerable yoke of a tyrant rises at last and throws off its chains, do you call that weakness? The man who, to save his house from the flames, finds his physical strength redoubled, so that he can lift burdens with ease which normally he could scarcely move; he who under the rage of an insult attacks and overwhelms half a dozen of his enemies—are these to be called weak? My friend, if a display of energy be strength, how can the highest exertion of it be a weakness?"

Albert looked at me and said, "Do forgive me, but I do not see that the examples you have produced bear any relation to the question."

"That may be," I answered; "I have often been told that my method of argument borders a little on the absurd. But let's see if we can't place the matter in another light by inquiring what a man's state of mind may be when he resolves to free himself from the burden of life—a burden which often seems so pleasant to bear. Surely, we are justified in discussing a subject such as this only in so far as we can put ourselves in another man's situation."

"Human nature," I continued, "has its limits. It can endure a certain

degree of joy, sorrow, and pain, but collapses as soon as this is ex-
ceeded. The question, therefore, is not whether a man is strong or
weak, but whether he is able to endure the measure of his suffering,
moral or physical. And in my opinion it is just as absurd to call a man a
coward who kills himself as to call a man a coward who dies of a malig-
nant fever."

"Paradox, all paradox!" cried Albert. "Not so paradoxical as you im-
agine," I replied. "You admit that we call a disease mortal when Nature
is so severely attacked and her strength so far exhausted that she cannot
possibly recover, no matter what the change that may take place."

"Now, my friend, apply this to the mind. Observe a man in his
natural, confined condition; consider how ideas work upon him, and
how impressions affect him, till at length a violent passion seizes him,
destroys all his powers of calm reflection, and utterly ruins him.

"It is in vain that a man of sound mind and cool temper recognizes the
condition of such a wretched being, in vain that he counsels him. Just as
a healthy man cannot impart his strength to an invalid."

Albert thought this too general. I reminded him about a girl who had
drowned herself a short time previously, and I related her story.

"She was a good creature, who had grown up in the narrow sphere of
her domestic chores and weekly appointed labor; one who knew no plea-
sure beyond a walk in the company of her friends on Sundays, dressed
in her best clothes, which she had got together gradually; or perhaps
going to a dance now and then during the holidays, and chatting away
her spare hours with a neighbor, discussing the scandals or the quarrels
of the village—trifles sufficient to occupy her heart. At length the
warmth of her nature is aroused by unfamiliar desires. She is flattered by
the attentions of men; her former pleasures seem to her more and more
insipid, till eventually she meets a young man to whom she is attracted
by a strange, new feeling; upon him she now rests all her hopes; she
forgets the world around her; she sees, hears, desires nothing but him,
and him only. He alone occupies all her thoughts. Unspoiled by the
empty indulgence of enervating vanity, her affection moving steadily
towards its object, she hopes to be his, and to realize, in an everlasting
union with him, all that happiness which she sought, all that bliss for
which she longed. His repeated promises confirm her hopes; embraces
and endearments, which increase the ardor of her desires, overpower
her soul. She floats in a dim, delusive anticipation of her happiness; and
her feelings become excited to their utmost tension. Finally she stretches
out her arms to embrace the object of all her wishes—and her lover
abandons her. Stunned and bewildered, she stands at the edge of an
abyss. All is darkness around her. No prospect, no hope, no consolation
—for she had lost the one in whom her entire existence was centered! She
sees nothing of the world before her, thinks nothing of the many others

who might fill the void in her heart; she feels deserted, forsaken by all the world; and, unseeing and impelled by the agony in her soul, she plunges into the deep, to end her sufferings in the broad embrace of death. You see, Albert, this is the story of thousands. And now tell me, is not this a case of physical infirmity? Nature can find no way out of the labyrinth of confusion and contradiction and the poor creature must die.

"Shame on him who can look on calmly and say, 'Foolish girl! She should have waited; she should have let time wear off the impression; her despair would have been eased, and she would have found another lover to comfort her.' One might as well say, 'The fool, to die of a fever! Why did he not wait till his strength was restored, till his blood became calm? All would have gone well, and he would have been alive now.'"

Albert, who still couldn't see the justice of the comparison, offered some further objections, among others, that I had taken the case of a mere ignorant girl. But how a rational being of sense, of more understanding and experience, could be excused, he was unable to comprehend. "My friend!" I exclaimed, "a man is a man; and whatever be the extent of his reasoning powers, they are of little avail when passion rages within and he feels himself confined by the narrow limits of human nature. Rather—but let us talk of this some other time," I said, and took my hat. My heart was over full; and we parted without having understood each other. How rare in this world is understanding!

August 15

There can be no doubt that in this world nothing but love alone makes us indispensable to each other. I know that Charlotte could not lose me without sorrow, and the children can't imagine my not coming to visit them every morning. I went this afternoon to tune Charlotte's piano. But I couldn't do it, for the little ones insisted on my telling them a story and Charlotte herself asked me to satisfy them. I gave them their supper, which they are now nearly as content to receive from me as from Charlotte, and I told them my favorite tale of the princess who was waited upon by hands. I learn a great deal doing this and am surprised at the impression my stories create. If I sometimes invent a minor episode which I forget the next time, they are quick to remind me that the story was different before, so that I now practice reciting them unchanged in a singsong tone which never changes. I've learned by this how much an author injures his work by altering it in a second edition, even though it may be improved from a literary point of view. The first impression is readily received. We are so constituted that we believe the most incredible things; and, once they are engraved upon the memory, woe to him who would endeavor to erase them!

August 18

Must it always be so—that the source of our happiness becomes the fountain of our misery?

The rich and ardent feeling which filled my heart with a love of Nature, overwhelmed me with a torrent of delight, and brought all paradise before me, has now become an insupportable torment—a demon which perpetually pursues me. When I used to gaze from these rocks upon the mountains across the river and upon the green valley before me, and saw everything around budding and bursting; the hills clothed from foot to peak with tall, thick trees; the valleys in all their variety, shaded with the loveliest woods; and the river gently gliding along among the whispering reeds, mirroring the clouds which the soft evening breeze wafted across the sky—when I heard the groves about me melodious with the music of birds, and saw the million swarms of insects dancing in the last golden beams of the sun, whose setting rays awoke the humming beetles from their grassy beds, while the subdued tumult around me drew my attention to the ground, and I there observed the hard rock giving nourishment to the dry moss, while the heather flourished upon the arid sands below me—all this conveyed to me the holy fire which animates all Nature, and filled and glowed within my heart. I felt myself exalted by this overflowing fullness, as if a god myself, and the glorious forms of an infinite universe stirred within my soul! Stupendous mountains encompassed me, abysses yawned at my feet, and cataracts fell headlong down before me; rivers rolled through the plains below, and the rocks and mountains resounded from afar. In the depths of the earth I saw the mysterious powers at work; on its surface, and beneath the heavens there teemed ten thousand living creatures. Everything is alive with an infinite variety of forms; and mankind safeguards itself in little houses and settles and rules in its own way over the wide universe. Poor fool! in whose petty estimation all things are little. From the inaccessible mountains, across the wilderness which no mortal foot has trod, far as the edge of the immeasurable ocean, the spirit of the eternal Creator breathes; and every speck of dust which He has made finds favor in His sight—Ah, how often then did the flight of a crane, soaring above my head, inspire me with the desire to be transported to the shores of the immeasurable ocean, there to drink the pleasures of life from the foaming goblet of the Infinite, and to realize, if but for a moment with the confined powers of my soul, the bliss of that Creator Who accomplishes all things in Himself, and through Himself!

My dear friend, the mere recollection of those hours consoles me. Even the effort to recall those ineffable emotions, and give them utterance, exalts my soul above itself, and makes me feel doubly the intensity of my present anguish.

It is as if a curtain had been drawn from before my eyes, and, instead of prospects of eternal life, the abyss of an ever-open grave yawned before me. Can we say of anything that it is when all passes away—when time, with the speed of a storm, carries all things onward—and our transitory existence, hurried along by the torrent, is swallowed up by the waves or dashed against the rocks? There is not a moment that doesn't consume you and yours—not a moment in which you don't yourself destroy something. The most innocent walk costs thousands of poor insects their lives; one step destroys the delicate structures of the ant and turns a little world into chaos. No, it is not the great and rare catastrophes of the world, the floods which sweep away villages, the earthquakes that swallow up our towns, that affect me. My heart is wasted by the thought of that destructive power which lies latent in every part of universal Nature. Nature has formed nothing that does not destroy itself, and everything near it. And so, surrounded by earth and air and all the active forces, I stagger on in sheer anxiety. The universe to me is an all-consuming, devouring monster.

August 21

In vain I stretch out my arms towards her when I awaken in the morning from my troubled dreams. In vain I seek her at night in my bed, when an innocent dream has happily deceived me, and I thought that I was sitting near her in the fields, holding her hand and covering it with countless kisses. And when I feel for her in the half confusion of sleep, and awaken, tears flow from my oppressed heart; and, bereft of all comfort, I weep over my dark future.

August 22

What misery, Wilhelm! My energies have degenerated into restless inaction. I cannot be idle, and yet I am unable to set to work. My powers of imagination are gone, I haven't any feeling for the beauties of Nature, and books are distasteful to me. Once we give ourselves up, we are lost. Many a time I wish I were a common laborer, so that when I awake in the morning I might at least have one clear prospect, one pursuit, one hope, for the day which has dawned. I often envy Albert when I see him buried in a heap of papers and documents, and I fancy that I would be happy were I in his place. This feeling has so often come over me that I have been on the point of writing to you and to the minister for the appointment at the embassy, which you assure me I might obtain. I believe it myself. The minister has long shown a regard for me, and has frequently urged me to seek employment. But it's just the whim of an hour. Then the fable of the horse recurs to me. Weary of its freedom, it let itself be saddled and bridled, and was ridden to death for its pains. I don't know what to do. For is not this craving for change the consequence of an impatient spirit which will forever pursue me?

August 28

If my misery could be cured at all, it would certainly be cured here among these people. Today is my birthday, and early in the morning I received a package from Albert. As I opened it, I found one of the pink ribbons which Charlotte wore in her dress the first time I saw her, and which I had several times asked her to give me. With it were two volumes in duodecimo of Wetstein's Homer—a book I had often wanted to own, to save me the trouble of carrying the large Ernesti edition with me on my walks. You see how they anticipate my wishes, how well they understand all those little attentions of friendship, so superior to the expensive presents of the great, which only humiliate us. I kissed the ribbon a thousand times, and in every breath inhaled the memory of those happy and unrecoverable days which filled me with the keenest joy. Such, Wilhelm, is our fate. I do not complain; the flowers of life are but illusions. How many fade away and leave no trace, how few yield any fruit; and the fruit itself, how rarely does it ripen! And yet there are flowers enough; should we let the little that does really ripen, rot, decay and perish unenjoyed?

Farewell! This is a glorious summer. I often climb into the trees in Charlotte's orchard, and with a fruit picker bring down the pears that hang on the highest branches. She stands below, and takes them as I hand them to her.

August 30

I'm such a fool! Why do I deceive myself? What is to come of all this wild, endless passion? I cannot pray except to her. My imagination sees nothing but her; nothing matters except what has to do with her. In this state of mind I enjoy many happy hours till at length I'm compelled to tear myself away from her again. Ah, Wilhelm, to what lengths does my heart often drive me! When I have spent several hours in her company till I feel completely absorbed by her figure, her grace, the divine expression of her thoughts, my mind becomes so excited, my sight grows dim, my hearing confused, my breathing oppressed as if by the hand of an assassin, and then my pounding heart seeks relief for my aching senses, only to confuse them more. Wilhelm, I'm sometimes uncertain whether I really exist. If in such moments I find no sympathy and Charlotte doesn't allow me the melancholy consolation of bathing her hand in my tears, I tear myself from her and roam through the country, climb some precipitous cliff, or make a path through a trackless wood, where I am wounded and torn by thorns and briers; and there I find some relief. Some! Often I lie down, overcome with fatigue and thirst; and sometimes, late in the night, when the full moon stands above me in the lonely woods, I sit on a crooked tree to rest my weary limbs, and there, exhausted and worn, I fall asleep in the subdued light. Oh Wilhelm! the hermit's cell, his sackcloth and belt of thorns would be relief compared with what I suffer. Adieu! I see no end to this wretchedness but the grave.

September 3

I must get away. Thank you, Wilhelm, for confirming my wavering purpose. For a whole fortnight I have thought of leaving her. I must. She is in town again, visiting a friend. And Albert—yes—I must get away.

September 10

Oh, what a night, Wilhelm! Now I can bear anything. I shall not see her again. Oh, why can't I flee to your arms and with floods of tears and raptures convey to you all the passions which overwhelm my heart! Here I sit gasping for breath, struggling to calm myself. I await the morning, at dawn the horses are to be at the door.

And she is sleeping calmly, little suspecting that she has seen me for the last time. I've torn myself free. I had the courage, in a conversation of two hours, not to betray my intention. Oh, Wilhelm, what a conversation it was!

Albert had promised to come with Charlotte to the garden immediately after supper. I stood on the terrace under the tall chestnuts and watched the setting sun. I saw it sink for the last time over this delightful valley and gentle stream. I had often visited the same spot with Charlotte, and watched that glorious sight; and now—I walked up and down the avenue which was so dear to me. A secret sympathy had frequently drawn me there even before I knew Charlotte; and we were delighted when, early in our acquaintance, we discovered that we loved the same spot, which is as romantic as any that the gardener's art has ever produced.

From between the chestnuts there is a broad view. I remember that I mentioned all this in a previous letter, and described the tall mass of beech trees at the end, and how the avenue grows darker and darker as it winds its way among them till it ends in an enclosure which has all the mysterious charm of solitude. I can recall the strange feeling of melancholy which came over me the first time I entered that dark retreat, at bright midday. I seemed to feel even then that it would some day be the scene of so much happiness and misery!

I had spent half an hour absorbed in the bittersweet thoughts of parting and seeing her again, when I heard them coming up the terrace. I ran to meet them and trembled as I took her hand and kissed it. When we reached the top of the terrace, the moon rose from behind the wooded hill. We talked about many things, and almost without noticing it approached the secluded spot. Charlotte entered and sat down, Albert beside her. I did the same, but I was so excited that I could not remain seated. I got up and stood before her, then walked to and fro, and sat down again. I was restless and miserable. Charlotte drew our attention to the beautiful effect of the moonlight, which threw a silver hue over the terrace in front of the beech trees. It was a glorious sight, all the more striking because of the complete darkness which surrounded the spot where we were. We remained silent; and after a while Charlotte said, "Whenever I walk by moonlight, it brings to my mind my beloved and departed friends, and I am filled with thoughts of death and afterlife. We shall live, Werther," she continued, with a firm but emotional voice; "but shall we know one another again? What do you think? What do you say?"

"Charlotte," I said, as I took her hand in mine, and my eyes filled with tears, "we shall see each other again—here and hereafter." I could say no more. Why, Wilhelm, should she put this question to me just at the moment when the anguish of our parting filled my heart?

"And," she continued, "do those departed ones know of us down here? Do they know when we are well that we recall their memory with the fondest love? In the quiet of evening, the shade of my mother always hovers round me, when I sit in the midst of her children, my children, when they are assembled about me as they used to be with her. Then I raise my anxious eyes to Heaven and wish she could look down upon us and see how I keep the promise I made to her on her deathbed to be a mother to her children. With what emotion do I cry out, 'Forgive me, dearest mother, forgive me if I cannot completely take your place! I do my best. They are clothed and fed; and, more important, they are cared for and loved. Could you but see, dear saint, the peace and harmony of our life, you would praise God with the deepest feelings of gratitude, to Whom, in your last hour, you addressed such fervent prayers for our happiness.'"

This is what she said! Oh, Wilhelm, who can do justice to her words? How can the cold dead letter convey the heavenly expressions of her spirit? Albert interrupted her gently: "This affects you too deeply, dear Charlotte. I know you dwell on such recollections with deep feeling, but I implore you—" "Oh, Albert!" she continued, "I am sure you do not forget the evenings when we three used to sit at the little round table, when Father was away, and the little ones had gone to bed. You often had a good book with you but seldom read it; the conversation of that wonderful soul was more than anything else—that beautiful, bright, gentle, and yet ever-active woman. God alone knows how I have often prayed in tears that I might be like her!"

I threw myself at her feet, and covered her hand with a thousand tears. "Charlotte," I exclaimed, "God's blessing and your mother's spirit are upon you!" "Oh if you had only known her!" she said, pressing my hand. "She was worthy of being known by you." I thought I should faint. Never had I received praise so magnificent. She continued: "And yet she was doomed to die in the prime of her life, when her youngest boy was six months old. Her illness was short, she was calm and resigned; it was only for her children, especially the youngest, that she felt unhappy. When her end drew near, she asked me to bring them to her. I took them in to her. The little ones knew nothing of their approaching loss; the elder ones were overcome with grief. They stood around the bed and she raised her hands and prayed over them; then she kissed them one after the other and sent them away. 'Be a mother to them,' she said to me. I gave her my hand. 'You are promising much, my child,' she said—'a mother's love and a mother's eye! I have often felt, by your tears of gratitude, that you know what that means; show it to your brothers and sisters. And be as obedient and faithful to your father as a wife; you will be his comfort.' She asked for him. He had gone out to conceal his intolerable anguish—he was completely broken.

"Albert, you were in the room. She heard someone moving about, inquired who it was, and asked you to approach. She looked at us both steadily, reassured that we should be happy—happy with each other." Albert embraced her and cried, "We are happy, and we always shall be!" Even Albert, tranquil Albert, had lost his composure; and I was moved beyond expression.

"And this woman," she continued, "had to leave us, Werther! God, must we part with everything we hold dear in this world? Nobody felt this more deeply than the children; they cried for a long time afterward and complained that the black men had carried away their dear mama."

Charlotte rose. I was so disturbed and shaken that I could not move, and held her hand. "We should go," she said; "it's late." She wanted to withdraw her hand, but I held it. "We shall see each other again," I cried; "we shall recognize each other under whatever conditions! I am going," I continued, "going willingly; but if I had to say forever, I could not bear it. Adieu, Charlotte; adieu, Albert. We shall meet again." "Yes; tomorrow, I suppose," she answered lightly. Tomorrow! how I felt the word! Oh! she little knew when she drew her hand away from mine . . . They walked down the avenue. I stood gazing after them in the moonlight, then threw myself on the ground, and wept, sprang up, and ran out on the terrace, and there below in the shade of the linden trees I saw her white frock gleaming as she disappeared near the garden gate. I stretched out my arms, and she vanished.

Book Two

October 20, 1771

We arrived here yesterday. The ambassador is indisposed, and will not go out for some days. If he were less unpleasant, all would be well. I see only too clearly that there are several trials in store for me. But courage; a light heart can bear anything. A light heart! I smile to find such a word coming from my pen. A little more lightheartedness would make me the happiest being under the sun. But must I despair of my talents and faculties, while others of far inferior gifts parade about with the utmost self-satisfaction? Gracious Providence, to Whom I owe all my powers, why didst Thou not withhold half the blessings I possess and give me in their place self-confidence and contentment?

But patience, patience! All will yet be well; you were quite right, my friend: since I have had to associate with other people and see what they do and how they live, I have become better satisfied with myself. For this is our nature, that we are ever anxious to compare ourselves with others; and our happiness or misery depends on the things and people with whom we compare ourselves. And nothing is more dangerous than solitude; our imagination, always disposed to rise high, nourished by the fantastic images of the poets, seems to project for us a chain of beings of whom we ourselves seem the most inferior. All things appear more perfect than they really are, and all seem superior to us. This is quite natural. We feel so often our own imperfections, and imagine that we perceive in others the qualities we do not possess, attributing to them also all that we have ourselves. And thus we form the idea of a perfect, happy man—a creature entirely of our own imagination.

But when, in spite of weakness and disappointments, we do our daily work in earnest, we shall find that with all false starts and compromises, we make better headway than others who have wind and tide with them; and it gives one a real feeling of self to keep pace with others or outstrip them in the race.

November 26, 1771

I am beginning to find life here more tolerable, considering all circumstances. The best thing is that I am busy; and the people I meet and their different ways keep me interested. I met Count C., and I respect him more and more every day. He is a man of understanding and great discernment; because he sees farther than other people, he is not cold in his manner but can inspire and return the warmest affection. He took an interest in me on one occasion, when I had to transact some business with him. From the very first word he realized that we understood each other, and that he could talk with me as he cannot with others. His frank and open kindness to me is beyond praise. There is nothing quite so pleasing and reassuring as to find an unusual mind in sympathy with our own.

December 24, 1771

As I expected, the ambassador annoys me. He is the most punctilious fool under heaven. He does everything step by step, as meticulous as an old woman; he is a man whom it is impossible to please, because he is never pleased with himself. I like to do work quickly and, when the job is finished, leave it at that. But he is likely to return my papers to me, saying, "They will do, but you might look them over again. One can always find a better word or a more appropriate particle." I completely lose my patience. Not a single "and" or any other conjunction must be omitted: he hates the inversions which I sometimes employ; and if we don't tune our sentences to the official key, he can't understand a word. It's dreadful to have to deal with such a fellow.

Count C.'s confidence is the only thing that cheers me. He told me frankly the other day that he was much displeased with the slowness and pedantry of the ambassador; that people like him make it difficult for themselves and others. "But," he added, "one has to put up with it, like a traveler who has to get across a mountain; if the mountain were not there, the road would be a good deal shorter and pleasanter; but there it is, and we must get over it."

The ambassador has noticed the Count's liking for me; this, too, annoys him, and he takes every opportunity to speak derogatorily of the Count. I naturally defend him, and that only makes matters worse. Yesterday he made me angry, for he seemed to imply criticism of me. "The Count," he said, "is a man of the world; he works easily and his style is good; but, like all literary people, he has no solid learning." He looked at me as if to see whether I had felt the dig. But he did not make me lose my temper; I despise a man who can think and act like this. However, I did make a stand, and answered with some warmth. The

Count, I said, was a man entitled to respect, both for his character and his knowledge. I had never met anyone whose mind was stored with more useful and extensive knowledge—who had, in fact, mastered such an infinite variety of subjects, and yet who retained all his feeling for the detail of ordinary business. This was all Greek to him and I took my leave, lest more of his twaddle should annoy me further.

As a matter of fact, you people are to blame for all this—you who talked me into this and had so much to say about an "active" life. An "active" life! If the fellow who plants potatoes and takes his corn to market is not more usefully employed than I am, then let me slave ten years longer in the galleys to which I am now chained.

Oh the gilded wretchedness, the boredom among the silly people who parade about in society here! The fighting for rank! How they watch and worry to gain precedence! What poor and contemptible passions are displayed in utter shamelessness! We have a woman here, for example, who never stops talking about her noble family and her estates. A stranger would think her a silly fool, whose head was turned by her pretensions to rank and property; but she is actually even more ridiculous—she is the daughter of a mere magistrate's clerk from this neighborhood. I cannot understand how human beings can so stupidly debase themselves.

Every day I observe more and more the folly of judging others by ourselves. I have so much trouble with myself, and my own heart is so restless, that I would be quite content to let others pursue their own ways, if they would only allow me to do the same.

What provokes me most is the extent to which distinctions of rank are carried. I know perfectly well how inevitable class distinctions are; indeed, I myself derive advantages from them; but I would not have these institutions prove a barrier to the small chance of happiness which I may enjoy on this earth. The other day, during one of my walks, I became acquainted with a Lady B., a very charming woman, who has remained natural in the midst of all this artificiality. Our first conversation pleased us both equally; and, on leaving, I asked permission to visit her. She consented so delightfully that I could hardly wait to see her again. She is not a native of this place but lives here with her aunt. The looks of the old lady were not exactly prepossessing. I paid her much attention, addressing the greater part of my conversation to her; and, in less than half an hour, I discovered what her niece later admitted to me, that her aged aunt, with but a small fortune and an even more limited range of understanding, enjoys no satisfaction except in the pedigree of her ancestors, no protection save in her noble birth, and no enjoyment but in looking down from her height over the heads of the humbler citizens. In her youth she was, no doubt, handsome, and probably spent her time inflicting her caprices on many a poor youth; in her later years she sub-

mittted to the yoke of a veteran officer, who, in return for her person
and her small independence, spent with her, so to speak, her brass age.
He is dead, and she is now a widow and deserted. She spends her iron
age alone and nobody would pay her any attention if her niece were not
so enchanting.

January 8, 1772

What strange beings they are, whose thoughts are completely occupied
with etiquette and ceremony, who for years devote all their mental and
physical energies to the task of getting one step ahead or moving up one
place at the table! Not that they have nothing else to do; on the con-
trary, as they go to infinite trouble for such petty trifles, they have no
time for more important matters. Last week a quarrel arose at a
sleighing party, and our amusement was spoiled.

The silly creatures cannot see that it is not rank which constitutes real
greatness; the man who occupies the first place seldom plays the princi-
pal part. How often are kings governed by their ministers, and ministers
by their secretaries? Who is really the chief? He, it seems to me, who
can see through the other, and possesses strength or skill enough to
make their power or passions serve his own designs.

January 20

I must write to you, dear Charlotte, from the tap room of this poor
country inn, where I have taken shelter from a severe storm. As long as
I stayed in that wretched place, D., among strangers—strangers to this
heart—I at no time felt an inner need to write you; but now in this
cottage, in this solitude, the world shut out, with the snow and hail
beating against the windowpanes, you are my first thought. The moment
I entered, your image came to my mind—O Charlotte, our sacred,
tender memories! Gracious Heaven, that happy moment of our first
meeting!

If you could see me now, dear Charlotte, in the whirl of dissipation—
how my mind dries up and my heart is never really full! Not one single
moment of happiness: nothing! nothing touches me. I stand before a
puppet show and see the little puppets move, and I ask myself whether it
isn't an optical illusion. I am amused by these puppets, or rather, I am
myself one of them; I sometimes grasp my neighbor's wooden hand, and
withdraw with a shudder. In the evening I resolve to enjoy the next
morning's sunrise, but I remain in bed; during the day I promise myself
a walk by moonlight, but I stay at home. I don't know why I get up nor
why I go to sleep.

The leaven which animated my life is gone; the charm which cheered me in the gloom of night, and aroused me from my morning slumbers, is no longer with me.

I have found but one person here to interest me, a Lady B. She resembles you, dear Charlotte, if anyone can possibly resemble you. "Ah!" you will say, "he has learned how to pay compliments." Yes, this is partly true. I have been very well behaved lately; I can't help it; I have developed a good deal of wit and the ladies say that no one understands flattery better (or lies, you will add, since the one invariably accompanies the other. Do you see?). But I must tell you of Lady B. She has a genuine soul, which one sees in her lovely deep blue eyes. Her rank is a torment to her, and of course satisfies none of her desires. She longs to get away from this whirl of fashion, and we often picture to ourselves a life of undisturbed happiness in a world of idyllic peace; and then we speak of you, dearest Charlotte; and she has to listen to my praises of you; no, she doesn't have to, she likes to hear me speak of you, and loves you herself.

Oh that I were sitting at your feet in that familiar little room, with the children playing around us! If they became troublesome to you, I would tell them some chilling story and they would gather round me quietly.

The sun is setting magnificently over the snow-covered countryside, the storm is over, and I must return to my cage. Adieu! Is Albert with you? and what is he . . . ? God forgive the question.

February 8

For a week now we have had the most wretched weather, but this is a blessing to me. Every lovely day I have had here has been thoroughly spoiled by someone or other. As long as we have rain, sleet, frost and storm, I congratulate myself that it cannot be worse indoors than outside, nor worse outside than within. When the run rises bright in the morning and promises a glorious day, I can't help saying, "There, now, they have another gift from Heaven, which they will be sure to spoil!" They destroy everything—health, reputation, happiness, amusement; and they do it through folly, lack of understanding or narrow-mindedness, and always, if you are to believe them, with the best of intentions. Sometimes I could implore them, on bended knees, not to be so furiously determined to destroy themselves.

February 17

I am afraid that my ambassador and I shall not get along together much longer. He is quite insufferable. His manner of doing business is so ridiculous that I often cannot help contradicting him and doing things my own way; and then, of course, he disapproves. He complained of me

lately on this account at court; and the minister reprimanded me—
gently, to be sure—but still, he did reprimand me. I was about to submit
my resignation when I received a private letter from him,[1] which I
accepted with the greatest respect for the high, noble, and generous
spirit which had dictated it. He tried to soothe my excessive sensibility,
respected my rather exaggerated ideas of duty, of good example, and of
perseverance in business, as the fruit of my youthful ardor—qualities
which he did not seek to eliminate, but only moderate, so that they
might have their proper play and be productive of good. I am now at
rest for another week, and no longer at variance with myself. Content-
ment and peace of mind are wonderful things; I only wish, dear friend,
that these precious jewels were a little less frail.

February 20

God bless you, my dear friends, and may He grant you that happiness
which He denies me!

I thank you, Albert, for having deceived me. I was waiting to hear
when your wedding day was to be; I intended on that day solemnly to
take down Charlotte's silhouette from the wall, and to bury it among my
other papers. Now you are married, and her picture is still up. Well, let
it remain! Why not? I know that I am still near you, that I still have a
place in Charlotte's heart—the second place, but I intend to keep it.
Oh, I would go mad if she could ever forget! Albert, that thought is
sheer hell! Farewell, Albert—farewell, angel from heaven—farewell,
Charlotte!

March 15

I have just had an annoying experience which will drive me away from
here. I am furious. It cannot be undone, and you alone are to blame;
you urged and impelled me to fill a post for which I was not suited. Now
I have reason to be satisfied, and so have you! But, that you may not
again attribute this to my impetuous temper, I am sending you, my dear
sir, a plain and simple account of the whole thing, as a chronicler of facts
would record it.

Count C. likes and respects me. That is well known, and I have men-
tioned it to you a hundred times. Yesterday I dined with him. It was the

---

[1] Out of respect for this excellent man this letter and another one which is
mentioned later on have not been included in the present collection. It seemed
unlikely that even the warmest gratitude of the reading public would excuse such
an impropriety.

day on which his aristocratic friends assemble at his house in the evening. I never once thought of the gathering, nor that we people of inferior rank do not belong to such society. Well, I dined with the Count, and after dinner we adjourned to the great hall. We walked up and down together and I conversed with him, and with Colonel B., who joined us; and in this manner the hour for the assembly approached. God knows, I was unsuspecting enough, when who should enter but the honorable Lady S., accompanied by her noble husband and that nobly hatched little goose, their flat-chested and tight-laced daughter. They passed by in the traditional manner, their eyebrows raised high and their noses aristocratically turned up. As I detest the whole breed, I decided to leave, and waited to take leave only till the Count had disengaged himself from their awful prattle, when Lady B. came in. As I always feel cheered when I see her, I stayed and talked to her, leaning over the back of her chair, and did not notice till a little later that she seemed uneasy and answered me in an embarrassed manner. I was struck by this. "Heavens!" I said to myself, "is she like the rest of them?" I felt irritated and was about to withdraw, but I remained, making excuses for her conduct, imagining that she did not mean it, and still hoping to receive some friendly recognition. The rest of the company now arrived. There was Baron F. in a complete wardrobe that dated from the coronation of Francis I; the Chancellor N. (here called—*in qualitate*—von N.) with his deaf wife; the shabbily dressed J., whose old-fashioned coat bore evidence of some modernization—all these people were coming in. I talked with some of my acquaintances, but they answered me curtly. I was preoccupied with Lady B., and did not notice that the women at the end of the room were whispering, that the murmur extended by degrees to the men, that Lady S. talked to the Count (this was all later related to me by Lady B.), till at length the Count came up to me and took me to the window. "You know our curious customs," he said, "I gather the company is a little displeased at your presence. I would not on any account wish to . . ." "I beg Your Excellency's pardon!" I exclaimed. "I ought to have thought of this before, but I know you will forgive this *faux pas*. I meant to leave," I added, "some time ago, but my evil genius detained me." I smiled and bowed to take my leave. He shook me by the hand, in a manner which expressed everything. I withdrew from the illustrious assembly, sprang into a carriage, and drove to M. to watch the setting sun from the top of the hill, and read that beautiful passage in Homer where Ulysses is entertained by the hospitable swineherd. How delightful all that was!

I returned home to supper in the evening. Only a few persons were still in the dining room. They had turned up a corner of the tablecloth and were playing at dice. The good-natured Adelin came in, laid down his hat when he saw me, approached and said quietly, "You have had a disagreeable time." "I?" I exclaimed. "The Count made you leave the assembly." "Let the Devil take the assembly!" I said. "I was glad to get some fresh air." "I am delighted," he added, "that you take it so lightly. I am only annoyed that everybody is talking about it." The whole thing began to irk me. I fancied that everyone who sat down and looked at me was thinking of this incident, and I became furious.

And now I could plunge a dagger into my heart when I hear myself pitied everywhere, and see the triumph of my enemies, who say that this is always the lot of the vain whose heads are turned with conceit, who affect to be above convention and similar nonsense. Say what you will of independence, but show me the man who can patiently put up with the laughter of rascals when they have an advantage over him. Only when their talk is empty nonsense can he suffer it with indifference.

March 16

Everything conspires against me. I met Lady B. today. I joined her, and when we were at a little distance from her companions, I could not help expressing my surprise at her changed manner toward me. "O Werther!" she said warmly. "You who know my heart, how could you so mistake my distress? How I suffered for you from the moment I entered the room! I saw it coming; a hundred times I was on the point of mentioning it to you. I knew that the S.'s and T.'s with their husbands would leave the room rather than remain in your company. I knew that the Count would not break with them: and now all this excitement!" "How do you mean?" I exclaimed, and tried to conceal my emotion, for all that Adelin had mentioned to me yesterday suddenly came back to me. "Oh, how much it has already cost me!" said this enchanting girl, her eyes filled with tears. I could scarcely control myself, and was ready to throw myself at her feet. "What do you mean?" I cried. Tears ran down her cheeks. She wiped them away without attempting to conceal them. "You know my aunt," she continued; "she was present: and you can imagine what she thought of the whole affair! Last night, and this morning, Werther, I had to listen to a lecture about my acquaintance with you. I had to hear you condemned and disparaged; and I could not—I dared not—say much in your defense."

Every word she uttered was a dagger in my heart. She did not feel that it would have been merciful of her to conceal everything from me. She told me all the gossip that would be further spread, and how the malicious would triumph; how they would rejoice over the punishment of my pride, over my humiliation for that want of esteem for others with which I had often been reproached. To hear all this, Wilhelm, in a tone

of the most sincere sympathy,—it overwhelmed me and I am still fu-
rious within. I wish I could find someone who dared to jeer at me about
all this. I would run a sword through him. The sight of his blood would
be a relief. A hundred times have I seized a knife to give ease to this
oppressed heart. I have heard of a noble race of horses that instinctively
bite open a vein when they are hot and exhausted by a long run, in order
to breathe more freely. I am often tempted to open a vein, to gain ever-
lasting liberty for myself.

March 24

I have tendered my resignation to the Court. I hope it will be accepted,
and you will forgive me for not having previously consulted you. I must
leave this place. I know you will all urge me to stay, and therefore—do
sweeten this news to my mother. I cannot do anything for myself: how,
then, should I be able to assist others? It will hurt her that I should have
stopped that wonderful course leading me to a councilorship and minis-
try, and now backwards, little oxen, to the stable! Argue as you will,
combine all the reasons which might have induced or compelled me to
remain—I am leaving; that is enough. But, that you may know where I
am going, I will tell you that Prince * * *, who has been much pleased
with my company, has heard of my intention to resign and has invited
me to his country house to pass the spring months with him. I shall be
left completely to myself; and as we see eye to eye on a good many
subjects, I shall try my luck and accompany him.

For Your Information: *April 19*

Thanks for both your letters. I delayed my reply, and withheld this let-
ter, till I had an answer from the Court. I feared my mother might apply
to the minister to defeat my purpose. But my request is granted, my
resignation is accepted. I shall not tell you with what reluctance it was
accorded, or what the minister wrote; you would only renew your lam-
entations. The Prince has sent me a present of twenty-five ducats, with a
few words that have moved me to tears. Now I won't need the money
from my mother, for which I wrote the other day.

May 5

I leave here tomorrow, and since my birthplace is only six miles away, I
intend to visit it again and recall the old, happy days of my childhood. I
shall enter at the same gate through which I left with my mother, when,
after my father's death, she moved away from that delightful retreat to

bury herself in that unbearable town of hers. Adieu, Wilhelm, you shall hear soon of my doings.

May 9

I have paid my visit to my native place with all the devotion of a pilgrim, and have experienced many unexpected emotions. Near the great linden tree, a quarter of an hour from the town, I got out of the carriage and sent it on ahead so that I might enjoy the pleasure of recollection more vividly and to my heart's content. There I stood, under that same linden tree which used to be the goal and end of my walks. How things have changed! Then, in happy ignorance, I yearned to go out into the world, where I hoped to find the stimulus and enjoyment which my heart desired; and now, on my return from that wide world, O my friend, how many disappointed hopes and unfulfilled plans have I brought back! As I saw the mountains which lay stretched out before me, I thought how often they had been the object of my dearest desires. Here I used to sit for hours, wishing to be there, wishing that I might lose myself in the woods and valleys that lay so enchanting and mysterious before me—and when I had to return to town at a definite time, how unwillingly did I leave this cherished place! I approached the town; and recognized all the well-known old summerhouses; I disliked the new ones, and all the changes which had occurred. I entered the gate, and all the old feelings returned. Dear friend, I cannot go into details; charming as they were, they would make dull reading. I had intended to lodge in the market place, near our old house. As I approached, I noticed that the school in which, as children, we had been taught by that good old lady, was converted into a shop. I called to mind the restlessness, the heaviness, the tears, and heartaches which I experienced in that confinement. Every step produced some particular impression. No pilgrim in the Holy Land could meet so many spots charged with pious memories, and his soul can hardly be moved with greater devotion. One incident will serve for illustration. I followed the stream down to a farm—it used to be a favorite walk of mine—and I paused where we boys used to amuse ourselves skipping stones upon the water. I remember so well how I sometimes watched the course of that same stream, following it with strange feelings and romantic ideas of the countries it was to pass through; but my imagination was soon exhausted. Yet I knew that the water continued flowing on and on . . . and I lost myself completely in the contemplation of the infinite distance. Exactly like this, my friend, so happy and so rich were the thoughts of the ancients. Their feelings and their poetry were fresh as childhood. And when Ulysses talks of the immeasurable sea and boundless earth, his words are true, natural, deeply felt, and mysterious. Of what use is it that I have learned, with every schoolboy, that the world is round? Man needs but little earth for his happiness, and still less for his final rest.

I am at present at the Prince's hunting lodge. He is a man with whom one can live quite well. He is honest and simple. There are, however, some curious characters about him whom I cannot quite understand. They are not dishonest, and yet they do not seem thoroughly honorable men. Sometimes I am disposed to trust them, and yet I cannot persuade myself to confide in them. It annoys me to hear the Prince talk of things which he has only read or heard of, and always from the point of view from which they have been represented by others.

He values my understanding and talents more highly than my heart, but I am proud of my heart alone. It is the sole source of everything—all our strength, happiness, and misery. Ah, the knowledge I possess anyone can acquire, but my heart is all my own.

May 25

I had a plan in my head of which I did not want to speak to you until it was accomplished; but now that it has not materialized, I may as well mention it. I wanted to go off to war, and had long been thinking about it. This was the chief reason for my coming here with the Prince, who is a general in the * * * service. I mentioned my intention to him during one of our walks together; but he dissuaded me, and I should have had to be really passionate about it, and not merely playing with the idea, to disregard his reasons.

June 11

Say what you will, I can't stay any longer. Why should I? I'm getting bored. The Prince is as gracious to me as anyone could be, and yet I am not in my element. There is, at any rate, little in common between us. He is a man of understanding, but quite of the ordinary kind. His conversation affords me no more amusement than I should derive from any well-written book. I shall remain a week longer, and then start again on my wanderings. My sketches are the best things I have done since I came here. The Prince has a feeling for art, and would be more sensitive still if his mind were not fettered by pseudo-scientific ideas and commonplace terminology. I often lose patience when, with glowing imagination, I express my feelings of art and nature, and he, thinking to be especially understanding, spoils everything with his clichés.

June 16

I am just a wanderer, a pilgrim on this earth. But what more are you?

June 18

Where am I going? I will tell you in confidence. I must stay here a
fortnight longer, and then I had a notion to visit the mines in * * *. But I
am only deluding myself. The fact is, I want to be near Charlotte again,
that's all. I smile at my own heart, and do its bidding.

July 29

No! it's fine as it is—all is well! I—her husband! Oh God, Who gave me
my life, if Thou hadst destined this happiness for me, my whole life
would have been one continued prayer of thanks! I will not complain—
forgive these tears, forgive these vain wishes. She—my wife! To have
held that dearest of Heaven's creatures in my arms! My whole body
shakes, Wilhelm, when Albert embraces her slender waist!

And dare I say it? Why not, Wilhelm? She would have been happier
with me than with him. Albert is not the man to satisfy the wishes of
such a heart. He lacks a certain sensibility; he lacks—put it any way you
like—their hearts don't beat in unison. At a passage in some beloved
book, when my heart and Charlotte's seem to meet, and in a hundred
other instances when our feelings are revealed by the story of some
other character. . . But, dear Wilhelm, he loves her with all his heart,
and such a love is worth a great deal.

I have been interrupted by an insufferable visitor. I have dried my
tears; my thoughts are elsewhere. Adieu, my dear friend!

August 4

I am not alone in my unhappiness. All men are disappointed in their
hopes and deceived in their expectations. I visited that good woman
under the linden. The eldest boy ran out to meet me; his shouts of joy
brought out his mother, who looked downcast. Her first words were:
"Alas! dear sir, my little Hans is dead." He was the youngest of her
children. I was silent. "And my husband has returned from Switzerland
empty-handed; and if some kind people had not helped him, he would
have had to beg his way home. He was taken ill with fever on his jour-
ney." I could say nothing, but gave something to the little one. She
offered me some fruit. I accepted, and left the place with a heavy heart.

August 21

I change at the turn of a hand. Sometimes a happy prospect seems to
open before me; but alas! it's only for a moment; and then, when I am
lost in dreams, I cannot help saying to myself, "What if Albert were to

die?—Yes, she would become—and I should be"—and so I pursue a chimera, till it leads me to the edge of an abyss before which I shudder.

When I leave through the same town gate, and walk along the same road which first took me to Charlotte, how different it all used to be! All, all is changed! No trace of that past world, no throb of my heart is the same. I feel like the ghost that has returned to the burnt-out castle which it had built in more splendid times, adorned with costly magnificence, and left lavishly furnished to a beloved son.

September 3

I sometimes cannot understand how another can love her so, dare love her, when I love nothing in this world so completely, so devotedly, as I love her, when she is my only thought, and I have nothing but her in the whole world.

September 4

Yes, so it is! As Nature turns to autumn, it becomes autumn within me and around me. My leaves are sear and yellow, and the trees near by have already lost their leaves. Do you remember my writing to you about a peasant lad shortly after my arrival here? I inquired again about him in Wahlheim. They said he was dismissed from his service, and no one knew anything further of him. I met him yesterday on the road, going to a neighboring village. I spoke to him and he told me his story. It touched me immensely, as you will easily understand when I repeat it to you. But why trouble you? Why not keep my anguish and sorrow to myself? Why distress you and give you a chance to pity and blame me? Unless this too is part of my destiny.

At first the lad answered my inquiries with a sort of subdued melancholy, which seemed more shyness than anything else; but as he began to recognize me, he spoke with less reserve, and openly admitted his faults and deplored his misfortune. I wish, dear friend, I could give true expression to his language. He confessed, indeed he told me with a sort of pleasurable recollection, that after my departure his passion for that woman grew daily, until at last he knew neither what he did or said, nor what was to become of him. He could not eat or drink or sleep; he felt suffocated; he did what he was not supposed to do, and forgot all orders; he seemed haunted by an evil spirit, till one day, knowing that the woman had gone upstairs, he had followed, or rather, been drawn after her. She would not listen to him, and he became violent. He does not know what happened, but he called God to witness that his intentions had always been honest and that he wanted nothing more sincerely than that they should get married and spend their lives together. After he had talked for awhile, he began to hesitate, as if there were something which he didn't have the courage to utter, till at length he admitted with some confusion that she had encouraged him now and again and had allowed him liberties. He broke off two or three times in his story, and assured me most earnestly that he had no wish to make her bad, as he put it; he loved her as sincerely as ever; he had never told the story before and had spoken of it to me only to prove that he was not completely worthless and mad. And here, my friend, I must start that old song which you know I always repeat. If I could only describe the man as he stood, and stands now before me—could only convey it all to you, you would feel that I do and must sympathize with his fate. Enough! You, who know my misfortune and my disposition, can easily understand what draws me toward every unfortunate being, but particularly toward this one.

As I reread this letter, I find I have forgotten to tell you the end of my tale; it is easily supplied. She fought him off, just as her brother appeared, who had long hated him and wanted him turned out of the house because, as his sister was childless, he was afraid that a second marriage might deprive his children of the handsome fortune they expected from her. The man was dismissed at once, and such a row was made about the whole business that she dared not take him back, even if she had wanted to. She has since hired another helper, with whom, they say, her brother is equally displeased, and whom she is likely to marry; but I am told that the brother is determined not to tolerate it.

This story is neither exaggerated nor embellished; as a matter of fact, I have told it in a very pale manner, and the conventional moral phrases that I have used may make it cruder than it should be.

This love, this constancy, this passion, is no poetical fiction. It is real and exists in its greatest purity amongst that class of people whom we call rude, uneducated. We—the would-be educated—who are so civilized that we are nothing. Read this story with respect, I beg of you. I am quiet today, as I write this; you see by my handwriting that I am not so excited as usual. Read this account, Wilhelm, and imagine that it might well be the story of your friend! Yes, it has happened to me; it will happen to me; and I am not half so brave, not half so determined as that poor wretch with whom I hardly dare to compare myself.

September 5

She had written a letter to her husband in the countryside, where he had official business. It began, "My dearest love, come back as soon as you can; I await you with all my love." A friend who came to the house brought word that, for certain reasons, Albert would not return immediately. The letter was not sent, and the same evening it fell into my hands. I read it, and smiled. She asked me why. "What a heavenly gift is imagination!" I exclaimed; "for a moment I thought that this was written to me." She changed the subject and seemed displeased. I was silent.

September 6

It cost me a great deal to part with that plain blue coat I wore the first time I danced with Charlotte, but I could not possibly wear it any longer. I have ordered a new one, exactly like the other, even to the collar and facings, and a new yellow waistcoat and a pair of breeches.

But it's not the same. I don't know why. . . . Perhaps in time I'll like it better.

September 12

She has been away for a few days to meet Albert. Today I visited her: she rose to greet me, and, overjoyed, I kissed her hand.

A canary flew from the mirror and settled on her shoulder. "Here's a new friend," she said and coaxed him to perch on her hand; "he's a present for the children. What a dear he is! Look at him! When I feed him, he flutters with his wings, and pecks so nicely. He can kiss me too—look!"

She held the bird to her mouth and he pressed her sweet lips as if he felt the bliss.

"He shall kiss you too," she added, and held the bird toward me. His little beak moved from her mouth to mine, and the touch of his peck seemed like the foretaste of the sweetest happiness.

"His kiss," I said, "is greedy; he wants food, and seems disappointed by these unsatisfactory endearments."

"He eats out of my mouth," she continued, and gave him a few morsels between her lips, smiling and happy to share her love so innocently.

I turned away. She shouldn't do this. She shouldn't excite my imagination with all this heavenly bliss nor awaken my heart from the slumber to which the monotony of life sometimes lulls it. And why not? She trusts me! She knows how much I love her.

September 15

It makes me furious, Wilhelm, to think that there should be people incapable of appreciating the few things of real value on this earth. You remember the walnut trees at St. under which I used to sit with Charlotte at the old vicar's—those glorious trees which so often filled my heart with delight, how intimately they enclosed the parsonage yard with their cool and wide branches! and how pleasing it was to remember the honest pastors who planted them so many years ago! The schoolmaster has frequently mentioned the name of one of them, which he learned from his grandfather. He must have been an excellent man; under the shade of those old trees his memory was sacred to me. With tears in his eyes the schoolmaster told us yesterday that those trees had been felled—cut down! I could kill the dog who struck the first blow. This I have to bear! If I had only two such trees in my own yard, and one died from old age, I should weep with real grief. But there is one remarkable thing about it—the feelings of the people—the whole village is angry; and I hope the vicar's wife will soon find out, when the villagers will no longer bring her butter and eggs and other presents, how much she has wounded the feelings of the people. It was she who did it—the wife of the present minister (our good old man is dead)—a haggard, sickly creature who has, of course, every reason to disregard the world as the world completely disregards her. The silly woman affects to be learned, pretends to examine the canonical books of the Bible, lends her aid to the newfangled reformation of Christendom, moral and critical, and shrugs her shoulders at the mention of Lavater's enthusiasms. Her health is broken, and she therefore takes no pleasure in the joys of God's earth. Only that sort of creature could have cut down my walnut trees! You see, I can't keep at all calm! Listen to her reasons: the falling leaves make the yard wet and dirty; the branches obstruct the light; boys throw stones at the nuts when they are ripe, and the noise affects her nerves and disturbs her profound reflections, as she weighs the merits of Kennicot, Semler, and Michaelis. When I saw that all the villagers, particularly the old people, were displeased, I asked why they allowed it. "Ah, sir!" they replied, "when the steward orders, what can we poor peasants do?" But one good thing has happened. The steward and the vicar (who for once thought to reap some advantage from his wife's whims) intended to divide the trees between them. The revenue office, being informed of it, revived an old claim to the ground where the trees had stood, and sold them to the highest bidder. There they lie! If I were the Prince, I should know how to deal with them all—vicar, wife, steward, and revenue office. Prince, did I say? If I were the Prince I should care little about the trees that grow in my country.

October 10

Just to look into her black eyes is a source of happiness for me! And what grieves me is that Albert does not seem so happy as he—hoped to be—as I—thought I would be—if—I don't like to use these dashes, but here I can't express myself in any other way; and I am probably explicit enough.

October 12

Ossian has superseded Homer in my heart. What a world into which that magnificent poet carries me! To wander over the heath, blown about by the winds, which conjure up by the feeble light of the moon the spirits of our ancestors; to hear from the mountaintops, mid the roar of the rivers, their plaintive groans coming from deep caverns; and the laments of the maiden who sighs and perishes on the moss-covered, grassy tomb of the warrior who loved her. I meet the grey bard as he wanders on the heath seeking the footsteps of his fathers; alas! he finds only their tombstones. Then, turning to the pale moon, as it sinks beneath the waves of the rolling sea, the memory of past ages stirs in the soul of the hero—days when the friendly light shone upon the brave warriors and their bark laden with spoils, returning in triumph. When I read the deep sorrow in his countenance, see his dying glory sink exhausted into the grave, as he draws new and heart-thrilling delight from the impotent shades of his beloved ones, casting a look on the cold earth and the tall grass, exclaiming, "The traveler will come—will come who has seen my beauty, and will ask, 'Where is the bard—the illustrious son of Fingal?' He will pass over my tomb, and seek me in vain!"—O friend, I would, like a true and noble knight, draw my sword, and deliver my lord from the long and painful languor of a living death, and dismiss my own soul to follow the demigod whom my hand had set free!

October 19

Ah! the void—the fearful void within me! Sometimes I think, if I could once—only once—press her to my heart, this void would all be filled.

October 26

Yes, I feel certain, Wilhelm, and every day more certain, that the existence of any being is of very little consequence. A friend of Charlotte's came to see her just now. I withdrew to another room and took up a book; but, finding I could not read, I sat down to write. I heard them talk quietly about all sorts of things, gossip of the town: one was going to be married; another was ill, very ill—"She has a dry cough, you can see the bones in her face, and she faints occasionally. I wouldn't give a penny for her life," said the friend. "N. is in very poor health, too," said Charlotte. "His limbs begin to swell already," answered the other; and my lively imagination carried me at once to the bedside of those poor people. I saw them struggling against death, with all the agonies of pain and horror. And these ladies, Wilhelm, talked of all this with as much indifference as if they were discussing the death of a stranger. And when I look around the room where I now am—when I see Charlotte's apparel lying about, and Albert's papers, and the furniture which is so familiar to me, even to the very inkstand which I am using—when I think what I am to this family!—all in all. My friends respect me; I often make them happy, and my heart seems as if it could not beat without them; and yet—if I were to die, if I were to leave this circle—would they feel—or how long would they feel—the void which my loss would make in their lives? How long? Yes, such is the frailty of man that even where he has the greatest certainty of his own being, where he makes the truest and most forcible impression—in the memory, in the heart of his beloved, there also he must perish—vanish—and that so soon!

October 27

I could tear open my breast and dash out my brains to think how little we can actually mean to each other. No one can give me those sensations of love, joy, rapture, and delight which I do not myself possess; and though my heart may be filled with bliss, I cannot make him happy who stands before me cold and indifferent.

October 27, in the evening

I possess so much, but my love for her absorbs it all. I possess so much, but without her I have nothing.

October 30

A hundred times I have been on the verge of embracing her. God! What a torture it is to see so much loveliness before one, and yet not dare to touch it! And touching with our hands is the most natural of human instincts. Do not children touch everything they see? And I?

November 3

God knows how often I lie down to sleep wishing and even hoping that I may never awaken again! And in the morning, when I open my eyes, I see the sun once more, and am wretched. If only I were a moody person, I might blame the weather, or an acquaintance, or disappointment, for my discontented mind; then at least this insupportable load of trouble would not rest entirely upon me. But ah! I feel all too clearly that I alone am to blame for my woe. To blame? No, my own heart contains the source of all my sorrow, as it previously contained the source of all my bliss. Am I not the same who once enjoyed an abundance of happiness, who at every step saw paradise open before him, and whose heart was ever ready to embrace the whole world? And this heart is now dead; no delight will flow from it. My eyes are dry, and my senses, no longer refreshed by soft tears, cause an anxious contraction of my brow. I suffer much, for I have lost the only joy of my life: that active, sacred power with which I created worlds around me—it is no more. When I look from my window at the distant hills, and behold the morning sun breaking through the mists, and illuminating the country around, which is still wrapped in silence, and the gentle stream winds among the willows, which have shed their leaves; when this magnificent scene lies there before me like a varnished picture, and all this glory cannot pump one single drop of happiness from my heart into my brain—there he stands, the poor fellow, in the face of God's glory, like a dry spring or an empty pail. I have often thrown myself to the ground and implored God for tears as the farmer prays for rain when the sky above him is brazen and the ground about him is parched.

But I feel that God does not grant sunshine or rain to our furious prayers. Those bygone days, whose memory now torments me—why were they so happy? Because I waited with patience for the blessings of His spirit and received the delight He poured over me with the grateful feelings of a thankful heart.

November 8

Charlotte has reproved me for my excesses—and with so much tenderness and goodness! I have been drinking a little more wine than usual. "Don't do it," she said; "think of Charlotte!" "Think of you!" I answered. "Need you tell me that? Whether I think of you deliberately or not, you are always before me! This morning I sat on the spot where, a few days ago, you stepped from the carriage, and—" She changed the subject to prevent me from getting deeper into it. My friend, I am lost; she can do with me what she pleases.

November 15

Thank you, Wilhelm, for your kind sympathy, for your well-meaning advice; and I implore you not to be disturbed. Let me endure to the end. In spite of my weariness, I still have strength enough to see it through. I respect religion—you know I do. I feel that it can give strength to the feeble and comfort to the afflicted. But does it affect all men alike? Look at the great world: you will see thousands for whom religion has

never existed, thousands for whom it will never exist, whether it be
preached to them or not; must it, then, necessarily exist for me? Does
not the Son of God Himself say that they are His whom the Father has
given to Him? Have I been given to Him? What if our Father should
want to keep me for Himself, as my heart sometimes tells me? I pray you,
do not misinterpret this. Do not see mockery in these innocent words.
I pour out my whole soul before you. Silence would have been better; I
do not like to waste words on a subject of which everyone else knows as
little as I do. What is the destiny of man but to fill up the measure of
his sufferings, and to drink his allotted cup of bitterness? And if that
same cup proved bitter to the Son of God, why should I affect a fool-
ish pride and call it sweet? Why should I be ashamed of shrinking at
that fearful moment when my whole being trembles between existence
and annihilation; when the remembrance of the past, like a flash of
lightning, illuminates the dark abyss of the future; when everything dis-
solves around me, and the whole world vanishes? Is it not the voice of a
creature oppressed beyond all resource, insufficient, irresistibly plung-
ing to destruction, and groaning deeply at its inadequate strength: "My
God! my God! why hast Thou forsaken me?" And should I feel ashamed
to utter these words? Should I not shudder at the moment which had
its fears even for Him Who folds up the heavens like a garment?

November 21

She does not see, she does not feel that she is preparing a poison which
will destroy us both; and I drink deeply of the draught that is to prove
my destruction. What is the meaning of those looks of kindness with
which she often—often? no, not often, but sometimes—looks at me,
that politeness with which she hears an involuntary expression of my
feeling, the tender pity for my suffering which she sometimes seems to
show?

Yesterday, as I was leaving, she took my hand and said, "Adieu, dear
Werther." Dear Werther! It was the first time she ever called me
"dear": it penetrated my whole being. I have repeated it a hundred
times and last night, as I was going to bed and talked to myself about
nothing in particular, I suddenly said, "Good night, dear Werther!" and
I could not help laughing at myself.

November 22

I cannot pray, "Let her be mine!" Yet she often seems to belong to me.
I cannot pray, "Give her to me!" for she is another's. I try to quiet my
suffering by all sorts of cool arguments. If I let myself go, I could com-
pose a whole litany of antitheses.

November 24

She feels what I suffer. This morning her look pierced my very soul. I found her alone, and said nothing; she looked at me. I no longer saw in her face the charms of beauty or the spark of her mind; these had disappeared. But I was struck by an expression much more touching—a look of the deepest sympathy and of the gentlest pity. Why was I afraid to throw myself at her feet? Why did I not dare to take her in my arms and answer her with a thousand kisses? She turned to her piano for relief and in a low and sweet voice accompanied the music with delicious sounds. Her lips never appeared lovelier; they seemed but just to open, that they might drink the sweet tones which came from the instrument, and return the delicate echo from her sweet mouth. Oh, if only I could convey all this to you! I was quite overcome, and bending down, pronounced this vow: "Never will I dare to kiss you, beautiful lips which the spirits of Heaven guard." And yet I want—but it stands like a barrier before my soul—this bliss—and then die to expiate the sin! Is it sin?

November 26

I often say to myself, "You alone are wretched; all others are happy; no one has ever been tormented like you." Then I read a passage of an ancient poet and it is as if I looked into my own heart. I have so much to endure! Have men before me ever been so wretched?

November 30

Never, it seems, shall I be at rest! Wherever I go, something occurs to upset me. Today—oh destiny! oh human nature!

At noon I went to walk by the river—I had no appetite. Everything around seemed gloomy; a cold and damp west wind blew from the mountains and heavy, grey clouds spread over the plain. I noticed at a distance a man in a shabby green coat, climbing among the rocks and apparently looking for herbs. When I approached, he turned round at the noise and I saw that he had an interesting face, in which a quiet melancholy, strongly marked by kindness, formed the principal feature. His long black hair was held in two coils by pins, and the rest was braided and hung down his back. As his dress indicated a person of lower rank, I thought he would not take it ill if I inquired about his business; I therefore asked what he was looking for. He replied, with a deep sigh, that he was looking for flowers and could find none. "But this is not the season," I observed, with a smile. "Oh, there are so many flowers!" he answered, as he came nearer. "In my garden there are roses and honeysuckles of two sorts: one sort was given to me by my father; they grow like weeds. I have been looking for them these two days, and can't find them. There are flowers out there, yellow, blue, and red; and that centaury has a very pretty blossom: but I can find none of them." I suspected something strange, and asked him in a roundabout way what he intended to do with his flowers. A curious twitching smile spread over his face. Holding one finger to his mouth, he implored me not to betray him; then he told me that he had promised to gather a nosegay for his sweetheart. "That's a fine idea," said I. "Oh!" he replied, "she has many other things as well; she is very rich." "And yet," I continued, "she likes your nosegays." "Oh, she has jewels and a crown!" he exclaimed. I asked who she was. "If the States-General would only pay me," he added, "I should be a different person. There was a time when I was well off; but that is past; now I am—" He raised his tear-filled eyes to heaven. "And you were happy once?" I asked him. "Ah, would I were so still!" was his reply. "I was as joyful and contented as a fish in water." An old woman who was coming toward us now called out: "Henry, Henry! where are you? We have been looking for you everywhere. Come and eat." "Is that your son?" I inquired, as I went toward her. "Yes," she said; "he is my poor, unfortunate son. The Lord has sent me a heavy cross." I asked how long he had been like this. She answered: "He has been as calm as he is at present for about six months. Thank Heaven that he has so far recovered. For a whole year he was quite violent and had to be chained down in a madhouse. Now he harms no one, but talks of nothing but kings and emperors. He used to be a good, quiet boy, who helped support me, and wrote a very fine hand. But all at once he became melancholy, was seized with a violent fever, grew distracted, and is now as you see. If I were to tell you, sir—" I interrupted her by asking what period it was in which he said he had been so happy. "Poor boy!" she exclaimed, with a smile of compassion, "he means the time when he was completely out of his mind—a time he never stops praising—when he was in the madhouse and unaware of his condition." I was thunderstruck. I put a piece of money in her hand and hastened away.

"When you were happy!" I exclaimed, as I returned quickly to the town, "happy as a fish in water!" God in heaven! is this the destiny of man? To be happy only before he has acquired his reason and again after he has lost it? Poor fellow! And yet I envy your fate; I envy the delusion to which you are a victim. You go forth with joy to gather flowers for your queen in winter, and grieve when you can find none, and cannot understand why they do not grow. And I—I wander forth without hope, without purpose; and I return as I came. You imagine what you would be if the States-General paid you. Happy mortal, who can ascribe your wretchedness to an earthly cause! You do not know, you do not feel, that in your own distracted heart and disordered brain dwells the source of that unhappiness which all the kings on earth cannot relieve.

Let that man die unconsoled who can deride the invalid for undertaking a journey to distant, healthful springs—which may only increase his sickness and hasten his painful death—or who can exult over the despairing mind of a sinner who, to obtain peace of conscience and relief from misery, makes a pilgrimage to the Holy Sepulchre. Each laborious step which hurts his wounded feet on rough and untrodden paths is balm for his troubled soul, and the journey of many a weary day brings nightly relief to his anguished heart. Will you dare call this illusion, you pompous fools? Madness! O God! Thou seest my tears. Thou hast allotted us our portion of misery: must we also have brethren to persecute us, to deprive us of our consolation, of our trust in Thee and in Thy love and mercy? For our trust in the virtue of the healing root or in the strength of the vine—what else is it but belief in Thee, from Whom all that surrounds us derives its healing and restoring powers? Father, Whom I know not—Who were once wont to fill my soul, but Who now hidest Thy face from me—call me back to Thee; be silent no longer! Thy silence cannot sustain a soul which thirsts after Thee. What man, what father, could be angry with a son for returning to him unexpectedly, for embracing him and exclaiming, "Here I am again, my father! Forgive me if I have shortened my journey to return before the appointed time! The world is everywhere the same—for labor and pain, pleasure and reward; but what does it all avail? I am happy only where thou art, and in thy presence I am content to suffer or enjoy." And Thou, Heavenly Father, wouldst Thou turn such a child from Thee?

December 1

Wilhelm! The man about whom I wrote to you—that man so happy in his misfortunes—was a clerk in the service of Charlotte's father. An unhappy passion for her, which he cherished, concealed, and eventually revealed, made him lose his position. This caused his madness. Think, as you read these dry words, what an impression all this has made on me! Albert told it as calmly as you will probably read it.

December 4

I implore you. It is all over with me. I cannot bear it any longer. Today I sat by Charlotte. She was playing on her piano all sorts of melodies, and with such—expression! Her little sister sat on my lap dressing her doll. Tears came into my eyes. I leaned down, and saw Charlotte's wedding ring; my tears fell—and as if by chance she began to play that favorite tune, that sweet air which has so often enchanted me. I felt comfort from a recollection of the past, of those earlier times when I heard that melody; and then I recalled all the sorrows and the disappointments which I had since endured—and then—I walked up and down the room, my heart choked with painful emotions. Finally, starting toward her with an impatient outburst, I said, "For Heaven's sake, stop it!" She stopped playing, and looked at me. Then she said, with a smile which went deep to my heart: "Werther, you are ill. Your dearest food is distasteful to you. Go, I ask you, and try to calm yourself." I tore myself away. God, Thou seest my torments, and will end them!

December 6

How her image haunts me! Waking or asleep, she fills all my thoughts! When I close my eyes, here, in my brain, where all the energies of inward vision are concentrated, are her black eyes. Here—I can't express it. But if I shut my eyes, there are hers: dark as the ocean, as an abyss they lie before me, and fill the nerves of my brain.

What is man—that much praised demigod? Do not his powers fail when he most requires their use? And whether he soar in joy or sink in sorrow, is he not inevitably arrested? And while he fondly dreams that he is grasping at infinity, is he not at that moment made doubly aware of the dull monotony of his existence?

The Editor to the Reader

I wish that we had so many documents by his own hand about our friend's memorable last days that I did not need to interrupt the sequence of his letters by a connecting narrative.

I have felt it my duty to collect accurate information from persons well acquainted with his history. The story is simple; and all accounts agree, except for some unimportant particulars. Only with respect to the character of the persons involved do opinions and judgments vary.

All that is left to do, then, is to relate conscientiously the facts which our persistent labor has enabled us to collect, to give the letters found after his death, and to pay attention to even the slightest fragment from his pen, especially since it is so difficult to discover the true and innermost motives of men who are not of the common run.

Sorrow and discontent had taken deep root in Werther's soul and gradually penetrated his whole being. His mind became completely deranged; perpetual excitement and mental irritation, which weakened his natural powers, produced the saddest effects upon him and rendered him at length the victim of a weariness against which he struggled with even greater effort than he had displayed in his other misfortunes. The anguish of his heart consumed his good qualities, his vivaciousness and his keen mind; he was soon a gloomy companion—increasingly unhappy, and the more unjust in his ideas, the more wretched he became. This, at least, is the opinion of Albert's friends. They insist that Werther had been unable to appreciate so steady and direct a man as Albert, who had found that happiness which he had so long wished for, and who meant to guard this happiness for the years to come. Werther could not understand such an attitude since he himself was inclined to squander his own substance every day, only to suffer privation and distress. Albert, they said, had in the meantime not changed at all; he was still the man whom Werther had known, honored and respected from the beginning. His love for Charlotte was unbounded; he was proud of her, and wanted her recognized by everyone as the noblest of human beings. Was he to blame for wishing to keep from her every appearance of suspicion? Or for his unwillingness to share this precious love with another, even for a moment, and however innocently? His friends admit that Albert frequently retired from his wife's rooms during Werther's visits; that he did so not from hatred or dislike for his friend, but rather from a feeling that his presence was oppressive to Werther.

Charlotte's father, who was confined to the house by indisposition, had sent his carriage for her, and she went out to him. It was a beautiful winter day, the first snow had fallen and covered the countryside.

The next morning Werther followed Charlotte, so that, if Albert could not meet her, he might accompany her home.

The clear weather had but little effect on his troubled mind. A heavy weight lay upon his soul, deep melancholy had taken possession of him. He was pursued by a host of the saddest images and his mind knew no change save from one painful thought to another.

As he was not at peace with himself, the condition of his fellow creatures was for him a perpetual source of concern and distress. He believed he had disturbed the happiness of Albert and his wife, and although he censured himself severely for this, he could not quite suppress a certain feeling of dislike for Albert.

On his way to Lotte, his thoughts dwelt on this subject. "Yes, yes," he said to himself, gnashing his teeth, "all this intimate, warm, tender and sympathetic love, this calm and lasting fidelity! What is it in reality but surfeit and indifference? Is he not infinitely more interested in any one of his miserable official duties than in his dear and incomparable wife? Does he appreciate his good fortune? Does he respect her as she deserves? He possesses her; very well—he possesses her; I know it—I have become accustomed to that thought, although it will drive me mad yet, it will kill me! And has his friendship for me really stood the test? Doesn't he regard my attachment to Charlotte as an infringement on his rights and my attentions to her as a silent rebuke for himself? I know perfectly well, I feel it, he dislikes me, he wants me to go, my presence is irksome to him."

He would often pause suddenly and stand still as if in doubt, and seem about to turn back; but he went on, and finally, engaged in such thoughts and soliloquies, somehow against his will, he reached the hunting lodge.

He entered, and, inquiring for Charlotte and her father, he noticed that the household was in a state of considerable confusion.

The eldest boy told him that an accident had occurred at Wahlheim, that a peasant had been murdered. This made little impression upon him. Entering the room he found Charlotte pleading with her father who, in spite of his illness, insisted on going to the scene of the crime in order to conduct an inquiry. The criminal was as yet unknown; the victim had been found dead at his own door that morning. Suspicions were aroused: the murdered man had been in the service of a widow, and the fellow who had previously held the job had been dismissed by her.

As soon as Werther heard this he cried excitedly: "Is it possible! I must go over there at once! I cannot stay a moment!" He hastened towards Wahlheim. He recalled the earlier meeting and did not doubt that the murderer was the man with whom he had so often spoken, and for whom he entertained so much regard.

His way took him past the linden trees to the house where the body had been carried. He felt a sudden horror at the sight of the spot that he remembered so fondly. The threshold where the neighbors' children had so often played together was stained with blood. Love and attachment, the noblest feelings of human nature, had been turned to violence and murder. The huge trees stood there, leafless and covered with hoarfrost; the beautiful hedgerows which had overgrown the low wall of the churchyard were bare, and here and there, half covered with snow, gravestones were visible.

As he came nearer the inn, in front of which the whole village was assembled, he suddenly heard shouts. A troop of armed peasants approached and everyone exclaimed that the criminal had been apprehended. Werther looked, and saw at once that it was the young man who had been so attached to the widow, and whom he had recently met prowling about with suppressed anger and ill-concealed despair.

"What have you done?" said Werther as he approached the prisoner. The young man turned his eyes upon him in silence, and then replied with perfect composure, "No one will marry her now, and she will marry no one." The prisoner was taken into the inn, and Werther left.

His mind was much excited by this terrible incident. For one moment he was lifted out of his usual feelings of melancholy, moroseness, and indifference to everything around him. He was seized by pity for the prisoner and felt an indescribable urge to save him from his impending fate. He felt for the man, thought his crime quite excusable, and identified himself so completely with the fellow that he was convinced he could make everyone view the matter in the light in which he saw it himself. He wanted to defend him, and began composing an eloquent speech for the occasion; and on his way to the hunting lodge he could not help uttering aloud all the things which he resolved to put before the judge.

On his arrival, he found Albert, and was a little irritated by this encounter. But he soon recovered himself and with much warmth expressed his views to the judge. The latter shook his head doubtingly; and although Werther urged his case with the utmost zeal, feeling, and determination, yet, as can be easily supposed, the judge was not much impressed by his appeal. On the contrary, he interrupted him, energetically contradicted him, and even rebuked him for being the advocate of a murderer. He demonstrated that, if Werther were right, every law would be violated and the public security utterly destroyed. He added that he could himself do nothing without assuming the gravest responsibility; that everything must proceed in due course, and go through the regular channels.

Werther, however, did not give in, and even suggested that the judge look away if someone tried to help the prisoner escape. But this proposal was, of course, rejected. Albert, who eventually took part in the discussion, agreed with the judge. At this Werther became enraged and took his leave in great anger after the judge had repeatedly said "No, he can't be saved."

How deeply these words must have struck him can be seen from a slip of paper which was found among his belongings, and which was undoubtedly written on that same day.

"You cannot be saved, unfortunate man! I see only too well that we cannot be saved!"

Werther was highly irritated at the remarks which Albert had made to the judge in this matter of the prisoner. He thought he could detect in them a little bitterness towards himself personally; and although, upon reflection, it could not escape his sound judgment that their view of the matter was correct, he felt the greatest possible reluctance to make such an admission.

A note of Werther's upon this point, expressive perhaps of his general feelings towards Albert, was found among his papers.

"What is the use of continually repeating to myself that he is a good and admirable man? It tears my heart, and I can't be just towards him."

On the same evening the weather was mild and Charlotte and Albert walked home together. From time to time she looked about her, as if she missed Werther's company. Albert began to speak of him, criticizing him, though most fairly. He alluded to his unfortunate attachment and wished it were possible to send him away. "I should like it for our sake," he added; "and I would ask you to do what you can to alter his behavior towards you. Convince him to visit you less frequently. The world is full of gossip, and I know that here and there people are talking about us." Charlotte made no reply, and Albert seemed to feel what her silence meant. At least from that time on he never spoke of Werther again; and when she brought up his name, he allowed the conversation to die, or else he changed the subject.

The vain attempt Werther made to save the unhappy murderer was the last feeble glimmering of a flame about to be extinguished. He sank only more deeply into a state of gloom and inactivity, and was nearly brought to distraction when he learned that he might be summoned as a witness against the prisoner, who now denied everything.

His mind became oppressed by the recollection of every misfortune in his past life. The annoyance he had suffered at the ambassador's, and his subsequent failures and troubles were revived in his memory. All this, he felt, gave him a right to be inactive. Without any energy left he seemed cut off from every pursuit and occupation which makes the business of everyday life. He became a victim of his own susceptibility, and of his restless passion for the most enchanting and beloved of women, whose peace he had destroyed. In this unvarying monotony of existence his days were consumed; and his powers became exhausted since he lived without purpose or design, until he seemed ever nearer his sorrowful end.

A few letters which he left behind, and which we here insert, afford the best proof of his anguish of mind and of the depth of his passion, as well as of his doubts and struggles, and of his weariness of life.

December 12

Dear Wilhelm, I am reduced to the state of mind of those unfortunate creatures who believe they are pursued by an evil spirit. Sometimes I am oppressed, not by apprehension or fear, but by an inexpressible inner fury which seems to tear up my heart and choke me. It's awful, awful. And then I wander about amid the horrors of the night, at this dreadful time of year.

Yesterday evening it drove me outside. A rapid thaw had suddenly set in: I had been told that the river had risen, that the brooks had all overflowed their banks, and that the whole valley of Wahlheim was under water! I rushed out after eleven o'clock. A terrible sight. The furious torrents rolled from the mountains in the moonlight—fields, trees, and hedges torn up, and the entire valley one deep lake agitated by the roaring wind! And when the moon shone forth, and tinged the black clouds, and the wild torrent at my feet foamed and resounded in this grand and frightening light, I was overcome by feelings of terror, and at the same time yearning. With arms extended, I looked down into the yawning abyss, and cried, "Down! Down!" For a moment I was lost in the intense delight of ending my sorrows and my sufferings by a plunge into that gulf! But then I felt as if rooted to the earth, and incapable of ending my woes! My hour is not yet come: I feel it. Oh, Wilhelm, how willingly would I have given up my human existence to merge with the wind, or to embrace the torrent! Won't this imprisoned soul some day be released for such bliss?

I turned with sadness toward a favorite spot beneath a willow where I used to sit with Charlotte after a long walk. It too was submerged and I could hardly make out the willow tree, Wilhelm! And her meadows, I thought, the countryside near her lodge, the arbor devastated by the floods. . . And a ray of past happiness fell upon me, as the mind of a prisoner is cheered by a dream of flocks and fields and bygone honors. But I stood firm!—I have the courage to die! Perhaps I should have—but here I now sit, like an old woman who gathers her own firewood and begs her bread from door to door to ease her joyless, waning life, and lengthen it by a few moments.

December 14

What is the matter with me, Wilhelm? I am afraid of myself! Is not my love for her the purest, most holy and most brotherly? Have I ever felt a single reprehensible desire? But I will make no protestations. And now—dreams! How right were the people who ascribed all these conflicting feelings to some strange supernatural power! Last night—I tremble as I say it—I held her in my arms. I pressed her to me and covered with countless kisses those dear lips of hers which murmured words of love in response. Our eyes were one in the bliss of ecstasy. God—am I wrong still to feel that happiness, to recall once more those rapturous moments with the deepest delight? Charlotte! Charlotte! I am lost! My senses are confused, for a week now I have been almost beside myself. My eyes are filled with tears—nowhere at ease, yet everywhere at home—I wish for nothing—I have no desires—better I were gone.

Under the circumstances narrated above, a determination to quit this world had now taken fixed possession of Werther's mind. Since his return to Charlotte this thought had been the object of all his hopes and wishes; it was to be no precipitate, rash act; he would proceed with calmness and with the most perfect deliberation.

His troubles and inner struggles may be seen from the following note, which was found, without date, amongst his papers, and seems to be the beginning of a letter to Wilhelm:

Her presence, her fate, her sympathy with mine, press the last tears from my withered brain.

To lift the curtain, to step behind it—that is all! And why all these doubts and delays? Because we don't know what it is like behind—because there is no return—and because our mind suspects that all is darkness and confusion, where we have no certainty.

Eventually the melancholy thought of death became more and more familiar to him; and his resolution was now final and irrevocable, as the following ambiguous letter addressed to his friend demonstrates:

December 20

I am grateful to you, Wilhelm, for having so well understood what I said. Yes, you are right: it is better that I should go. Your suggestion that I should return to you does not quite please me; at least, I should like to make a little excursion on the way, particularly as we may now expect the frost to last, and the roads to be good. I am delighted that you will come to fetch me; only postpone it for a fortnight, and await another letter from me. One should not pluck the fruit before it is ripe, and a fortnight sooner or later makes a great difference. Ask my mother to pray for her son, and to forgive me for all the unhappiness I have caused her. It has ever been my fate to sadden those to whom I owed joy. Adieu, my dearest friend. May every blessing of heaven be upon you. Farewell.

We hardly dare to express in words the emotions with which Charlotte's soul was filled during the whole of this time, both in relation to her husband and to her unfortunate friend. But, knowing her character, we may form some idea of her frame of mind; a beautiful soul may be able to fathom her emotions and feel with her.

It is certain that she was determined to keep Werther at a distance; and if she hesitated, it was only from a sincere feeling of pity, knowing what it would cost him—indeed that he would find it almost impossible to comply with her wishes. But for various reasons she felt at that time more inclined to be firm. Her husband kept silent about the whole matter, as she herself had never made it a subject of conversation. But she felt all the more bound to prove to him by her conduct that her views agreed with his.

On the same day—it was the Sunday before Christmas—on which

Werther had written the last-mentioned letter to his friend, he came in the evening to Charlotte's house and found her alone. She was busy arranging some toys for her brothers and sisters which were to be distributed to them on Christmas Day. He talked of the pleasure of the children, and about those times when the unexpected opening of the door and the appearance of the Christmas tree, decorated with fruit and candy, and lighted up with wax candles, causes such paradisical joy. "You shall have a present, too, a little roll of wax tapers, and something else, if you behave well," said Charlotte, concealing her embarrassment under a sweet smile. "And what do you call behaving well? What am I to do, what can I do, dearest Charlotte?" said he. "Thursday night," she answered, "is Christmas Eve. The children are all to be here, and my father, too. There will be a present for each; you must come too, but not before that time." Werther was taken aback. "I beg of you; it has to be," she continued. "I beg you, for my own peace of mind. We can't go on like this any longer." He turned away from her, walked hastily up and down the room, muttering, "We can't go on like this any longer!" Charlotte, seeing the violent state into which these words had thrown him, tried to divert his thoughts by all sorts of questions, but in vain. "No, Charlotte!" he exclaimed; "I will never see you again!" "Why?" she answered. "Werther, you can, you must see us again; only control yourself. Oh! why were you born with that excessive, that ungovernable passion for everything that is dear to you?" Then, taking his hand, she said: "I beg of you, be calmer; your talents, your understanding, your knowledge, will furnish you with a thousand delights. Be a man, and conquer this unhappy attachment towards a person who can do nothing but pity you." He gritted his teeth and looked at her gloomily. She held his hand. "Only one moment of clear thinking, Werther," she said. "Don't you see that you are deceiving yourself, that you are seeking your own destruction? Why must you love me, me only, who belongs to another? I fear, I fear, that it is only the impossibility of possessing me that makes your desire for me so strong." He drew back his hand, with a fixed, angry look in his eyes, and cried, "Wise, very wise. Did Albert furnish you with this idea? It is politic, very clever." "Anyone might say it," she answered. "Is there not a woman in the whole world who could make you happy? Bring yourself to look for her, I swear that you will find her. I have long feared for you, and for us all: you have confined yourself to us for too long. Make an effort: a short journey will distract you. Seek and find an object worthy of your love; then return and let us enjoy together the happiness of a most perfect friendship."

"This speech," replied Werther, with a cold smile, "this speech ought to be printed for the benefit of all teachers. Dearest Charlotte, allow me but a little rest, and all will be well." "But, Werther," she added, "do not come again before Christmas Eve." He was about to make some answer when Albert came in. They greeted each other coolly, and with mutual embarrassment paced up and down the room. Werther made some casual remarks; Albert did the same, and their conversation soon dropped. Albert asked his wife about one or two household matters; and, finding that they had not been done, he used some expressions which, to Werther's ear, sounded harsh. He wished to go, but could not; and remained till eight o'clock, his uneasiness and dissatisfaction continually increasing. At length, the table was laid for supper, and he took his hat and stick. Albert asked him to stay; but Werther, suspecting a polite gesture, thanked him curtly and left.

Werther returned home, took the candle from his servant, and retired to his room alone. He talked to himself for some time, wept aloud, walked excitedly up and down his room; finally, without undressing, he threw himself on the bed, where he was found by his servant at eleven o'clock, when the latter ventured to enter his room and asked whether he might take off his master's boots. Werther let him do it, but ordered him not to come in the morning till he was called.

On Monday morning, December 21, he wrote the following letter to Charlotte, which was found, sealed, on his desk after his death, and was given to her. I shall insert it in sections; as it appears, from several circumstances, to have been written in that manner.

My mind is made up, Charlotte: I am resolved to die! I am writing you this without any romantic sentimentality, on this morning of the day when I am to see you for the last time. When you read this, my dearest, the cool grave will cover the stiff remains of that restless and unhappy man who, in the last moments of his life, knows no greater bliss than to converse with you! I have passed a dreadful night—or rather, a propitious one; for it has given me resolution, it has fixed my purpose. I am resolved to die. When I tore myself away from you yesterday, my senses were in tumult and disorder; my heart was oppressed, hope and pleasure had fled from me forever, and a cold horror had seized me. I could scarcely reach my room. I threw myself on my knees, and God, for the last time, granted me the bitter consolation of tears. A thousand ideas, a thousand schemes raced through my mind, till at last one fixed, final thought took possession of my heart. I intend to die. I lay down; and in the morning, in the quiet hour of awakening, I felt the same determination. I intend to die! It is not despair, but the certainty that I have reached the end, and must sacrifice myself for you. Yes, Charlotte, why should I not say it? One of us three must go: it shall be Werther. O Beloved! this heart, excited by rage and fury, has often had the monstrous impulse to murder your husband—you—myself! Now, it is decided. And in the bright, quiet evenings of summer, when you wander toward the mountains, let your thoughts turn to me: recollect how often you watched me coming to meet you from the valley; then, look toward the churchyard to my grave, and, by the light of the setting sun, mark how the evening breeze waves the tall grass which grows above my tomb. I was calm when I began this, but now, when I see it all so vividly, I am weeping like a child.

About ten in the morning, Werther called his servant, and, as he was dressing, told him that in a few days he intended to go away, and bade him therefore take out his clothes and prepare them for packing, call in all his accounts, fetch home the books he had lent, and give a two months' advance to some poor people to whom he usually gave a weekly allowance.

He had his meal in his room, and then mounted his horse and went to visit the judge, who, however, was not at home. He walked pensively in the garden, and seemed anxious to bury himself in melancholy memories.

The children did not let him alone for long. They followed him, skipping and dancing, and told him that after tomorrow—and another day—and one day more, they were to receive their Christmas presents from Charlotte; and they related all the wonders which their imaginations promised them. "Tomorrow—and again tomorrow," said he, "and one day more!" And he kissed them tenderly. He was about to go, but the younger boy stopped him to whisper something in his ear. He told him that his elder brothers had written beautiful New Year's wishes—so big—one for Papa, and another for Albert and Charlotte, and one for Werther; and they were to be presented early in the morning, on New Year's Day. This quite overwhelmed him. He made each of the children a present, mounted his horse, left his regards for Papa, and rode away with tears in his eyes.

He returned home towards five o'clock and ordered the maid to keep up his fire; he told his servant to pack his books and linen in the trunk downstairs, and to sew his clothes up in a bundle. It was probably then that he wrote the following passage from his last letter to Charlotte:

You aren't expecting me. You think I'll obey you and not visit you again till Christmas Eve. Oh, Charlotte, today or never again! On Christmas Eve you will hold this letter in your hand; you will tremble, and moisten it with your tears. I will, I must! Oh, how glad I am that I have made up my mind!

In the meantime, Charlotte found herself in an odd state of mind. After her last conversation with Werther, she realized how hard it would be to part from him, and how he would suffer if he had to go.

She had in Albert's presence casually mentioned that Werther would not return before Christmas Eve; and soon afterwards Albert went on horseback to see an official in the neighborhood with whom he had to transact some business that would detain him all night.

Charlotte was sitting alone. None of her family were near and her thoughts turned to her own situation: she was married to the man whose love and fidelity she trusted, to whom she was deeply devoted and who, with his steadiness and honesty, seemed heaven-sent to ensure her happiness. She knew what he would always be to her and the children. On the other hand, she had grown so fond of Werther; from the very first hour of their acquaintance she had felt the sympathy between them, and their long association and many common experiences had made an indelible impression upon her heart. She had become accustomed to sharing with him every thought and feeling, and his departure threatened to create a void in her life which it would be impossible to fill. How she wished that she might change him into her brother, that she could induce him to marry one of her own friends, and that she could re-establish his friendship with Albert.

In her mind she passed all her intimate friends in review, but found something objectionable in each, and could decide upon none to whom she would consent to give him.

Amid all these reflections she felt, for the first time, deeply though half unconsciously, that it was her secret wish to keep him for herself. But she realized that she could and must not do so. Her own heart, usually so clear and light and always able to find a way out of trouble, was oppressed with a load of distress that seemed to bar any prospect of happiness. She was depressed, and a dark cloud obscured her vision.

It was half past six when she heard Werther's step on the stairs. She recognized his voice, as he enquired if she were at home. Her heart beat furiously—we might almost say, for the first time—at his arrival. It was too late to deny her presence and as he entered she said with a sort of excited confusion: "You didn't keep your word!" "I promised nothing," he answered. "But you should have complied at least for my sake," she continued. "I asked you for the sake of your peace of mind and my own."

She scarcely knew what she said or did as she sent for some friends in order not to be alone with Werther. He put down several books he had brought with him, then enquired about some others, and she began to hope that her friends might arrive shortly and at the same time that they might stay away. The maid returned to say that neither friend could come.

For a moment she felt that the girl, with whatever work she had to do, should remain in the adjoining room, but she changed her mind. Werther, meanwhile, walked impatiently up and down. She went to the piano and began to play a minuet—but it didn't sound right. She pulled herself together and sat down quietly beside Werther, who had taken his usual place on the sofa.

"Have you brought nothing to read?" she enquired. He had nothing. "There in my drawer," she continued, "is your own translation of some of the songs of Ossian. I have not read them yet, I always hoped to hear you recite them; but it never seemed possible to arrange it." He smiled, and fetched the manuscript. A tremor ran through him as he took it in his hand, and his eyes were filled with tears as he looked at it. He sat down and read.

"Star of descending night! fair is thy light in the west! thou liftest thy unshorn head from thy cloud; thy steps are stately on thy hill. What dost thou behold in the plain? The stormy winds are laid. The murmur of the torrent comes from afar. Roaring waves climb the distant rock. The flies of evening are on their feeble wings; the hum of their course is on the field. What dost thou behold, fair light? But thou dost smile and depart. Thy waves come with joy around thee; they bathe thy lovely hair. Farewell, thou silent beam! Let the light of Ossian's soul arise!

"And it does arise in its strength! I behold my departed friends. Their gathering is on Lora, as in the days of other years. Fingal comes like a watery column of mist! his heroes are around; and see the bards of song—gray-haired Ullin! stately Ryno. Alpin with the tuneful voice! the soft complaint of Minona! How are ye changed, my friends, since the days of Selma's feast, when we contended, like gales of spring as they fly along the hill, and bend by turns the feebly whistling grass!

"Minona came forth in her beauty, with downcast look and tearful eye. Her hair flew slowly on the blast that rushed unfrequent from the hill. The souls of the heroes were sad when she raised the tuneful voice. Often had they seen the grave of Salgar, the dark dwelling of white-bosomed Colma. Colma left alone on the hill, with all her voice of song! Salgar promised to come; but the night descended around. Hear the voice of Colma, when she sat alone on the hill!

"*Colma:* It is night; I am alone, forlorn on the hill of storms. The wind is heard on the mountain. The torrent is howling down the rock. No hut receives me from the rain; forlorn on the hill of winds!

"Rise, moon, from behind thy clouds! Stars of the night, arise! Lead me, some light, to the place where my love rests from the chase alone! His bow near him unstrung, his dogs panting around him! But here I must sit alone by the rock of the mossy stream. The stream and the wind roar aloud. I hear not the voice of my love! Why delays my Salgar; why the chief of the hill his promise? Here is the rock, and here the tree; here is the roaring stream! Thou didst promise with night to be here. Ah, whither is my Salgar gone? With thee I would fly from my father, with thee from my brother of pride. Our races have long been foes: we are not foes, O Salgar!

"Cease a little while, O wind! stream, be thou silent awhile! Let my voice be heard around; let my wanderer hear me! Salgar! it is Colma who calls. Here is the tree and the rock. Salgar, my love, I am here! Why delayest thou thy coming? Lo! the calm moon comes forth. The flood is bright in the vale; the rocks are gray on the steep. I see him not on the brow. His dogs come not before him with tidings of his near approach. Here I must sit alone!

"Who lie on the heath beside me? Are they my love and my brother? Speak to me, O my friends! To Colma they give no reply. Speak to me: I am alone! My soul is tormented with fears. Ah, they are dead! Their swords are red from the fight. Oh, my brother! my brother! why hast thou slain my Salgar? Why, O Salgar! hast thou slain my brother? Dear were ye both to me! what shall I say in your praise? Thou wert fair on the hill among thousands! he was terrible in fight! Speak to me! hear my voice! hear me, sons of my love! They are silent, silent forever! Cold, cold, are their breasts of clay! Oh, from the rock on the hill, from the top of the windy steep, speak, ye ghosts of the dead! Speak, I will not be afraid! Whither are ye gone to rest? In what cave of the hill shall I find the departed? No feeble voice is on the gale: no answer half drowned in the storm!

"I sit in my grief: I wait for morning in my tears! Rear the tomb, ye friends of the dead. Close it not till Colma comes. My life flies away like a dream. Why should I stay behind? Here shall I rest with my friends, by the stream of the sounding rock. When night comes on the hill—when the loud winds arise, my ghost shall stand in the blast, and mourn the death of my friends. The hunter shall hear from his booth; he shall fear, but love my voice! For sweet shall my voice be for my friends: pleasant were her friends to Colma.

"Such was thy song, Minona, softly blushing daughter of Torman. Our tears descended for Colma, and our souls were sad! Ullin came with his harp; he gave the song of Alpin. The voice of Alpin was pleasant; the soul of Ryno was a beam of fire! But they had rested in the narrow house; their voice had ceased in Selma! Ullin had returned one day from the chase before the heroes fell. He heard their strife on the hill; their song was soft, but sad! They mourned the fall of Morar, first of mortal men! His soul was like the soul of Fingal; his sword like the sword of Oscar. But he fell, and his father mourned; his sister's eyes were full of tears. Minona's eyes were full of tears, the sister of car-borne Morar.

She retired from the song of Ullin, like the moon in the west, when she foresees the shower, and hides her fair head in a cloud. I touched the harp with Ullin; the song of mourning rose!

"*Ryno:* The wind and the rain are past; calm is the noon of day. The clouds are divided in heaven. Over the green hills flies the inconstant sun. Red through the stony vale comes down the stream of the hill. Sweet are thy murmurs, O stream! but more sweet is the voice I hear. It is the voice of Alpin, the son of song, mourning for the dead! Bent is his head of age; red his tearful eye. Alpin, thou son of song, why alone on the silent hill? why complainest thou, as a blast in the wood, as a wave on the lonely shore?

"*Alpin:* My tears, O Ryno! are for the dead—my voice for those that have passed away. Tall thou art on the hill; fair among the sons of the vale. But thou shalt fall like Morar; the mourner shall sit on thy tomb. The hills shall know thee no more; thy bow shall lie in thy hall unstrung!

"Thou wert swift, O Morar! as a roe on the desert; terrible as a meteor of fire. Thy wrath was as the storm; thy sword in battle as lightning in the field. Thy voice was a stream after rain, like thunder on distant hills. Many fell by thy arm: they were consumed in the flames of thy wrath. But when thou didst return from war, how peaceful was thy brow! Thy face was like the sun after rain, like the moon in the silence of night; calm as the breast of the lake when the loud wind is laid.

"Narrow is thy dwelling now! dark the place of thine abode! With three steps I compass thy grave, O thou who wast so great before! Four stones, with their heads of moss, are the only memorial of thee. A tree with scarce a leaf, long grass which whistles in the wind, mark to the hunter's eye the grave of the mighty Morar. Morar! thou art low indeed. Thou hast no mother to mourn thee, no maid with her tears of love. Dead is she that brought thee forth. Fallen is the daughter of Morglan.

"Who on his staff is this? Who is this whose head is white with age, whose eyes are red with tears, who quakes at every step? It is thy father, O Morar! the father of no son but thee. He heard of thy fame in war, he heard of foes dispersed. He heard of Morar's renown; why did he not hear of his wound? Weep, thou father of Morar! Weep, but thy son heareth thee not. Deep is the sleep of the dead—low their pillow of dust. No more shall he hear thy voice—no more awake at thy call. When shall it be morn in the grave, to bid the slumberer awake? Farewell, thou bravest of men! thou conqueror in the field! but the field shall see thee no more, nor the dark wood be lightened with the splendor of thy steel. Thou hast left no son. The song shall preserve thy name. Future times shall hear of thee—they shall hear of the fallen Morar!

"The grief of all arose, but most the bursting sigh of Armin. He remembers the death of his son, who fell in the days of his youth. Carmor was near the hero, the chief of the echoing Galmal. Why burst the sigh of Armin? he said. Is there a cause to mourn? The song comes with its music to melt and please the soul. It is like soft mist that, rising from a lake, pours on the silent vale; the green flowers are filled with dew, but the sun returns in his strength, and the mist is gone. Why art thou sad, O Armin, chief of sea-surrounded Gorma?

"Sad I am, nor small is my cause of woe! Carmor, thou hast lost no son; thou hast lost no daughter of beauty. Colgar the valiant lives, and Annira, fairest maid. The boughs of thy house ascend, O Carmor! But Armin is the last of his race. Dark is thy bed, O Daura! deep thy sleep in the tomb! When shalt thou wake with thy songs—with all thy voice of music?

"Arise, winds of autumn, arise; blow along the heath! Streams of the mountains, roar; roar, tempests in the groves of my oaks! Walk through broken clouds, O moon! show thy pale face at intervals; bring to my mind the night when all my children fell—when Arindal the mighty fell, when Daura the lovely failed. Daura, my daughter, thou wert fair—fair as the moon on Fura, white as the driven snow, sweet as the breathing gale. Arindal, thy bow was strong, thy spear was swift on the field, thy look was like mist on the wave, thy shield a red cloud in a storm! Armar, renowned in war, came and sought Daura's love. He was not long refused: fair was the hope of their friends.

"Erath, son of Odgal, repined: his brother had been slain by Armar. He came disguised like a son of the sea; fair was his skiff on the wave, white his locks of age, calm his serious brow. Fairest of women, he said, lovely daughter of Armin! a rock not distant in the sea bears a tree on its side: red shines the fruit afar. There Armar waits for Daura. I come to carry his love! She went— she called on Armar. Naught answered, but the son of the rock. Armar, my love, my love! why tormentest thou me with fear? Hear, son of Arnart, hear! it is Daura who calleth thee. Erath, the traitor, fled laughing to the land. She lifted up her voice—she called for her brother and her father. Arindal! Armin! none to relieve you, Daura.

"Her voice came over the sea. Arindal, my son, descended from the hill, rough in the spoils of the chase. His arrows rattled by his side; his bow was in his hand, five dark-gray dogs attended his steps. He saw fierce Erath on the shore; he seized and bound him to an oak. Thick wind the thongs of the hide around his limbs; he loads the winds with his groans. Arindal ascends the deep in his boat to bring Daura to land. Armar came in his wrath, and let fly the gray-feathered shaft. It sung, it sunk in thy heart, O Arindal, my son! for Erath the traitor thou diest. The oar is stopped at once: he panted on the rock and expired. What is thy grief, O Daura, when round thy feet is poured thy brother's blood?

The boat is broken in twain. Armar plunges into the sea to rescue his Daura, or die. Sudden a blast from a hill came over the waves; he sank, and he rose no more.

"Alone, on the sea-beat rock, my daughter was heard to complain; frequent and loud were her cries. What could her father do? All night I stood on the shore: I saw her by the faint beam of the moon. All night I heard her cries. Loud was the wind; the rain beat hard on the hill. Before morning appeared, her voice was weak; it died away like the evening breeze among the grass of the rocks. Spent with grief, she expired, and left thee, Armin, alone. Gone is my strength in war, fallen my pride among women. When the storms aloft arise, when the north lifts the wave on high, I sit by the sounding shore, and look on the fatal rock.

"Often by the setting moon I see the ghosts of my children; half viewless they walk in mournful conference together."

A torrent of tears which streamed from Charlotte's eyes and gave relief to her oppressed heart stopped Werther's reading. He threw down the sheets, seized her hand, and wept bitterly. Charlotte leaned upon her other arm and buried her face in her handkerchief; both were horribly agitated. They felt their own fate in the misfortunes of Ossian's heroes—felt this together, and merged their tears. Werther's eyes and lips burned on Charlotte's arm; she trembled, she wanted to go, but grief and pity lay like a leaden weight upon her. She took a deep breath, recovered herself, and begged Werther, sobbing, to continue—implored him with the very voice of Heaven! He trembled, his heart ready to burst; then taking up the sheets again, he read in a broken voice: "Why dost thou awake me, O breath of Spring, thou dost woo me and say, 'I cover thee with the drops of heaven'? But the time of my fading is near, the blast that shall scatter my leaves. Tomorrow shall the traveller come; he that saw me in my beauty shall come. His eyes will search the field, but they will not find me."

The whole force of these words fell upon the unfortunate Werther. In deepest despair, he threw himself at Charlotte's feet, seized her hands, and pressed them to his eyes and to his forehead. An apprehension of his terrible plan seemed to strike her. Her thoughts were confused: she held his hands, pressed them to her bosom; and, turning toward him with the tenderest expression, her burning cheek touched his. The world vanished about them. He clasped her in his arms tightly, and covered her trembling, stammering lips with furious kisses. "Werther!" she cried with choking voice, turning away. "Werther!" and, with a feeble hand, pushed him from her. And again, more composed and from the depth of her heart, she repeated, "Werther!" He did not resist, released her, and threw himself before her. Charlotte rose, and with confusion and grief, trembling between love and anger, she exclaimed, "This is the last time, Werther! You shall never see me again!" Then, casting one last, loving glance at the unhappy man, she rushed into the adjoining room and locked the door. Werther held out his arms, but did not dare detain her. He lay on the floor with his head resting on the sofa for half an hour till he heard a noise which brought him to his senses. It was the maid, who wanted to set the table. He walked up and down the room; and when he was alone, he went to Charlotte's door, and, in a low voice, said, "Charlotte, Charlotte! but one word more, one last adieu!" She did not answer. He waited, pleaded again, and waited. Finally he tore himself away, crying, "Adieu, Charlotte, adieu forever!"

He came to the town gate. The guards, who knew him, let him out without a word. It was raining and snowing. He knocked at the gate again at about eleven. His servant saw him enter the house without his hat but did not dare say anything. As he undressed his master, he found that his clothes were wet. His hat was afterward found on the point of a rock overhanging the valley. It is inconceivable how he could have climbed to the summit on such a dark, stormy night without losing his life.

He went to bed and slept late. The next morning his servant, who brought in his coffee, found him writing. He added the following passage to his letter to Charlotte.

For the last, last time, I open these eyes. Ah! they will see the sun no more. A dim and misty day hides it. Yes, Nature! Mourn! Your friend, your lover, draws near his end! There is nothing like this feeling, Charlotte, and yet, it is most akin to a diffused dream, when you say to yourself—This is the last morning! The last! Charlotte, no word can adequately express this feeling. The last! Here I stand in all my strength— tomorrow I shall lie outstretched and inert. To die! What does it mean? We are but dreaming when we speak of death. I have seen many people die; but, so limited is our nature that we have no clear conception of the beginning or the end of our life. At this moment I am my own—or rather I belong to you, my beloved!—and the next we are parted, severed—perhaps forever! No, Charlotte, no! How can I, how can you, pass away so completely? We *are!* Pass away. . . a mere word, an empty sound, without feeling. Dead, Charlotte! laid in the cold earth, in the dark and narrow grave! There was a woman who was everything to me in my helpless youth. She died. I followed her hearse and stood by her grave when the coffin was lowered; when I heard the creaking of the ropes as they were loosened and drawn up, when the first shovelful of earth was thrown in, and the melancholy coffin returned a muffled sound, which grew fainter and fainter till all was completely covered over, I threw myself beside the grave; my heart was shaking, moved, shattered; my soul torn—but I knew not what had happened, what was to happen to me. Death! the grave! I do not understand the words.

Forgive, oh, forgive me! Yesterday! it should have been the last moment of my life! You angel!—for the first—first time in my life I felt rapture glow within my inmost soul. She loves me, loves me! The sacred fire of your lips still burns upon mine. New torrents of delight overwhelm my soul. Forgive me, forgive!

I knew that you loved me. I knew from the first entrancing look, the first pressure of your hand, but when I was away from you, when I saw Albert at your side, my doubts and fears returned.

Do you remember the flowers you sent me when at that dreadful party you could neither speak to me nor give me your hand? Half the night I was on my knees before those flowers; they were to me the pledges of your love. But those impressions faded, as the believer gradually loses the sense of grace which his God conveyed to him so abundantly in sacred, visible symbols.

All this passes away, but no eternity could extinguish the living flame which was kindled yesterday by your lips, and which now burns within me. She loves me! These arms have embraced her, these lips have trembled upon hers. She is mine! Yes, Charlotte, you are mine forever!

And what does it mean that Albert is your husband? Husband? He may be, in this world; and in this world is it a sin to love you, to wish to tear you from his embrace? A sin? Very well! I suffer the punishment, but I have tasted the full delight of my sin. I have drunk a balm that has restored my soul. From this moment on you are mine. Yes, Charlotte, mine! I go before you. I go to my Father, to your Father. I will bring my sorrows before Him and He will give me comfort till you come. Then will I fly to meet you. I will hold you, and remain with you in eternal embrace, in the sight of the Infinite.

I do not dream. So near the grave, I see more clearly. We *shall* exist! we shall see each other again! see your mother! I shall find her, and pour out my inmost heart to her. Your mother—your image!

About eleven o'clock Werther asked his servant if Albert had returned. He answered: "Yes," he had seen his horse go past; upon which Werther sent him the following note, unsealed:

"Would you lend me your pistols for a journey I am about to undertake? Adieu."

Charlotte had slept little that night. Her fears were realized in a way that she could neither have foreseen nor have avoided. She, who was usually so tranquil, was feverishly disturbed. A thousand painful sensations rent her heart. Was it the passion of Werther's embraces? Was it anger at his daring? Was it the contrast between her present condition with those days of innocence, peace and self-confidence? How could she face her husband and confess a scene which she had no reason to conceal and which she yet felt unwilling to avow? They had so long preserved a silence toward each other—and should she be the first to break it by this unexpected admission? She was afraid that the very news of Werther's visit would annoy him, and now—this sudden catastrophe! Could she hope that he would see her as she was and judge her without prejudice? Could she honestly wish that he read her inmost soul? On the other hand, could she deceive him to whom all her thoughts had always been as clear as a crystal, and from whom she never would or could conceal a single thought? All this made her anxious and distressed. Again and again her mind returned to Werther, who was now lost to her, but whom she could not bring herself to let go, and for whom, she knew, nothing was left but despair if she should be lost to him.

A shadow of that estrangement which had lately come between herself and Albert fell over her thoughts. Two such intelligent and well-meaning people had begun to keep silent because of certain unspoken differences of opinion—each preoccupied with his own right and the other's wrong, making things worse and worse until eventually it became impossible to disentangle the knot at the crucial moment on which all seemed to depend. If mutual trust had earlier brought them together again, if love and understanding had helped them open their hearts to each other, our friend might still have been saved.

But we must not forget one other curious circumstance. As we can gather from Werther's correspondence, he had never concealed his anxious desire to quit this world. He had often discussed the subject with Albert, and Charlotte and her husband had on occasion talked about it. Albert was so opposed to the very idea that, with a kind of irritation unusual in him, he had more than once given Werther to understand that he doubted the seriousness of his threats, and not only turned them into ridicule but persuaded Charlotte to share his feelings. This put her heart somewhat at ease when she thought of the melancholy subject, but it also prevented her from communicating to her husband the fears she felt at that time.

Albert returned and was greeted by Charlotte with an embarrassed embrace. He was himself in a bad mood; his business was unfinished, and he had found the neighboring official, with whom he had to deal, an obstinate and narrow-minded person. The bad roads, too, had irritated him.

He enquired whether anything had happened during his absence, and Charlotte hastily answered that Werther had been there on the evening before. He then asked after the mail and was told that a letter and several packages had been left in his study. He thereupon retired, leaving Charlotte alone. The presence of her husband, whom she loved and honored, made a fresh impression on her heart. The recollection of his generosity, kindness, and affection calmed her agitation; a secret impulse prompted her to follow him; she took her work and went to his study, as was often her custom. He was busy opening and reading his mail. It seemed as if some of it contained disagreeable news. She asked some questions; he gave short answers and went to his desk to write.

An hour passed, and Charlotte's feelings became more and more melancholy. She felt the extreme difficulty of explaining to her husband, even if he were in a better mood, the weight that lay upon her heart; and her depression became all the more distressing as she tried to hide her grief and to control her tears.

The arrival of Werther's boy caused her the greatest embarrassment. He gave Albert a note, which the latter calmly handed to his wife, saying, "Give him the pistols.—I wish him a pleasant journey," he added, turning to the servant. These words fell upon Charlotte like thunder; she rose from her seat, half conscious of what she did. She walked slowly to the wall, took down the pistols with a trembling hand, wiped the dust from them, and hesitated. She would have delayed longer had not Albert hastened her with an impatient look. She gave the fatal weapons to the boy without being able to utter a word. As soon as he had gone, she folded up her work and went to her room, in a state of immeasurable uncertainty. Her heart prophesied all sorts of catastrophes. At one moment she was on the point of going to her husband, throwing herself at his feet, and confessing everything: all that had happened on the previous evening, her own guilt, her apprehensions. Then she saw that such a step would be useless; she could not hope to induce Albert to visit Werther. The table was laid and a kind friend who had come to ask a question or two helped to sustain the conversation. They pulled themselves together, talked about this and that, and were able to forget.

When the servant brought the pistols to Werther, the latter received them with transports of delight when he heard that Charlotte had given them to him with her own hand. He had bread and wine brought in, sent his servant to dinner, and then sat down to write:

"They have passed through your hands—you have wiped the dust from them. I kiss them a thousand times—you have touched them. Heavenly Spirits favor my design—and you, Charlotte, offer me the weapon. You, from whose hands I wished to receive my death. Now—

my wish is gratified. I asked my servant. You trembled when you gave him the pistols, but you bade me no farewell. Ah! Not one farewell! How could you shut your heart against me on account of that one moment which made you mine forever? Oh, Charlotte, ages cannot efface the impression—I feel you cannot hate him who loves you so!"

After dinner he called his servant, told him to finish packing, destroyed many papers, and then went out to settle some small debts. He returned home, then went out again beyond the gate in spite of the rain, walked for some time in the Count's garden, and farther into the surrounding countryside. Toward evening he came back and wrote:

"Wilhelm, I have for the last time seen fields, wood, and sky. Farewell to you, too! And you, dearest mother, forgive me! Console her, Wilhelm. God bless you both! I have settled all my affairs! Farewell! We shall meet again, and be happier."

"I have ill rewarded you, Albert, but you will forgive me. I have disturbed the peace of your house. I have sowed distrust between you. Farewell! I will end it all. And oh! that my death may restore your happiness! Albert, Albert! make the angel happy, and may God's blessing be upon you!"

He spent the rest of the evening going through his papers; he tore up and burned a great many; he sealed a few packages and addressed them to Wilhelm. They contained some short essays and disconnected aphorisms, some of which I have seen. At ten o'clock he ordered his fire to be made up, and a bottle of wine to be brought to him. He then sent his servant to bed; his room, as well as the apartments of the rest of the domestics, was situated in the back of the house. The boy lay down without undressing that he might be the sooner ready for his journey in the morning, as his master had told him that the coach horses would be at the door before six o'clock.

After eleven

All is silent around me, and my soul is calm. I thank Thee, God, that Thou hast given me strength and courage in these last moments!

I step to the window, my dearest, and can see a few stars through the passing storm clouds. No, you will not fall. The Almighty sustains you, and me. I see the brightest lights of the Great Bear, my favorite constellation. When I left you, Charlotte, and went out from your gate, it was always in front of me. With what rapture have I so often looked at it! How many times have I implored it with raised hands to witness my happiness! and still—But what is there, Charlotte, that does not remind me of you? Are you not everywhere about me? and have I not, like a child, treasured up every trifle which your saintly hands have touched?

Beloved silhouette! I now return it to you, and I pray you to preserve it. Thousands of kisses have I pressed upon it, and a thousand times did it gladden my heart when I left the house or returned.

I have asked your father in a note to protect my body. At one corner of the churchyard, looking towards the fields, there are two linden trees—there I wish to lie. Your father can, and doubtless will, do this for his friend. You ask him, too! I don't expect of pious Christians that their bodies should be buried near the corpse of a poor, unhappy wretch like me. Ah, I could wish to lie in some remote valley by the wayside, where priest and Levite would bless themselves as they pass by my tomb, and the Samaritan shed a tear.

You see, Charlotte, I do not shudder to take the cold and fatal cup, from which I shall drink the frenzy of death. Your hand gave it to me, and I do not tremble. All, all the wishes and the hopes of my life are fulfilled. Cold and stiff I knock at the brazen gates of Death.

Oh that I might have enjoyed the bliss of dying for you! how gladly would I have sacrificed myself for you, Charlotte! And could I but restore your peace and happiness, with what resolution, with what joy would I meet my fate! But it is given to but a chosen few to shed their blood for those they loved, and by their death to kindle a hundredfold the happiness of those by whom they are beloved.

Charlotte, I wish to be buried in the clothes I wear at present; you have touched them, blessed them. I have begged this same favor of your father. My spirit soars above my coffin. I do not wish my pockets to be searched. This pink bow which you wore the first time I saw you, surrounded by the children—Oh, kiss them a thousand times for me, and tell them the fate of their unhappy friend! I think I see them playing around me. The darling children! How they swarm about me! How I attached myself to you, Charlotte! From the first moment I saw you, I knew I could not leave you! Let this ribbon be buried with me; it was a present from you on my birthday. How eagerly I accepted it all! I did not think that it would all lead to this! Be calm! I beg you, be calm!

They are loaded—the clock strikes twelve. So be it! Charlotte! Charlotte, farewell, farewell!

A neighbor saw the flash and heard the shot; but, as everything remained quiet, he thought no more of it.

At six in the morning, the servant enters Werther's room with a candle. He finds his master stretched on the floor, blood about him, and the pistol at his side. He calls to him, takes him in his arms, but there is no answer, only a rattling in the throat. He runs for a surgeon, for Albert. Charlotte hears the bell; a shudder seizes her. She awakens her husband; both arise. The servant, in tears, stammers the dreadful news. Charlotte falls senseless at Albert's feet.

When the surgeon arrived, Werther was lying on the floor; his pulse beat, but his limbs were paralyzed. The bullet had entered the forehead over the right eye; his brains were protruding. He was bled in the arm; the blood came, he was still breathing.

From the blood on the chair, it could be inferred that he had committed the deed sitting at his desk, and that he had afterwards fallen on the floor and had twisted convulsively around the chair. He was found lying on his back near the window. He was fully dressed in his boots, blue coat and yellow waistcoat.

The house, the neighbors, and the whole town were in an uproar. Albert arrived. They had laid Werther on the bed. His head was bandaged, and the pallor of death was upon his face. His limbs were motionless; a terrible rattling noise came from his lungs, now strongly, now weaker. His death was expected at any moment.

He had drunk only one glass of the wine. *Emilia Galotti* lay open on his desk.

Let me say nothing of Albert's distress or of Charlotte's grief.

The old judge hastened to the house upon hearing the news; he kissed his dying friend amid a flood of tears. His eldest boys soon followed him on foot. In speechless sorrow they threw themselves on their knees by the bedside, and kissed his hands and face. The eldest, who was his favorite, clung to his lips till he was gone; even then the boy had to be taken away by force. At noon Werther died. The presence of the judge, and the arrangements he had made prevented a disturbance; that night, at the hour of eleven, he had the body buried in the place that Werther had chosen. The old man and his sons followed the body to the grave. Albert couldn't bring himself to. There was concern for Charlotte's life. The body was carried by workmen. No clergyman attended.

ELECTIVE AFFINITIES

Translated by Judith Ryan

Translator's Note: *Despite Margaret Fuller's praise for its beauty, pathos, and "irresistible fatality," * Elective Affinities *never really gained entry into the American reader's canon of favorite literary masterpieces. In undertaking this new translation, I was eager to win for Goethe's novel the devoted following it deserves. This meant that the translation itself would need to remain as invisible as possible. Imitation can never quite capture the ring of authenticity. To have borrowed the style of, say,* Mansfield Park—*a work that appeared only five years later and that bears its own elective affinity to Goethe's novel—would have made a period piece out of a book that continues, even today, to fascinate those who know it in the original. I wanted it to be read as a novel rather than as a translation.*

For this reason, the language has been kept comparatively plain, except in the speech of those two old-fashioned souls, Mittler and the schoolmaster, and in the novella told by the English visitors, who are said to be speaking "strangely accented French." Proper names are given in English forms, where they exist; sentence rhythms have been accommodated to an English pronunciation of the more unusual ones, such as Ottilie or Luciane; and those who know the German original will scarcely object to the appearance of young "Nanny" in the guise of "little Nan." The most obstinate problem was posed by Goethe's use of the present tense to narrate extended sequences in the action. While present-tense narration is occasionally used in English, it tends to be something of a tour de force; the English speaker finds it hard to tolerate over long stretches. I was reluctant, nonetheless, to flatten Goethe's narrative by giving it in the past tense throughout. Instead, I reserve the present tense for two special scenes, Chapters Thirteen and Eighteen of Part Two, and even then only for the high points of those episodes. Readers interested in Goethe's use of tenses are advised to consult the original.

I would like to thank all those who read versions of this translation, as well as those of my family and friends who submitted to my persistent questioning about matters of usage. To my mother, who not only read the translation in its earliest form but, even more importantly, was the chief influence that made me a reader and writer, I owe a special debt of gratitude.

J. R.

Part One

Chapter One

Edward—as we shall call a well-to-do baron in the prime of his life—
had been spending the finest hours of an April afternoon grafting freshly
cut shoots onto young rootstocks. He had just finished this task and was
putting his tools back in their box, contemplating his work with plea-
sure, when the gardener arrived and examined with delight his master's
contribution to their combined efforts.

"Have you seen my wife, by any chance?" asked Edward, starting to
move on.

"Over in the new gardens," replied the gardener. "The moss hut she
is building in the cliff face opposite the house will be finished today. It
has turned out very nicely and is sure to please you, your lordship. You
have an excellent view: the village down below, the church, whose spire
you hardly notice from up there, a little to the right; and opposite, the
manor-house and the gardens."

"Yes," returned Edward. "A few yards from here I could see the
people working."

"Then," the gardener continued, "the valley opens up to the right
and you can see over the vast expanses of trees clear into the distance.
The climb up the cliff is very prettily arranged. Her ladyship knows how
to do these things; it's a pleasure to work for her."

"Go to her," said Edward, "and ask her to wait for me. Tell her I
want to see and enjoy her new creation."

The gardener hurried off and Edward soon followed.

He climbed down the terraces, checking on greenhouses and nursery-
beds as he passed, until he came to the water, then, across a small
bridge, to a place where the path went off in two directions to the new
gardens. He avoided the path that led, through the churchyard, fairly
directly to the cliff, and went instead by the other one, which wound its
way gently up through some charming shrubbery somewhat further to
the left; and where both joined again he sat down for a moment on a
conveniently placed bench before beginning the actual climb up, which

took him over all kinds of steps and stairs along a narrow, increasingly steep path that finally led to the moss hut.

Charlotte was there at the doorway to greet her husband; she asked him to sit down so that he could take in at a glance the various scenes that showed the landscape as if framed by door and window. He enjoyed what he saw, anticipating that spring would soon enliven the scene even more. "I would make only one observation," he added; "the hut seems a little small."

"But there's enough room for the two of us," Charlotte responded.

"Well, of course," said Edward, "I suppose there's room for a third person, too."

"Why not?" Charlotte replied, "and a fourth as well. We'll have other places for larger groups."

"Now that we are alone and uninterrupted here," said Edward, "and in a quiet, happy frame of mind, I must confess that for some time now I have had something on my mind that I feel compelled—that I would like—to confide to you, and haven't been able to bring myself to mention."

"I knew there was something," replied Charlotte.

"And I will admit," continued Edward, "that if I weren't pressed by tomorrow's mail, if we didn't have to come to a decision today, I would perhaps have kept it to myself even longer."

"Well, what is it?" asked Charlotte in an open, amiable tone.

"It has to do with our friend the Captain," answered Edward. "You know the unfortunate position he is in, like so many others, quite without fault of his own. How disturbing it must be to a man of his education, talents and skills to be without employment and—I won't conceal any longer what I want for him: I would like us to invite him here for a time."

"That's something that needs to be carefully weighed, and considered from different angles," replied Charlotte.

"I'll be glad to give you my views on the subject," responded Edward. "In his last letter there is a subdued tone of profound dissatisfaction; not that he is in any particular need, for he is quite able to live frugally, and I have taken care of the basic necessities; and it doesn't bother him to accept help from me, since we have been in each other's debt so much all our lives, off and on, that we can't calculate the actual status of our respective debit and credit—what bothers him is the fact that he has lost his job. His sole pleasure and passion lies in his many-sided talent and training, and his ability to use it for the benefit of others every hour of every day. And now to be idle, or to take up his studies again and learn new skills when he cannot use what he already has in full measure—in short, my dear, it is a distressing position, doubly and triply agonizing to him in his present isolation."

"But I thought," said Charlotte, "that he had been made various offers. I myself had written to a number of energetic friends on his behalf, and, to the best of my knowledge, not without results."

"Quite so," replied Edward; "but even these various opportunities, these offers cause him new distress and dissatisfaction. None of the positions is really appropriate. He would not have any influence; he would have to sacrifice himself, his time, his convictions, his whole being—and that he cannot do. The more I think about it the more aware I am of this, and the more keenly I wish to see him here with us."

"It's very fine and admirable of you," replied Charlotte, "to show such empathy with your friend's situation; but permit me to ask you to think of your own and ours."

"I have done so," Edward answered. "We have only advantages and pleasures to expect from having him with us. I won't speak of the expense, which will not be much for me in any event if he joins us here; especially considering that his presence won't cause us the slightest inconvenience. He can stay in the right wing of the house, and everything else will fall into place. How good this will be for him, how pleasant things will be in his company, and how many advantages it will bring us! For a long time I have wanted to have the estate and its environs surveyed; he will undertake and direct this task. Your plan is to manage the property yourself as soon as the contracts of the present tenants are up. But how risky this plan is! Think of the technical advice he can give us! I'm only too aware how much we need a man like him. The farmers know what's what, but they communicate it in a confused and deceitful way. The specialists from the academies in town are doubtless clear and organized, but they don't have direct experience of these things. My friend has both, I can guarantee that; and then there are a hundred other ramifications that, I like to think, will also be of interest to you and that I foresee will have many positive results. I am grateful that you have listened to me so amiably; now take your time, speak frankly and tell me all you have to say; I won't interrupt you."

"Very well, then," replied Charlotte. "I will begin with a generalization. Men think more about the present and about particular details, and rightly so, since they are called to act and have influence; women on the other hand think more of the broader connections in life, and this too quite rightly, since their fate and the fate of their families is bound up with these connections and it is precisely the ability to make connections that is demanded of them. So let us take a look at our present and past life and you will admit that inviting the Captain does not quite fit in with our original intentions, plans and arrangements.

"How I like to think back to the time when we first knew each other! In our youth we were very much in love with each other; but we were separated; you from me because your father, from an insatiable desire for possessions, married you off to a rich woman somewhat older than you; and I from you because, having no particular prospects, I had to give my hand to a well-to-do man I respected but did not love. Later on we were free again; you earlier, when the old lady left you considerable property; I later, just when you returned from your travels. So we found each other again. We took pleasure in our recollection, we were fond of what we recalled, and there was no hindrance to our living together. You urged that we get married; I didn't agree right away, for since we are about the same age I have doubtless aged more, being a woman, than you have as a man. But in the end I did not want to deny you what you saw as your sole happiness. You wanted to recover in my company from all the excitements of life at court, in the army and on your travels; you wanted to enjoy life and find yourself again; but with me alone. I sent my only daughter to boarding school, where she is, admittedly, receiving a more varied education than would be possible here in the country; and not only did I send my daughter to school, I also sent Ottilie, my beloved niece, who might best have grown up under my tutelage learning the arts of housekeeping. All this was done with your consent, and merely so that we could live for ourselves alone, so we could attain early on the long-desired happiness we had not been able to have until so late. So we began our life in the country. I took over the inside of the house, you the outside and the overall management. I have set things up so as to accommodate you, to live for you alone; let us try for a time at least to see how we can get along in this way with each other's company."

"Since, as you say, the broader connections are really women's natural element," Edward replied, "we men should either not listen to you when you develop an argument or simply decide at the outset to give in to your opinion—and I grant that you've been right, Charlotte, until today. The plans for our life with which we have up to now been so intensely involved are well thought-out; but are we never to add to them, never to expand upon them? Are my gardening and your landscaping to be for hermits only?"

"Very good!" replied Charlotte, "very well! Only we should not admit anything alien or intrusive. Remember that the amusements we had planned were designed more or less for the two of us alone. First, you planned to recount the content of your travel diaries to me in proper sequence, while at the same time organizing various of your papers on the subject, and with my help and interest piece together those valuable but disordered pages and notebooks to form a rounded picture that would give pleasure to ourselves and others. I promised to help you with the fair copy, and we imagined that it would be so agreeable, so charming, so warm and cozy to journey again in memory through a world we were not destined to see together. Why, we've already made a start on it! And then you have taken up your flute again in the evenings while I accompany you on the piano; and there is no lack of visits back and forth between us and the neighbors. I for one have built up out of all this the first really happy summer I've ever looked forward to in my life."

"If only," Edward replied, rubbing his forehead, "I didn't keep thinking, while you go over all that so sensibly and lovingly, that the Captain's presence would not interfere with any of it, but rather would enliven it and give it new incentive. In addition, he shared in some of my travels, remembers much of them, and what's more, from a different perspective: we have only to put it all together and it would immediately round out the picture."

"Then let me confess to you honestly," answered Charlotte with some impatience, "that this plan is at odds with my intuition. I have an inner feeling that doesn't augur well."

"That kind of argument would make you women irrefutable," said Edward; "first you're so sensible that one can't contradict you, so loving that one immediately gives in, so sensitive that one doesn't want to hurt you, so full of forebodings that one feels quite alarmed."

"I'm not superstitious," Charlotte responded, "and I don't set any store by obscure intimations, when that is all they are; but for the most part they are subconscious memories of good or bad consequences that our own or other people's actions have had. Nothing has more impact on any situation than the arrival of a third party. I have seen friends, siblings, lovers, spouses whose relationships have been totally altered, whose situations have been completely reversed by the accidental or deliberate addition of a new person."

"That can happen, I suppose," Edward replied, "with people who live unreflectingly, but not with those who are more aware and enlightened by experience."

"Awareness, my dear," replied Charlotte, "is an inadequate, indeed sometimes a dangerous weapon for the one that bears it; and the upshot of all this is, in any event, that we shouldn't be too hasty. Give me a few more days: don't make the decision now!"

"As things stand," responded Edward, "we will still be too hasty even in several days' time. We've each had our turn to put the arguments for and against; all we have to do is decide, and really the best thing would be for us to toss a coin."

"I know you like to bet or gamble when something needs to be decided," Charlotte said, "but I would think it wicked to do so in such a serious instance as this."

"But what shall I write to the Captain?" cried Edward. "For I must write at once."

"A calm, sensible, comforting letter," replied Charlotte.

"Which is to say no letter at all," retorted Edward.

"And yet in many instances," Charlotte answered, "it is the kind and necessary thing to write nothing rather than not write at all."

Chapter Two

Edward was left alone in his room; and Charlotte's rehearsal of his life, her recollection of their mutual situation and their plans for the future had put his volatile mind into a pleasant state of excitement. As long as he had been near her, in her company, he had felt so happy that he had begun to conceive a friendly, sympathetic, but calm and noncommittal letter to the Captain. But when he went to his desk and took up his friend's letter to read it over again, the sorry plight of that excellent man came immediately to mind; all the emotions that had tormented him during the past few days returned, and he felt it impossible to abandon his friend to such a worrisome situation.

Edward was not used to denying himself what he wanted. Spoilt from early childhood, he had been the only child of rich parents who had managed to talk him into a strange but highly advantageous marriage to a much older woman. She in turn had coddled him, repaying his decent behavior to her with the greatest generosity. After her death, he had been his own master, traveling independently and able to indulge in any amount of diversion and change of scene, not desirous of anything extravagant, but eager for many and various experiences, free-spirited, charitable, gallant, and, if need be, brave—what on earth could stand in the way of his desires!

Up to now everything had gone as he had wished—he had even gained Charlotte after wooing her with persistent, even sentimental faithfulness; and now, for the first time, he saw himself contradicted and frustrated, at the very moment when he wished to re-establish his ties with his childhood friend and, as it were, round off his entire existence. He felt irritated and impatient, took up his pen several times and laid it down again, unable to settle in his mind what he wanted to write. He did not want to act against his wife's wishes, but he could not act according to them; he was expected to write, in his present state of impatience, a calm letter, but this would have been quite impossible. The most natural thing was to seek a delay. In a few brief words he begged his friend's forgiveness for not having written earlier and for not writing at length now, and promised to send him a more meaningful and reassuring letter very soon.

Charlotte took advantage of an opportunity the following day, in the course of a walk to the same part of the garden, to take up their conversation again, perhaps in the conviction that desires can never be more surely blunted than when they are repeatedly discussed.

This reiteration suited Edward well. He expressed his feelings in a friendly and pleasant tone: for even though he was excitable and could easily get worked up, his strong desire becoming too urgent and his persistence making one impatient, his arguments were nonetheless always tempered by such a thorough-going consideration of the other person that one was forced to find him charming even when he was being annoying.

Thus it was that on this morning he first got Charlotte into a most cheerful mood, then contrived through winning turns of phrase to quite disarm her, with the result that she finally exclaimed: "You doubtless want me to grant my lover that which I denied my husband."

"At least, my dear," she continued, "you should know that your wishes and the charming urgency with which you have expressed them have not left me untouched or unmoved. They force me to make an admission. I, too, have concealed something from you until now. I'm in a similar state of mind to you, and have put myself under the same pressure that I've expected you to bear."

"I'm glad to hear that," said Edward; "I see that spouses sometimes have to have a disagreement in order to find out something about each other."

"Well now, let me tell you," said Charlotte, "that with regard to Ottilie I'm in the same position as you are with regard to the Captain. It distresses me greatly to think of that poor child at boarding school, where she feels under such pressure. My daughter Luciane, who is born for society, is receiving at school an education for society, quickly picking up languages, history and other knowledge imparted to her and playing her musical exercises and variations with the greatest ease and fluency; with her lively nature and quick memory you might say she forgets everything and recalls it again in an instant; she distinguishes herself from all the others by her free and natural behavior, her graceful dancing and her tasteful ease of conversation, and makes herself, through her innate ability to lead, the queen of her small circle of friends; and the lady in charge of that establishment regards her as a budding goddess who will truly blossom in her care, who will do her credit, win confidence and attract other young people to the school. Thus, whereas the first pages of the principal's letters and monthly reports are always hymns in praise of such a fine creature, though of course I know very well how to translate them into my own prose, in contrast what she says at the end about Ottilie is no more than excuse heaped on excuse for the fact that a growing girl, in other respects so lovely, is unable to develop talents or skills. The few words she adds are no mystery to me, since I recognize in the dear child the whole character of her mother, my dear companion, who grew up alongside me and whose daughter I know I could turn into a lovely creature if I myself could be her teacher and mentor.

"But seeing that it does not fit into our plans and since one should not push and pull at one's life so much, constantly bringing something new into it, I would rather put up with this situation. I can even repress my concern when my daughter, who well knows how dependent poor Ottilie is on us, willfully exploits her natural advantages at Ottilie's expense and so in essence undoes the good deed we have done the child.

"But is there anyone so educated as not occasionally to press his advantages in the cruelest way at the cost of others? Is there anyone so high and mighty as not sometimes to suffer such ill-treatment? Ottilie's virtue only grows by these trials; nevertheless, now that I have come to see more clearly how embarrassing this situation is, I've taken steps to find another place for her. I expect to receive an answer at any moment, and then I will not hesitate to act. That, my dear, is the situation I'm in. You see that in our faithfulness to our friends we both have the same worries. Let us bear them together, since two wrongs do not make a right."

"What strange people we are," said Edward, smiling. "If we can just banish our worries from our minds we think we have taken care of them. For important matters we are able to give up a lot, but to make sacrifices in small things is a demand we can seldom live up to. My mother was like that. As long as I was living at home during my boyhood and youth, she couldn't stop worrying about me every minute. If I came back late from riding I must have had an accident; if I got wet in a drizzle, I was sure to catch a fever. Yet once I went away on my travels I hardly seemed to belong to her anymore.

"When you think about it," he continued, "we're both behaving foolishly and irresponsibly in leaving two of the noblest souls, both so dear to us, in anxiety and distress just to avoid risk to ourselves. If this is not selfish, what is? You take Ottilie, let me have the Captain, and in God's name let's hazard the experiment!"

"It might be worth venturing," said Charlotte anxiously, "if the risk were to us alone. But do you think it wise to have the Captain as a house guest along with Ottilie—a man of approximately your age, an age (I hate to flatter you like this to your face) when a man really begins to be worthy of love and able to give love, and a girl as lovely as Ottilie?"

"I simply can't think," replied Edward, "how you can prize Ottilie so highly! I can only assume it's because your affection for her mother has carried over to her. She is pretty, that is true, and I recall that the Captain drew my attention to her when we returned a year ago and met her with you at your aunt's house. She is pretty, and has especially beautiful eyes; but I don't recall that she made the slightest impression on me."

"That's creditable of you," said Charlotte, "for I was there, too; and even though she's much younger than I, the presence of your older friend was evidently so attractive that you ignored the budding beauty-to-be. That's one of the things about you that make me so glad to be sharing life with you."

But though she seemed to speak so frankly, Charlotte was concealing something. She had deliberately introduced Ottilie to Edward upon his return from his travels in order to put her beloved ward in the way of a fine match: for she had no longer thought of herself in connection with Edward. The Captain had also been put up to drawing Edward's attention to Ottilie; but stubbornly mindful of his earlier love of Charlotte, Edward looked neither left nor right, happy merely in the knowledge that now at last it was possible to win what he had so much desired, but which circumstances had made him renounce, as it seemed, forever.

The couple was just about to walk down to the manor through the new gardens when a servant came hurrying up toward them, laughing loudly from below. "My lord and lady, come quickly! Mr. Mittler has just burst into the courtyard. He called out for us all to come down and said we should go looking for you and ask if there were need of him. 'If there's need of me!' he called after us, 'do you hear? But quickly, quickly!'"

"The funny fellow!" exclaimed Edward, "has he not come at the right moment, Charlotte? Hurry back!" he told the servant, "tell him we need him very much indeed. Ask him to please dismount. Look after his horse, show him into the drawing-room and give him something to eat; we'll be there directly."

"Let's take the shortest way back, " he said to his wife, and set off along the path across the churchyard which he usually avoided. But how amazed he was when he saw that even here Charlotte had provided for sentiment. With the greatest care for the old monuments, she had ordered and arranged everything so that it seemed to make a pleasant spot on which both eye and imagination might happily dwell.

She had done honor to even the oldest gravestone. She had stood the stones up along the wall, inserting and arranging them according to their dates; in this way, the church's high foundation acquired charm and variety. Edward felt strangely moved as he stepped through the low gate; he pressed Charlotte's hand and there were tears in his eyes.

But their comical guest soon dispelled his tears. For Mittler, not content to rest at the manor, had ridden straight on through the village to the churchyard gate, where he stopped and called out to his friends: "You're not joking, are you? If you really need me I'll stay till noon. But don't hold me up—I have a lot to do today."

"Since you've taken the trouble to come so far," Edward called out to him, "ride right in. We've met at a solemn spot, and look how nicely Charlotte has decorated this place of mourning."

"I'm not going in there," said the rider, "either on horseback or by carriage or on foot. The dead rest in peace, and I have nothing to do with them. I won't give in until I'm dragged in there one day feet first. Well, were you really serious?"

"Oh yes, indeed!" cried Charlotte, "really serious! It's the first time since we were married that we've been confused and in trouble and not known how to resolve it."

"You don't look so troubled," he responded; "but I'll believe you. If you're playing a trick on me, then I won't help you out in the future. Come after me quickly; my horse can probably do with a rest."

Soon all three were together in the drawing-room; the meal was brought in, and Mittler told them what he had done and what he planned to do that day. This eccentric man had formerly been a minister of religion and had distinguished himself in that office with his unceasing activity and his success in resolving all kinds of quarrels, especially those within families and between neighbors, in the first instance between separate individuals, and later in whole communities and amongst groups of property owners. As long as he had held his ministry not a single couple had got divorced, and the county courts were left free of suits from his district. He soon realized he needed to know more about the law. He began to study it exclusively, and soon felt himself the equal of the most skillful lawyer. His sphere of influence expanded in the most amazing way, and he was about to be called to the capital in order to complete from above what he had begun at a lower level, when he won a sizable prize in the lottery. He bought himself a fairly large estate, leased it out to tenant farmers and made it the center of his activity, with the firm intention—or rather following his old habits and inclinations—not to waste his time in any household where there was no help to give and no quarrel to resolve. Those who are superstitious about names maintain that the name Mittler, meaning mediator, had obligated him to take on this strangest of all vocations.

Once dessert had been served, the guest earnestly urged his hosts not to withhold their tale any longer, since he had to leave right after coffee. The couple related their problem in some detail; but hardly had Mittler grasped the gist of the matter than he leaped up from the table in annoyance, dashed to the window and ordered the servants to saddle his horse.

"Either you don't know me," he exclaimed, "you don't understand me, or else there is some mischief here. Is this a quarrel? Is help really necessary here? Do you think that I'm in this world just to give advice? That's the stupidest thing one can do. Let everyone do as he sees fit and act as he must. If it turns out well, let him enjoy his happiness and wisdom; if it goes ill, then I am at hand. If a person wants to get rid of something unpleasant, he always knows what he wants; a person who wants something better than he has is stone blind—yes, yes! You may well laugh—such a person is playing blind man's bluff: he finds his object perhaps; but what is it? Do what you wish: it's all the same! Invite your friends or have them stay away: it's all the same! I've seen the most sensible projects fail, the stupidest ones succeed. Don't rack your brains about it. If things go wrong one way or another, don't rack them either. Just send for me and I'll help you. Till then, your servant!"

And so he leaped onto his horse without waiting for coffee.

"Now you see how very little a third party can really help," said Charlotte, "when things are not quite working out between two people who are close to each other. Now we are surely more confused and uncertain, if that is possible, than before."

Both would doubtless have remained undecided a while longer had not a letter from the Captain arrived in response to Edward's last missive. He had decided to take one of the positions that he had been offered, even though it was in no way an appropriate one. He would have to kill time with rich and elegant people, who themselves were putting all their faith in his ability to provide them distraction.

Edward perceived this situation very clearly and elaborated upon it pointedly. "Do we want our friend to be in such a position?" he cried: "You can't be so cruel, Charlotte!"

"When all's said and done," replied Charlotte, "that funny fellow Mittler is probably right. All such undertakings are risky. No one can predict what will come of them. New arrangements can give rise to good or bad fortune without our really being to praise or to blame. I don't feel strong enough to deny your request anymore. Let's take the risk. All I ask is that it be for a short time only. Let me try more actively to speak on behalf of the Captain, using my influence and connections more energetically and persuasively to find a position that will be satisfying to someone of his character."

Edward gave his wife the most charming and profuse thanks. Free and relieved, he hastened to communicate his plans to his friend. Charlotte had to add her approval herself in a postscript, joining with Edward in his friendly invitation. She wrote with fluent and sincere charm, yet with uncharacteristic haste; and in the end—something that seldom happened to her—she smeared the page with an annoying inkblot that only grew larger when she tried to erase it.

Edward made a joke of this, and as there was still some room on the page, he added a second postscript to the effect that their friend should take it as a sign of the impatience with which they awaited him, and make as much haste with his journey as they had with writing to him.

The messenger having left, Edward could not express his gratitude more convincingly than by repeatedly insisting that Charlotte should immediately bring Ottilie home from school.

She asked for time to think about it, and suggested to Edward that he might like to spend the evening with a little musical diversion. Charlotte played the piano very well; Edward played the flute, but not so smoothly, for although he had taken pains with it at times, he had not had the patience and persistence necessary to develop his talent. So he played his part very unevenly—some passages well, if a little too fast; but haltingly in other spots, not having practiced them enough—and thus it would have been difficult for anyone else to manage a duet with him. But Charlotte could handle it; she slowed down and let herself be carried along again by him, thus performing the dual task of a good conductor and a prudent housewife, who both know how to maintain proper measure in everything, even if individual passages may not always be in time.

Chapter Three

The Captain arrived. He had sent a most thoughtful letter on ahead, which set Charlotte's mind completely at rest. His perceptiveness concerning himself and his clearsightedness about his own position and that of his friends seemed to augur well.

As usual amongst friends who have not seen each other for a while, their first conversations were lively, in fact almost exhausting. Towards evening Charlotte proposed a walk to the new gardens. The Captain was charmed by the whole area and noticed every beautiful spot that the new pathways had brought to light and enhanced. He had a practiced, yet undemanding eye; and even where he clearly saw what might be more desirable, he did not upset people showing him around their property by expecting more than circumstances allowed or recalling greater perfections seen elsewhere.

When they reached the moss hut, they found it most delightfully decorated, just with evergreens and artificial flowers, yet interspersed with such lovely bunches of natural wheat and other products of field and orchard that they did credit to the artistic sense of the arrangers.

"Although my husband does not care to have his birthday or name day celebrated, he surely won't take it ill of me if we dedicate these wreaths to a threefold occasion."

"Threefold?" asked Edward. "Of course!" replied Charlotte. "Our friend's arrival should certainly be cause for celebration; and then you two have evidently not remembered that today is your name day. Is not the one of you just as much an Otto as the other?"

The two friends gave each other their hand across the small table. "You've just reminded me," said Edward, "of that childhood bargain. When we were children we were both called Otto; but once we were at boarding school together and it began to cause confusion, I voluntarily gave up that fine, laconic name to my friend."

"And in doing so you were not being in any way generous," said the Captain. "For I well recall that you liked the name Edward better, since when spoken by fair lips it sounds particularly attractive."

So now all three were sitting around the same table at which Charlotte had so energetically opposed inviting the Captain. In his contentment Edward did not wish to remind his wife of that occasion; but he couldn't refrain from saying, "There would be plenty of room for a fourth person here, too."

At this moment hunting horns could be heard from the manor house, as if to confirm and reinforce the good wishes and intentions of the friends gathered together. They listened silently, each withdrawn into himself and sensing with redoubled pleasure his own contentment at the happy arrangement.

Edward was the first to break the silence by standing up and leaving the moss hut. "Let us take our friend," he said to Charlotte, "up to the very top of the rise, so that he won't have the impression that our property is restricted to this narrow valley; the view is freer and there's more room to breathe."

"Then for now we will have to clamber up the tortuous old footpath," replied Charlotte; "but I hope that very soon my new steps and stairs will lead more conveniently to the top."

And so, over rocks, through bushes and shrubbery, they reached the summit, which formed a whole series of fertile ridges without a single flat spot. The village and manor house could no longer be seen. Down below they saw an expanse of ponds; beyond them green hills, whose contours they followed; and finally steep cliffs forming a clearly defined vertical boundary to the furthest watery expanses, in whose surface their majestic outlines were mirrored. Down in the valley, where a rapidly flowing brook ran into the ponds, was a half-hidden mill, forming together with its surroundings an inviting resting-place. Heights and depths, bushes and woodland alternated throughout the whole semi-circular view, and the leaves on the trees promised greater fullness later in the season. Separate groups of trees caught the eye at various spots. In particular a clump of poplars and plane trees stood out most attractively near the edge of the middle pond, at their feet. The trees were in their prime: fresh, healthy, reaching upward and outward.

Edward drew his friend's particular attention to this group of trees. "I planted them myself in my youth," he said. "They were young saplings I salvaged when my father, who was planting a new part of the manor gardens, had them dug out one summer. They will doubtless show their gratitude this year, as ever, by putting forth new shoots."

In happy good humor the friends returned home. Their guest was shown to a pleasant spacious room in the right wing of the manor house, where he soon set up his books, papers and instruments, organizing them in preparation for his usual activities. But during the first days of his stay Edward did not leave him in peace; he showed him around everywhere, now on horseback, now on foot, and acquainted him with the property and its surroundings; at the same time he expressed his long-cherished desire to become more familiar with his estate and make better use of it.

"The first thing we should do," said the Captain, "is to survey the whole property with a compass. This is an easy and enjoyable task, and even though it does not give perfectly accurate results, it is still useful and makes a satisfying start; in addition, it can be done without much assistance and you can be sure of completing it. If you are thinking of doing more accurate surveying, then we can easily take further advice."

The Captain was most experienced in this type of map-making. He began at once, having brought the necessary equipment with him. He showed Edward and a number of hunters and peasants how to help him with the work. The weather during the day was favorable; and the evenings and early morning hours were spent drawing and cross-hatching the map. Soon the whole was colored with water paints, and Edward saw his estate taking shape on paper like a new creation. He felt that he was seeing it now for the first time; and for the first time it really seemed to belong to him.

This gave occasion for them to discuss the whole area, noting that planting could be undertaken much better when one could see the total picture than when one was obliged to tinker with nature on the basis of random impressions.

"We will have to point this out to my wife," said Edward.

"No, better not!" replied the Captain, who did not like to see his own opinions at cross purposes with those of others and who had learned that people's views are too many and various to be brought to a consensus by even the most rational considerations. "Better not!" he said, "it would just confuse her. As with everyone who takes up such projects out of a dilettantish interest in them, it is more a question of her keeping busy than of anything specific being accomplished. It's a matter of toying with nature, developing a preference for this spot or that; such people don't dare remove this or that obstacle, aren't bold enough to sacrifice anything; they can't imagine what the end effect will be; it works out, it doesn't work out, they change—change perhaps what should be left alone and leave what should be changed, and in the end it is just a jumble that delights and stimulates but cannot satisfy."

"Be honest with me," said Edward. "You're not happy with her landscaping."

"If she had managed to carry out to perfection her original idea, which is very fine, I would have no objection to make. She has worked her way up through the rock laboriously, if you will, and now makes everyone clamber up there just as laboriously. You can't walk freely either beside or behind one another. Every moment your regular pace is thrown out of step. And one could raise all kinds of similar objections."

"Couldn't that have been easily remedied?" asked Edward.

"Very easily," responded the Captain; "she would just have had to cut away one corner of the cliff, not a very impressive one either, since it consists of small pieces of rock; and then she would have given a beautiful curved rise to the path and at the same time acquired enough stones to support those spots that are narrow or crumbling. But we should keep this in confidence, for otherwise she will get confused and irritated. And it's best to leave what has been done as it is. But if you want to spend more money and go to more trouble, you could do a number of things above the moss hut and over the rise, creating some very pleasant effects."

In this way the two friends were well occupied by the tasks of the present, but even so they did not lack pleasurable and lively recollections of the past. In these Charlotte also participated. They planned, too, to make a start on the travel diaries as soon as the most immediate work was finished, and thus to call the past to mind in this way as well.

In other respects Edward had less to talk about when he was alone with Charlotte, the more so since the Captain's seemingly justified criticism of her landscape efforts still weighed on his mind. For a long time he kept his peace about what the Captain had said; but finally, when he saw his wife beginning to lay steps and pathways from the moss hut up to the top of the rise, he could no longer restrain himself, and after some roundabout remarks, revealed his new view of the matter.

Charlotte was dismayed. She was intelligent enough to see that these views were right; but what she had done was not in accord with them, and now she had taken all that trouble; she had thought it right, she had thought it desirable, and even the criticized parts were in each and every detail dear to her; she resisted Edward's attempt to convince her, she defended her little creation, scolding the men for extending themselves in all directions and setting themselves a task that had arisen jocularly, conversationally, without thought of the costs that a more ambitious plan would be certain to bring with it. She was hurt, upset, distressed; she could not let go of her old ideas, yet she could not quite refute the new ones either; but in her decisive way, she halted her work forthwith and took time to reflect on the matter and let it grow on her.

But now that she had nothing to occupy her days, while the men were going about their tasks with growing intimacy, taking special care with the garden beds and glass houses, as well as continuing their usual noble pursuits, such as hunting, buying and trading horses, grooming and breaking them in, Charlotte felt more lonely by the day. She carried on her correspondence with more than usual energy, especially on behalf of the Captain, yet she still had many a lonely hour. All the more gratifying and diverting were the reports she received from the boarding school.

Appended to a long letter from the principal, who expatiated in detail, as usual, about the pleasing progress of Charlotte's daughter, was a brief postscript, together with an enclosure from a male assistant. Both of these will now be given here.

THE PRINCIPAL'S POSTSCRIPT

As for Ottilie, your ladyship, I can only repeat what I have said in my previous reports. I cannot reproach her, yet I cannot be pleased with her. As ever, she is modest and agreeable to others; but this diffident, servile behavior of hers is something I cannot approve. You recently sent her money and various dress fabrics. She has made no use of the former; and the fabrics, too, lie there untouched. Of course she keeps her things very neat and tidy but seems to change her clothes only when cleanliness and orderliness demand. I find, too, that I cannot praise her extreme restraint with respect to food and drink. There is no surplus at our table; yet I like to see nothing more than when the children eat their fill of tasty, nourishing dishes. Food that has been prepared and served according to well-considered principles should be eaten up. I cannot bring Ottilie to clean her plate. Instead, she contrives to cover for some forgetfulness on the part of the servants, just in order to avoid having to eat a particular dish or the dessert. However, one does need to bear in mind in this connection that—as I found out only fairly recently—she sometimes suffers from pain on the left side of her head which, though passing, is evidently severe and might mean something serious. So much for this otherwise so pretty and lovable child.

THE SCHOOLMASTER'S ENCLOSURE

Our excellent principal usually allows me to read the letters in which she communicates her observations of her pupils to their parents and guardians. Those directed to your ladyship I always read with redoubled attention and pleasure; for while we must congratulate you on a daughter who combines all those shining virtues which assure one's rise in the world, I at least must count you no less lucky in having as your ward a child born for the welfare and comfort of others and surely for her own good fortune as well. Ottilie is practically the only pupil about whom I disagree with our honored principal. I by no means take it ill of this energetic person that she demands visible, tangible fruits of her labors; but there are also hidden fruits, and these are the ones that contain the most fertile seeds and that sooner or later grow to be most beautiful. This is most certainly the case with your ward. As long as I have taught her, I have observed her going ahead evenly, slowly, slowly forward, never backward. If ever it were necessary to begin at the beginning with a child, it is certainly so with her. She cannot grasp what does not follow from what has gone before. She stands helpless, unable to proceed in the face of a perfectly easy topic that has no connection in her mind with anything else. But if one can find the connections and make them clear to her, she can understand the most difficult material.

On account of this slow progress she lags behind her fellow pupils, who, with their quite different talents, are forever hastening ahead, learning and remembering with ease even the most disconnected facts and applying them without difficulty. Ottilie learns nothing, is incapable of learning anything in an accelerated program of instruction, as is the case with various subjects taught by hasty and impatient teachers. Complaints have been made about her handwriting and about her inability to learn the rules of grammar. I have looked into these complaints more closely: it is true that she writes slowly and stiffly, if you will, but not hesitantly or unpleasingly. What I have taught her bit by bit of the French language (which is not actually my subject) she easily understood. One strange thing is, however, that though she knows many things quite well, she seems to know nothing when she is questioned about them.

If I may close with a more general observation, I should say the following: she does not learn like a person being educated, but like a person destined to teach; not like a pupil, but like a future instructor. Perhaps it will seem strange to your ladyship that as a teacher and educator I have no higher praise for someone than declaring her like myself. Your greater insight, your deeper understanding of people and society will surely place the best construction on my inadequate but well-intended words. You will doubtless assure yourself that there is much joy to be hoped for from this child. I commend myself to you with the request that you permit me to write again when I find I have something significant and gratifying to relate.

Charlotte was pleased to receive this letter. What it contained was consonant with her own view of Ottilie; at the same time she could not help smiling at the teacher's sympathy for the girl, which seemed warmer than that occasioned by the usual insights into the virtues of a pupil. With her calm and objective way of thinking, she let this circumstance rest, as she had so many others; she valued the perceptive man's interest in Ottilie, for experience had taught her how very precious true affection is in a world where indifference and antipathy are firmly ingrained.

Chapter Four

The topographical map on which the estate and its surroundings had been drawn in pen and wash—with graphic accuracy in a relatively large scale, its precision thoroughly checked by the Captain's trigonometric measurements—was soon finished: for there was hardly anyone needing less sleep than this active man, who regularly devoted his days to the task at hand and who thus had always accomplished something by evening.

"Now," he said to his friend, "let us move on to our next task, the description of the property. For this, we must make a sufficient start on the work to be able to draft leases and suchlike later on. Only let us establish one principle: separate all business matters from life. Business demands earnest discipline, life demands spontaneity; business demands clear logic, but life often finds inconsistency necessary—indeed it can be desirable and entertaining. If you are sure in the one, then you can be all the freer in the other, instead of finding freedom undermining certainty and canceling it out."

Edward sensed a slight reproach in these suggestions. Though not by nature disorganized, he could never bring himself to arrange and classify his papers. He did not keep matters that had to do with other people separate from those that had to do with himself; just as he did not clearly enough distinguish between business and busyness, entertainment and diversion. Now things were made easy for him in that a friend assumed this task, a second self undertaking the separation that a single self is often reluctant to perform.

In the Captain's wing they set up a repository for matters of present moment and an archive for those of past relevance; they transferred all documents, papers and reports from various containers, storerooms, cabinets and chests, and in an amazingly short time the enormous pile had been put into the most satisfying order, all classified in separate pigeon-holes. What they needed was found in greater perfection than they had hoped. In this task an old copyist, with whom Edward had always been dissatisfied in the past, proved especially useful to them, spending his days and even part of the night at his desk.

"I scarcely know the man anymore," Edward said to his friend, "it's hard to believe how energetic and useful he is."

"That's because we give him nothing new until he has taken his time to finish the old," replied the Captain. "This way he manages to get a great deal done; if we interrupt him, he cannot accomplish anything."

While the friends spent their days together in this manner, they did not fail to sit with Charlotte regularly in the evenings. If there was no company from neighboring towns and estates, as was often the case, then their talk and reading were mostly devoted to topics concerning the welfare, advantages and comfort of bourgeois society.

Charlotte, who was in any event accustomed to taking advantage of the present moment, derived some personal benefits from her husband's good humor. By the Captain's good offices, various household arrangements she had long desired but had not been able to achieve were put into effect. The household apothecary, which had until now contained but few supplies, was stocked up, and Charlotte, instructed by their conversation and by the books they were reading, was able to exercise her helpful, active nature more effectively and more frequently than before, both in the course of their conversations and in connection with the books they were reading.

As they were thinking about the most common emergencies, which for that very reason all too often took people by surprise, they provided themselves with all sorts of necessary life-saving equipment, the more so in that with so many lakes, rivers and dams nearby accidents of this kind occasionally did happen. The Captain took special care with this equipment, and Edward let a remark escape him about how such an incident had been a turning-point in his friend's life. But since the Captain remained silent and seemed anxious to avoid confronting some sad memory, Edward stopped short, and Charlotte, too, who was no less informed about the general circumstances of that event, let these remarks pass.

"While we may well be proud of all these precautionary measures," said the Captain one evening, "we still lack the most essential thing, a good man who knows how to make use of them. I can suggest an army surgeon I know who can be had for very little money, an excellent man in his field, who in many instances treated sudden complaints of mine better than any famous doctor. After all, here in the country first aid is always what is most lacking."

This man, then, was immediately engaged, and husband and wife were pleased that certain monies left over for arbitrary expenditures were thus turned to useful account.

So Charlotte made her own use of the Captain's knowledge and energy, and began to feel quite content with the way things stood at present and reassured about how they might turn out in the future. She was usually prepared to ask many questions, and as she enjoyed life, she tried to eliminate anything potentially dangerous or fatal. The lead glaze on pottery and the verdigris of copper containers had caused her a great deal of concern. She now asked to have these things explained, and so it was only natural for them to go back to the basic principles of physics and chemistry.

An accidental, but nonetheless welcome basis for discussions of this kind was provided by Edward's predilection for reading aloud. He had a very agreeable deep voice and had formerly been popular and much in demand for his lively and expressive recitation of poetry and rhetorical pieces. Now other subjects interested him; he read from other texts, and for some time had chosen by preference works on physics, chemistry and technology.

One of his idiosyncrasies, which many other people doubtless share, was that he couldn't bear to have someone reading over his shoulder. This was a natural result of his earlier readings from poetry, plays and stories, and stemmed from the intention, as appropriate for the reader as for the poet, actor, or story-teller, to employ surprise effects, make dramatic pauses and raise the audience's expectations. Of course it totally nullifies the intended effect if someone reads on ahead silently. For this reason he usually sat so that there was nobody behind him. With only three of them this precaution was unnecessary, and since in this instance he had no need to excite emotions or catch the imagination off guard, he did not think to heed where he sat.

But one evening he noticed, after he had casually taken his place, that Charlotte was looking at the pages. His old impatience flared up, and he reprimanded her in a rather unfriendly tone. "If only people would give up such irritating habits once and for all, as well as a few other things that are annoying when you're in company. If I read to someone, isn't it just the same as if I were explaining something orally? The written or printed words take the place of my own feelings and intentions, and do you think I would take the trouble to talk intelligibly if there were a window in my forehead or my breast so that the person to whom I wish to relate my thoughts and feelings one by one would know in advance what I'm aiming at? When someone reads over my shoulder I always feel as if I were split in two."

Charlotte, whose tact distinguished itself in circles large and small by her ability to cover for any disagreeable, violent or even just too boisterous remark, interrupt a conversation dragging on too long or stimulate a flagging one, was even now not abandoned by her good gifts. "You will certainly forgive my rudeness when I tell you what just happened. I heard you reading about affinities, and then I thought of an affinity that has recently developed, much to my concern, between two cousins of mine. My attention came back to your reading and I realized that you were talking of inanimate objects, so I took a look at the page to reorient myself."

"It is a figure of speech that has distracted and confused you," said Edward. "The book is dealing with minerals and different types of earth, but man is a real Narcissus—he finds his own image everywhere and sees the whole world against the backdrop of his own self."

"Quite so!" continued the Captain. "That's how man sees everything that lies outside him: his foolishness and wisdom, the willed random nature of his own actions—these he imputes to animals, plants, the elements and the gods."

"Could you perhaps just briefly explain," replied Charlotte, "since I don't want to lead too far away from the topic at hand, what is actually meant here by 'affinities'?"

"I'll be glad to do so," replied the Captain, to whom Charlotte had turned; "though of course only to the extent I can, based on what I learned from books about it ten years ago. Whether this view is still held by scientists and if it accords with their more recent theories I cannot say."

"It is terrible that one can't learn anything for life anymore," exclaimed Edward. "Our ancestors held firm to what they had learned in their youth; but we have to learn everything over again every five years if we are not to be totally behind the times."

"We women are not so particular," Charlotte said, "and to be honest, I really just want to understand the meaning of the word: for nothing makes one look more foolish in company than using an unusual or technical expression wrongly. I would just like to know the sense of the term in this context. Let's leave the scientific explanations to experts—who, as I've often noticed, don't seem to be able to agree on anything anyway."

"But where to begin, to come as quickly as possible to the heart of the matter?" Edward asked the Captain after a pause. Reflecting a moment, the Captain then answered:

"If you will permit me to take what may seem like a roundabout route, we'll soon be where we want to be."

"You have my full attention," said Charlotte, laying her needlework aside.

And so the Captain began: "With all natural objects the first thing we notice is their relation to themselves. It may seem strange to mention something so obvious, but we can only move on to the unknown when we are clear about the known."

"I thought we might make it easier for her and ourselves," Edward interrupted, "by using examples. Just think of water, oil or mercury, and you will see what we mean by the unity or connectedness of their parts. These substances retain their unity unless it is broken by some outside force. When the external influence is gone, they immediately join together again."

"Of course," agreed Charlotte. "Raindrops tend to come together in streams. And when we were children we found it fascinating to play with mercury, dividing it into little balls and letting it run together again."

"Then perhaps I may mention in passing another important point," added the Captain. "This pure and perfect cohesiveness natural to fluids is always characterized by a definite tendency to form round shapes. Falling water drops are round; you mentioned drops of mercury yourself; and even molten lead, if it has time to solidify as it falls, ends up in the shape of a ball."

"Let me go from there," said Charlotte, "and see if I can guess what you are driving at. Just as everything has a relation to itself, so it also has a relation to other things."

"And this will differ according to the different nature of the objects,"

Edward rapidly went on. "In some cases they come together readily like old friends and acquaintances, meeting and uniting, without any change in their own nature—wine and water mix this way; but others persistently refuse to blend and cannot be united even by mechanical mixing or rubbing—when shaken together, oil and water, for example, separate again right away."

"It's not hard to recognize in these basic forms people one has known," said Charlotte; "in particular, they call to mind social groups we have lived in. But what is most similar to these lifeless objects are the larger groups that confront one another in the world, the trades and the professions, the nobility and the middle classes, soldiers and civilians."

"All the same, though," said Edward, "just as these groups can be brought together by law and manners, so in the chemical world there are mediators to bind substances that repel each other."

"That is how we combine oil and water," interposed the Captain, "by using alkaline salt."

"Not too fast with your lecture," said Charlotte; "I want to show that I can keep up. I imagine we have now come to the 'affinities', is that so?"

"Exactly," replied the Captain, "and we will soon get to know them in the full force of their definition. Those kinds of substance that rapidly combine and interact when brought together are what we call 'related.' It is easy to see this relatedness, or 'affinity,' with alkalis and acids, which, though opposites (and perhaps even because of this), most determinedly seek each other out, combine, modify each other and form through their interaction a new compound. Just think of calcium, which has the greatest and most obvious propensity to combine with all sorts of acids. As soon as our chemical supplies arrive, we'll show you various experiments that are quite fascinating and will give you a clearer idea of all this than words, names and technical terms."

"Let me confess," said Charlotte, "that when you call these strange substances 'related' I think not so much of blood relationships as of intellectual or spiritual ones. In the human world this is how truly meaningful friendships come about; for natures that are opposites make for a more intimate union. So I am prepared to wait for your demonstrations of these mysterious effects. And now," she said, turning to Edward, "I won't interrupt your reading anymore. Now that I understand these things better, I'll be able to follow it with closer attention."

"But now that you've called on us," Edward said, "you can't get away so easily: for the complex cases are actually the most interesting. From them you can really begin to understand the degrees of affinity, be they nearer and stronger or weaker and more remote. It really starts to get fascinating when the relationships bring about separations."

"Does that distressing word, which one hears so often in social life," cried Charlotte, "also occur in science?"

"Indeed it does," replied Edward. "It used even to be a special honor to call chemists 'separating,' or analytical scientists."

"But they are not called that anymore, I presume," said Charlotte, "and rightly so. Bringing things together is a greater and much more creditable art. A specialist in unifying things would be welcome in any branch of life at all.—But now that you're so caught up in your topic, let me hear a few examples."

"Then let's take up where we left off," said the Captain, "with what we have defined in our discussion so far. What we call limestone, for example, is more or less pure calcium oxide, closely bound together by a volatile acid better known in its gaseous state. If you put a piece of limestone in dilute sulphuric acid, the acid attacks the lime and turns it into gypsum; the instable, gaseous acid evaporates in the form of sulphur. In this instance both a separation and a combination have taken place, and it almost seems justified to speak of 'elective affinities,' since it actually appears as if the substances choose one combination in preference to the other."

"I hope you will forgive me," said Charlotte, "just as I forgive the scientist. But I would never speak of a choice here, but rather of necessity—and scarcely even that; since in the last analysis it is probably just a question of opportunity. Opportunity makes relationships just as it makes thieves; and when you speak of your natural substances, the choice seems to me to be entirely with the chemist who brings them together. But once they have been brought together, then God preserve them! In the case you mentioned I feel sorry for the poor sulphur, forced to float around again in the formless air."

"But then it just has to combine with water," said the Captain, "thus becoming a mineral spring and helping to refresh the sick and the healthy."

"That's all very well for the gypsum," said Charlotte, "it is a solid, self-sufficient body that can take care of itself, whereas the sulphur, in its banishment, must undergo all kinds of suffering before it can return to earth again."

"If I am not mistaken," said Edward, smiling, "there is a hidden barb in your words. Admit it, you mischievous creature! When all's said and done you see me as the calcium, attacked by the Captain in the form of sulphuric acid, removed from your gracious presence and turned into recalcitrant gypsum."

"If it's your conscience that leads you to make such remarks," responded Charlotte, "then I won't need to worry. These figures of speech are clever and amusing, and who doesn't like to have a little fun with analogies? But human beings are so many stages higher than these basic substances, and although we've been rather free with such spendid words as 'elective' and 'affinities,' we might do well to take a look at ourselves and give due thought to the meaning of such words in this connection. I for my part know plenty of cases where apparently inseparable intimacies between two people were dissolved by the accidental arrival of a third party, and one of those who seemed so firmly united was driven out into the empty air."

"Chemists are much more gallant," said Edward, "they add a fourth substance so that no one substance ends up alone."

"That's true," said the Captain; "and the strangest and most significant cases are those where the attraction, affinity and separation can be shown to take place in a crosswise pattern; where four substances, originally united by twos, are brought together and, abandoning their original combinations, join to make new compounds. In this kind of separation and combination, repulsion and attraction, some higher destiny really does seem to manifest itself; one almost feels like endowing such substances with the ability to excercise choice and will, so that the term 'elective affinities' seems perfectly justified."

"Can you give an example?" asked Charlotte.

"One shouldn't just rely on words in this sort of case," said the Captain. "As I said, when I can demonstrate these experiments for you, they will become much clearer and easier to grasp. For now I will just have to make do with technical terms that are rather daunting and won't give you a real idea of the matter. One has to see these substances, which are seemingly inanimate, but in actuality always full of potential life, interacting before one's eyes—one has to watch with some empathy as they seek each other out, attract, attack, destroy, swallow up, devour each other, finally emerging from their former close connection in a new, fresh and unexpected form. This is the point at which one attributes an eternal soul, or even common sense and intelligence to them, since our own senses hardly suffice to observe them properly and our intellect is hardly adequate to understand them."

"I don't deny," said Edward, "that the strangest terms cause difficulty, seem ridiculous even, to someone who hasn't come to accept them through the evidence of his own eyes and intellect. But in the meantime, perhaps we can explain by means of letter symbols the experiment the Captain has just described."

"If you don't think it pedantic," answered the Captain, "I'll be happy to use symbols for the sake of brevity. Think of a substance A, existing as a compound with substance B, unable to be sundered from B by force or any other means; and then think of a substance C, related in the same way to substance D. Now bring the two compounds together: A will combine with D and C with B in such a way that it will be impossible to say which elements separated or recombined first."

"Well now!" said Edward. "Until we can see these things with our own eyes, let us regard these formulae as metaphors and derive from them a lesson for our immediate use. You, Charlotte, are A, and I am your B— for in reality I depend on you alone and stay by you, as A stays with B. C is clearly the Captain, who at the moment is pulling me away from you somewhat. Now if you don't want to end up floating around in the air, we will have to procure a D for you, and that, without a doubt, is our charming young Ottilie, to whose arrival you can really no longer raise any objection."

"Good," said Charlotte, "although I don't think your example exactly fits our case. But I think it's lucky that we are all in agreement here today and that these reflections on natural and elective affinities have paved the way for a more intimate exchange of thought. I will admit, then, that I have made up my mind this afternoon to invite Ottilie to join us, since my faithful caretaker and housekeeper is about to leave and get married. This decision results from my view of the matter and what I hope to gain from it; the advantages I see in it for Ottilie you will now read aloud to us. I won't look over your shoulder—but of course I already know what the letter says. But do read it, go ahead!" And with these words she took out a letter and handed it to Edward.

Chapter Five

THE PRINCIPAL'S LETTER

Your Ladyship will forgive me, I am sure, for the brevity of this letter, for now that the public examinations are over, I have to report the outcome of the past year's work to the parents and guardians of all our pupils. But in this case there is no need for me to write at length, as I can say a lot in a few words. Your daughter proved to be the best in her class in every respect. The enclosed report card, as well as her own letter describing the prizes she has won and telling how pleased she is at her great success should give you reassurance and gratification. My own pleasure is somewhat diminished by the prospect of not being able to keep such a proficient young lady with us much longer. I send your Ladyship my regards and will take the liberty of communicating to you very shortly my views on the course I think might be most advantageous for her. My assistant has kindly offered to write to you about Ottilie.

THE SCHOOLMASTER'S LETTER

Our honored principal has asked me to write to you about Ottilie, in part because what we have to report is, to her mind, embarrassing, and in part because she would rather have me make the apologies she owes you.

As I was well aware how hard it is for our dear Ottilie to articulate

what she knows and show what she can do, I was somewhat anxious at
the prospect of the public examination—all the more so in view of the
fact that it is impossible to prepare for it and that Ottilie is not the sort of
student who can be prepared, as is so often the case, to create the super-
ficial appearance of having mastered the material. The outcome only
confirmed my apprehension; she did not receive a prize and is one of
those who failed to receive a diploma. What more can I say? In pen-
manship the others formed their letters less well, but wrote with a freer
hand; in arithmetic they were all faster, and difficult problems, which
Ottilie solves much better, were not set. In French many outtalked and
outdid her; in history she could not immediately recollect names and
dates; in geography she failed to take political divisions into account. In
music there was neither time nor leisure for her to play the few simple
tunes she knows. In drawing she would definitely have won first place:
her outlines were clean and the execution careful and well-conceived.
But unfortunately she had taken on too large a project and was unable
to finish.

When the pupils had stepped down and the examiners conferred
about the results, in the course of which we teachers were allowed at
least to say our modest piece, I soon saw that they either had nothing at
all to say about Ottilie or else made only indifferent, if not negative re-
marks. I hoped that by frankly presenting the sort of person she is I
might be able to create a more favorable impression, and I attempted to
do so with redoubled efforts, not only out of firm conviction but also
because I myself had been in a similar situation in my younger days. The
examiners listened attentively to what I had to say; but when I had
finished, the head of the commission remarked in a friendly but curt
fashion: "Talent is presupposed; but it has to become accomplishment.
This is the aim of all education, it is the clear and distinct desire of the
parents and guardians and the subconscious, unvoiced wish of the chil-
dren themselves. This is the object of the examination in which pupils
and teachers are tested alike. From what you have said we can be opti-
mistic about the child, and indeed it is praiseworthy of you to attend so
closely to your pupils' potential. If you can transform her talent into
accomplishment in the course of the next year, you can be certain that
we will not fail to do justice to you and your favorite pupil."

I had already inwardly accepted the consequence of this speech, but I
had not anticipated something even worse which then took place. Our
dear principal, who, like a good shepherd, did not wish to lose—or, as
was here the case, to see unadorned—a single one of her sheep, could
not conceal her displeasure once the examiners had left and said to
Ottilie, who was standing quite calmly at the window while the others
exclaimed over their prizes: "Now tell me, in heaven's name, how can
anyone seem so stupid when in fact she is not?" Ottilie answered, quite

unperturbed: "You must excuse me, dear madam; but it so happens that I have one of my headaches today, rather a bad one." "How can we be expected to know that!" replied that otherwise so sympathetic woman, turning away angrily.

Well, that is true, no one could know; for Ottilie's face shows no change of expression and I have never even noticed her raising her hand to her forehead.

That was not all. The day's triumph made your Ladyship's daughter, otherwise alert and generous, exuberant and aggressive. She danced about the room with her certificates and prizes and even shook them in Ottilie's face. "You really messed things up today!" she cried. Quite calmly, Ottilie replied: "But this isn't the final judgment, after all." "But *you'll* still always be last!" cried your daughter, prancing off.

To everyone else Ottilie appeared unperturbed, but not to me. Whenever she tries to suppress some unpleasant and keenly felt emotion, her face flushes unevenly. The left cheek reddens for a moment while the right turns pale. I saw this sign and could not refrain from doing something about it. I took our principal aside and spoke seriously with her about the matter. That excellent woman saw her mistake. We conferred for quite some time and, without going into any more detail, I would like to tell your Ladyship our conclusions and our request: that you take Ottilie home for a time. You can easily reconstruct our reasoning yourself. If you decide on this course, I will make further suggestions about how the dear child should be treated. Once your daughter has left us, as we assume will be the case, then we will gladly welcome Ottilie back.

One thing which I might forget when I write again: I have never observed Ottilie demand, or even urgently request, anything. However there are times, though very seldom, when she tries to refuse something demanded of her. She does this with a gesture irresistible for anyone who has grasped its meaning. She presses the palms of her hands together and holds them up, then brings them towards her breast, bending forward a little and looking at the person making the request with such an expression that one gladly gives up all that one might wish to demand. If you ever see her make this gesture—which is not likely when she is in your care—then think of me and spare Ottilie.

Edward had read this letter aloud, not without smiling and shaking his head from time to time. And he couldn't resist making comments about the various people and situations.

"Enough!" cried Edward at last, "it is decided, she shall come here! That would take care of your worries, my dear, and we men can proceed with a suggestion we have in mind. It is essential for me to move into the right wing with the Captain. The evening and morning hours are the best time for us to work together. And you and Ottilie will have plenty of room for yourselves on your side of the house."

Charlotte accepted this suggestion, and Edward began to talk about the shape their lives would now take. Amongst other things, he exclaimed, "It's really very obliging of my niece to have a little headache on the left side; I sometimes have one on the right. If we have it at the same time and are sitting opposite each other, I leaning on my right elbow and she on her left, our heads inclined in opposite directions on our hands, it will make a charming set of mirror images."

The Captain claimed that this was a dangerous thought, but Edward exclaimed: "Just you watch out, my friend, for D! What will B do when C is taken from him?"

"I thought that would be obvious," responded Charlotte.

"Of course," cried Edward: "he will return to his A, his alpha and omega!" he exclaimed, jumping up and clasping Charlotte firmly to his breast.

Chapter Six

Ottilie's carriage had arrived. Charlotte went out to meet her; and the lovely child hastened towards her, fell at her feet and clasped her knees.

"Why such humility?" asked Charlotte, feeling somewhat embarrassed and trying to raise her up. "It's not meant that way," replied Ottilie, not moving from her previous position. "It's just that I so like to think of the time when I was no taller than your knee and felt so confident of your love."

She got up, and Charlotte embraced her warmly. She was introduced to the men, who immediately treated her as a special guest. Indeed, beauty is welcome the world over. She seemed to follow the conversation closely, but without taking part in it.

The next morning Edward said to Charlotte: "She is a charming, entertaining young woman."

"Entertaining?" replied Charlotte with a smile. "She didn't open her mouth once."

"Really?" said Edward, appearing to reflect. "How very strange!"

Charlotte had only to give the new arrival a few hints about the household. Ottilie quickly, indeed—which was even more remarkable—intuitively grasped its organization. She soon saw what she had to do for the group as a whole and for each as an individual. Things were done punctually. She knew how to give orders without seeming bossy, and if something was forgotten, she did the task herself.

As soon as she saw how much time she had left to herself, she asked Charlotte to make up a schedule for her which was to be strictly observed. She did what was asked of her in the manner described by the schoolmaster in his letter to Charlotte. They let her have her way, and only now and again did Charlotte try to suggest something different. Occasionally she gave her used pens in an attempt to make her write with a freer hand; but soon even these pens were sharply cut again.

The women had agreed to speak French when they were alone; and Charlotte persisted with this all the more since Ottilie was less taciturn in the foreign language, its exercise having been made one of her duties. In so doing she often seemed to say more than she intended. Charlotte was particularly charmed by occasional, but accurate and lovingly detailed descriptions of the boarding school. Ottilie became a beloved companion to her, and she hoped in due course to have in her a trusted friend.

In the meantime Charlotte took out again Ottilie's old school reports to remind herself of what the principal and the teacher had said about the dear child and to compare it with her own impression of her personality. For Charlotte believed that one cannot get to know soon enough the character of a person one has to live with, so that one knows what to expect from them, what aspects of their personality can be improved and what must be accepted and allowed for once and for all.

Of course she found nothing new as she perused the papers again, but what she did know became clearer and more distinct. Thus Ottilie's modest habits of eating and drinking, for example, began to really worry her.

The first thing the women took up was Ottilie's wardrobe. Charlotte wished Ottilie to wear richer, more fashionable dresses. So the dear, diligent child set to work right away cutting out fabrics she had been given earlier and fitting them, with little help from others, quickly and most attractively. Her new, fashionable clothes greatly improved her: for since people's charm is conveyed through external appearances, so one seems to see them afresh, and ever more charmingly, when their characteristics are conveyed in new surroundings.

Thus she became for the men, as she had been from the outset, all the more—to make no bones about it—a real joy to behold. For just as the emerald pleases, indeed even heals the sight to some degree with its splendid color, so human beauty has an even greater influence on our inner and outer senses. Whoever beholds it cannot be touched by evil; he feels at one with himself and the world.

So in many ways the little group had profited from Ottilie's arrival. The two men kept more regularly to the hours, the minutes even, that had been arranged for their meetings. They never kept the women waiting any longer than was proper at mealtimes, or for tea, or for a walk. And especially in the evening, they did not leave the table so hastily. Noticing this, Charlotte observed the two men. She tried to work out whether one of the two was more responsible for it, but she could detect no difference. Both were generally sociable. During their conversations they seemed to bear in mind the sort of topic that might make Ottilie join in, subjects suited to her intelligence and education. When reading aloud or recounting stories, they stopped until she returned to the room. They became gentler and altogether more communicative.

In response, Ottilie's diligence increased daily. The more she got to know the house, the people, the circumstances, the livelier her participation became, the quicker she was to understand every glance, every gesture, half a word, a mere sound. Her calm attentiveness, her unperturbed activity never changed. Thus her sitting, standing, coming, going, fetching, carrying, sitting down again was a constant alternation, an ever charming, and, as it seemed, never restless movement. In addition, one hardly heard her, so lightly did she tread.

This care and diligence of Ottilie's was a great pleasure to Charlotte. But one thing that didn't seem appropriate to her she did not conceal from Ottilie. "It is a commendable attention," she said to her one day, "to stoop and pick up something someone has dropped. In this way we show that we wish to be of service to that person; but in society we have to bear in mind to whom we show such respect. I won't lay down the law as to how you should behave towards women. You are young. Towards older and more important people it is your duty, towards your peers an act of politeness and towards younger and more lowly people one of human kindness; but it is not proper for a woman to show such humble servitude towards a man."

"I will try to get out of the habit," replied Ottilie. "But in the meantime you will forgive me this incorrect behavior when I tell you how I came to acquire it. They taught us history at school; I haven't remembered as much of it as I doubtless should; for I didn't know what use it might be to me. But certain incidents have remained very vividly in my mind, amongst them the following. When Charles I of England was standing before those who presumed to be his judges, the gold knob of the stick he was carrying fell to the ground. Used to having someone help him on such occasions, he seemed to look round and expect someone to do him this small service. But no one moved; he bent down himself and picked up the knob. I was so keenly moved by this, rightly or wrongly, that from that moment on I have been unable to see anyone drop something without bending to pick it up myself. But since, as you say, it is not always proper, and," she continued with a smile, "I cannot always tell my little story, I will restrain myself in the future."

In the meantime the useful work the two men felt moved to undertake continued without interruption. Indeed, each day they found something new that needed to be done.

When they went into the village one day they noticed, to their displeasure, how much, in terms of order and cleanliness, it fell short of those villages where land is a more precious commodity.

"You recall," the Captain said, "how we formed the desire, during our trip through Switzerland, to give the last touch to a country garden estate by setting up a village situated like this one, not in the Swiss style of architecture, but in their style of neatness and cleanliness, which are so conducive to good use of the land."

"That would be quite possible here, for example," replied Edward. "The hill where the manor is situated forms a protruding angle around which the village is built in an almost regular semi-circle; through it flows the brook, against whose floods one villager has protected his house with stones, another with posts, another with wooden beams and yet another with planks, with no one helping another, but rather causing injury and danger to others and himself. So the path goes awkwardly up and down, through water, over stones. If the people were willing to put in some work themselves, it would be possible without great subsidy to erect a semi-circular wall here and raise the path behind it to the level of the houses, thus making a most attractive area, encouraging neatness, and eliminating for good all this inadequate piece-work with a single, larger-scaled undertaking."

"Let us try it," said the Captain, scanning and sizing up the land quickly.

"I don't like to deal with townspeople and peasants if I am not in a position to actually give orders," said Edward.

"You're quite right," replied the Captain, "I've had trouble with dealings like that before. How hard it is for people to weigh what they have to give up against what they stand to gain! How hard to desire the results and not dislike the efforts needed to obtain them! Many people even confuse the means and the ends, taking pleasure in the one without keeping the other in mind at all. Everything bad has to be fixed at the spot where it appears, and nobody bothers about its actual origin or what else it bears on. That's why it's so hard to consult on these things, especially with common folk, who understand everyday affairs quite well but seldom look beyond tomorrow. And if a communal project means that one person's profit is another one's loss, there's no way of reaching agreement. Everything of benefit to the general welfare should really be supported by absolute decree."

While they were standing talking, a fellow who looked to be more brazen than needy came up to beg from them. Not liking to be bothered by interruptions, Edward reprimanded him, after several unsuccessful attempts to turn him away more peacefully; but as the man shuffled off, grumbling and even scolding back at him, insisting on the rights of beggars, who could be refused alms but should not be insulted because they were as much under the protection of God and the king as anyone else, Edward completely lost his temper.

To calm him down, the Captain then said: "Let us take this incident as a challenge to extend our country legislation. Charity is necessary; but it is better not to give it personally, especially in one's own home town. There one should be consistently moderate in all things, even in one's good deeds. Too much generosity encourages beggars instead of sending them on their way; on the other hand when traveling one can well appear like good fortune itself by giving some poor person on the street an unexpectedly large gift. The location of the village and the manor make it easy for us to solve this problem; I have been thinking about it for some time.

"At one end of the village there is the inn, at the other an honest old couple; in both places you should leave a small sum of money. Not the beggar entering, but the beggar leaving the village gets some; and since both houses are directly on the roads that lead by the manor, everyone who intends to come up to the house will be referred to these two spots."

"Come," said Edward, "let's do that right away, we can always straighten out the details later."

They went to the innkeeper and the old couple, and the matter was soon disposed of.

"I am well aware," said Edward, as they walked back up to the house, "that everything in the world depends on bright ideas and firm decisions. You have rightly judged my wife's landscape gardening, and have even given me some tips for improvement which, I must confess, I passed on to her right away."

"I suspected as much," responded the Captain, "but I don't think you did the right thing. You have confused her; she has dropped her work entirely and is annoyed with us on this one point: she avoids speaking of it and has not invited us back to the moss hut, although she spends her spare time with Ottilie up there."

"We shouldn't let ourselves be put off by that," Edward replied. "Once I am convinced that an idea is good and think it could and should be done I cannot rest until it is. After all, we usually manage to make our wishes felt. Let us bring out those illustrated English estate descriptions tonight, and afterwards your map of the property. We should present it first as a general problem and as something of a joke; the talk will soon enough become serious."

The books were consulted accordingly. They showed in each instance a map of the area and a view of the landscape in its natural state, then on separate flaps the change artfully made to utilize and enhance its original good properties. From this the transition to their own estate, their own surroundings, and what could be made of them, was an easy one.

Now it became a pleasant task to consult the map the Captain had made, although at first it was hard to tear themselves away from Charlotte's original conception of the project. They did find an easier path up the hill, however; and they made plans to build a summer house on the upper part of the rise in front of a delightful little wood; it would be connected with the manor in that it could be seen from the windows of the big house, and from it one would be able to ramble back towards the house and the gardens.

The Captain, who had considered everything carefully and done all the surveying, mentioned again the path in the village, the wall beside the brook, and the landfill that would be thus necessitated. "By creating a convenient path to the top of the hill," he said, "I will gain exactly the right amount of stone needed for the wall. In that the one is connected with the other, both become cheaper and can be finished more expeditiously."

"But now comes my worry," said Charlotte. "A certain sum of money will have to be spent; and when one knows what is needed for such a project, one can spread it out over several months, if not weeks. I am in charge of expenses; I shall pay the bills and keep the books myself."

"You don't seem to have too much trust in us," said Edward.

"Not when it comes to your personal desires," responded Charlotte. "We women can control our desires better than you."

The arrangements were made, the work was soon begun, with the Captain ever present and Charlotte the almost daily witness of his serious and decisive management. He for his part got to know her better, and the two of them found it easy to work together and achieve results.

In business it is just as in dancing: those who keep the same rhythm become indispensable to each other. Mutual good will is the inevitable result, and that Charlotte felt this way towards the Captain now that she had got to know him better was clearly proved by the fact that she quite calmly let him tear up a lovely resting-place which she had specially selected and decorated in her first landscaping efforts, but which did not fit into his plans; yet she didn't feel the least resentment about it.

Chapter Seven

Now that Charlotte was working together with the Captain, Edward, consequently, spent more time with Ottilie. He had in any event been quietly growing fond of her for some time. She was helpful and obliging to everyone; and he flattered himself, in his vanity, that she was more so towards him. There was no doubt about it: she had already taken note of the dishes he liked and how he liked them done. How much sugar he took in his tea, and other things of this sort, did not escape her notice. She took special care to prevent all drafts, since he was unusually sensitive to them, a fact that sometimes brought him into conflict with his wife, who liked to have plenty of fresh air. Ottilie also knew what was what in the flower garden and orchard, and tried to foster what would please him and to prevent anything that might irritate him. The result was that she soon became a kindly guardian angel, indispensable to him, and sorely missed when she was not there. In addition, she seemed more open and communicative whenever they were alone together.

Edward had retained as he grew older a childish streak to which Ottilie's youthfulness greatly appealed. They liked to recall former times when they had met: these memories went back to the first period of Edward's love for Charlotte. Ottilie claimed to remember the two of them as the most handsome couple at court; and when Edward said that she could not possibly remember something from so far back in her childhood, she insisted that she did recall one particular incident in perfect detail: how she had once hidden her face in Charlotte's lap when he had come into the room—not from fear, but from childish surprise. She might have added: because he had made such an impression on her, because she had liked him so much.

This regrouping had brought almost to a halt many projects that the two men had previously begun, with the result that they now had to take stock of things once more, and draft various plans and write certain letters. So they went up to their office, where they discovered that the old copyist had nothing to do. They set to work and soon found tasks for him, not noticing that they were handing over many jobs that they had formerly done themselves. The Captain had trouble with the very first memorandum, Edward with the very first letter he began. They struggled for a time with drafts and revisions, until at last Edward, whose work was going the least smoothly, asked how late it was.

At this point they discovered that, for the first time in years, the Captain had forgotten to wind his pocket chronometer; and although they didn't quite realize it, they seemed to sense that time was becoming indifferent to them.

But just as the men's activity was slowing down, the women's began to increase. Indeed, it is generally true that the life of a family, consisting of a certain set of persons and an unavoidable set of circumstances, contains within itself, like a wine-vat, any extraordinary affection or growing passion, and some time can elapse before this new ingredient sets up a noticeable fermentation and over-flows the top.

In the case of our friends their growing mutual affections had the most delightful effects. They became more free and open with each other, and a general good will was born of their individual fondness for one another. Each one felt content and was glad to see the others happy as well.

Such a mood elevates the spirit and expands the heart, and everything one plans and does tends towards the infinite. Thus the friends no longer remained confined to the house. Their walks extended farther and farther, and while Edward hastened on ahead with Ottilie to choose which way they would go and to blaze the trail, the Captain followed steadily with Charlotte, deep in serious conversation, delighting in newly discovered spots and unexpected views, in the wake of their more impetuous leaders.

One day their walk took them through the gate of the right wing of the house down to the inn, over the brook towards the lakes, whose contours they followed as far as one could go along the water, since the bank suddenly ceased to be negotiable, being cut off first by a bushy hill and further on by steep rocks.

But Edward, who knew this area from his hunting expeditions, went ahead with Ottilie along an overgrown path in the knowledge that the old mill, hidden between the rocks, could not be far off. Soon, however, the little-used path stopped and they found themselves lost in thick bushes amongst moss-covered boulders. Not for long though, for soon the sound of the mill-wheel showed them they were close to the spot they were looking for.

Stepping out onto a cliff, they saw the quaint old black wooden building in the valley below them, shaded by steep rocks and high trees. They decided to climb down without further ado over the mossy crags, with Edward going first; and when he looked up and saw Ottilie stepping lightly without the slightest fear, balancing gracefully from stone to stone after him, he thought she was a heavenly being floating above him. And if, at the tricky spots, she grasped his extended hand from time to time, he couldn't deny that this was the most delicate female creature who had ever touched him. He almost wished she might stumble or slip so that he could catch her in his arms and press her to his heart. But in fact he would on no account have done so, and for more than one reason: he was afraid he might upset or hurt her.

We will soon see his reason for this. Once he had reached the bottom and was sitting opposite her at the rustic table, having asked the kindly miller's wife for some milk and sent the hospitable miller to fetch Charlotte and the Captain, Edward began to speak somewhat hesitantly:

"I have a request, dear Ottilie: and I hope that even if you do not grant it you will forgive me for asking it. You make—quite properly— no secret of the fact that you wear a miniature on your breast underneath your dress. It is a portrait of your father, that fine man whom you scarcely knew and who deserves in every way a place next to your heart. But do forgive me: the portrait is large and cumbersome, and its metal frame and glass make me quite anxious when you lift up a baby or carry some object before you, when the carriage sways or when we force our way through bushes, as just now, when we were climbing down the cliffs. It terrifies me that some unforeseen jolt, fall, or push could cause you bodily harm. For my sake, take the miniature not out of your mind or out of your room—indeed, give it the most beautiful, the most sacred place in your apartment; but remove from your breast that object whose presence there seems to me, in my perhaps exaggerated anxiety, so dangerous."

Ottilie, who had sat pensively while he spoke, was silent a while; then, calmly and unhesitatingly, looking more to heaven than towards Edward, she unfastened the chain, took out the picture, pressed it to her forehead and handed it to her friend, saying: "Please look after it until we get home. I cannot show you in any better way how much I value your kindness and concern."

Her friend did not dare press the picture to his lips, but clasped her hand and held it to his eyes. Theirs were perhaps the two most beautiful hands that had ever met. He felt as if a weight had fallen from his heart, as if a dividing wall had been torn down between him and Ottilie.

Guided by the miller, Charlotte and the Captain arrived by an easier route. The friends greeted each other, and enjoyed the refreshments. They did not want to go back the same way, so Edward suggested a path on the other side of the brook from which one could again catch a glimpse of the lakes, although it was not altogether an easy climb. Now they went through mixed woodland, with a good view of the countryside and its various villages, plots and dairy farms with their fertile green sur-roundings. The first thing they came to was a farmstead nestled at the peak amongst the woods. From the top of the gentle hill they had the most beautiful view of the richness of this countryside in all directions, and from this they came to a charming little clump of trees; stepping out, they found themselves on the cliff opposite the manor house.

How glad they were to see it so unexpectedly. They had circum-scribed a separate little world; they were now standing on the spot where they planned to erect the new building, and could look into the windows of their own house again.

They went down to the moss hut, and it was the first time that all four had sat there together. Nothing was more natural than for them to agree that the path they had just taken, slowly and with some difficulty, should be laid out in such a way that they would be able to stroll along it together pleasantly and comfortably. Everyone had a suggestion to make, and they calculated that the route back to the house, which had taken them several hours to traverse, could be done in an hour if it were properly constructed. And they were just projecting a decorative bridge, which would shorten the route at the point below the mill where the brook flowed into the lakes, when Charlotte put an end to their high-flying fantasies by reminding them of the costs this particular plan would involve.

"I have a solution for that," replied Edward. "That farmstead in the wood, so prettily situated but financially so unprofitable, could be sold and we could use the proceeds for the new project. In this way we would have the pleasure, each time we took that marvelous walk, of enjoying the interest of well-invested capital, whereas at the moment we will be annoyed to find, when we tally everything up at the end of the year, that the farm has brought us only a very meagre income."

Thrifty manager that she was, Charlotte could say nothing against this. The matter had been brought up earlier. Now the Captain wanted to draw up a plan for dividing the plots of land amongst the farmers; but Edward favored a speedier and more convenient solution. The present tenant farmer, who had already made a bid for it, should receive it and pay the money in instalments, and they would complete the landscaping project in stages as his money came in.

This sensible, moderate arrangement was certain of everybody's approval, and soon the whole company saw in their mind's eye the new paths meandering through the landscape and envisaged themselves discovering the most delightful resting-places and vantage points.

In order to call everything more vividly to mind, they took out the map that very evening as soon as they were home. They traced the path they had taken on the map and noted ways for improving it at certain spots. They talked over all their earlier suggestions and compared them with their newest plans, agreeing once again on the location of the new building opposite the manor and thus completing the circular arrangement of paths.

Ottilie had said nothing to all this, when Edward moved the map, which had been lying in front of Charlotte, over in Ottilie's direction and asked her what she thought of it. She hesitated a little, and he gently encouraged her, telling her to speak up, since things were still open, and nothing was settled yet.

Putting her finger on the highest part of the rise, Ottilie said: "I would build the summer house here. You wouldn't see the manor from there, of course, since it would be hidden by the clump of trees; instead, you would be in a new and different world, with the village and all the houses hidden from sight. The view of the lakes, towards the mill, the hills, mountains and countryside, is extraordinarily beautiful; I noticed it as we went past."

"She's right!" exclaimed Edward. "Why didn't it occur to us? That's what you mean, isn't it, Ottilie?" He took a pencil and drew in rough, bold strokes a long rectangle on the rise.

The Captain was taken aback; he didn't like to have his careful, cleanly drawn map disfigured in this way; but after gently expressing his displeasure, he controlled himself and took up the idea. "Ottilie is right," he said. "After all, don't we all enjoy taking a long drive to drink coffee or eat fish that we would not have enjoyed so much at home? We like to have a little change and to see different things. Your ancestors very sensibly built the manor here, for it is protected from the winds and close to all our everyday needs; but a building intended more for social occasions than to be actually lived in would be well placed up there and could give us some delightful hours in the good seasons of the year."

The more they talked it over the better the idea seemed, and Edward could not conceal his triumph that Ottilie had thought it up. He was as proud of it as if it had been his own invention.

Chapter Eight

The Captain surveyed the spot the very next morning and drew a preliminary sketch, and once they had all reconfirmed their decision on the site, he made an exact plan with an estimate of costs and an account of everything that was necessary. All kinds of preparations had to be made. The sale of the farmstead was taken up right away. Together, the two men found new things to keep them occupied.

The Captain pointed out to Edward that it would be a nice gesture, that in fact it was his obligation, to celebrate Charlotte's birthday by laying the foundation stone. It didn't take much to overcome Edward's long-standing dislike of such festivities, for it occurred to him that Ottilie's birthday, which came later, could be celebrated in a similar way.

Charlotte, who took the new landscaping plans very seriously and thought them actually rather risky, spent her time checking through the estimates and making out a schedule of deadlines and expenditures. The group saw each other less during the daytime, and the result was that they were all the more eager to meet in the evening.

In the meantime, Ottilie had taken over the management of the household completely, as one might have expected, given her quiet, self-assured manner. Her whole attention was turned more toward household things than to the world or outdoor life. Edward soon noticed that she only went on walks out of politeness, stayed outside longer in the evening merely out of social duty and often enough found some household task as an excuse for going inside again. Soon he managed to arrange their walks so that they were home again before sundown, and he began to read poetry aloud—something he had not done for quite some time—especially poems into which he could inject an expression of pure but passionate love as he read them.

In the evening they usually sat around a small table at their customary places: Charlotte on the sofa, Ottilie in an armchair opposite her, and the men on the other two sides. Ottilie sat to Edward's right, where he placed the lamp when he was reading. Soon Ottilie moved closer, so she could look over his shoulder: for she placed more trust in her own eyes than in someone else's lips. And Edward, for his part, moved nearer, to make it easier for her in every way; indeed, he often paused for longer than necessary, so that he would not have to turn the page until she was also finished.

Charlotte and the Captain, noticing this, smiled at each other now and again; but both were surprised by another indication of Ottilie's secret affection.

One evening, which had been partly spoiled for the little group by some annoying visitors, Edward suggested that they stay together a while longer. He felt like playing his flute, which he had not done for a long time. Charlotte looked for the sonatas they usually played together, and when she could not find them, Ottilie admitted, with some hesitation, that she had taken them up to her room.

"And you can accompany me on the piano, you really want to?" exclaimed Edward, his eyes shining with joy. "I think I can manage," replied Ottilie. She brought the music and sat down at the piano. Their audience was attentive, and surprised to see how well Ottilie had worked up the piece by herself, but what surprised them even more was how well she could keep up with Edward. "Keep up" is not actually the right word: for while Charlotte, with deliberate skill, was able to slow down at one spot and speed up at another to keep pace with her husband's erratic playing, Ottilie, who had heard the sonata played by the two of them several times, seemed to have learned it in the same manner as Edward was accustomed to play it. She had so taken over his faults that a whole new piece resulted, one that did not entirely keep to the correct tempo, but was nonetheless exceedingly pleasant and charming. The composer himself would have enjoyed hearing his work so delightfully distorted.

The Captain and Charlotte observed this strange and unexpected event with the unspoken feelings one often has towards a child's actions when, because of their worrisome consequences, one cannot approve of them and yet cannot scold, in fact must even feel envious. For in reality the affection between Charlotte and the Captain was growing just as much as that of the other two, and all the more dangerously maybe, in that they were more serious, more sure of themselves, and better able to control themselves.

The Captain had already begun to sense that habit threatened to bind him irresistibly to Charlotte. He forced himself to avoid those hours when Charlotte came out into the gardens by getting up very early in the morning to give his orders and then withdrawing to his wing of the house. The first few days Charlotte thought this was accidental; she looked for him wherever he might be likely to be; then she realized what he meant by it, and her respect for him grew all the more.

But if the Captain avoided being alone with Charlotte, he was all the more concerned with speeding up the progress of the landscaping so as to celebrate her birthday more dazzlingly. While he had the gently rising path laid down from behind the village, he also had men working from the summit downwards, under the pretext of excavating rock, and had carefully arranged it so that the two parts of the path should be joined the night before her birthday. The cellar for the new house on the hill had been hastily dug out rather than carefully excavated, and a beautiful foundation stone with panels and covering slabs had been hewn.

The external activity, all these secret, loving plans, and the internal, more or less repressed emotions that accompanied them had a somewhat dampening effect on the company when they were together; hence Edward, who sensed that something was missing, suggested one evening that the Captain get out his violin and accompany Charlotte on the piano. The Captain could not deny the general request, and so the two performed a most difficult piece of music together, with feeling, fluency and ease, much to the pleasure of the listening couple. Plans were made to repeat the performance and to practice together often.

"They play better than we do, Ottilie!" said Edward. "Let us admire them, but let us have our own joy together as well."

Chapter Nine

Charlotte's birthday had arrived and everything was ready: the wall that formed a higher barrier between the village road and the water, and also the path past the church. This joined for a while the path Charlotte had laid out, before winding its way up the cliff with the moss hut to its left, first above and then, after a complete reversal of direction, beneath it, as it gradually reached the top.

A large group had gathered for the occasion. At church they found the parishioners assembled in their finest array. After the service the boys, youths and men led on, as had been arranged; then came the lords and ladies with their guests and retinue; and finally the girls and women.

At the turn in the path a raised clearing had been made; here the Captain asked Charlotte and the guests to pause. From this point they could survey the whole path with the group of men, who were well ahead, and the women following them, who were just now passing by. In this splendid weather, it was a most charming sight. Charlotte was touched and delighted, and pressed the Captain's hand with feeling.

They followed the steadily advancing throng which had now formed a circle around the place where the house was to be erected. The builder and his men, as well as the noblest guests, were invited to step down into the excavation where the foundation stone, propped on one side, was ready to be laid. A mason in his best finery, with his trowel in one hand and his hammer in the other, gave a handsome speech in rhymed verses that can only be inadequately reproduced in prose.

"Three things," he began, "are necessary for a building: that it be rightly situated, that it have a good foundation, and that it be properly constructed. The first is the owner's responsibility; for as in towns and cities it is up to the prince and the community to decide where building may be done, so in the country it is the prerogative of the landowner to say, 'this is where my house will stand and nowhere else.'"

Edward and Ottilie did not dare look at each other at this point in the speech, even though they were standing across from each other.

"The third thing, the actual completion of the building, involves all kinds of different tradespeople; indeed, there are few that are not called upon to share the work. But the second thing, the foundation, is the mason's task and—let us state this boldly—the chief business of the whole undertaking. It is a serious matter, and our invitation to you is a serious one, for this ceremony takes place in the depths of the earth. Here in this narrow, hollowed-out space you do us the honor of appearing as witnesses to our secret task. Very soon we shall lower this well-hewn stone, and soon these walls of earth, now graced by fine and important persons, will not be visible—they will be filled in.

"We could easily just lower this stone, whose corner marks the right-hand corner of the building, whose rectangular form represents, in miniature, the building's rectangular shape, and whose horizontal and vertical planes stand for the true level of all its walls; we could do so because it would rest evenly by virtue of its own weight. But here there shall be no lack of mortar, the substance that binds stone to stone; for just as people who are naturally fond of each other stay together better when they are bound together by the law, so stones that have already been shaped to fit together are held together better by its cohesive powers; and as it is not proper to be idle when others are working, you will doubtless not refuse to participate."

Hereupon he handed his trowel to Charlotte, who tossed some mortar under the stone. Many others were persuaded to do likewise and soon the stone was lowered, whereupon the hammer was handed to Charlotte and the others so that, by tapping it three times, they could properly bless the union of stone and earth.

"The mason's work," the speaker continued, "though now in the open air, takes place, if not in secret, then for a secret purpose. The leveled ground is filled in, and even in the case of the walls we build above ground, one hardly thinks of us in the end. The work of stone-mason and stonecutter is more in evidence, and we even have to accept it when the painter completely obliterates all traces of our work, making it his own by covering it up, smoothing it out and coloring it.

"Who else, then, is more justified than the mason in doing what he does right to please himself? Who has more reason for confidence in his own worth? When the house has been completed, the floor smoothed out and tiled, and the exterior ornamented, he can still see through all these layers and recognize the regular, well-laid joints that give the whole building its shape and stability.

"But just as someone who has done an evil deed fears that it will come to light in spite of all his precautions, so anyone who has secretly done good must expect that this too will be revealed against his will. This is why we are going to make this foundation stone a memorial as well. Here in these different hollowed-out spaces we shall place various items to bear witness for remote posterity. These sealed metal containers hold written messages; on these metal plates all kinds of memorable things have been engraved; in these fine glass bottles we are burying our best aged wine, marked with its vintage; we have not forgotten to include all kinds of coins minted this year; all this we owe to the generosity of our master. There is plenty of space left here yet, if any guest or observer wishes to bequeath anything to posterity."

After a brief pause the workman looked around; but as usual in such situations, no one was prepared; they had all been taken by surprise. At last a lively young officer spoke up: "If I am to contribute anything that has not yet been placed in this treasure chamber, then I must cut off a couple of buttons from my uniform; they certainly deserve to go down to posterity." No sooner said than done! And now many others had similar ideas. The womenfolk did not hesitate to throw in their little hair combs; scent bottles and other pretty objects were not spared; but Ottilie, absorbed in the sight of all the things that had been contributed, hesitated until she was roused by an encouraging word from Edward. Then she unfastened the golden chain around her neck on which her father's portrait had hung, and laid it gently on top of the other treasures, whereupon Edward rather hastily made sure that the well-fitting cover was immediately set in place and joined fast.

The young journeyman, who had been the most active during all this, took up his orator's pose once again and continued: "We are laying this stone for all time, to ensure that the present and future owners will have the longest possible enjoyment of this house. But insofar as we are also burying a treasure, as it were, we reflect, during this most fundamental of tasks, on the transience of all things human; we contemplate the possibility that this firmly sealed cover may be opened again, which could not happen unless everything else that we have not yet even finished building were to be destroyed.

"But for this very reason—so that it may be finished—away with thoughts of the future, back to the present! Let us, after today's ceremony, move ahead with our work right away, so that none of the tradesmen who are to continue on our foundation may stand idle, so that the building may rise and be completed rapidly and so that the master of the house, with his relatives and guests, may enjoy the surrounding landscape from windows that are not yet there. Now let us drink to the health of our lords and ladies and all present!"

And so he drained a fine crystal glass at one draught and threw it into the air; for it is a sign of the highest joy to destroy the vessel one has used at such a happy moment. But that is not what happened on this occasion: the glass did not return to the ground, yet there was no miracle involved.

To speed up the progress of the building the ground had been completely excavated at the opposite corner and the walls had even been begun, and for that purpose scaffolding had been put up to the necessary height.

For the benefit of the workers the scaffolding had been covered with boards for the occasion, and a crowd of spectators had been allowed up onto them. The glass went in this direction and was caught by one of the onlookers who regarded this accident as a good omen for himself. Finally, without letting anyone else hold it, he showed it around, and on it the letters E and O most delicately intertwined could be seen engraved: it was one of the glasses that had been made for Edward in his childhood.

Once the workmen had left the scaffolding, the nimblest of the guests climbed up to look around. They could not praise enough the beautiful views on every side. How much more one can see from a vantage-point, even if it is only one story up! Further out in the countryside several new villages came into view; the silver streak of the river could be seen distinctly, and indeed one person claimed he could even see the towers of the capital. At their back, behind the wooded hills, rose the blue summits of a far-off mountain range, and the nearby countryside could be seen in its entirety. "Now all that needs to be done," said one guest, "is to combine the three small lakes to make a big one; then the view would have all the grandeur you could want."

"That could doubtless be done," said the Captain, "for at one time they formed a single mountain lake."

"Only I beg you to spare my clump of planes and poplars that stand so handsomely beside the middle pond," said Edward. "Look," he turned to Ottilie, leading her forward a couple of paces and pointing down below, "I planted these trees myself."

"How long have they been there?" asked Ottilie. "About as long," Edward replied, "as you have been alive. Yes, my dear, I planted them when you were still in the cradle."

The company returned to the manor house. After dinner they were invited to take a walk through the village to see the new improvements. The Captain had ordered the inhabitants to gather in front of their houses; they were standing, now in rows, but grouped naturally in families, partly occupied with their evening's work, partly resting on the new benches. It had been made their pleasant duty to take up this neat and orderly pose at least on Sundays and holidays.

A closed and affectionate circle, such as had been formed amongst our friends, is always unpleasantly disrupted by a larger group. All four were glad to find themselves alone again in the large drawing room; but this cozy feeling was somewhat disturbed by a letter that was handed to Edward announcing other guests for the next day.

"As we suspected," exclaimed Edward to Charlotte; "the count could not stay away; he is coming tomorrow."

"Then the baroness is not far behind," replied Charlotte.

"No indeed!" answered Edward. "She's arriving tomorrow too, from her part of the world. They ask for a place to stay for the night, and mean to travel on together the day after tomorrow."

"Then we must get things ready in good time, Ottilie!" said Charlotte.

"What would you like to have done?" asked Ottilie.

Charlotte gave her orders in a general outline, and Ottilie went off.

The Captain enquired about the relationship of these two people, which he knew about only in a general way. Earlier on, the two of them, already married to others, had fallen passionately in love. Two marriages were wrecked, not without scandal; divorce was contemplated. This had been possible for the baroness, but not for the count. They had to act as if they had parted, but their relationship continued; and if they could not spend their winters together in the capital, they made up for it during the summer on pleasure trips and at spas. They were both a little older than Edward and Charlotte, and all of them were close friends from the time when they had been at court together. They had always stayed on good terms, even though they did not approve of everything about their friends. But this time their arrival was in a sense quite inconvenient for Charlotte, and if she were to have examined the reason more closely, she would have had to say that it was on account of Ottilie. The chaste and virtuous child should not see such an example so early.

"They could have stayed away a few days longer," said Edward, as Ottilie came back in again, "until we had completed the sale of the farm. The contract is ready, and I have one copy of it here; but we need a second one, and our copyist is very ill." The Captain offered to copy it, and so did Charlotte, but there were some objections to this. "Give it to me!" cried Ottilie urgently.

"You won't be able to get it finished," said Charlotte.

"Indeed, I need it by early the day after tomorrow, and it is very long," said Edward. "It will be ready," cried Ottilie, the paper in her hands already.

The next morning, while they were watching for their guests, whom they did not want to miss, from the top floor windows, Edward said: "Who is that riding so slowly along the road?" The Captain described the rider more closely. "Then I wasn't mistaken," said Edward. "For all the details you can see so clearly go very well with the general picture which I can see quite well. It's Mittler. But why on earth is he riding so very slowly?"

The figure approached, and it was Mittler indeed. He was warmly welcomed as he came up the stairs. "Why didn't you come yesterday?" called Edward, as he came nearer.

"I don't like loud parties," responded Mittler. "But today I have come to make up for it and celebrate my dear Charlotte's birthday with you all in peace and quiet."

"How can you spare so much time?" Edward asked jocularly.

"You owe my visit, for what it is worth, to a thought I had yesterday. I spent half the day very happily in a house where I had helped make peace, and then I heard that a birthday was being celebrated here. I suppose you can call it selfish, but I thought to myself: you only wish to share the happiness of those you have brought back together. Why don't you celebrate as well for once with friends who live in peace and cherish it? No sooner said than done! Here I am, as I vowed I would be."

"Yesterday you would have found many guests, today you'll find few," said Edward. "You will find the count and the baroness, with whom you have had dealings before."

Looking immediately for his hat and riding whip, their eccentric but much liked guest jumped up from their midst: "Must I be dogged by an evil star, as soon as I want to relax and enjoy myself? But why should I act out of character? I shouldn't have come, and now I'm obliged to leave—for I refuse to stay under the same roof as those people. And beware: they bring nothing but ill luck! They are like a fungus that spreads over everything!"

They tried to assuage him, but in vain. "Anyone who attacks the state of marriage," he declared, "who undermines this foundation of all moral society by word or deed, will have to reckon with me; or else, if I cannot better him, I will have nothing to do with him. Marriage is both the base and the pinnacle of culture. It makes barbarians tame, and it gives the most cultivated of people an opportunity to demonstrate their gentleness. It must be indissoluble; it brings so much luck that individual misfortunes cannot be weighed against it. And why speak of misfortune? Misfortune is really impatience that comes over people from time to time, and then they like to see themselves as unlucky. If you let the moment pass, you will think yourself fortunate that something that has stood the test of time still exists. There is no sufficient reason for separation. The human condition is so highly charged with joy and sorrow that one cannot calculate what two spouses owe each other. It is an infinite

debt that can only be paid in eternity. It may be unpleasant at times—
I can well believe it—but that is right and proper. Are we not also
married to our conscience, which we would often like to get rid of, since
it is more disagreeable than any man or woman could ever be?"

He would have gone on speaking in this forceful way for a long time
had not postillion blasts announced the arrival of the count and baron-
ess, who were driving into the courtyard from two directions at the
same time, as had been arranged. While the companions hastened to
meet them, Mittler concealed his presence, ordered his horse to be
brought to the inn and rode off in high dudgeon.

Chapter Ten

The guests had been welcomed and led inside; they were pleased to see
once more the house and the rooms where they had spent so many happy
days, but which they had not visited for a long time. The friends were
very glad to see them again, too. The count and baroness were two of
those fine and noble creatures who are almost more attractive in middle
age than in youth; for even though they may have lost something of their
first bloom, they inspire not only affection but a definite sense of inti-
macy. Thus, the couple made a particularly agreeable impression now.
Their easy manner of accepting and coping with what life brought, their
poise and apparent spontaneity were infectious, and there was a great
propriety and a total lack of artificiality about everything they did.

This impression made itself felt in the little group immediately. The
new arrivals, who had come straight from the world of society, as was
apparent from their clothing, equipment and everything else about
them, made a kind of contrast to our friends with their countrified ways
and secret passions. But the difference soon diminished as old memories
and present interests mingled, and a fast-paced, lively conversation
rapidly bound them all together.

It did not take long, however, before they split into groups. The
women retired to their wing of the house and found much to talk about
as they began to exchange confidences and look at the newest patterns
and styles of morning gowns, hats and the like. The men occupied them-
selves with the new carriages and the horses which were trotted out, and
they immediately began to barter and trade.

They did not come together again until dinner time. They had
changed their clothes, and once again the new arrivals showed them-
selves to advantage. Everything they were wearing was new and un-
familiar and yet had already been worn enough to be easy and comfort-
able.

Their conversation was lively and varied, since everything and nothing captures the attention in the presence of such people. They spoke French so as to prevent the servants from following, and touched with capricious pleasure upon high and not so high spheres of society. The conversation dwelt on one point longer than was proper when Charlotte asked after a childhood friend and discovered to her surprise that she was to be divorced very shortly.

"It is distressing," said Charlotte, "when you believe your absent friends are in comfortable circumstances or think a dear friend is well settled, and before you turn around you hear that their fate is uncertain and they are about to take new and perhaps uncertain paths."

"Actually, my dear," responded the count, "we are ourselves to blame when we are surprised in this way. We like to regard the things of this world, marital relationships in particular, as more or less lasting, and with respect to the latter point, we are led by the comedies we see so often into harboring such fantasies, which do not accord with the way of the world. In a comedy we see marriage as the end-point of a desire whose fulfilment has been delayed by the obstacles of several acts, and in the very moment when it is attained the curtain falls, and this momentary contentment stays with us. In real life it is different; the play keeps on going backstage, and when the curtain goes up again, we don't care to see or hear any more of it."

"It can't be so bad," said Charlotte smiling, "since I note that people who have retired from this stage are often quite eager to play a part on it again."

"There is nothing to be said against that," said the count. "It is pleasant to take on a new role again, and when one knows the world, one understands that with marriage, too, it is that bond fixed for eternity amidst so much other change in the world that causes the difficulty. One of my friends, whose high spirits mostly express themselves in suggestions for new laws, claimed that every marriage should only be contracted for a period of five years. This, he said, was a nice odd number, a sacred number, and a period just sufficient to get to know one another, produce a number of children, separate, and, the nicest part of it, become reconciled again. He used to exclaim: 'How happily the first years would pass! Two or three years would go by very pleasantly. Then one party, eager to see the relationship continue, would become increasingly attentive the closer the end of the contract approached. The indifferent or even dissatisfied partner would be charmed and won over. They would forget, as we do the hours in good company, that time was passing, and would be most pleasantly surprised to notice, after the deadline was already passed, that the contract had been extended without a word having ever been spoken.'"

Clever and amusing as this was, and however easily one could give a profound moral significance to this jocular idea—as Charlotte was well aware—she did not care for such discussions, especially in view of Otti-lie's presence. She knew very well that nothing was more dangerous than talk that is too free and that treats criminal or reprehensible actions as though they were common everyday, or even praiseworthy ones; and certainly everything pertaining to marriage comes into this category. She attempted therefore in her skillful way to change the topic; but when she did not succeed she was sorry that Ottilie had arranged every-thing so well that she did not have to leave the table. The quiet, con-siderate child communicated with the steward by nods and gestures, so that everything turned out splendidly, even though a couple of new and inept servants were involved.

And so, oblivious to Charlotte's attempts to distract him, the count continued to talk on this topic. Although he did not usually monopolize a conversation, this matter weighed too heavily on his heart, and the difficulty he was having in obtaining a divorce from his wife made him bitter about marriage in general, however much he desired to marry the baroness.

"That same friend," he went on, "made yet another suggestion for a new law: a marriage should only be regarded as indissoluble when it was the third marriage of one or both. For this was incontrovertible evidence that marriage was something this person could not do without. Now it would also be known how they had behaved in their previous relationships, and whether they had bad habits, which more frequently lead to separations than do bad characters. We should find out about one another; and we should keep an eye on married people as well as un-married ones, since we could not know what might come to pass."

"That would greatly increase society's interest," said Edward; "for indeed, when we are married, nobody bothers about our virtues or our faults anymore."

"If such a law came into effect," the baroness interjected, smiling, "our dear host and hostess would have happily passed successfully through two stages and could prepare themselves for the third."

"It turned out well for them," said the count; "in their case death was glad to do what the courts are usually unwilling to."

"Let us leave the dead in peace," replied Charlotte, not altogether in jest.

"Why?" asked the count, "since we can think of them with honor. They were modest enough to content themselves with a few years in return for the many good things they left behind."

"If only," the baroness said, suppressing a sigh, "the best years did not have to be sacrificed in such cases!"

"Indeed," replied the count, "that would be cause for despair if it weren't the case that in the world things generally fail to turn out as we hope. Children don't hold to what they promise; young people seldom do, and if they do keep their word, the world breaks it for them."

Charlotte, who was happy that the conversation had taken a different turn, added serenely, "We should get used soon enough to enjoying good things in bits and pieces."

"Certainly," the count responded, "you have both enjoyed good times. When I think back to the years when you and Edward were the handsomest couple at court! Today, there are no longer such glorious events or such splendid figures. When the two of you danced together all eyes were on you, and how everyone vied for your attention, while you had eyes only for each other!"

"Now that so much has changed," said Charlotte, "I suppose that we can listen to such praise in all modesty."

"I often secretly reproached Edward for not having been more persistent," the count said; "for when all was said and done his parents, eccentric as they were, would have given in; and it is no small thing to gain ten years of youth."

"I must take his part," broke in the baroness. "Charlotte was not entirely blameless, nor totally blind to the charms of others, and even though she loved Edward with all her heart and had secretly chosen him for her future husband, I nonetheless saw how much she sometimes tormented him, so that it was easy to persuade him to take the unfortunate step of going away, traveling, and weaning himself from her."

Edward nodded towards the baroness and seemed grateful for her support.

"And then again," she continued, "I must add something to excuse Charlotte: the man who wooed her at that time had long distinguished himself by his fondness for her and, once one got to know him better, he was no doubt more likeable than you others care to admit."

"My dear," replied the count a little heatedly, "let us just admit that he was not quite indifferent to you, and that Charlotte had more to fear from you than from any other. I find it a very charming trait in women that they retain their affection for a man so long and do not let it be disturbed or discontinued by a separation of any kind."

"Perhaps men possess this good quality even more," replied the baroness; "at least I have noticed in you, dear count, that no one has more power over you than a woman you once were fond of. I have noticed that you try harder to please such a person than your attachment of the moment."

"One has to put up with such reproaches, no doubt," said the count; "but as regards Charlotte's first husband, the reason for my dislike was that he split asunder the finest couple, a couple truly predestined for each other, who, once brought together, would not have had to fear a five-year contract or have needed to look towards a second or indeed a third marriage."

"We shall try to make up for what we have missed," said Charlotte.

"You must keep to that," said the count. "Your first marriages," he continued with some vehemence, "were truly marriages of the most hateful kind, and unfortunately marriages in general have something— if you will pardon the strong expression—idiotic about them; they spoil the most delicate relationships, and the only reason for them is the vulgar sense of security that at least one of the parties desires to gain. Everything is taken for granted, and the couple seems to have united for the sole purpose of permitting them to go their separate ways."

At this moment Charlotte, who was anxious to break off this conversation once and for all, made a bold attempt to change the topic. She succeeded, and the discussion turned to more general matters. Edward, Charlotte, and the Captain could take part, and even Ottilie was drawn in; and they enjoyed their dessert in the best of spirits, to which the rich array of fruits arranged in decorative little baskets, and the most color-ful display of flowers in splendid vases were an excellent accompani-ment.

The talk turned, as well, to the new gardens, which were inspected as soon as dinner was over. Ottilie retired under the pretext of some domestic duty; in fact, however, she sat down to copy out the document. The Captain conversed with the count; later Charlotte joined him. When they had reached the top of the rise and the Captain kindly has-tened back down to fetch the map, the count said to Charlotte: "I am extremely impressed by this man. He is highly informed. And by the same token, he seems to do his work very seriously and systematically. What he has achieved here would be most significant in a more elevated sphere of society."

Charlotte heard the count's praise with deep pleasure. Yet she con-trolled herself and confirmed his opinion clearly and calmly. But how surprised she was when the count went on to say: "It is very convenient that I should have met him just now. I know a position to which the man is completely suited, and by recommending him I can both ensure his good fortune and cement a noble friendship of mine in the happiest manner."

Charlotte was thunderstruck. The count was not aware there was any-thing amiss; for women, accustomed to restraint at all times, retain a cool exterior even in the most extraordinary circumstances. But she no longer heard what he was saying as he went on: "When I have made up my mind about something, I act swiftly. I have already composed my letter in my head and I am anxious to write it down. Give me a horse and messenger, and I will send it off this evening."

Charlotte felt inwardly torn. Taken aback by this suggestion, as also by her own reaction, she could not utter a word. Fortunately, the count went on discussing his plans for the Captain, and their advantages were only too apparent to Charlotte. At this point the Captain came back and unrolled his map for the count. With what new eyes she saw the friend she was about to lose! With a perfunctory nod she turned aside and hurried down to the moss hut. Halfway there, the tears were streaming from her eyes, and once in the little hermitage she flung herself down in its narrow space and gave herself up totally to sorrow, passion and despair such as she would not have dreamed in the slightest way possible just a few moments earlier.

Edward, for his part, had gone down to the lakes with the baroness. That astute lady, who liked to be informed of everything, soon noticed in the course of a tactful conversation that Edward was very fulsome in his praise of Ottilie. She managed to get him going little by little, and in such a natural way, that in the end she had no doubt that here was passion not just budding, but already full-blown.

Married women, even when they do not like each other, still secretly take each other's side against young girls. Her worldly mind saw too quickly the consequences of such a love affair. In addition, she had spoken with Charlotte about Ottilie early that morning. She had expressed her disapproval of the child's living in the country, especially in view of her retiring manner, and had suggested that she send Ottilie to a friend of hers in town who was very devoted to the education of her only daughter and was looking for a suitable companion for her, one who could be like a member of the family and could enjoy the same advantages. Charlotte had agreed to think it over.

Now her glimpse into Edward's state of mind made the baroness strengthen her intention, and the faster her decision took shape, the more she appeared to play up to Edward. For no one was more in control of herself than this woman, and composure in extraordinary situations leads us to dissimulate even in everyday circumstances. Furthermore, exerting so much control over ourselves tends to make us extend this control to others, in order, as it were, to compensate for inward loss by outward gain.

This attitude is mostly accompanied by a kind of secret malicious pleasure in the other's blindness, in the way they fall into the trap unawares. We take pleasure not merely in our present success, but also in the other's future humiliation. And so the baroness was malicious enough to invite Edward and Charlotte to the wine harvest on her estate, responding to Edward's question whether they might bring Ottilie with them in a way he could interpret favorably if he wished.

Edward began to wax enthusiastic over the splendid countryside, the great river, the hills, cliffs and vineyards, the ancient castles, the boating parties, the joys of the wine harvest, grape-pressing and so forth, and in the innocence of his heart he said he was looking forward to the impression such scenes would make on Ottilie's naive mind. At this moment they saw Ottilie approaching, and the baroness said hastily to Edward that he had better say nothing of this planned autumn trip; for usually things one has looked forward to long in advance do not take place. Edward promised, but obliged her to quicken her step as they went to meet Ottilie, and finally he hurried on several paces ahead of her towards the lovely child. His whole being radiated with heartfelt pleasure. He kissed her hand, and pressed into it a bouquet of field flowers he had gathered along the way. Seeing this, the baroness felt a kind of inward bitterness. For even though she did not approve of the immorality of this love, she could not help but envy this young nobody of a girl its engaging charm.

When the company sat down to dinner, a completely different mood had taken hold of them. The count, who had written his letter and sent off the messenger before the meal, conversed with the Captain, whom he could examine all the more shrewdly and unobtrusively because he had managed to sit beside him that evening. The baroness, on the count's right, thus had little entertainment either from Edward, who from thirst to begin with, then from excitement took a good deal of wine and was talking animatedly with Ottilie, whom he had drawn to his side, nor from Charlotte who, on her other side next to the Captain, was finding it difficult, indeed almost impossible, to conceal her inner agitation.

The baroness had ample time to make her observations. She noticed Charlotte's discomfiture, and because she knew only about Edward's relationship with Ottilie, she was easily convinced that Charlotte too was worried and annoyed at her husband's behavior. She began to consider how she could best achieve her aims.

Even after dinner the group was divided. The count, who wished to sound out the Captain thoroughly, had to take a very indirect route to find out what he wanted to know from this restrained, in no way boastful, and altogether reticent man. The two of them paced together up and down one side of the drawing-room, while Edward, stimulated by wine and desire, talked gaily with Ottilie by the window, whereas Charlotte and the baroness went quietly back and forth on the other side of the room. Their silence and the way they kept pausing idly finally brought the rest of the company to a standstill. The women withdrew to their wing, the men to theirs, and so the day seemed to have come to a close.

Chapter Eleven

Edward accompanied the count to his room and was glad to let the conversation induce him to stay a while. The count became involved in thoughts of former times, remembering vividly Charlotte's beauty which, connoisseur that he was, he described with some ardor. "A pretty foot is a great gift of nature. It's the sort of charm that's indestructible. I watched her walking today; even now one is tempted to kiss her shoe, and repeat the somewhat barbaric, but deeply felt compliment of the Sarmatians, whose highest toast to a loved and honored person is drinking from her shoe."

The turn of a pretty foot was not the only topic of conversation between the two friends. From Charlotte they went on to talk of old episodes and adventures, and finally came to the obstacles that had been put in the way of these two lovers and the trouble they had gone to, the clever plans they had devised just to be able to tell each other their love.

"Do you remember," continued the count, "the adventure I helped you through so graciously and generously when their royal highnesses were visiting her uncle at his rambling country house? The day had been spent in stuffy formal festivities; part of the night at least was to pass in free and loving conversation."

"You had taken good note of the way to the ladies' quarters," said Edward. "We reached Charlotte without incident."

"Who," the count went on, "had given more thought to propriety than to my comfort and had kept a very ugly chaperone with her; so that, while you had a fine time conversing with words and glances, I suffered a most unpleasant fate."

"Just yesterday," responded Edward, "when we heard that you were coming, I was recalling the incident with my wife, especially the tale of our return. We lost our way and came upon the guardroom. Since we knew our way back from there quite well, we thought we could get through without any trouble and go past the guard on duty, as we had past the others. But how great was our amazement when we opened the door! The hall was all laid out with mattresses on which the huge men were stretched out asleep. The solitary guard awake at his post looked at us in astonishment; but in our youthful exuberance and bravado we stepped quite calmly over the stretched-out boots without waking a single one of those snoring giants."

"I had a great urge to stumble," said the count, "so as to make some noise; just think of the strange resurrection we would have seen then!"

At this moment the clock struck twelve.

"It's midnight," said the count, smiling, "and just the right time. I must ask a favor of you, my dear baron; lead me today as I led you then; I promised the baroness I would visit her tonight. We haven't exchanged a word alone all day, we haven't seen each other for so long, and nothing is more natural than to wish for a quiet hour together. Show me how to get there and I'll find my own way back; and in any event I won't have to stumble over any boots."

"I'll be glad to do you the favor," replied Edward; "but the three women are together in the same wing. Who knows if we might not find them together and if, whatever business we feign, we wouldn't make rather a strange impression."

"Don't worry!" said the count; "the baroness will be waiting for me. I know she will be alone in her room now."

"Well, it's easy to get there," responded Edward, taking a light to show the count down a secret stairway that led into a long corridor. At the end of the corridor Edward opened a small door. They climbed up a spiral staircase; on a narrow landing at the top Edward gave the light to the count, showing him a secret door in the wall to the right which opened at the first try, swallowing up the count and leaving Edward behind on the dark landing.

Another door at the left led to Charlotte's bedroom. Hearing voices, he stopped and listened. Charlotte was speaking to her chambermaid. "Is Ottilie in bed yet?" "No," answered the other, "she's still downstairs writing." "Then light the nightlamp," said Charlotte, "and leave me: it's late. I'll put out the candle myself and put myself to bed."

Edward was delighted to hear that Ottilie was still writing. "She's doing it for me!" he thought exultantly. He saw her sitting huddled in the darkness, writing away; he imagined himself approaching and seeing her turn towards him; he felt an uncontrollable longing to be near her once more. But there was no passage from here to the mezzanine where her room was. Now he found himself right outside his wife's door; a strange confusion took hold of him; he tried to open the door, and, finding it locked, knocked gently, but Charlotte did not hear.

She was pacing agitatedly up and down in the larger room next door. She repeated to herself again and again what she had turned over and over in her mind since the count had made that unexpected suggestion. The Captain seemed to stand before her. He filled the house and gave life to their walks—and now he was to leave, all was to become empty! She told herself everything possible, and anticipated, as we so often do, the feeble comfort that even such grief is assuaged by time. She cursed the time that would be need to assuage it; she cursed the death-like time that would come when it was assuaged.

So when at last she began to weep, it was all the more welcome in that this was rare with her. She flung herself upon the sofa and gave herself up to her grief. Edward, for his part, could not leave the door; he knocked again, and a third time a little more loudly, with the result that Charlotte heard it quite clearly through the stillness of the night and jumped up startled. Her first thought was: it might, it must be the Captain; her second: it could not be! She thought she had just imagined it; but she had heard it, she hoped, she was afraid she had heard it. She went into the bedroom, stepped quietly to the door in the wall. She scolded herself for her fears: "Perhaps the baroness needs something!" she said to herself, and called out in a calm and measured tone: "Is anyone there?" A soft voice answered: "It's me." "Who?" returned Charlotte, not recognizing the voice. She imagined the Captain's form outside the door. She heard, somewhat more loudly: "Edward!" She opened the door and her husband stood before her. He greeted her in a jocular tone. She managed to respond in the same vein. He cloaked the mysterious visit in mysterious explanations. "But the real reason I've come," he said finally, "I must now confess. I made a vow to kiss your shoe this very night."

"You haven't thought of that in a long time," said Charlotte.

"So much the worse," replied Edward, "and so much the better!"

She had sat down in an easy chair in order to conceal her light night-gown from his gaze. He knelt down before her and she couldn't stop him from kissing her shoe, and, when it stayed in his hand, grasping her foot and pressing it tenderly to his heart.

Charlotte was one of those women who, moderate by nature, still retain in marriage, without consciously trying, the ways of a girl in love. She never sought to arouse her husband, in fact she hardly even responded to his desire; but, without coldness or stern words of refusal, she yet resembled a loving bride who still feels some inner shyness even about what is now permitted. And so this evening she had ambivalent feelings about Edward. How much she wished her husband would go away: for the imagined figure of her friend seemed to stand there and reproach her. But what should have put Edward off just attracted him the more. Signs of emotion could be seen on her face. She had been weeping, and while weak personalities mostly lose their charm by weeping, those we usually think of as strong and composed gain infinitely. Edward was so loving, so affectionate, so urgent; he begged to stay with her, not demanding it but trying to persuade her now seriously, now teasingly, never thinking of his marital rights; and in the end he impulsively put out the candle.

In the dim lamplight secret affections began to hold sway, and imagination took over from reality. Edward clasped none other than Ottilie in his arms; Charlotte saw the Captain more or less distinctly before her mind's eye, and so things present and absent mingled, curiously enough, in the most charming and delightful manner.

And yet the present will not be deprived of its monstrous rights. They spent part of the night in playful conversation, which had all the freer rein in that the heart had no part in it. But when Edward woke up the next morning beside his wife the daylight seemed to him to shine in ominously on a crime; he crept from her side, and upon awakening she found herself, strangely enough, alone.

Chapter Twelve

When the company met again at breakfast, an alert observer could have read the different feelings and emotions from the bearing of each individual. The count and baroness met with the comfortable serenity of a loving couple who have once more assured each other of their mutual affection after a forced absence; whereas Charlotte and Edward, looking almost rueful and ashamed, stepped up to greet the Captain and Ottilie. For such is the nature of love that it recognizes no right but its own, and all other rights vanish before it. Ottilie was happy as a child; after her fashion, one could almost call her talkative. The Captain appeared earnest; after a conversation with the count which had awakened all the impulses that had for some time been dormant within him, he was too keenly aware that he was not living up to his potential here and was in essence merely killing time in half-active idleness. Hardly had the two guests left than other visitors arrived, which Charlotte welcomed since she felt the need to be distracted and to forget herself; Edward on the other hand found it inconvenient, as he was doubly desirous of being with Ottilie; and Ottilie likewise found it inconvenient, since she had not yet finished her copy of the document that was so urgently needed the next morning. Thus when the guests departed at a late hour of the day, she immediately hastened to her room.

Evening had come. Edward, Charlotte and the Captain, who had accompanied their visitors part of the way on foot before they got into their carriage, agreed to take a walk to the lakes. A boat that Edward had ordered at considerable cost and from some distance away had just been delivered. They were eager to test how well it handled.

It was tied up against the bank of the middle lake not far from several old oak trees which they were planning to keep for that purpose in the future. Here a landing-place was to be constructed and an aesthetically pleasing bench was to be placed beneath the trees, which would serve as a landmark for anyone rowing on the lake.

"Where will be the best place for the landing on the other side?" asked Edward. "I would think near my plane trees."

"They are a little too far over to the right," said the Captain. "If the landing-place were to be further down, it would be closer to the house; but we shall have to think about it."

The Captain was already standing in the stern of the boat and had grasped one oar. Charlotte got in, Edward followed and took hold of the other oar; but just as he was about to push off, he thought of Ottilie, and that this excursion on the lake would delay him. Who knew when they would get back! Without further ado he decided to jump out again, handed the oar back to the Captain and, making a hasty apology, hurried back to the house.

There he heard that Ottilie had shut herself in her room to write. Despite the feeling that she was doing something for him, he was keenly distressed not to see her right away. His impatience increased by the second. He paced up and down in the drawing-room, and tried to interest himself in this and that without success. It was she he wished to see, and by herself, before Charlotte and the Captain returned. Night fell and the candles were lit.

Finally she entered, all glowing with loveliness. The feeling of having done something for her friend had transfigured her. She placed the original and the copy in front of Edward on the table. "Shall we check them against each other?" she said, smiling. Edward did not know what to reply. He looked at her; he looked at the copy. The first pages had been written with the greatest of care in a delicate feminine hand; then the writing seemed to change, becoming lighter and freer; but how astonished he was when he glanced over the last pages! "For heaven's sake!" he exclaimed, "what is this? That's my own handwriting!" He looked at Ottilie, and then back at the pages. The end especially was just as if he had written it himself. Ottilie said nothing, but she gazed into his eyes with the greatest of content. Edward held out his arms: "You love me!" he cried, "Ottilie, you love me!" and they clasped each other in their arms. Who caught hold of the other first no one could have made out.

From this moment on the world was transformed for Edward; he was not the same—the world was not the same. They stood face to face, he held her hands, they gazed into each other's eyes, about to embrace again.

Charlotte and the Captain entered. Edward smiled secretly at their apologies for having stayed away so long. 'How much too early you have returned!' he said to himself.

They sat down to dinner and exchanged opinions about the day's visitors. Edward, excited by love, spoke well of each of them, always indulgently and often approvingly. Charlotte, who did not altogether agree with him, noticed his mood and teased him, who was usually the severest critic of the guests who had departed, for being so mild and considerate today.

In a tone of fiery and fervent conviction Edward cried: "If one loves just a single being with all one's heart, everyone else appears lovable, too!" Ottilie looked down, and Charlotte gazed straight ahead.

The Captain joined in, remarking: "Respect and honor have a similar effect. We become aware of what is admirable in the world when we have had the chance to experience this feeling in relation to a single object."

Charlotte retired to her room early to give herself up to the memory of what happened that evening between her and the Captain.

When Edward had leaped to shore and pushed off the boat, leaving his wife and friend to the unstable element, Charlotte had found herself face to face with the man for whom she had suffered so much already. Sitting before her in the twilight, he moved the boat forward in no particular direction with his two oars. She felt a profound sadness such as was rare for her. The circling of the boat, the splashing of the oars, the breeze trembling over the surface of the water, the rustling of the reeds, the last flights of birds, the twinkling and blinking of the first stars: all this seemed ghostly in the quiet all around. She felt as if her friend were taking her far away to abandon her and leave her to her fate. She was strangely moved, but could not weep.

Meanwhile, the Captain described to her how he thought the gardens should be laid out. He praised the fine qualities of the boat, which could easily be handled with a single person at the oars. She would learn how to do it herself, he said; it was an enjoyable feeling to float alone on the water from time to time and to be one's own ferryman and steersman.

At these words his companion thought of their imminent separation. 'Is he saying this deliberately?' she wondered. 'Does he know already? Does he suspect? Or is he saying this by accident, and predicting my fate without knowing it?' A great melancholy, a great impatience took hold of her; she begged him to pull to shore as soon as possible and to return to the house with her.

It was the first time the Captain had been out rowing on the lakes, and although he had taken general soundings of their depths, he was not familiar with individual spots. It began to grow dark; he rowed towards a place where he thought there would be a convenient spot to get out and near where he knew there was a footpath leading to the manor. But as Charlotte somewhat anxiously repeated her wish to reach land soon, he was distracted from this course. With renewed efforts he approached the bank, but alas, some distance away he felt his way obstructed; the boat had become stuck, and his attempts to get free were in vain. What were they to do? He had no choice but to get into the water, which was shallow enough, and carry his companion onto dry land. Strong enough not to falter or make her nervous, he succeeded in bringing his lovely burden ashore; but she had nonetheless clasped her arms anxiously around his neck. He held her firmly and pressed her to him. Only when they had reached the grassy bank did he set her down, not without confused emotions. She still clung about his neck; he clasped her anew in his arms and pressed a fervent kiss upon her lips; but in that very moment he lay at her feet, kissed her hand and cried: "Charlotte, will you forgive me?"

The kiss which her friend had dared to give and which she had almost returned brought Charlotte back to consciousness. She pressed his hand, but did not help him up. Bending down to him and placing one hand on his shoulder, she exclaimed: "We cannot prevent this moment from being a turning-point in our lives; but it is in our hands to make it worthy of us. You must depart, dear friend, and you shall depart. The count is making preparations to improve your position: this both pleases and pains me. I did not want to mention it until it was certain; but this moment forces me to reveal the secret. I can only forgive you, forgive myself, insofar as we have the courage to change our external situation, since it is not within our power to change our feelings." She lifted him up and grasped his arm for support, and so they returned silently towards the manor.

But now she was standing in her bedroom, where she was bound to see and feel herself as Edward's wife. In the face of all these contradictory emotions, her practical nature and considerable experience came to her aid. Always used to being poised and in control, she did not find it difficult even now to regain by serious reflection the serenity she desired: indeed, she had to smile at herself when she thought of the extraordinary visit she had had the night before. But soon she was gripped by strange premonitions, by a joyful, anxious trembling that dissolved into pious hopes and wishes. Moved, she knelt down and repeated the vow she had sworn to Edward at the altar. Friendship, affection, renunciation passed like vivid images before her mind's eye. She felt herself inwardly restored. Soon a sweet tiredness took over her and she fell gently asleep.

Chapter Thirteen

Edward for his part was in a very different state. Sleep was so far from his mind that he didn't even think of undressing. He kissed a thousand times the copy of the document with its beginning in Ottilie's hesitant handwriting; he scarcely dared kiss the end, where he thought to see his own. "If only it were another document!" he said to himself; and yet it was, all the same, the loveliest assurance that his dearest wish had been fulfilled. Would it not remain, after all, in his possession, and would he not continue to press it to his heart, even once it had been sullied by the signature of a third party?

The waning moon rose above the wood. The warm night tempted him out of doors; he roamed about, the most restless and yet the happiest of mortals. He walked through the gardens; they were too confined for him; he hastened out into the fields, and they were too free. He felt drawn back to the house, and found himself beneath Ottilie's windows. There he sat down upon a terrace step. "Walls and bars may part us now," he said to himself, "but our hearts are still together. If she were here she would fall into my arms and I into hers; what need is there of greater certainty!" All around him it was still, not a breeze stirred; it was so quiet that he could hear the busy tunneling of animals for whom day and night are one. He gave himself up to happy fantasies, finally falling asleep and not waking until the sun arose with its majestic gaze and banished the early mists.

Now he was the first one awake on the estate. He thought the workers too tardy. They came, but there seemed to be too few of them, and the tasks planned for the day too limited to accomplish all his desires. He demanded more workers, was promised them, and they were supplied in the course of the day. But even these were not enough to let him see his plans carried out with dispatch. The project ceased to give him plea-sure; it must be completed, and for whom? The paths must be made level so that Ottilie could walk on them with ease, the benches must be set in place so that Ottilie could rest upon them. At the new house, too, he did what he could; the roof was to be in place by Ottilie's birthday. In Edward's thoughts, in Edward's actions there was no longer any mod-eration. The knowledge of loving and being loved urged him on to infinite extravagance. How changed was the aspect of every room, everything around him! He no longer knew his own house. Ottilie's presence consumed everything; he was totally absorbed in her, no other thought occured to him, no pang of conscience warned him; all that was repressed in him burst forth and his whole being streamed toward Ottilie.

The Captain observed this passionate activity and was anxious to pre-vent its tragic consequences. This whole landscape, which was now being single-mindedly forced into shape, had been part of his plans for a quiet, friendly life together. He had accomplished the sale of the farm-stead, the first payment had been made, and Charlotte had deposited it in her cash-box as arranged. But in the very first week she was forced to be more stringent, patient and organized than ever; for this hasty way of proceeding would quickly swallow up what had been set aside.

Many tasks had been started and there was still much to be done. How could he leave Charlotte in this position! Talking it over together, they decided instead to hasten the work that had been originally planned and to borrow money for this purpose which would be paid back on the dates when the payments from the sale of the farmstead fell due. This could be done almost without loss by means of a mortgage; it gave them a freer hand and meant they could accomplish more at once, since everything was underway and the workers were already on the job; it would achieve their purpose without delay or confusion. Since this concurred with his own plans, Edward agreed eagerly.

But inwardly Charlotte persisted with her earlier plans and projects, and in the same spirit her friend stood staunchly by her. But this very situation only deepened their intimacy. They discussed Edward's pas-sion frankly and conferred about it together. Charlotte drew Ottilie closer to her and watched her more strictly, and the more she became aware of her own feelings, the better she understood the girl's. She saw no hope but to send the child away.

Now it seemed to her a fortunate turn of events that Luciane had accounted for herself so excellently at school; for her great-aunt, having heard about this, was anxious to have her come and live with her, to enjoy her company and to introduce her to society. Ottilie could return to boarding school, the Captain would depart without financial difficulty; and everything would be as it had been a few months ago, in fact better. Charlotte hoped soon to mend her relationship to Edward, and she worked this out so cleverly in her thoughts that it only confirmed her delusion that they could go back to their earlier, more restricted way of life, and that explosive passions could once more be brought under control.

Edward meanwhile found the obstacles that were being put in his way unduly great. He soon noticed that he and Ottilie were being kept apart, that it was being made difficult for him to talk to her alone, to come near her even, except in the presence of several other people; annoyed about this, he got angry about other things as well. Whenever he managed a brief word with Ottilie it was not only to assure her of his love, but also to complain of his wife and the Captain. He was not aware that his extravagance was exceeding their budget; he blamed Charlotte and the Captain bitterly for not having kept to the first contract; yet he himself had agreed to the second, indeed he had instigated and necessitated it.

Hatred is blind, but love is more so. Ottilie, too, began to feel less friendly to Charlotte and the Captain. Once when Edward told Ottilie that he believed the Captain had not behaved quite honestly in view of his friendship and his relation to the family, Ottilie said carelessly: "Even before I didn't like the dishonest way he treated you. Once I heard him say to Charlotte, 'If only Edward would spare us his awful flute-playing! One can't hope for improvement, and it's so annoying to the listener.' You can imagine how pained I was to hear that, when I so much enjoy playing your accompaniments."

Hardly had she uttered the words than she realized she should not have; but now it was out. Edward's expression changed. Never had anything upset him more; his dearest enthusiasms were insulted. He had not aimed for more than innocent amusement, far from any trace of ambition. What pleased and amused him should be treated tactfully by his friends. He gave no thought to how dreadful it was for others to have their hearing assaulted by his amateurish talent. He was insulted, furious, unable to forgive. He felt himself absolved from all the bonds of duty.

His need to be with Ottilie, to see her, to whisper to her and confide in her grew with every day. He decided to write to her suggesting a secret exchange of letters. The slip of paper on which he had written his brief note lay on his desk and was whisked away by the wind when the valet entered to curl his hair. The servant had the habit of picking up little scraps of paper to test the heat of the curling-iron; now he took up the billet-doux, pressed it hastily, and it was singed. Edward, seeing the mistake, snatched it from his hand. A few minutes later he sat down again to write it over; but it didn't quite come out right the second time. He had some qualms, he felt somehow uneasy; but he overcame this. He pressed the letter into Ottilie's hand the first moment he was able to get near her.

Ottilie did not fail to answer him. He put her reply unread into his waistcoat, which, being fashionably short, could not keep it in place. It worked its way out and fell on the floor without his noticing. Charlotte saw it and picked it up, handing it to him after a fleeting glance at it. "Here is something you wrote," she said, "which you may not wish to lose."

He was taken aback. 'Is she play-acting?' he thought. 'Does she know what's in the letter, or has the similarity of the handwriting misled her?' He hoped and believed the latter. He had been warned, doubly warned; but his passion was blind to those strange chance signs by which a higher power speaks to us; and because his desires led him on, he felt with all the more displeasure the constraints under which he seemed to be being kept. The group's friendly spirit vanished. His heart was hardened, and when he was obliged to be with his friend and his wife, he could not find within him his former affection for them, nor was he able to bring it back to life. Feeling discomfited by his secret self-reproaches, he resorted to a kind of humor, which, being loveless, lacked his usual grace.

Charlotte's inner resolve helped her through all these trials. She was well aware how earnest her intention was to renounce such beautiful, noble passions.

How much she wished she could help the other two! Distance, she rightly felt, would not alone suffice to heal such an evil. She decided to speak to the dear child; but she could not; the recollection of her own vacillation hampered her. She tried to talk about it in general terms, but these applied equally well to her own position, which she hesitated to broach. Every hint she tried to give Ottilie referred her back to her own heart. She was anxious to warn her but was aware that she herself might be in need of warning.

Silently she kept the lovers apart, and things were not improved. Tactful allusions that escaped her from time to time had no effect on Ottilie; for Edward had already convinced her of Charlotte's affection for the Captain and persuaded her that Charlotte herself desired the divorce which he was now hoping to obtain in a decent and proper manner.

Borne up by her feelings of innocence and within grasp of the happiness she desired, Ottilie lived only for Edward. Strengthened in all her good works by her love for him, happier in her activities at the thought of him, more open towards others, she thought she was in heaven on earth.

Thus all of them together, each in their own way, continued their daily life, with or without real reflection; everything seemed to take its accustomed course. For even in the most terrible situation, when everything is at stake, people live on as if it were nothing of moment.

Chapter Fourteen

Meanwhile a letter had come for the Captain from the count—two letters in fact—one suitable for showing others, setting forth fair prospects for the future and another, containing a definite offer of a significant position at court and in society right away, promotion to major, a respectable salary and other benefits. By reason of various accompanying circumstances this one was to be kept secret for the moment. Accordingly, the Captain informed his friends only of his more distant hopes, concealing those that were near at hand.

In the meantime he went on vigorously with his present business, quietly making arrangements for everything to go ahead unhindered in his absence. Now it suited him very well to establish deadlines for a number of tasks and to let Ottilie's birthday hasten their completion. And now the two friends, though without express agreement, enjoyed working together. Edward was very pleased that their finances had been increased by taking out the loans; the whole project moved forward apace.

The Captain would have preferred to advise against combining the three lakes into a large one. The lower dam would have to be strengthened, the middle ones removed, and the whole matter was in many respects seriously questionable. Both of these interrelated tasks had already been begun, however, and here a young architect, a former pupil of the Captain, came in very handy. By employing competent tradesmen for some aspects of the work and contracting out other parts of it where this was possible, the architect moved the work along and gave it continuity and certainty; this secretly pleased the Captain, since he would not be missed when he left. For it was a principle of his not to leave unfinished any business he had undertaken until he could find a suitable substitute. Indeed, he scorned those selfish boors who, to make their departure more keenly felt, create havoc all around them by trying to destroy what they will not continue to be involved with.

So they worked with unceasing efforts to the greater glory of Ottilie's birthday, not uttering the thought or even quite frankly admitting it to themselves. Jealousy aside, Charlotte's attitudes would prevent it being a real celebration. Ottilie's youth, her circumstances, her relation to the family did not entitle her to appear as queen of the day. And Edward did not want to mention it, for he wanted the festivities to be a pleasant surprise, something very spontaneous and natural.

They reached an unspoken agreement on the pretext that this day, apropos of nothing, would see the completion of the summer house and that they could then invite the villagers and their own friends to a celebration.

But Edward's love was boundless. Just as he desired to make Ottilie his own, so he knew no limit to giving gifts and making sacrifices and promises. Charlotte's suggestions as to what he could give Ottilie for her birthday were far too unworthy. He spoke with the valet who ordered his clothing and was in constant consultation with merchants and fashion dealers; this man, who knew not only the most delightful of gifts but also the best way of presenting them, immediately ordered in town the loveliest little chest, covered with red morocco, studded with steel pins and filled with gifts worthy of such a container.

He made yet another suggestion to Edward. They had some fireworks which they had kept forgetting to use. These could easily be added to. Edward took up the idea, and his valet promised to see to its execution. The plan was to remain secret.

Meanwhile, as the day drew nearer, the Captain had arranged for the sort of policing he felt necessary whenever a crowd of people comes together. Moreover, he had made provisions against begging and any other unpleasantness that might mar the charm of a festivity.

Edward and his confidant had splendid plans for the firework display. It was to take place on the middle lake in front of the great oak trees; the spectators were to gather on the opposite side beneath the plane trees in order to see the effects from the proper distance. From here they could observe in comfort and safety the reflections in the water and those fireworks that were to float on the surface.

Under another pretext, Edward had the space beneath the plane trees freed of brush, grass and moss, and their magnificent growth in height and breadth could be seen for the first time on the cleared ground. Edward took great pleasure in the sight. "It is about this time of year that I planted them. How long ago would it be?" he wondered. As soon as he got home, he looked up some old diaries which his father had kept in excellent order, especially during stays in the country. To be sure, this planting would not be mentioned in them, but another important domestic event that Edward remembered well as having taken place on the same day would have to be noted. He leafed through several volumes and located the event. But how astonished, how delighted he was to find an amazing coincidence! The day, the year on which he had planted the trees was also the day, the year of Ottilie's birth.

Chapter Fifteen

At last the morning Edward had longed for dawned, and a crowd of guests gradually began to arrive; for a great number of invitations had been sent out and many who had missed the foundation stone laying and had heard what a delightful occasion it had been were all the more eager not to miss this second ceremony.

Before the banquet the carpenters appeared in the manor courtyard, accompanied by music and carrying a richly decorated wreath consisting of numerous rings of leaves and flowers balanced on top of each other in layers. They spoke their greeting and, as custom demanded, asked the women for silk scarves and ribbons to deck themselves out. While the lords and ladies were dining, the carpenters' procession went on its jubilant way. After stopping awhile in the village, where they also deprived the women and girls of many a ribbon, they finally came to the rise where the newly finished summer house stood. A large crowd went with them to join the many who were waiting there.

Charlotte restrained the company a little after the meal. She did not wish to have a solemn, formal procession, so they made their way gradually in separate groups without any particular order. Charlotte hung back with Ottilie, which did not improve matters; for as Ottilie was the last to arrive, it seemed as if the fanfare had waited for her alone and the ceremony could only begin now that she had arrived.

To disguise the unfinished appearance of the house it had been decorated with green branches and flowers according to instructions from the Captain; but unbeknown to the latter Edward had had the architect fashion the date out of flowers on the window sill. That may have been acceptable enough; but the Captain had been able to intervene just in time to prevent Ottilie's name from shining forth from the gables. He managed tactfully to avert this plan and to remove those floral letters that had already been completed.

The wreath was placed on top and could be seen far and wide. The ribbons and scarves fluttered colorfully in the breeze and a short speech was for the most part carried away by the wind. The ceremony was over, and dancing was about to begin on a leveled area near the house marked off by greenery. A finely dressed carpenter's apprentice led a lively farmer's maid toward Edward and invited Ottilie, who was standing next to Edward, to dance with him. The two couples were promptly joined by others, and soon enough Edward changed partners, taking Ottilie's hands and dancing around the space with her. The younger lords and ladies happily joined in the villagers' dance, while the older ones looked on.

Then, before everyone went their way along the paths, it was agreed that they would meet again at sundown by the plane trees. Edward, who was the first to arrive, got everything organized, conferring with his servant, who, together with the firework-specialist, was in charge of the display on the other bank.

The Captain was not pleased to see the arrangements that were being made; he was about to speak with Edward about the large crowd of spectators that was expected, but Edward begged him hastily to leave this part of the ceremony to him alone.

The villagers had already made their way onto the marked-off dikes where the sod had been removed and the earth was uneven and not very firm. The sun sank, twilight came, and refreshments were served to the company beneath the plane trees while they were waiting for it to grow darker. They thought the spot incomparably delightful, and looked forward to enjoying from here the future prospect of a wide, picturesquely framed lake.

A calm evening with not a breath of wind promised the right setting for the night's festivities; but suddenly a terrible cry arose. Great clumps of earth had broken away from the dike and several people could be seen plunging into the water. The ground had given way beneath the pushing and shoving of the ever-increasing throng. Everybody wanted to have the best place, and now no one could go either forward or backward.

They all leaped up, more to see what was happening than to help; for what was there to do in a spot no one could reach? The Captain hastened forward with several other stalwarts, urged the crowd immediately down from the dike towards the banks to make way for the helpers trying to rescue those who were sinking. Soon they were all on dry land, either by their own efforts or by those of others, except for one young boy who in his alarm had moved away from the dike instead of towards it. He seemed to be losing strength: only once or twice did a hand or foot come up out of the water. Alas, the boat was on the other side, filled with fireworks; unloading could only proceed slowly, delaying the rescue. The Captain made his decision: with all eyes upon him, he threw off his outer clothing, and everyone's confidence was restored by his strong, powerful figure. A shout of surprise went up from the crowd all the same as he plunged into the water, and all eyes followed him as the practiced swimmer soon reached the boy and brought him—dead, as it seemed—back to the dike.

Meanwhile the boat rowed up, the Captain got in and checked with those present whether all had really been saved. The doctor came and took charge of the corpse-like boy; Charlotte joined them and begged the Captain to look after himself, return to the manor and change his clothes. He hesitated, but finally some sensible and clear-headed people who had been nearby and had helped with the rescue themselves gave him their word of honor that everyone had been saved.

Charlotte watched him return home, but suddenly remembering that wine, tea, and whatever else might be necessary was under lock and key and that in such instances people usually lose their heads, she hurried through the scattered company still left beneath the plane trees. Edward was busy trying to talk everyone into staying; in a few moments he intended to give the sign for the fireworks to begin. Charlotte went up to him and begged him to postpone an amusement that was no longer appropriate and that no one could enjoy just now; she reminded him of his duty towards the boy and his rescuer. "The doctor will do what is necessary," replied Edward. "He has the right equipment, and our interference would just hamper him."

Still persisting, Charlotte motioned to Ottilie, who immediately turned to go. Edward took her hand and exclaimed. "Let us not end this day at the sickbed! Ottilie is too good to be a sister of charity. Those given up for dead will be resurrected and the living will dry themselves off without our help."

Charlotte went away silently. Several people followed her, and others went in their wake; in the end nobody wished to be the last, and so all departed. Edward and Ottilie found themselves alone beneath the plane trees. He insisted on remaining, however urgently, however fearfully she begged him to return with her to the manor. "No, Ottilie!" he cried, "extraordinary events do not move along the smooth path of custom. This evening's sudden accident brings us together all the sooner. You are mine! I have vowed and sworn it to you so often now; let us no longer vow and swear it, let it be so."

The boat drifted over from the other bank. It was the servant who asked with some embarrassment what should be done now with the fireworks. "Set them off!" Edward called to him. "For you alone I planned it, Ottilie, and now you alone shall witness it! Allow me to sit beside you and enjoy it with you." With modest restraint he sat down beside her but did not touch her.

Rockets roared up, cannons thundered, balls of fire rose, squibs curved down and burst, catherine wheels hissed, first separately, then in pairs, then all together and with increasing violence, in succession and at once. Edward, his heart aflame, watched these fiery apparitions with eager satisfaction. Susceptible and agitated as she was, Ottilie found this roaring and flashing, bursting and fading more distressing than pleasurable. She leaned shyly against Edward, and her closeness, her trust in him completed his feeling that she belonged to him entirely.

Darkness scarcely held sway again when the moon rose to light their way back. A figure with hat in hand stepped up to them and begged them for alms, since he had been neglected on this festive day. The moon shone upon his face, and Edward recognized the features of the insolent beggar. But happy as he was, he couldn't be angry with him; it didn't occur to him that he had expressly forbidden begging on this day. He didn't search long in his pocket, but gave him a gold coin. He would gladly have made anyone happy, so boundless did his own happiness seem.

At the manor everything had turned out as desired. The doctor's efforts, the provision of all necessary remedies, Charlotte's assistance— all this had worked together and the boy had been restored to life. The guests dispersed, both to see something of the fireworks from a distance and to wend their way to the quiet of home after the confusion of the scenes they had witnessed.

The Captain, too, after hastily changing his clothes, had actively helped them with their first-aid measures; once all was calm, he found himself alone with Charlotte. He gently confided that he was soon to leave. She had gone through so much this evening that this disclosure made little impression on her; she had seen her friend sacrifice himself, she had seen him save and be saved. These miraculous events seemed to her to be significant, but not unhappy portents for the future.

Edward came in with Ottilie and was told of the Captain's imminent departure. He suspected that Charlotte had been informed of the details earlier, but he was too absorbed with himself and his own plans to take it ill.

On the contrary, he was pleased and eager to hear about the fine and honorable position that had been offered to the Captain. His unbridled thoughts ran on impatiently ahead of realities. He saw the Captain united with Charlotte and himself with Ottilie. He could not have received a greater gift on this festive day.

But how astonished was Ottilie when she went into her room and found the precious little chest on her table! She opened it right away. Inside, everything was so beautifully packed and arranged that she hardly dared to disturb it, to touch it even. Muslin, cambric, silk, scarves and lace vied with each other in fineness, elegance, and costliness. Jewelry had not been forgotten, either. She understood the intention behind it: to clothe her several times over from head to foot. But it was all so precious and unfamiliar that she did not dream of thinking it was hers.

Chapter Sixteen

The next morning the Captain had disappeared, leaving behind him a letter of genuine gratitude to his friends. He and Charlotte had taken a reticent and halting leave of each other the previous evening. She felt it was a permanent separation and was resigned to this; for in the count's second letter, which the Captain had finally shown her, there was mention of a most advantageous marriage prospect, and although he paid no attention to this point, she regarded it as definite, and renounced her claims to him completely.

On the other hand she believed she could demand from others the same control that she exerted over herself. It had not been impossible for her, so the same should be possible for others. In this spirit she began her talk with her husband, the more frankly and confidently in that she felt the matter should be dealt with once and for all.

"Our friend has left us," she said; "we are together again as before, and it is up to us whether we wish to return completely to our former circumstances."

Edward, hearing only what flattered his passion, thought that these words of Charlotte's referred to their previous widowhood and meant, if only indirectly, to suggest some prospect of divorce. So he answered smilingly: "Why not? We would only have to come to an agreement."

He saw himself much deceived when Charlotte replied: "We also have to decide how to change Ottilie's situation; for now we have two different opportunities to place her in desirable cirumstances. Since my daughter has moved to her great-aunt's, Ottilie can return to boarding-school; or she can be taken into a respectable family where she can enjoy together with an only daughter all the advantages of an education appropriate to her social standing."

"Nonetheless," answered Edward with tolerable calmness, "Ottilie has become so spoiled by our congenial company that any other would hardly be agreeable to her."

"We have all been spoiled," said Charlotte, "not least you. But this is a turning-point that calls for reflection and urges us to think seriously of the best for all members of our little circle and not to neglect any sacrifice this might entail."

"I don't find it right in any event that Ottilie be sacrificed," replied Edward, "and that would be the case if she were to be cast amongst strangers at this time. The Captain met good fortune when he came here; we can see him go without concern, indeed with pleasure. Who knows what is in store for Ottilie; why should we act hastily?"

"What is in store for us is fairly clear," retorted Charlotte with some feeling, and as she meant to have it out once and for all, she continued: "You are in love with Ottilie, you have become accustomed to her. Love and affection are growing on her side, too. Why should we not put into words what every hour proclaims and confesses? Shouldn't we have at least enough prudence to ask ourselves what will come of it?"

"While this is hard to answer right away," Edward replied, with great self-control, "it can certainly be said that one always decides to wait and see what the future will bring at precisely those times when one cannot tell how a thing will turn out."

"To predict what will happen needs no great wisdom in this case," replied Charlotte, "and this much can be said in any event: that neither of us is young enough anymore to tread blindly along a path we should not or do not wish to take. No one can take responsibility for us now; we must look to our own interests, be our own counselors. We are expected not to go to extremes, to act neither reprehensibly nor even foolishly."

"Can you take it amiss," said Edward, who could not reply in kind to his wife's frank and proper manner, "can you reproach me for being concerned for Ottilie's happiness? And not just her future happiness, which we cannot foresee, but her present happiness? Don't deceive yourself; imagine honestly Ottilie torn from our company and thrown in with strangers—I for my part am not so cruel as to wish such a change upon her."

It was not hard for Charlotte to perceive her husband's stubbornness behind his mask. Now she realized for the first time how far apart they had grown. With some emotion she cried, "Can Ottilie be happy when she has torn us asunder, taken a husband from me and a father from his children?"

"I thought things had been taken care of for our children," said Edward smiling coldly; but in a more amiable tone he added: "Why leap to such extreme conclusions?"

"Extremes are the neighbors of passion," Charlotte remarked. "As long as there is still time, do not reject the good advice and help I am offering us. In unclear situations the one who sees most clearly must be the one to act. This time I am that person. Dearest, dearest Edward, let me have my way! Can you expect me just to give up my well-earned happiness, my dearest rights, yourself?"

"Who's saying that?" responded Edward in some embarrassment.

"You yourself," Charlotte answered; "by wishing to keep Ottilie here, are you not admitting all that will follow? I won't put pressure on you; but if you can't control your impulses, you can at least no longer deceive youself."

Edward felt how very right she was. A word spoken is a terrible thing when it suddenly utters what the heart has long allowed; and to avoid confronting this for a moment, Edward replied: "I don't even know what you have in mind."

"It was my intention," answered Charlotte, "to think the two suggestions over with you. Both have their advantages. In view of the child's present character, boarding-school would be the most appropriate; in view of her future development, the broader, less restricted alternative is more promising." She then described the two plans to her husband in some detail, saying in conclusion: "As for my own opinion, placing her with the lady would be preferable to the boarding-school for a number of reasons, most particularly because I do not wish to increase the affection, indeed, the passion of that young man who took such a liking to Ottilie while she was there."

Edward pretended to agree with her, but only to gain a little time. Charlotte, who was anxious to come to a decision, promptly seized the opportunity offered by Edward's failure to contradict her immediately and arranged Ottilie's departure for the next few days, having already prepared everything in secret.

Edward was horrified. He felt himself betrayed and saw his wife's loving words as a cunningly rehearsed plan to sever him forever from his happiness. He pretended to leave everything to her; but in reality he had made his own decision. To gain some breathing-space, to avert the imminent, unimaginable disaster of Ottilie's being sent away, he decided to leave home—not quite without informing Charlotte, whom he allowed to believe that he did not wish to be present at Ottilie's departure, indeed that he did not wish to see her anymore again. Thinking she had won out, Charlotte urged him to go ahead with this plan. He called for his horses, gave his valet the necessary instructions about packing and following him, and as if with one foot in the stirrup, he sat down to write.

EDWARD TO CHARLOTTE

The evil that has befallen us, my dear, may or may not be curable; one thing my instinct tells me: if I am not to despair at this moment, I must gain time—for myself, for us all. The sacrifice I am making entitles me to make demands. I am leaving home and will not return until prospects are better and calmer. In the meantime, the house shall be yours, but Ottilie's too. I want to be sure she stays with you, not with strangers. Look after her, treat her as usual, but more lovingly, more kindly, more sensitively. I undertake not to attempt to make any secret contact with her. Let me know nothing for a time about your way of life; I will assume the best. Think the same of me. Only I beg you, most fervently, most urgently: do not try to lodge Ottilie elsewhere or to change her situation! Once outside your house and gardens, entrusted to strangers, she shall belong to me, and I will come to take her. But if you respect my affection, my desires, my grief, if you bear with my delusion and my hopes, then I will not resist recovery if the occasion presents itself.

These last words flowed from his pen, but not from his heart. And when he looked at them on paper, he began to weep bitterly. To think that he should renounce in any way the joy, or even the despair, of loving Ottilie! Now the full force of what he was doing came to him. He was leaving without knowing what was to come of it. He was not to see her again at the moment, in any event; and what certainty could he promise himself that he would see her again ever? But the letter had been written; the horses were standing at the door; he feared that at any moment he would catch sight of Ottilie somewhere and that his decision would in that instant be nothing. He pulled himself together, reflecting that it would be possible for him to return at any time and that, indeed, his absence might bring him nearer to his heart's desires. On the other hand he pictured Ottilie turned out of the house if he were to stay. He sealed the letter, hastened downstairs and mounted his horse.

As he was riding by the inn, he saw in the arbor the beggar to whom he had been so generous the night before. The man was sitting comfortably at his dinner, and stood up and bowed respectfully, reverently even, towards Edward. This very figure had been there yesterday when he was walking arm in arm with Ottilie; now he reminded him painfully of the happiest hour of his life. His sufferings were intensified, his sense of what he was leaving behind was unbearable; he looked back once more at the beggar: "How I envy you!" he exclaimed; "you still can feast on yesterday's alms, but I no more on yesterday's bliss!"

Chapter Seventeen

Hearing someone riding away, Ottilie went to the window and caught sight of Edward's receding figure. She thought it strange that he was leaving the house without having seen her or said good morning to her. Becoming restive, she grew increasingly concerned when Charlotte took her off on a long walk, spoke of many things and, deliberately as it seemed, did not mention her husband. So she was doubly distressed to find, on their return, the table set for two only.

We do not like to do without seemingly trivial things we are used to having, but doing without becomes really painful when we are deprived of something significant. Edward and the Captain were absent, Charlotte had set the table herself for the first time in a long while, and Ottilie felt as if she had been demoted. The two of them sat opposite each other; Charlotte spoke quite freely about the Captain's new employment, saying there was little hope they would see him again soon. The only comforting thought Ottilie had in view of this was that Edward might have ridden off after his friend to accompany him part of the way.

But when they left the table, she saw Edward's carriage beneath the window, and when Charlotte rather irritably asked who had ordered this, she was told that his valet had done so, since he wanted to pack up some additional things. It took all of Ottilie's self-control to conceal her amazement and distress.

The valet came in and asked for several items, amongst them one of his master's mugs, a few silver spoons, and various things that suggested to Ottilie a lengthy journey and a prolonged absence. Charlotte refused these requests quite bluntly: she did not understand what he was talking about; after all, he had the master's belongings under his own lock and key. The cunning fellow, whose sole purpose was of course to speak to Ottilie and to entice her out of the room under some pretext or other, apologized and persisted in his demands, which Ottilie wished to grant; but Charlotte refused, the valet was forced to leave, and the carriage drove off.

It was a terrible moment for Ottilie. She did not understand it, she could not fathom it; but she sensed that Edward was torn from her for quite some time. Charlotte tactfully left her alone. We dare not depict her grief and tears. Her suffering was beyond measure. She prayed to God to help her through this one day; she survived the day and the night, and when she came to, she felt as if she were a different being.

She had not got a grip on herself, nor had she submitted to her fate, but she was still there after such a great loss, and she had more fears yet to face. Her first concern, now that consciousness had returned, was that since the men had been sent away, she might be sent away, too. She had no knowledge of Edward's threats, which had ensured her staying with Charlotte; but Charlotte's behavior relieved her mind a little. Charlotte tried to keep the dear child occupied and allowed her only rarely and reluctantly out of her sight; and although she knew that words can do little to counteract a determined passion, she did know the power of awareness and reflection, and so she brought up a number of topics between herself and Ottilie.

Thus it was a great comfort to Ottilie when Charlotte deliberately observed from time to time: "How very grateful people are when our calmness helps them get over the dilemmas their enthusiasms have led them into! Let us take pleasure in continuing with what the men have left unfinished. In this way we will be making the best of preparations for their return, preserving and continuing in a temperate fashion what their wild and impatient manner might have destroyed."

"Now that you mention temperate behavior, dear aunt," replied Ottilie, "I can't conceal my thoughts about men's lack of temperance, especially when it comes to wine. How often has it worried and distressed me to see how pure reason, intelligence, consideration of others, charm and even likeableness vanish for hours at a time and how often, instead of all the good deeds a fine man may be capable of doing, confusion and disaster threaten to break loose! How frequently does this give rise to hasty decisions!"

Charlotte agreed, but did not continue the discussion; for she was only too aware that Ottilie was thinking here of Edward alone, who—not always, but more often than necessary—enhanced his pleasure, conversation, and activities with the aid of wine.

If this remark of Charlotte's had made Ottilie think of the men, and Edward in particular, she had all the more cause to do so when Charlotte spoke of the Captain's imminent marriage as a quite well-known and definite matter. This gave things a different complexion than Edward's earlier assurances had led her to imagine. All this increased Ottilie's attentiveness to every word, every hint, every deed, every action of Charlotte's. Ottilie had become cunning, watchful, suspicious.

Meanwhile Charlotte in her perceptive way took stock of everything around her, working deftly, rationally, constantly urging Ottilie to participate. Fearlessly she pared down her household; indeed, in the cold light of day she saw their emotional upheavals as a kind of happy fate. For if they had continued with their expenditures, they could easily have got out of their depth and would have disturbed, if not destroyed, their rich fortune and happiness with their aggressive behavior.

She did not interrupt the work in the gardens. She continued, rather, whatever was needed for its future development; but she left it at that. When her husband returned he would have enough to do to satisfy him.

In these projects and activities she could not praise highly enough the work the architect was doing. Soon the lake lay spread out before their eyes and the newly made banks were decked with varied and graceful plantings and lawns. All the rough work had been completed on the new house and the weatherproofing had been taken care of; and there Charlotte stopped, at a point where it could be taken up again with pleasure later. She remained calm and serene throughout; but Ottilie only appeared to do so, watching solely for signs of whether Edward was expected soon or not. This was the only interest she took in anything.

For this reason she welcomed arrangements that were made to gather together the farmers' boys and have them keep the newly enlarged gardens neat. This had originally been Edward's plan. An attractive sort of uniform was made for the boys, which they put on in the evening after they had washed and scrubbed themselves well. The outfits were kept in the big house and entrusted to the care of the most sensible and reliable of the boys: the architect oversaw the whole arrangement, and before you knew it they had developed a certain adeptness. It turned out that they were easy to train, and they performed their tasks as if these were a sort of drill exercise. Indeed, when they marched by with their picks, garden shears, rakes, trowels, hoes and fan-shaped brooms, while others followed them with baskets to remove weeds and stones, and others again pulled the big, heavy iron roller behind them, it made a charming and delightful procession. It inspired the architect to sketch an appealing succession of poses and activities for a summer-house frieze; but Ottilie for her part saw it merely as a kind of parade, soon to welcome home the returning master.

This encouraged her to plan to greet him with something similar. The village girls had always been taught to sew, knit, spin and perform other womanly tasks. These virtues had increased now that measures had been taken to ensure the beauty and cleanliness of the village. Ottilie had always lent a hand, but irregularly, according to inclination or opportunity. Now she planned to do so more systematically and consistently. But one cannot make a corps out of a group of girls as one can with a group of boys. She followed her common sense, and without really thinking it through, she simply tried to inculcate in each girl devotion to home, parents, brothers and sisters.

This succeeded with many of them. But one lively little girl was said to have no aptitude and to be quite unwilling to do anything around the house. Ottilie could not take it ill of the girl, for the child was especially fond of Ottilie. The girl sought out Ottilie, ran and walked with her whenever she was allowed. At these moments the child was active, lively and untiring. Her affection for her lovely mistress evidently fulfilled some need. At first Ottilie merely tolerated the child's companionship; then she became fond of her herself; in the end they were inseparable, and little Nan accompanied her mistress everywhere.

Ottilie often took the path to the garden, finding pleasure in the way it flourished. The berries and cherries were coming to an end but little Nan especially enjoyed the late ones. As for the other fruit, which promised such a rich harvest this autumn, the gardener constantly had his master in mind and never ceased to wish he were back. Ottilie liked listening to the kind old soul. He knew his trade thoroughly and was full of Edward's praises.

When Ottilie said how pleased she was that the grafts had taken so well this spring, the gardener replied doubtfully: "I only wish that our good master could enjoy them. If he were here this fall he could see what fine varieties we still have in the garden from his father's time. Present-day fruit growers are not as reliable as the monks used to be. You find decent enough names in the catalogs; but you graft and train them and in the end, when they bear fruit, it isn't worth the trouble to have such trees in the orchard."

But the faithful servant's most frequent enquiry, every time he saw Ottilie, was about the date of the master's return. And when Ottilie was unable to tell him, the good man, not without a certain unspoken sorrow, showed that he thought she did not trust him, and she was embarrassed by the sense of ignorance she was thus forced to acknowledge. Yet she could not keep away from these borders and flower-beds. What they had in part sown together, everything they had planted together was now in full bloom; it scarcely needed any care except watering, which little Nan was always ready to do. With what emotions Ottilie contemplated the late flowers which were just beginning to show and whose full glory was to have displayed itself on Edward's birthday to express her affection and gratitude! Sometimes she pictured it as a celebration; but the hope of seeing this festival was not always equally vivid. Doubts and cares constantly nagged at her.

She could not reach a genuine and frank agreement with Charlotte either, for the two women's situations were too different. If everything remained the same, if they returned to a regular way of life, Charlotte would gain in present happiness, and a joyous prospect for the future would open before her, but Ottilie would lose all. We may indeed say all; for she had first found life and happiness in Edward, and in her present state she felt an infinite emptiness of which she had formerly had no notion. For a heart that has lost feels its loss. Desire turns into despair and impatience, and a woman's spirit, accustomed to waiting and hoping, longs to step out of its charmed circle and do something active to ensure its happiness.

Ottilie had not renounced Edward. How could she, indeed, even though Charlotte, against her own conviction, cunningly acted as if the matter were settled, and assumed in all she said that they had agreed there could be a friendly and dignified relationship between her husband and Ottilie. And yet how often Ottilie knelt at night, once she had locked herself into her room, before the open chest and contemplated the birthday presents of which she had used nothing, the cloth she had not cut or made up. How often did the dear girl hasten at sunrise out of the house where she had once found her entire bliss and go out into the open, which had never appealed to her before. She did not even care to remain on dry land. She leaped into the boat and rowed out into the middle of the lake; then she took out a travel book and, letting herself be rocked by the waves, she read and dreamed herself in foreign parts, and always she found her friend there; she had ever remained dear to his heart, and he to hers.

Chapter Eighteen

We should not be surprised to hear that that curiously active man we have met already, Mittler, having received word of the disaster that had taken place among the group of friends, was anxious to demonstrate and practice his friendship and his counselling skills in this case, even though none of the parties had called upon his help. Still it seemed advisable first to wait a while; for he knew very well that it is harder to help educated people than uneducated people in their moral confusions. So he left them to themselves for a time; but finally he could endure it no more, and hastened to find Edward, whose whereabouts he had already discovered.

His path led him to a pleasant valley through whose charming green meadow with its many trees a lively brook now wound its way, now rushed along. On the gentle hills were fertile fields and well-stocked orchards. The villages were not too close, the whole landscape had a peaceful aspect, and the separate parts, though they would not have made a good painting, made a very good place to live.

A well-preserved farmstead with a neat, modest dwelling, surrounded by gardens, finally came into view. He suspected that this was where Edward was now staying, and he was right.

We can say this much of our solitary friend: he had secretly given himself up completely to the sensation of his passion, concocting many a plan and nourishing many a hope. He could not but admit to himself that he desired to see Ottilie here, that he wished to bring her or entice her here, and that he had other thoughts, too, permissible and impermissible, which he did not deny himself. Then his fantasy ranged around through all sorts of possibilities. If she was not to be his, legitimately his, then he would give over the title of his property to her. There she should live alone, quietly and independently; she should be content and—so his self-tormenting imagination led him on—should even be happy with another.

So the days passed in continual vacillation between hope and sorrow, tears and bliss, plans, preparations and despair. The sight of Mittler did not surprise him. He had long expected his arrival, and so it was half welcome to him. In that he thought him to have been sent by Charlotte, he had armed himself with all kinds of excuses, postponements and indeed with definite proposals; in that he hoped to hear from Ottilie, however, Mittler was as dear to him as an angel from heaven.

How annoyed and irritated was Edward, then, when he heard that Mittler had not been sent by them, but had come of his own initiative. His kind feelings vanished, and conversation was desultory at first. But Mittler knew very well that a mind preoccupied by love has an urgent need to express itself and pour out its innermost concerns to a friend; and hence he was content, after some aimless talk, to drop his accustomed role for once and to play the confidant rather than the mediator.

When, accordingly, he gently reproached Edward for his solitary existence, his friend replied: "Oh, I cannot conceive how I could spend my time more pleasantly! I think continually of her, I am constantly near to her. I have the incomparable advantage of being free to imagine where Ottilie is, where she walks, where she stands, where she rests. I see her in my mind's eye doing what she always does, working and busying herself—of course always things that flatter me most. And that is not all; for how can I be happy when I am far from her! Now my imagination conjures up what Ottilie should do to come closer to me. I write sweet, confiding letters to myself in her name, I answer them and keep the two sets of letters together. I have promised not to make a move towards her, and I will keep that promise. But what prevents her from turning to me? Has Charlotte perhaps been so cruel as to demand a sacred promise from her not to write to me, to send me no news of herself? It would be natural, and probable, and yet I find it outrageous and unbearable. If she loves me, as I believe, as I know she does, why does she not make up her mind, why does she not dare flee, and fling herself into my arms? That is what she should do, I sometimes think; that is what she *could* do. If anything stirs in the hall, I look toward the door. "She is about to enter!" I think, I hope. Ah, but since the possible is impossible, I imagine that the impossible must be possible. That at night, when I wake up and the lamp casts an uncertain light about the room, her figure, her spirit, an intimation of her might float by, come nearer, take hold of me, just for a moment, to give me a kind of certainty that she is thinking of me, that she is mine.

"One pleasure alone remains for me. When I was near to her, I never dreamed of her; but now, when I am far from her, we are united in dream, and curiously enough, now that I have got to know other likeable people in the neighborhood, her image appears to me in my dreams, as if she wished to say: 'Look where you will! You will not find anything more beautiful or lovable than me.' And so her image blends into all my dreams. All I experienced with her mingles and runs together. Now we are signing a contract; there is her hand and mine; the two dissolve, the two intertwine. These glorious phantasms of the imagination are not without pain. Sometimes she does something to spoil the pure idea I have of her, and then I feel more keenly how much I love her, for then I am anxious beyond description. Sometimes she teases and torments me in a way quite unlike her usual manner; but then her image changes, her lovely round heavenly face lengthens: it is someone else. But I am tormented nonetheless, dissatisfied and shattered.

"Do not smile, dear Mittler—or do smile if you wish. I am not ashamed of this dependency, this mad and foolish passion, if you will. No, I have never loved before; now I am discovering for the first time what it means to love. Everything until now in my life was a prelude, a procrastination, a way to make time pass, to kill time, until I met her, until I loved her, wholly and truly loved her. People have reproached me, not directly, but behind my back, of being dilettantish and just toying with most things. It may be so; but I had never found the thing in which I could prove myself a master. I'd like to see someone who surpasses me in the talent of loving.

"To be sure, it is a pathetic talent, one fraught with tears and suffering; but it is so natural to me, so very much my own that it is most unlikely that I will ever give it up."

Although those heartfelt, forceful words gave vent to Edward's feelings, they also made him realize in sudden, vivid detail the strangeness of his condition. Overcome by the painful tug of emotions, he burst into tears, which flowed the more freely because his heart had been softened by confessing his feelings.

Now that Edward's distressing outburst of passion had made the aim of his journey seem less attainable, Mittler's quick temperament and uncompromising common sense were the harder to disguise. He expressed his disapproval without mincing words. Edward should control himself, he said, he should do justice to his manhood, he should not forget that the better part of valor was to pull oneself together in misfortune and bear pain with serenity and dignity, so as to be highly esteemed, honored, and held up as an example.

Upset and distressed as Edward was by the most agonizing emotions, these words inevitably seemed vain and empty to him. "He who is happy and content may well speak," Edward burst out; "but he would be ashamed if he saw how unbearable he is to one who is suffering. Infinite patience is thought to be possible, but in his rigid way of thinking the contented person is not willing to recognize infinite suffering. There are cases—there are indeed!—in which any comfort is base and it is our duty to despair. After all, does not the noble Greek, who knows how to depict heroes, not scorn to show his figures weeping over painful dilemmas. Even in a proverb he says: 'Good are men who have tears.' Away with him who is dry-eyed and dry-hearted! A curse on those happy souls for whom the unhappy are but a spectacle. An unhappy man is expected to bear himself nobly in the most terrible physical and mental distress, and for the sake of their applause at his decease to die in honor like a gladiator before their eyes. My dear Mittler, I thank you for your visit; but you would do me a great service if you would take a look around the garden or the countryside. We shall meet again. I will try to become more composed and more like yourself."

Mittler preferred to go on rather than break off a conversation he would not be able to resume so easily another time. It suited Edward, too, to continue their talk, which was in any event moving towards his goal.

"Of course," said Edward, "thinking and talking around and about does not help at all; but in the course of this conversation I have become truly aware of my own situation for the first time, felt clearly for the first time what decision I should take, what decision I have come to. I see my present and future life before me; I just have to choose between misery and pleasure. Dear friend, help me obtain the divorce that is necessary, that has already in effect taken place; obtain Charlotte's agreement for me! I shall not explain at greater length why I think it can be had. Go to her, my good fellow. Bring peace to us all and make us all happy!"

Mittler was taken aback. Edward went on: "My fate and Ottilie's cannot be separated, and we will not perish. Look at this glass! Our initials are engraved on it. A joyous guest threw it into the air; no one was to drink out of it again, it was to be shattered on the stony ground; but someone caught it. I got it back again at a high price, and now I drink from it every day to convince myself that all friendships forged by fate are indestructible."

"Alas," cried Mittler, "what patience I must have with my friends! Now I am confronted with superstition, to my mind the most pernicious thing that can visit men, and hence an abomination to me. We toy with prophecies and dreams and so give meaning to our everyday life. But when life itself takes a more meaningful turn, when all around us is noise and turbulence, the storm is only made more terrible by such fancies."

"In this uncertainty of life, amidst these hopes and fears," exclaimed Edward, "leave the troubled heart some guiding star to which it can look and by which it can make its way."

"I would accede to that," replied Mittler, "if one could only hope there were some logic to it, but I have always found that people don't heed the warning signs, they notice only those that flatter their hopes, and optimism is the only thing that really exists for them."

Since even Mittler felt himself dragged down into the darker regions which made him increasingly uncomfortable the longer he spent there, he was somewhat more willing to take up Edward's urgent request to go and see Charlotte. What arguments did he have to counter Edward at this point? All he could do, even by his own lights, was to gain time and find out how the women felt.

He hurried off to see Charlotte, whom he found as usual composed and serene. She was glad to tell him about all that had happened; for Edward's words had only let him see the effects of what had happened. For his part, he approached the matter cautiously, but could not make himself mention the word divorce even in passing. How puzzled, amazed and—as could be expected from someone of his views— delighted he was, then, when Charlotte, after relating all kinds of unpleasant things, finally said: "I must trust and hope that all will come right again, and that Edward will return. How can it be otherwise, since I am now in a certain condition?"

"Have I understood you aright?" Mittler broke in. "Completely," replied Charlotte. "A thousand blessings on this news!" he cried, clapping his hands. "I know how powerfully this works upon a man's mind.

How many marriages have I thus seen hastened, strengthened, restored! Such expectancy is better than a thousand words; it is indeed the greatest expectation we can have. But," he continued, "for my own part, I would have every cause to be annoyed. In this case I see that not even my own vanity is flattered. You can give me no thanks for my efforts. I feel like my friend the doctor who was successful with all the cures he undertook out of charity upon the poor, but could seldom cure a rich person who was willing to pay him well. Luckily this case is about to cure itself, since all my trouble, all my good words would have come to nothing."

Charlotte now asked him to take the news to Edward, to bring him a letter from her and see what he could do and what could be restored. But he refused to do so. "All has been done already," he exclaimed. "Write your letter! Any messenger will do. I must turn to where my help is needed more. I will come back only to congratulate you; I will come to the christening."

Now, as so often before, Charlotte was dissatisfied with Mittler. His hasty nature could do much good, his overhastiness was the cause of many a failure. No one was more prone to act on the spur of the moment than he.

Charlotte's messenger reached Edward, who received him with something of a start. The letter could as easily mean no as yes. For some time he did not dare open it, and how stunned he was when he had read it, turned as if to stone by the following passage with which it ended:

"Recall those romantic hours of the night when you came to your wife as a lover, when you drew her irresistibly to you and clasped her in your arms as a mistress, a bride. Let us revere this strange accident as ordained by heaven, to create a new bond for our relationship in the very moment when the joy of our life threatened to dissolve and fade away."

What took place in Edward's soul from now on would be hard to describe. In such a predicament old habits and inclinations finally reappear to while away time and give life meaning. Hunting and war are always ready ways out for the nobleman. Edward longed for external danger to preserve his internal balance. He longed for death, since life threatened to become unbearable; indeed, it was a comfort to him to think that he would be no more and that in this way he would make his friends and loved ones happy. No one opposed his desire, since he kept his decision secret. In all due formality he drew up his will; it was sweet to him to be able to leave the estate to Ottilie. He made provisions for Charlotte, for the unborn child, for the Captain, for his servants. The war that had recently broken out again suited his plans well. Halfhearted military affairs had greatly annoyed him during his youth; that was why he had left the service. Now it was a glorious feeling to set out under a general of whom he could say to himself: under his leadership death is probable and victory certain.

Ottilie, learning of Charlotte's secret, was as stunned as Edward, and more so; she withdrew into herself. She had no more to say. She could not hope, and she dared not wish. Her diary, from which we intend to quote some excerpts, gives us nonetheless some insight into her innermost feelings.

Part Two

Chapter One

In everyday life we often experience what in epics we are accustomed to praise as a poetic technique: that when the central characters move away, disappear, become inactive, a second or third person, scarcely noticed before, steps in right away to fill the empty spot, and, by showing the full extent of his activity, seems to us worthy of attention, sympathy, and indeed of praise and distinction.

So once Edward and the Captain had departed the architect became more important by the day, since it was on him that the organization and completion of so many tasks depended. In carrying them out he proved himself exact, sensible and energetic, and at the same time he supported the women in all sorts of ways and knew how to help them while away the long, uneventful hours. His very appearance was the kind that inspires confidence and affection. A youth in every sense of the word, he was well built, slender, somewhat on the tall side, modest but not fearful, confiding but not overbearing. He was glad to take over all their cares and worries, and because he was good at doing calculations, the household was soon no secret to him, and his good influence made itself felt in everything. He was usually the one to receive strangers, and he knew how to turn away unexpected visitors or else to prepare the women in such a way that there was no inconvenience.

One of these visitors, a young lawyer, caused him considerable trouble. Sent along one day by a neighboring nobleman, the lawyer mentioned something which, though not in itself of particular significance, nonetheless greatly moved Charlotte. We have to refer to this incident since it set various things in motion that might otherwise have remained dormant.

Let us recall the changes that Charlotte had made in the churchyard. All the monuments had been removed from their places and set against the wall or around the foundation of the church. The remaining space had been made level. Apart from a wide path that led to the church and along past it to the gate on the other side, the rest had been planted with various sorts of clover, whose green leaves and blossoms looked most

175

attractive. The plan was to place new graves in a certain order from the end, but each time the ground was to be leveled again and planted with clover. No one could deny that this arrangement made a pleasant and dignified sight for churchgoers on Sundays and holidays. Even the aged minister, who clung to old habits and who had not been especially happy with this provision at first, now took pleasure in it when, like Philemon, he sat with his Baucis under the old linden trees by the back door and saw instead of the clumsy graves a lovely, colorful carpet before him. It was, furthermore, to benefit his household, since Charlotte had had the use of the spot made over to the parsonage.

But in spite of this a number of parishioners had disapproved early on of the fact that the markers had been taken from the places where their forebears lay, and thus, so to speak, their memory had been erased; for the well-preserved monuments showed who had been buried, but not where, and the location was really the most important thing, many claimed.

This view was shared by a neighboring family who had reserved many years ago a plot for them and theirs in this general resting-place, and who had made a small endowment to the church for this purpose. Now the young lawyer had been sent to revoke the endowment and to indicate that they would not continue to pay, since the condition upon which the payments had hitherto been made had been canceled unilaterally and all their requests and counter-arguments had not been given due consideration. Charlotte, who was responsible for the new arrangement, wished to speak to the young man herself; and he presented his own and his client's arguments energetically, but not aggressively, giving them all a great deal to think about.

"You will understand," he said, after a short introduction in which he justified his intrusion, "you will understand that the lowliest and the highest are equally desirous of marking the spot where their relatives are buried. The poorest farmer, burying his child, has a kind of comfort in placing a light wooden cross on the grave and decorating it with a wreath, so that the memory shall remain at least as long as the grief, even though such a marker, like sorrow itself, is obliterated by time. Well-to-do families make these crosses of iron and secure and protect them in various ways, thus ensuring that they last for several years. But since these sink and lose their lustre in the end, the rich have no greater concern than to erect a stone which will be sure to last for several generations and can be renewed and refurbished by their offspring. Yet it is not the stone we care about, but what lies beneath it, what has been entrusted to the earth beside it. It is not just a question of the memorial, but of the person, not of the memory, but of the presence. I can feel close to my dear departed more readily and more fervently through a grave than through a monument, for a monument is nothing much in itself; but spouse, relatives, and friends should gather around a grave as around a mile-stone, even after they themselves are deceased, and the living should retain the right of ejecting and removing strangers and ill-wishers from the side of their departed loved ones.

"I believe, therefore, that my client is completely in the right to revoke his endowment; it is only proper, since members of his family have been injured in a way that cannot be made good. They are deprived of the sweet sorrow of bringing a tribute to the dead and of the hope and comfort of resting beside them in the course of time."

"This matter is not so significant," replied Charlotte, "that one should trouble to file a lawsuit over it. I so little regret what I have done that I will be glad to make restitution to the church for its financial loss. But I must honestly admit that your arguments do not convince me. The pure idea of a final equality for all, at least after death, seems more comforting to me than this stubbornly rigid attempt to continue our personages, dependencies, and circumstances.—What is your opinion?" she asked, turning to the architect.

"In such a matter," he replied, "I am hesitant either to argue or to tip the scale. Let me, in all modesty, say something germane to my art and my way of thinking. Since we are no longer so fortunate as to be able to clasp to our hearts an urn with the remains of our loved ones, and since we are neither so rich nor so cold-blooded as to embalm them and preserve them in large, ornate sarcophagi, indeed since we do not even have space in the churches for ourselves and our relatives, but are compelled to use the open ground, we have every reason to approve of the fashion you have introduced, milady. If members of a parish lie in rows beside one another, they rest in close proximity to their dear ones; and if we are in the end to be entrusted to the earth, I find nothing more natural and proper than that graves set up in random order and now gradually sinking be leveled without dividing marks, so that the cover they all bear may be made lighter for each."

"And they should all pass away without any hint of a memorial, without anything to foster their memory?" asked Ottilie.

"Not at all!" continued the architect; "we should not give up their memory, merely their actual resting-place. It is very much in the interest of architects and sculptors that people should expect their art and craft to produce a lasting monument to their lives and hence I would like to see well-conceived and well-executed memorials, not scattered about separately and at random, but set up in one place where a certain permanence can be expected. Since even the pious and the rich must forgo the privilege of being buried in the church itself, let us at least set up there or in fine halls around the cemeteries memorials and inscriptions. There are thousands of different motifs that can be suggested, thousands of different decorations that can be used."

"If artists are really so creative," replied Charlotte, "tell me why they can never get away from the form of small obelisks, broken columns or funeral urns. Instead of the thousand inventions you boast of, I have only seen a thousand repetitions."

"That may be so in these parts," answered the architect, "but not everywhere. And in any event designs and their proper application are a tricky matter. In this particular case there are many problems involved in giving something so serious an attractive appearance and not making something unpleasant displeasing as art. With respect to designs for monuments of all kinds, I have collected many and occasionally display them; but the best monument is always a portrait of the deceased. More than anything else this gives us an impression of who the person was; it is the best text for much or little music; but it must have been done when the person was at his prime, though people usually neglect to do so. No one thinks of preserving the living form, and if they do, they do it inadequately. A mask is hastily made of the deceased, set upon a stone, and called a bust. How rarely can the artist breathe life into it again!"

"Without meaning to, perhaps," said Charlotte, "you have given this conversation a distinct turn to my advantage. The portrait of a person is independent, you will admit; wherever it stands, it is self-sufficient, and we do not demand that it mark the actual gravesite. But shall I confess a peculiar reaction I have? I don't even care much for portraits: they always seem to be a silent reproach; they refer to something distant and departed, and remind me how hard it is for us to do proper justice to the present. If we think how many people we have seen and known, and admit how little we have meant to them and they to us, what an unsettling thought that is! We meet the wise and witty without conversing with them, scholars without learning from them, travelers without expanding our horizons, kind souls without returning their kindness.

"And, sad to say, this is not the case with fleeting acquaintances only. Groups and families behave this way towards their dearest members, cities towards their most respected citizens, peoples towards their most splendid princes, nations towards their finest men.

"I once heard someone ask why one speaks well of the dead unreservedly, but of the living always with a certain degree of hesitation. The answer was that we have nothing to fear from the dead whereas the living could cross us at some future point. That's how far from disinterested our concern for the memory of others is; it's mostly just vain egotism, whereas it should be our sacred duty to keep our relation to the living active and alive."

Chapter Two

Inspired by this incident and the discussions it had aroused, they went the next day to the cemetery, where the architect made a number of happy suggestions for decorating and making it more pleasant. But his work was also to extend to the church, a building that had caught his eye from the very first.

Several hundred years old, the church had been built in the fine old German style and decorated very tastefully. Presumably the architect of a nearby convent had agreed to exercise his taste and his fancies on this smaller building, and it was still a pleasantly solemn sight to behold, despite the fact that the new interior, set up for protestant services, detracted somewhat from its serene majesty.

It was not hard for the architect to persuade Charlotte to grant him a modest sum of money to restore it to its original form, both inside and out, and to make it harmonize better with the cemetery in front of it. He himself was a very skilled craftsman, and they planned to retain several of the carpenters who were working on the house until this pious task was finished as well.

Now it was time to take a closer look at the building itself with its grounds and annexes, and so they discovered to the architect's great astonishment and delight a little side chapel of more delicate and more brilliantly conceived proportions and more charmingly and assiduously decorated. It included many carved and painted objects from its Catholic period, when the various festivals were marked, each in its own way, with all kinds of pictures and sacred objects.

The architect could not resist including the chapel in his project right away, aiming to restore this narrow space as a special monument to former times and tastes. He had already imagined the empty surfaces decorated according to his own fancy and was looking forward to practicing his artistic talent on them; but for the moment he kept this secret from the others.

First of all he showed the ladies, as he had promised, various drawings and sketches of old grave monuments, urns and other related objects, and when the conversation turned to the simple gravemounds of the Nordic tribes, he brought out his collection of weapons and utensils that had been found there. He kept everything very neatly in portable drawers and compartments on carved, cloth-covered boards, with the result that these ancient, solemn objects took on a somewhat prettified air, and could be looked at with the same enjoyment as the display cases of a fashion dealer. And once he had started these exhibitions, he brought forth part of his treasures every evening to fill their need of entertainment in their solitude. Most of these objects were German in origin: silver plates, heavy old coins, seals and other things of this kind. All these things turned the friends' thoughts to ancient times, and when he finally illustrated his conversations with the earliest prints, woodcuts and copper engravings, and the church similarly moved closer to the past day by day as it was painted and decorated, they almost had to ask themselves if they were really living in modern times, and if it were not a dream that customs, habits, fashions and convictions were now quite different.

After this preparation, a large portfolio he brought out finally was particularly effective. It mainly contained sketches of figures, which, because they had been traced directly from the original pictures, had completely retained their ancient character—and how very attractive they all found it! An aura of the greatest purity radiated from each of the figures; all were surely, if not noble, at least virtuous. Calm composure, happy recognition of the One above, silent acquiescence in loving anticipation was written on every face, in every gesture. The old man with the bald head, the curly-haired boy, the lively youth, the earnest man, the transfigured saint, the hovering angel, all seemed blissful in their innocent sufficiency and pious expectation. The most everyday doings seemed to shine with divine life, and a worshipful aspect appeared to clothe every character.

Most of us look towards such a sphere as towards a vanished golden age, a paradise lost. Perhaps Ottilie alone could feel at home here.

Who could now have resisted the architect's suggestion of decorating the spaces between the vaults of the ceiling according to these models, thus putting his mark on a place where he had already had such success. He was somewhat wistful about this; for he well recognized that his stay in such perfect company could not be prolonged forever and would perhaps soon have to be broken off.

These days, moreover, though not rich in external events, still gave occasions to more serious talk. We will take this opportunity, then, to reproduce some passages from Ottilie's notebooks, to which we can think of no more appropriate transition than an image that comes to mind upon perusal of these touching pages.

The English navy has a particular device: every rope of the royal fleet, from the thinnest to the thickest, is twined in such a way that a red thread goes through it all, a thread that cannot be removed without undoing the whole rope and by which even the smallest pieces can be recognized as belonging to the crown.

In the same way a thread of love and devotion runs through Ottilie's diary, binding everything together and giving a unique mark to the whole. It makes these notes, reflections, extracts and mottoes the peculiar property of the writer; it conveys their meaning for her. Even a single one of these selections we are about to reproduce bears the most decisive testimony to this fact.

FROM OTTILIE'S DIARY

To rest at last beside the person one loves is the pleasantest thought one can have if one thinks beyond the end of life. "To be called unto one's own" is such a heart-warming expression.

There are many monuments and memorials that can bring the dear departed nearer to us. None has as much significance as does a picture. To converse with the portrait of a loved one, even if the likeness is poor, has a certain charm, just as there is a certain charm to arguing with a friend. One has the pleasant sensation of being at odds, yet unable to separate.

Sometimes we converse with someone present as if with a picture. He does not need to speak, or look at us, or concern himself with us; we see him, we feel our relationship with him, indeed our bonds can grow without his doing anything, without his noticing that we are treating him as if he were a picture.

We are never satisfied with portraits of people we know. I have always pitied portrait painters for this reason. So seldom do we demand the impossible, yet in this case we do. Portrait painters are expected to bring everyone's relation to the person, as well as the person's likes and dislikes, into the picture; they are not merely to depict the person as they see him, but as everyone would see him. It does not surprise me that such artists gradually grow inflexible, indifferent and obstinate. This would be of no consequence if it did not mean one had to do without the portraits of so many dearly loved friends.

It is true that the architect's collection of ancient weapons and utensils buried with the dead in earth mounds and cliffs shows how useless it is to trouble about the survival of one's personality after death. And how contradictory we are! The architect admits to having opened such ancestral gravemounds, and yet he continues to concern himself with monuments for generations to come.

But why be so pedantic about it? Is everything we do for eternity? Do we not dress in the morning, only to undress again in the evening? Do we not travel in order to come home again? And why should we not wish to rest in peace beside our own people, be it only for a single century?

When one sees the many sunken gravestones worn thin by the steps of churchgoers, the churches themselves fallen into ruin above their tombs, then life after death can seem like a second life entered as if into a picture whose inscription lingers longer than in the real life we live. But even this picture, this second existence vanishes sooner or later. Time will not be robbed of its rights—over monuments as over human beings.

Chapter Three

It is so enjoyable to do something you are not really good at that we should not criticize a dilettante who practices an art he will never master, or blame an artist who takes it into his head to go beyond the limits of his own field and enter a neighboring one.

It is with such indulgent thoughts in mind that we should consider the architect's plans for decorating the chapel. The paints had been prepared, measures taken, sketches drawn. He had laid aside any claim to originality; he kept to his outlines; his only concern being to distribute the floating or seated figures skillfully and to decorate the space tastefully.

The scaffolding was up, the work proceeded, and since some striking parts had been completed, he could not object to a visit from Charlotte and Ottilie. The life-like angel faces, the vivid draperies on the heavenly blue background were delightful to behold, their quiet piety inspiring the viewer to recollection and producing a very delicate effect.

The women had climbed up the scaffolding to where he was working, and Ottilie scarcely noticed how smoothly and easily what she had learnt before in her lessons at school suddenly seemed to come into its own. She took paint and brush and, following the architect's instructions, began neatly and skillfully to draw an elaborately draped garment.

Charlotte, who was pleased to see Ottilie occupied and distracted in some way, left the two to their work and went away to think her own thoughts and to work through by herself the worries and concerns she could not share with anyone else.

When ordinary mortals are driven by everyday problems to behave emotionally and fearfully, we are moved to smile with pity, but we look with awe upon a spirit bearing the seed of a powerful fate, that must await its development and neither can nor may hasten the good or evil, the happiness or the misery, that is to come of it.

Edward had answered the messenger Charlotte had sent to him in his seclusion in a friendly and sympathetic tone, but with dignified composure rather than loving intimacy. Shortly afterwards he had disappeared, and his wife was unable to obtain news of him until at last, by accident, she saw his name in the newspapers amongst those who had distinguished themselves in an important battle. Now she knew what path he had taken and she discovered that he had escaped great dangers; but she was immediately convinced that he would embark on even greater ones, and she could easily conclude that he would be unlikely to let himself be held back from the most extreme acts in every sense of the word. She kept these constant cares to herself, and turn them as she might, she could find no way of looking at them that set her mind at ease.

Ottilie, unaware of all this, had in the meantime taken great interest in the painting and had easily obtained Charlotte's permission to continue with it regularly. Now the work proceeded rapidly, and the azure heaven was soon peopled with suitable inhabitants. Their constant practice lent Ottilie and the architect a freer manner in their later pictures which visibly improved. Even the faces, which had been left to the architect alone, gradually took on a quite particular character: they all began to look like Ottilie. The presence of this lovely creature must have made a vivid impression upon the young man, who had not yet drawn from nature or art, so that gradually nothing was lost between the eye and the hand, and indeed in the end both worked in unison. In short, one of his last faces was so well done it seemed as if Ottilie herself were looking down from the heavenly vault.

The arched ceiling was now finished. They had decided to leave the walls plain and simply to cover them with a lighter brown paint; the delicate columns and the decorative sculptures were to stand out in a darker color. But as one thing leads to another in such affairs, they decided to add garlands of flowers and fruit, joining, as it were, heaven and earth. Here Ottilie was thoroughly in her element. The gardens provided the loveliest patterns, and even though the wreaths were very richly embellished, they were finished sooner than expected.

But the whole still looked crude and bare. The scaffoldings had been pushed together, the boards tossed on top of each other, the uneven floor disfigured by all kinds of spilled paint. The architect thus asked the women to grant him eight days' time, during which they would not enter the chapel. One fine evening he begged them at last to go and see it together; but he did not wish to accompany them, and immediately took his leave.

"Whatever he may have planned in the way of a surprise for us," said Charlotte when he had gone, "I don't feel like going just now. You go on your own and tell me about it. I'm sure he has created something very charming. I will enjoy it first in your description, and then in reality."

Well aware that Charlotte had to be careful in many ways, avoiding all emotions and most particularly any untoward surprises, Ottilie set out for the chapel right away, looking instinctively for the architect. He was nowhere to be seen, however, and must have been hiding. She found the church open and went in. It had been finished earlier, and had been cleaned up and dedicated. She went over to the door of the chapel, whose bronze weight opened easily before her and surprised her with an unexpected view of a familiar place.

From its single high window came solemn, multi-colored light; for the window had been exquisitely put together from panes of stained glass. The whole chapel thus took on an unfamiliar aspect and created a special atmosphere. The beauty of the vault and walls was enhanced by a decorative floor consisting of specially shaped bricks laid in an attractive pattern and set in mortar. The architect had had the bricks and the colored panes made in secret, and was thus able to put them all together in a very short time. Seating had also been provided. Amongst the antiques belonging to the church had been several finely carved choir stalls, and these were now arranged most charmingly along the walls.

Ottilie was delighted to see the familiar parts that now appeared as an unfamiliar whole. She stopped, walked back and forth, looked and looked again; finally she sat down on one of the seats, and it seemed to her, as she gazed up and all around, as if she were alive and not alive, conscious and unconscious; as if all this might vanish from her sight and she from herself; and it was not until the sun left the window it had hitherto lit so brightly that Ottilie came to herself and hastened towards the manor.

She was not unaware of the remarkable date on which this surprise had fallen. It was the eve of Edward's birthday. She had hoped, of course, to celebrate it very differently. How everything was to have been decked out in honor of the day! But now the whole autumnal array of flowers was unpicked. The sunflowers still turned their faces to heaven, the asters still peeped forth modestly, and those that had been bound into wreaths had been used as patterns for decorating a place that, if it was to be more than an artist's whim—if it was to be used for anything—was only suitable to be their common grave.

She could not help thinking of the noisy activity with which Edward had celebrated her birthday; she thought of the newly-built house under whose roof they had hoped to spend so many pleasant hours. The fireworks exploded once more in her mind's eye, and the lonelier she felt, the clearer they seemed in her imagination; but she only felt all the more alone. No longer was she leaning on his arm, and she had no hope that she would ever find support in it again.

FROM OTTILIE'S DIARY

I must note down one of the young artist's remarks: "As with the craftsman, so one observes most clearly in the pictorial artist that man can take the least possession of what most truly belongs to him. His works leave him as birds leave the nest in which they have been hatched."

More than others, an architect has a most curious fate in this respect. How often does he apply his every mental and emotional energy to create spaces from which he himself is excluded! Royal halls owe their splendor to him, but he cannot enjoy them at their most effective. In temples he must exclude himself from the most sacred places; no longer may he tread upon the steps whose moving solemnity he conceived, just as the goldsmith may only revere from afar the monstrance he has created from gold and precious stones. With the key to the palace the builder gives over to the rich all its pleasures and comforts, and has no chance to enjoy any of it himself. Must not art thus separate itself from the artist when the work, like a child that has been provided for, no longer interacts with the father? And how beneficial it must have been for art when it was designed almost exclusively for the public and as everyone's property, and thus also belonged to the artist!

There is one grim notion held by ancient civilizations that might seem terrifying to us. They imagined their forebears to be sitting in silent conversation on thrones arranged in a circle in large caves. If the newcomer entering were sufficiently worthy, they stood and bowed in welcome. Yesterday, while I was sitting in the chapel, I noticed that several carved seats had been placed in a circle opposite my own, and the thought seemed pleasant and agreeable to me. "Why can you not sit still?" I thought to myself, "sit silent and withdrawn for a long, long time, until at last the friends would come for whom you would stand and whom you would show to their places with a friendly bow." The stained glass panes turn the day into solemn twilight, and someone should donate an eternal lamp, so that the night, too, should not remain completely dark.

Turn it how one will, one always imagines oneself seeing. I think we dream solely to prevent ourselves from ceasing to see. It may come to pass that the inner light bursts forth from us all at once, and then we will have no need of any other.

The year is dying away. The wind blows through the stubble and finds nothing it can stir; only the red berries on those slender trees seem anxious to remind us of more cheerful things, as the rhythm of the thresher makes us think what life and nourishment lie hidden in the mown sheaves.

Chapter Four

After events like these, that thrust upon her a sense of transience and decay, how strangely must Ottilie have been affected by the news, which could no longer be concealed from her, that Edward had given himself up to the changing fortunes of war. None of the thoughts this might give rise to escaped her. Luckily a human being can comprehend only a certain measure of misfortune; any more either destroys us or leaves us cold. There are situations in which fear and hope become one, cancel each other out and are lost in dark apathy. How could we otherwise know our dearest friends to be in hourly danger, and still carry on our ordinary lives?

So it was as if a good spirit had undertaken to protect Ottilie. Suddenly, in the midst of this silence where she seemed to be sinking in her solitary inactivity, a wild crowd burst in, giving her plenty to do in an external way and bringing her out of herself, while also stimulating in her a sense of her own strength.

Charlotte's daughter, Luciane, had hardly left boarding-school to enter society, hardly found herself surrounded by all the people who had come to visit her aunt, than her desire to please actually found a response, and a very rich young man soon conceived a passionate desire to marry her. A considerable fortune gave him the right to call the best of everything his, and he seemed to lack nothing other than a perfect wife who, like everything else he had, would be the envy of the world around him.

These family matters had kept Charlotte very busy, occupying her whole mind and correspondence, insofar as this was not directed towards finding out more news of Edward; and for this reason Ottilie had spent more time alone recently than before. She knew, of course, of Luciane's planned arrival; she herself had made the necessary domestic arrangements; but no one had dreamed that her visit was to be so soon. They had meant to write and make the date more precise, when suddenly the storm broke in upon the house and upon Ottilie.

Maids and servants arrived, carriages came with cases and trunks, and one would have thought that two or three loads of people were already in the house; but now the guests appeared in person: Luciane, her great-aunt, several friends, and her fiancé, who was himself not unaccompanied. The whole entryway was full of cases, valises and other leather containers. The many boxes and bags could hardly be sorted out. There was no end to the dragging about of luggage. In the meantime it began to pour with rain, which caused a good deal of inconvenience. Ottilie coped with this bustle and tumult by calmly going about her business, indeed her serene and capable manner showed itself at its best; for within a brief while she had arranged and put away everything. All were installed in their rooms, all were comfortable and had what they needed, and they all thought themselves well served because they were not prevented from helping themselves.

Now the whole company would have liked to have a little peace and quiet after such an arduous journey, and Luciane's fiancé would have liked to speak with her mother and assure her of his intentions; but Luciane could not rest. It so happened that she had a chance to do some horse-riding. Her fiancé owned fine horses, and they had to go riding right away. Wind and weather, rain and storm were of no account; it was as if the only thing in life were getting wet and then getting dry again. If she felt like going out for a walk, she never thought what clothes she had on and what shoes she was wearing; she had to inspect the gardens of which she had heard so much. What they could not see on horseback they dashed through on foot. Soon she had seen everything and passed judgment on it. It was hard to contradict her, considering the fast pace at which she moved. The whole household suffered, but the housemaids had the worst of it, being kept constantly busy with washing and ironing, unpicking and sewing seams up again.

Hardly had she exhausted the house and its surroundings than she felt obliged to call on the neighbors. In view of the speed at which they rode and drove, the neighborhood spread out for quite some distance. The manor house was overwhelmed with return visits, and so that no one would miss anybody, "at home" days were soon decided on.

And while Charlotte tried to arrange business matters with her aunt and with the future bridegroom's financial adviser, and Ottilie and the servants, setting in motion hunters and gardeners, fishermen and shop-keepers, managed to see to it that nothing was lacking despite the constant press of visitors, Luciane continued to behave like a fiery comet dragging a long tail after it. The usual entertainments soon seemed quite tasteless to her. She hardly allowed the older guests to spend a quiet hour at cards: anyone who was still in the slightest way active—and who could resist her charming persuasion?—had to join in, if not in dancing, then at least in lively games of forfeit, wagers and riddles. And although all of this, especially the forfeits, were centered upon herself, no one— no man in particular, whatever kind of person he might be—went quite without a prize; in fact, she enjoyed winning over older people of consequence by finding out their birthdays and name-days and celebrating them ostentatiously. She had a great talent for this, with the result that, since all were favored, each thought himself her particular favorite, a weakness of which even the oldest in the group was most noticeably guilty.

While her intention seemed to be to charm men of importance, rank, reputation, fame or some other significance, and to put prudence and good sense to shame by winning over even the most cautious to her strange, wild ways, she also gave the young people their due; there was a day, hour, and occasion when she managed to delight and captivate each and every one of them. Thus she soon had her eye on the architect, who gazed so unaffectedly from beneath his long black curls, stood so calm and straight, at something of a distance, answered all questions so concisely and sensibly, but did not seem inclined to participate in anything else, that she finally decided, half unconsciously, half by cunning design, to make him the hero of the day and so to win him for her court.

It was not for nothing that she had brought so much luggage, and indeed more had been sent on after her arrival. She had made provision for an endless change of clothing. While she enjoyed changing three or four times a day from morning to night in a succession of dresses perfectly customary in society, she appeared from time to time in masquerade, as a peasant woman or a fishergirl, a fairy or a flower seller. She did not disdain to dress up as an old lady, which made her young face look out all the more freshly from under her hood; and in truth, so much did she mingle the real and the imaginary that one might have been dealing, directly or indirectly, with a sprite straight out of an operetta.

Her main use for these costumes, however, were pantomimes and dances in which she was very skilled at acting out various parts. A cavalier from her entourage had undertaken to accompany her mimes with a little piano music; they only needed to confer briefly, and were in harmony right away.

One day, during the intermission of a lively ball, she was asked, spontaneously as it seemed, but actually as part of a prearranged plan of her own, to give one of these performances. She pretended to be surprised and embarrassed, and contrary to her usual custom, she made them press her for some time. She pretended she could not make up her mind, left the choice to others, and asked, as if improvising, for a theme. At last her piano-playing assistant, with whom she had presumably arranged it all in advance, sat down at the piano and, beginning to play a funeral march, begged her to act the part of Artemisia which she had practiced to such superb effect. She took up the request, and after a brief absence she appeared with measured tread to the sad, soft tones of the funeral march, dressed as the royal widow, bearing an urn of ashes before her. Behind her was borne a large blackboard and a well-sharpened piece of chalk in a golden pen holder.

One of her adjutants and admirers to whom she had whispered something went over to the architect, to beg, urge and virtually push him into enacting the part of the builder drawing the tomb of Mausoleus, which made him not at all a passive, but a genuinely active participant in the drama. Despite his external awkwardness—and indeed, in his plain black well-fitting modern dress he cut a strange figure in contrast to the funereal drapes, crepes, fringes, jet, tassels and coronets—he nonetheless pulled himself together, but that only made him the stranger to behold. He positioned himself with the greatest earnestness in front of the large blackboard, which was held by two pages, and drew most carefully and accurately a tomb perhaps more appropriate for a Lombard than a Carian king, but so beautifully proportioned, so earnestly conceived, so brilliantly decorated that it was a pleasure to watch it taking shape and to admire it when it was finished.

During this whole time he had scarcely turned towards the queen, but had devoted his complete attention to his task. Finally, when he bowed before her to indicate that he thought he had carried out her orders, she held out the urn towards him and gave him to understand that she wished to see it depicted on the top of the tomb. He did so, if unwillingly, since it did not fit with the rest of his sketch. As far as Luciane was concerned, she was released at long last from her state of impatience; for it had not been her intention at all to have an accurate drawing from him. If he had just sketched, in a few strokes, something vaguely resembling a monument and spent the rest of the time attending to her it would have been more to her liking. But his way of proceeding caused her quite some embarrassment; for although she tried to vary to some extent her expressions of sorrow, her orders and suggestions, her approval of the sketch that was gradually taking shape, and several times almost pulled the architect around in order to create some interaction between them, his acting was just too stiff. The result was that she had to rely on the urn far too often, pressing it to her heart and gazing heavenward, looking in the end (since such situations can only get more intense) more like a widow of Ephesus than a queen of Caria. The performance dragged on; the pianist, usually patient enough, was at a loss to know what key to modulate to next. He was so relieved when he saw the urn on the pyramid that he moved unconsciously into a happy theme. Although the performance lost its character, the party was thoroughly cheered, and they broke up right away, expressing their pleasure and admiration to the lady for her superb acting and to the architect for his artistic and charming drawing.

Luciane's fiancé, in particular, went to speak with the architect. "It's a pity," he said, "that your drawing is so impermanent. Permit me at least to have it brought to my room so I can talk with you about it." "If you like," the architect said, "I can show you carefully executed drawings of similar buildings and monuments; this is only a hastily improvised sketch."

Ottilie, standing nearby, came up to them. "Do not forget to show the baron your collection some time," she said to the architect; "he is interested in art and antiquity; I would like you to get to know each other better."

Luciane whirled up and asked: "What are you talking about?"

"A collection of art works," answered the baron, "which this gentleman owns and which he would like to show us some time."

"He should bring them at once!" Luciane cried. "You will bring them at once, won't you?" she added in a cajoling tone, clasping his hands winningly.

"I don't think it is the right moment," replied the architect.

"What!" exclaimed Luciane imperiously. "You refuse to obey your queen's commands?" Then she began to beg him coquettishly.

"Don't be so stubborn!" whispered Ottilie.

The architect went off with a bow; the gesture said neither yes nor no.

Scarcely had he gone than Luciane started chasing her greyhound around the room. "Oh dear!" she cried, accidentally bumping into her mother, "how unhappy I am! I didn't bring my monkey with me; I was persuaded not to, but it is just the servants' laziness that has robbed me of the pleasure. I will send for him; someone shall go and get him. If I could only see a picture of him I would be happy. I will make sure to have his portrait painted, and it shall never leave my side."

"Perhaps I can make up for it," replied Charlotte, "by having a whole book of the most amazing monkey pictures brought down from the library." Luciane shrieked with joy, and the large volume was brought in. The sight of these repulsive creatures, so like human beings and made even more so by the artist, pleased Luciane tremendously. But what she liked most was to find in each and every one of these animals a resemblance to people they knew. "Doesn't he look like uncle?" she exclaimed heartlessly, "and this one like our gift shop man M . . . , that one like pastor S . . . , and this one is what's-his-name incarnate. At bottom, monkeys are the original Dandies—I don't understand how they can be excluded from the very best society."

It was in the very best society that she was saying this, but nobody took it ill of her. They were so used to making concessions to her charm that in the end they also made concessions to her rudeness.

Meanwhile Ottilie was talking to Luciane's fiancé. She hoped that the architect would come back and rescue the party from all this monkey business with his tasteful and serious collection. Anticipating this, she had been discussing it with the baron and telling him about various details. But the architect did not come, and when he finally did, he mingled amongst the crowd. He had not brought anything back with him nor did he behave as if there had been any suggestion of his doing so. For a moment Ottilie was—how to put it?—annoyed, impatient, rebuffed; she had put in a good word for him, and she had hoped to give Luciane's fiancé a pleasant hour, since for all his love for her he appeared to be pained by Luciane's behavior.

The monkeys had to give way to a cold platter. Party games, dancing even, and finally a sort of listless sitting around and chasing after vanished pleasures lasted, as was so often the case, until long after midnight. For Luciane had already got into the habit of being unable to get up in the morning and unable to go to bed at night.

About this time events are noted much more rarely in Ottilie's diary; maxims and sayings referring to life and drawn from life take their place. Considering that most of them are presumably not her own thoughts, it is probable that she was given some book from which she copied out what suited her purpose. Much else of more personal relevance is doubtless revealed by the red thread.

FROM OTTILIE'S DIARY

The reason we are so eager to look into the future is that our secret desires wish to shape to our own advantage the vague forms moving about there.

We do not find ourselves at a large party without tending to think that chance, which brings so many people together, will bring our friends to us as well.

One can live as reclusive a life as one will, but before one turns around one has become a debtor or a creditor.

If we meet someone who owes us thanks, we immediately think of it. How often it may be that we meet someone to whom we owe thanks and do not give thought to it!

It is natural to communicate; cultivation is the ability to receive the communication in the sense in which it was given.

No one would say much in company if we only knew how often we misunderstand others.

In repeating what others have said, we change it for the sole reason, presumably, that we have not understood it.

Anyone who gives a long speech in public without flattering the audience is ill received.

Every word that is uttered provokes its opposite.

Both contradiction and flattery make for poor conversation.

The nicest parties are those where an amiable respect prevails amongst all present.

People reveal their character by nothing more clearly than by what they find laughable.

The laughable results when we see something that, in a harmless way, goes against custom.

Sensual people often laugh when there is nothing to laugh about. Whatever excites them, their inner delight comes through.

Sensible people find practically everything laughable, rational people practically nothing.

People took it ill of an older man that he was courting a young woman. "It is the only way to rejuvenate oneself," he replied, "and that is something everyone wants to do."

We are patient about letting ourselves be reproached, punished or made to suffer for our faults; but we become impatient when we are required to give them up.

Certain faults are essential to a particular individual's existence. We would be upset if old friends gave up certain habits.

We say, "He will die soon," when people do something contrary to their nature.

What faults may we be permitted to keep, or even to cultivate? Those which flatter others more than hurt them.

Passions are faults or virtues intensified.

Our passions are veritable phoenixes. At the very moment when the old one is burning down, a new one is already rising up from the ashes.

Great passions are like incurable diseases. What could heal them is what makes them really dangerous.

Passion is transfigured and made milder when it is confessed. The golden mean is perhaps nowhere more desirable than in what we tell or withhold from those we love.

Chapter Five

Thus Luciane constantly whipped up a frenzy before her in a sociable whirlwind. Her court increased daily, in part because her activity excited and attracted many, in part because she knew how to gain the friendship of others by means of little favors and attentions. She was extremely generous; for since the affection of her aunt and her fiancé had led them to give her so many beautiful and expensive things at once, she appeared not to own anything of her own and not to know the value of the objects she had accumulated. Thus she did not hestitate for a moment to take off a precious shawl and place it around the shoulders of a woman who seemed to be too poorly dressed in comparison to the others, and she did so in such a cunning, teasing fashion that no one could reject the gift. One of her followers always had a purse and was under instructions to enquire about the oldest and sickest in the places they visited in order to relieve their condition at least temporarily. This gave her an excellent reputation in the whole region, although it was sometimes a nuisance, since it attracted a far too tiresome number of needy sufferers.

Nothing enhanced her reputation so much, however, as her persistent and ostentatiously kind treatment of an unfortunate young man who, though otherwise handsome and well-formed, avoided appearing in society because he had lost his right hand, honorably to be sure, in battle. This mutilation so depressed him and he was so distressed at having to tell every new acquaintance about his injury that he preferred to hide himself away, spending his time on studies and reading, and wishing once and for all to have nothing to do with society.

The young man's way of life was no secret to her. She insisted he join her, first at small parties, then at larger ones, then at the very largest. She was more charming to him than to anyone else; in particular she knew how to make his loss into an advantage by insisting on helping and busily trying to be a substitute hand for him. At table he had to sit beside her; she cut up his meal for him so that he only had to use his fork. If he had to give up his place near her for older or nobler guests, she extended her attention the length of the whole table, and the servants had to hasten and make up for the attentions lost by distance. Finally she encouraged him to write with his left hand; he had to address all his attempts to her, and so, far or near, she was continually in touch with him. The young man did not know what had happened to him, and indeed he began a new life from this moment on.

One might perhaps think that such behavior would meet with her fiancé's disapproval; on the contrary. He gave her great credit for these efforts and was all the more at ease about it in that he knew her almost exaggerated manner of turning aside everything in the slightest way compromising. She wanted to have her way with everyone, and they all ran the risk of being pushed, pulled or otherwise teased; but no one dared take the liberty of treating her that way, no one could encroach on her at will, no one could in the slightest way respond in kind to the liberties she took; and so she kept others most strictly within the bounds of propriety while constantly overstepping them herself.

Altogether one might have thought it a principle of hers to expose herself equally to praise and blame, affection or dislike. For though in many ways she tried to win people's friendship, she usually spoilt it again through her spiteful tongue which spared nobody. Thus no visit was made in the neighborhood, she and her company were nowhere received in fine houses and residences without her showing in the most open way, on her return, that she was inclined to see only what was laughable in all human relationships. In one place there were three brothers who had been overtaken by age while they were politely letting each other have the first chance at marriage; in another there was a small, young wife with a huge, old husband; in yet another, by contrast, a lively little man with a clumsy giantess. In one house you stumbled over a child at every move; another household, even with crowds of guests present, did not seem complete to her, since there were no children. Old married couples with no legal heirs should see to it that they were soon buried, so that there would be laughter in the house again. Young couples should travel, since keeping house was not right for them. And she treated objects—buildings, furniture and tableware— the same way as she treated people. Wall decorations, in particular, incited her to mocking remarks. From the oldest hangings to the newest wallpaper, from the most venerable family portraits to the most frivolous new engravings, all were the butt of her criticism, all were torn to shreds, as it were, by her scornful comments, so that it was amazing anything still existed for five miles around.

There was perhaps no actual malice in her critical manner; she was, no doubt, usually incited to it by mischievous egotism; but a genuine bitterness had crept into her relationship with Ottilie. She looked with scorn upon the dear child's steady, quiet industry, which everyone else noticed with praise; and when the talk turned to Ottilie's interest in the gardens and glass houses, she laughed at it, expressing—in complete disregard of the deep winter all about—her puzzlement that neither blossoms nor fruits were to be seen. Then, too, she began to bring in so much greenery, twigs and anything that happened to be in bud, to lavish daily upon the decoration of the rooms and the table, that Ottilie and the gardener were distressed in no small measure to see their hopes destroyed for next year and perhaps for some time to come.

She was equally unwilling to leave Ottilie to the peaceful household routine in which she moved so comfortably. Ottilie was to go along on the outings and sleigh rides, she was to attend the balls that took place in the neighborhood; she was not to be put off by snow or cold or violent evening storms, since after all, others did not die from them. The delicate child suffered considerably, but Luciane did not gain anything by this; for although Ottilie went very simply attired, she was, or at least seemed to the men, the most beautiful. A gentle power attracted all the men to her, whether she was in the first or the last place in the great halls; indeed, Luciane's fiancé himself often talked with her, all the more since he desired her advice and help in a matter that was troubling him.

He had come to know the architect well, had spoken a great deal about historical matters with him in connection with his collection of art works, and had come to value his talent in other things too, especially after seeing the chapel. The baron was young and rich; he was a collector and was interested in building; his enthusiasms were keen, his knowledge limited; and he believed that he had found in the architect the man with whose help he could achieve more than one of his aims. He had spoken with Luciane about his plan; she praised him for it and was very pleased with the suggestion, but perhaps more because she wished to separate the young man from Ottilie—for she thought she could observe a kind of affection on his part—than because she intended to use his skills for her projects. For even though he had played an active part in her improvisations and had offered various services on one occasion or another, she thought that she herself could manage things better; and since her ideas were in the main commonplace, the talent of a skilled valet would serve as well as that of the most superior artist. Her imagination could not rise above a sacrificial altar or a wreath, whether on a plaster head or a live one, whenever she wished to pay a festive compliment on birthdays or anniversaries.

Ottilie was able to inform Luciane's fiancé fully about the architect's position in the household. She knew that Charlotte had been looking for a post for him, for if all these guests had not arrived, the young man would have departed as soon as the chapel had been completed, since all construction had to stop during the winter; and for this reason it was very desirable that the talented artist be employed and supported by another patron.

Ottilie's personal relationship to the architect was quite pure and innocent. His personable, industrious presence had pleased and delighted her like that of an older brother. Her feelings for him remained on the quiet passionless level of blood relationship; for there was no more room in her heart; it was filled to overflowing with love for Edward, and only God, who is present in all things, could possess her heart with him.

But the more the winter advanced, the wilder the weather became and the more unpassable the roads, the more tempting it was to spend the shortening days in such good company. After brief ebbs the crowd again flooded the house at various times. Officers from rather distant garrisons joined them, the cultivated ones much to their own advantage, the coarser ones to the annoyance of the group. There was also no lack of civilians, and one day the count and baroness drove up together quite unexpectedly.

Their presence provided what had been missing to form a veritable court. The men of rank and propriety surrounded the count, and the ladies paid homage to the baroness. The general surprise at seeing them both happily together was soon dispelled by the news that the count's wife had died, and a new wedding would take place as soon as was proper. Ottilie remembered their first visit and the discussion of marriage and divorce, uniting and separating, hope, expectation, resignation and renunciation. The very couple who had then had no prospects at all was now before her, so close to their heart's desire, and her bosom heaved with an involuntary sigh.

Scarcely had Luciane heard that the count was a music-lover than she contrived to arrange a concert; she wanted them to hear her sing and accompany herself on the guitar. She played the instrument quite well and had a pleasant voice; but as for the words, they were as unintelligible as when any German beauty sings to the guitar. Yet everyone assured her that she had sung with great expression, and she could be satisfied with the loud applause. But now a curious mishap occurred. Present at the party was a poet whose favor she especially wished to win, being eager to have some songs of his dedicated to her, and so on this evening it was mainly songs of his that she presented. Like everyone else, he was perfectly polite to her, but she had expected more. She pressed him several times, but got no response, until finally out of impatience she sent one of her entourage to him to sound him out and see if he had not been delighted to hear his excellent poems so excellently performed. "My poems?" he replied in astonishment. "I beg your pardon, sir," he added, "but I heard nothing but vowels and not even all of those. Still, I owe it to her to show my thanks for such a charming thought." Luciane's envoy was silent, and kept what he had heard to himself. The poet tried to get out of the affair with a few fine-sounding compliments. Luciane did not conceal her desire to have something composed especially for her. If it had not been too impolite, he could have presented her with the alphabet, so she could dream up her own eulogy to some existing melody. But she was not to be released from the affair without insult. Shortly afterwards she discovered that on that very

evening he had written a charming little poem, expressing some devo-
tion, set to one of Ottilie's favorite melodies.

Like other people of her kind, who always confuse what becomes
them and what does not, Luciane now decided to try her luck at recita-
tion. Her memory was good, but her delivery, truth to tell, was lifeless,
emphatic but not passionate. She recited ballads, stories and everything
else usually heard at such performances. She had taken on the unfortu-
nate habit of accompanying her recitations with gestures, which had the
disagreeable effect of confusing, rather than uniting, pieces that were
really epic or lyrical with the dramatic.

The count, a perceptive man who soon had the measure of the com-
pany, its interests, passions and amusements, encouraged Luciane—
fortunately or unfortunately—to take up a new kind of performance
which suited her personality very nicely. "There are so many handsome
people here," he said, "who are certainly not incapable of imitating
artistic gestures and poses. Have you never attempted to present actual
well-known paintings? Such imitations, though they require laborious
preparation, produce an unbelievably charming effect."

Luciane quickly realized that she would be in her element. Her fine
build and full figure, her regular yet impressive face, her light-brown
braids, her slender neck, all was as if calculated for a portrait; and if she
had only known that she looked better when she stood still than when
she was in motion (for sometimes she accidentally made an oddly grace-
less movement), she would have devoted herself with increased zeal to
this natural picture-making.

They searched out copper engravings after famous paintings, select-
ing first van Dyck's "Belisarius." A tall, well-built man of a certain age
was to represent the seated blind general, and the architect the soldier
standing in front of him and looking on with melancholy sympathy—a
figure he actually did resemble somewhat. Luciane had, with a modesty
of sorts, chosen the young woman in the background counting out
generous alms from her purse into her open hand, while an old lady
appears to take her to task and suggest that she is giving too much.
Another woman actually giving alms was not forgotten.

They went to great trouble over this and other pictures. The count
gave the architect some ideas about how they could be presented, and
the architect immediately set up a stage and took care of the lighting.
They were deeply involved in preparations when they realized that this
sort of undertaking demands considerable expense and that many re-
quirements could not be fulfilled in the country in the middle of winter.
So to prevent things from coming to a standstill Luciane had practically
her entire wardrobe cut up for the various costumes indicated, whimsi-
cally enough, by the artists.

The evening arrived, and the presentation took place before a large audience and to general acclaim. An impressive musical overture heightened expectations. The Belisarius picture was the first to be shown. The characters were so well cast, the colors so well chosen, the lighting so artistic that one seemed indeed to be in another world, except that the presence of real figures instead of painted ones created a kind of unsettling sensation.

The curtain fell and opened again several times by general request. A musical interlude entertained the company, which was to be surprised by a picture of a nobler sort. It was the well-known painting by Poussin: Ahasuerus and Esther. This time Luciane had given herself a better role. As the fainting queen she revealed all her charms and had, most cleverly, selected only attractive, well-proportioned young women to represent the girls surrounding and supporting her: but none of them could vie with her in the slightest. Ottilie did not take part in this or in the other pictures. To represent the Zeus-like king on his golden throne they had chosen the most robust and handsome man of the group, with the result that the picture achieved an incomparable perfection.

For the third picture they had chosen Terburg's "Paternal Admonition." Who is not familiar with Wille's splendid engraving of this painting! A noble, knightly father sits with crossed feet, apparently admonishing his daughter. We see her only from behind, a splendid figure in a richly draped white satin dress, but her whole bearing seems to suggest that she is pulling herself together. That the father's scolding is not angry or belittling is apparent from his expression and gestures; and as for the mother, she appears to conceal some slight embarrassment as she looks into a glass of wine she is about to drink.

In this picture Luciane was to appear in her greatest glory. Her braids, the shape of her head and neck were incredibly beautiful, and her waist, of which little could be seen in today's mock classical dress, revealed itself to great advantage in the older costume as extremely delicate, light and slender; and the architect had taken care to lay the folds of the white satin in the most cunningly natural way, so that without question, the tableau vivant, to everyone's delight, far surpassed the original. There was no end of curtain calls, and the very natural desire to see the front of such a beautiful creature, visible only from the back, became so strong that one impatient clown called out, using the words you sometimes put at the end of a page, "Tournez s'il vous plaît"—and everyone clapped assent. But the actors were too well aware where their advantage lay, and understood the sense of the painting too well to yield to this general request. The daughter, seemingly ashamed, stood still and did not let the audience see the expression on her face; the father remained in his reproving posture, and the mother did not take her nose and eyes from the transparent glass in which, though she appeared to drink, the level of the wine never sank.—What more shall we say of the

small pieces that followed, for which Dutch inn and market scenes had
been selected!

The count and baroness departed, promising to return in the first
happy weeks of their approaching marriage, and Charlotte now hoped,
after two difficult months, that she could get rid of the other guests too.
She was sure her daughter would be happy once the first whirl of young
bridehood had settled; for the bridegroom thought himself the luckiest
man on earth. With his great fortune and steady character, he appeared
curiously flattered to possess a woman admired by all. He had a strange
way of relating everything to her, and through her to himself, so that he
felt distressed if a new arrival did not turn his whole attention to her
right away but sought to establish a closer friendship with himself with-
out particularly heeding her—as older people, especially, often did in
view of his good qualities. The problem of the architect was soon solved.
In the New Year, he was to follow the bridegroom and spend the carniv-
al season in town with him; and Luciane looked forward to the greatest
pleasure from a repeat performance of the paintings that had been so
beautifully presented, and from a hundred other things, the more so in
that her aunt and fiancé seemed to think any expense modest if it were
necessary for her amusement.

Now they were to go their separate ways, but this could not be done in
any ordinary way. They were commenting jokingly that Charlotte's win-
ter supplies would soon be used up, when the gentleman who had por-
trayed Belisarius and who was, to be sure, rich enough, cried out impul-
sively, captivated by Luciane's charms which he had long admired:
"Then let us go Dutch! Come and use up my supplies, and then we'll
continue in turn." No sooner said than done: Luciane took up the idea.
The next day they were all packed and the crowd invaded another
estate. There they had plenty of space, but fewer comforts and ameni-
ties. This gave rise to many improprieties, which highly delighted
Luciane. Their life grew wilder and wilder. There were hunts in the
deepest snow and every other kind of discomfort imaginable. Neither
men nor women could absent themselves, and so they went hunting and
riding, sleighing and shouting from one estate to another, until they
finally approached the capital; and there the tales and stories of what
amusements were taking place at court and in town gave their imagina-
tion a new turning, and Luciane and her entire train, her aunt having
gone on ahead, were drawn irresistibly into another circle of existence.

FROM OTTILIE'S DIARY

We take everyone in the world as they present themselves; but they
have to present themselves as something. It is easier to put up with
difficult people than insignificant ones.

One can force anything upon society except that which has internal consistency.

We do not get to know people when they come to us; we must go to them to find out what they are like.

I think it is fairly natural to criticize visitors, and to judge them as soon as they have left in terms that are not the kindest, for we have a right, so to speak, to measure them by our standards. Even fair and sensible people hardly restrain themselves from sharp criticism on such occasions.

On the other hand, once we have visited others and seen their surroundings, their habits and the way they conform to or influence their necessary and unavoidable circumstances, then we would have to be stupid or malicious to find laughable what should seem to us in many respects admirable.

What we call good manners has the purpose of achieving what would otherwise only be attained by force, or not even by that.

Knowing how to behave with women is the very basis of good manners.

How can human nature and human individuality be reconciled with well-bred behavior?

Individuality should be brought out by good breeding. We all like to do something of significance as long as it causes us no trouble.

An educated soldier enjoys the greatest advantages in life as in society in general.

Crude army folk never act out of character, but because their strength generally conceals good humor one can get along with them if need be.

No one is more irritating than an ill-bred civilian. One can expect him to show refinement, since he has nothing to do with anything crude.

When we live with people who have a highly developed sense of what is proper, we get anxious on their behalf when someone does something inappropriate. This is why I always feel for Charlotte when someone tilts their chair, which is something she absolutely cannot stand.

No one would come into a private room with glasses on if they knew that we women right away lose our interest in looking at them or conversing with them.

Intimacy is always laughable when it takes the place of respect. No one would take off his hat when he had hardly finished lifting it in greeting if he knew how absurd it looks.

There is practically no external mark of politeness that does not have an underlying moral basis. Proper upbringing would ideally consist in transmitting the convention and the reason for it at one and the same time.

Behavior is a mirror in which everyone shows his own face.

There is a politeness of the heart; it is akin to love. The most natural kind of external politeness is derived from it.

Voluntary dependency is the most beautiful condition, and how could it be possible without love?

We are never further from our desires than when we imagine we have already attained them.

No one is more enslaved than he who thinks he is free when he is not.

No one has the right to call himself free unless he is aware that he is at that very moment conditioned. If he dares to call himself conditioned then he feels himself to be free.

There is no other remedy to another person's superior virtues than to love him.

There is something terrible about a fine man who lets himself be taken advantage of by fools.

No man, they say, is a hero to his valet. That is because a hero can only be recognized by a hero. But the valet is no doubt able to recognize the merits of his own kind.

There is no greater consolation for mediocrity than that genius is not immortal.

Great men are always connected to their own century by some weakness.

One tends to think people are more dangerous than they are.

Fools and wise people are equally harmless. But the half-foolish and the half-wise are the most dangerous.

One cannot escape from the world with greater certainty than through art, and one cannot relate to it with greater certainty than through art.

Even at the moment of greatest happiness or greatest misery we have need of the artist.

Art concerns itself with what is difficult and good.

To treat difficult things lightly gives us an idea of the impossible.

The closer one comes to one's goal the more the difficulties increase.

To sow is easier than to reap.

Chapter Six

One compensation for the disturbance this visit caused Charlotte was that she came to understand her daughter better, and here her knowledge of the world served her well. It was not the first time that she had come across such an unusual personality, though she had never before seen it in such an extreme form. But experience taught her that people like this can mature and become very charming and likable, as their self-centeredness is blunted and their obsessive activity harnessed under the influence of family and various life experiences. As a mother Charlotte was for this reason more ready to tolerate behavior others might find disagreeable and to hope for improvement more than a parent should, where others only wanted to enjoy Luciane's company or at least not to be bothered by it.

But Charlotte was to suffer in a most unexpected way after her daughter's departure, for it was not her reprehensible behavior, but what could have been thought praiseworthy that had left a bad impression. Luciane seemed to have vowed not only to be happy with those who are happy and sad with those who are sad, but on occasion also, as if to exercise her contrariness to the full, to make the happy annoyed and the sad happy. Whenever she visited a household, she always enquired about the weak and sick who could not appear in company. She visited them in their rooms, acted the doctor, and urged them to take strong medicines from the traveling pharmacy she always had with her. As can be imagined, such treatments succeeded or failed as chance would have it.

In this type of benevolence she was quite cruel; she could not be talked out of it, as she was firmly convinced that her actions were beyond reproach. But one experiment turned out a moral failure, and it was this one that caused Charlotte distress, both because of its consequences and because it was the subject of everyone's gossip. She did not hear about it until Luciane had left; Ottilie, who had been a party to it, was obliged to give her a detailed account.

One of the daughters of a respected family had been so unfortunate as to have caused the death of a younger sibling, and she was unable to recover or pull herself together again. She kept to her room and could not bear to see her family except one at a time, for she was quick to suspect that when several of them got together they talked about her and the state she was in. To each of them individually she could speak reasonably and converse for hours.

Luciane heard of this, and secretly decided to visit the house and work a miracle by bringing the young woman back into society. This time she was more cautious than usual, managed to see the disturbed girl alone and, as far as the others could make out, to gain her confidence through music. But in the end she made a mistake: one evening, precisely so as not to attract everyone's attention, she suddenly introduced the lovely, pale creature, thinking her sufficiently well prepared, to a bright, glittering party; and perhaps she might even have been successful, had not the company behaved foolishly in its anxious curiosity, gathering around the sick girl, then turning away, confusing and upsetting her by putting their heads together and whispering. Her delicate nerves could not take it. She ran away shrieking terribly, as if a monster had attacked her. Distressed, the party dispersed in all directions, and Ottilie helped the others take the girl, who had fainted dead away, back to her room.

In the meanwhile Luciane had thoroughly scolded the group, after her fashion, without thinking at all that she alone was to blame. She did not allow this failure, and various others, to restrain her enthusiasm for this kind of undertaking.

The sick girl's condition had become worse since then, and indeed the problem increased so much that her parents could not keep the poor creature at home, but had to place her in a public institution. Charlotte had no recourse other than to exercise particular tact, and thus assuage to some degree the pain her daughter had caused the family. The affair had made a deep impression on Ottilie; she pitied the poor girl all the more in that she was convinced, as she could not help admitting to Charlotte, that she could have been restored to health if properly treated.

In this way, since people usually talk more about unpleasant events than pleasant ones, they came to speak of a minor misunderstanding that had confused Ottilie: the evening when the architect had refused to show his collection, even though she had begged him so politely. This refusal of his had always remained on her mind, and she did not herself know why. Her feelings were quite justified; for what a girl like Ottilie demands should not be refused by a young man like the architect. In reply to her gentle reproaches, however, he gave a fairly convincing explanation.

"If only you knew," he said, "how roughly even educated people treat the most precious works of art, you would forgive me for not wishing to bring mine out at a big party. No one knows to pick up a medallion by the edge; they run their fingers over the most beautiful impressions and the cleanest backgrounds, they rub the most valuable pieces between thumb and forefinger, as if this were the way to examine objects of art. Without thinking that one should take hold of a large sheet with both hands, they reach with one hand for an invaluable engraving, an irreplaceable drawing, just as an impudent politician grabs a newspaper and lets one know in advance his opinion of world events by crushing it. No one realizes that if twenty people handle a work of art that way one after another, the twenty-first won't have much left to see."

"Have I ever given you cause to worry about that?" Ottilie asked. "Have I ever damaged anything in your collection without meaning to?"

"Never," replied the architect, "never! That couldn't happen with you; you instinctively do the proper thing."

"In any event," Ottilie went on, "it would not be a bad idea if future books of etiquette were to include, after the chapters about how to behave at meals, a long and detailed chapter about how to behave in museums and archives."

"Curators and collectors would certainly be happier about showing their pieces," the architect responded.

Ottilie had long since forgiven him, but since he seemed to take her reproach to heart and assured her again and again that he was glad to show his collection and glad to work for his friends, she realized that she had hurt a sensitive soul, and she felt she owed him something. Thus she could not well refuse him a request he made right after this, even though her instinctive reaction was that she could not see how to grant him his wishes.

The problem was this. He had been extremely distressed that Luciane's jealousy had excluded Ottilie from the living pictures; he had also regretted that Charlotte, who had not been feeling well, had only been present intermittently at this more dramatic part of the social entertainment. Now he did not want to leave without having shown his gratitude by giving a presentation even more beautiful than the previous ones in honor of one of his friends and for the entertainment of the others. Perhaps, unbeknown to himself, there was another secret motive here: it was hard, indeed it seemed to him impossible to leave this house and family, to go from Ottilie's sight which had nourished his entire existence for the last little while with its calm, steady, friendly gaze.

Christmas was approaching, and it suddenly occurred to him that the living pictures had actually originated in what was known as the creche—those pious representations made in this holy season of the divine mother and her child in their apparent lowliness, honored first by shepherds, then by kings.

In his mind's eye he had conjured up in complete detail the possibility of such a presentation. A fair and beautiful babe had been found; there was no lack of shepherds and shepherdesses; but without Ottilie there was no way of carrying out the project. The young man had elevated her, in his mind, to the mother of God, and if she were to reject his proposal there was no question in his eyes that the project must be dropped. Ottilie, half embarrassed at his suggestion, referred his request to Charlotte. The latter was glad to give her permission, and by friendly persuasion she helped Ottilie to overcome her reservations about presuming to portray that holy figure. The architect worked night and day so that all would be ready by Christmas eve.

He literally did work night and day. He had few other needs in any event, and Ottilie's presence was food and drink to him; working for her he seemed to need no sleep, busying himself on her account he seemed to need no nourishment. On the holy evening everything was ready and prepared. He had managed to get some fine wind instruments together to introduce the presentation and create the appropriate atmosphere. When the curtain went up, Charlotte was genuinely suprised. The scene before her had been represented so often that a new impression could hardly be expected. But the reality which had here been turned into a picture had its own charms and delights. The whole room was dark rather than partially lit, and yet no detail of the scene was unclear. By a clever lighting device, the artist had realized the exquisite notion of having all light radiate from the infant; the figures in the foreground, shaded and illuminated only by side-lights, served to conceal the mechanism. Happy girls and boys stood round, their fresh faces clearly lit from below. There were angels there, too, their own radiance dimmed by the divine light, their ethereal bodies made duller and more opaque by comparison with the divine body in human form.

Fortunately the baby had fallen asleep in the most charming pose, and nothing disturbed the picture of the mother raising a shawl with infinite grace to reveal the hidden treasure beneath. At this moment the image seemed caught and transfixed. Physically blinded, mentally stunned, the villagers around seemed to have just turned their dazzled eyes away and, in their curiosity and delight, to be taking another look, more in amazement and pleasure than in admiration and veneration, although these expressions had not been forgotten, but were reserved for several older figures.

Ottilie's form, posture and expression, however, surpassed anything an artist has ever depicted. A discriminating connoisseur, seeing this presentation, would have been struck with anxiety that something might move; he would have worried whether he would ever have pleasure in anything again. But alas, there was no one there who could have appreciated the full effect. Only the architect, dressed as a tall, slender shepherd observing the scene from the side over the heads of those who were kneeling, had the greatest pleasure in it, despite his imperfect vantage point. And who can describe the expression of the newly created queen of heaven? The purest humility, the most charming air of modesty in the face of a great and undeserved honor, an incredible, unmeasurable bliss was written on her face, expressing both her own inner feelings and her conception of the role she was playing.

Charlotte found the lovely picture delightful, but it was mainly the baby that moved her. Her eyes filled with tears, and she was vividly aware of the fact that she would soon have a similar little creature on her own lap.

The curtain had fallen, partly to give the actors a rest, partly to make a scene-change. The artist had planned to transform the first scene of night and humble circumstances into a scene of daylight glory, and had thus prepared an unusually bright illumination from all sides that was to be lit up during the intermission.

Ottilie's greatest consolation at this quasi-theatrical performance was that apart from Charlotte and a few other members of the household no one else could see this pious mummery. Thus she was quite disturbed when she heard during the intermission that a stranger had arrived and been greeted by Charlotte in the drawing room. Who it was she could not find out. She submitted to her role so as not to make a disturbance. Lamps and candles were lit, and she was surrounded by infinite brightness. The curtain went up on a surprising sight for the spectators: the whole scene was flooded with light, and instead of the shadow, which had disappeared entirely, only the colors could be seen, and these had been cleverly chosen to create a wonderfully muted effect. Looking out from under her long eyelashes, Ottilie noticed a man sitting next to Charlotte. She did not recognize him, but she thought she could hear the voice of the teacher from her boarding school. A strange sensation took hold of her. How much had happened since she had last heard the voice of her devoted teacher! Like a bolt of lightning her joys and sorrows flashed in sequence before her mind's eye. 'Can you dare confess all this to him?' she wondered. 'And how unworthy you are to appear before him in this sacred role. How strange it must be for him to see you in masquerade, when he has only ever seen you as your ordinary self.' Thoughts and feelings clashed within her with incredible rapidity. Her heart was paralyzed, her eyes filled with tears as she forced herself to remain in her fixed pose; and how relieved she was when the baby began to stir and the artist saw himself constrained to signal for the curtain to fall!

While the embarrassment of not being able to rush out and welcome a valued friend had been added to Ottilie's other emotions in the last few moments, she now felt even more embarrassed. Should she go to meet him decked out in this unwonted array? Should she change? She did not stop to decide, but changed her clothes, trying all the while to collect and calm herself. She did not feel at ease until she could greet the new arrival in her familiar dress.

Chapter Seven

Seeing that he had every good wish for his patrons' well-being, the architect was glad to know, now that he had to take his leave at last, that they were in the good company of the schoolmaster they so esteemed. But when he thought about the kindness they had shown him, he found it somewhat painful to find himself so rapidly and, as it may have seemed in his modesty, so completely replaced. He had hesitated a while yet, but now he was forced to go; for he did not wish to see with his own eyes what he could not prevent when he was absent.

To cast a ray of sunshine on these rather sad feelings, the ladies gave him a farewell gift of a vest; with a secret feeling of envy towards the lucky future recipient, he had seen them both putting hours of knitting into it. Such a gift is the nicest one a loving admirer can receive; for when he thinks about the tireless work of the pretty fingers that made it, he cannot help flattering himself with the thought that in the course of all that diligence the heart cannot have been quite unfeeling.

Now the women had a new guest to look after. They liked him and hoped to make him feel at home with them. Women have their own unchanging inner goals, from which nothing on earth can make them stray; but in external, social affairs they are more than willing to be led by the man with whom they are concerned at any given moment; and so, by refusal and acceptance, insistence and compliance, they are actually in charge of things and in the world of manners no man can escape their rule.

In accordance with his own desires and inclination, the architect had proved and practiced his talents to the ladies' pleasure and at their service, and their occupations and distractions had been organized around these intentions. By contrast, the presence of the schoolmaster very soon introduced a different way of life. His great talent was his ability to express himself well and discourse upon human situations, especially about the education of the young. This made for a perceptible contrast to their former way of life, the more so in that the schoolmaster did not entirely approve of the work that had preoccupied them exclusively all this time.

He said not a word about the tableau vivant that had met him on his arrival. But when they proudly showed him the church, the chapel and their surroundings, he could not refrain from expressing his opinions and reactions. "For my own part," he said, "I do not care for this juxtaposition, this commingling of the sacred and the sensual; I do not care for certain rooms to be dedicated, decorated and decked out for the sole purpose of exciting and nourishing a sense of piety. No place, even the most common, should disturb the awareness of the divine which is with us everywhere and can make any spot a temple. I like to see divine services held in the same room where we dine, hold parties, and enjoy games and dancing. The highest, the supreme attributes of man have no corporeal form, and we should avoid bodying them forth except in noble deeds."

Charlotte, who already knew his opinions in their general outline and was to find out even more about them, soon found an activity that was just right for him. She had her gardeners' boys, whom the architect had rounded up just before his departure, march up and down in the large hall, looking very fine in their bright, clean uniforms, with their coordinated movements and natural liveliness. The schoolmaster inspected them after his fashion and, using various questioning techniques, soon revealed the children's characters and abilities. Within less than an hour he had inconspicuously done some real teaching and helped them make real progress.

"How do you do it?" Charlotte asked when the boys had gone away again. "I listened very closely; what came out was perfectly well known, and yet I don't know how I could manage to get them to express themselves so logically in such a short time with so much conversational give and take."

"Perhaps the tricks of one's trade should be kept secret," said the schoolmaster. "But I cannot conceal from you the very simple principle which makes it possible to achieve all this and more. Take a subject, a theme, a concept—whatever you wish to call it; keep a good grip on it; be clear about it in every detail; and then it will be easy for you, in conversation with a group of children, to see what parts they have already learned, where their interests still need to be awakened and where they are still in need of instruction. The answers to your questions may be inappropriate, they may go off in tangents as much as you like, but as long as your counter-questions bring their attention back to the subject, as long as you do not let yourself be diverted from your own view of it, the children are in the last analysis obliged to think, see and understand just exactly what the teacher desires to teach them. The teacher's greatest mistake is to let his pupils lead him off into byways, to be unable to keep their attention on the point at issue. Try it next time, and you will be greatly amused by the method."

"How charming," said Charlotte. "Good teaching, then, is just the opposite of good living. In social conversation it is not proper to dwell on one topic, but the main principle in teaching is to work against all distractions."

"Variation without distraction would be the finest motto for life and the classroom, if only that desirable balance were so easy to maintain!" said the schoolmaster, who was about to continue, when Charlotte asked him to look at the boys again, whose cheerful procession was just moving across the courtyard. He expressed his pleasure at the fact that the children were encouraged to dress uniformly. "Men should wear a uniform from childhood," he said, "because they have to get used to acting in concert, losing themselves amongst their peers, obeying as a group and working for society as a whole. In addition, any kind of uniform encourages a military attitude and brisk, upright deportment, and in any event all boys are born soldiers; you just have to look at their games of battle and contest, storming and attacking."

"By the same token you will not reprimand me," added Ottilie, "for not dressing the girls in the same fashion. When I introduce them to you, I hope to delight you with a colorful mixture."

"I fully approve," replied the schoolmaster. "Women should in principle be dressed in different colors, each after her own fashion, so that she can learn what suits her and is appropriate for her. A more important reason, too, is that women are destined to be alone and act alone their whole lives long."

"That seems very paradoxical to me," replied Charlotte. "After all, we are almost never by ourselves."

"Oh yes indeed!" said the schoolmaster, "you are alone with respect to other women. Whether a woman be regarded as a lover, a bride, a wife and mother, she is always isolated, always alone—and intentionally so. This is the case with even the vainest woman. Each woman by nature excludes any other; for we demand of each individually what the whole sex is obliged to accomplish. This is not the case with men. One man requires another; he would invent another if one did not exist; a woman could live for an eternity without thinking of producing another of her kind."

"If true things are said in strange ways," replied Charlotte, "in the end strange things appear true. Let us draw the best conclusions from what you have just said and yet, as women, cleave to women and work together with them, so that men will not have too great an advantage over us. Indeed, you will have to put up with a slight malicious pleasure, which we will feel more keenly now any time gentlemen do not get on with each other especially well."

Soon afterwards the sensible man examined with great care the way in which Ottilie treated her little pupils, and expressed his distinct approval of it. "You are quite right," he said, "to educate your subordinates only for their most immediate usefulness. Cleanliness makes the children look upon themselves with pleasure, and the battle is won if they are encouraged to do what they have to happily and with self-confidence."

To his great satisfaction he saw that nothing had been done superficially and for the sake of appearance, but rather with inner conviction and in the service of necessity. "How few words would suffice," he exclaimed, "to formulate the whole business of teaching, if only people had ears to hear!"

"Do you want to try me?" Ottilie asked amiably.

"Gladly," he replied; "but you must not give away the secret. Boys should be educated to be servants and girls to be mothers, then everything will work out very suitably."

"Mothers . . .," responded Ottilie. "Women might be willing to accept that, since, even if they don't become mothers, they have to accommodate themselves to being maids; but our young men would think themselves too good to be servants, since you can easily tell that they each think themselves more capable of giving the orders."

"That's why we should not tell them," said the schoolmaster. "We work our way into life by flattery, but life does not flatter us. How many people freely allow what in the end they have to do anyway? But let us drop these irrelevant remarks!

"I think you are very fortunate that you can apply the right principles to your pupils. When your youngest girls carry dolls around and mend a few old rags for them, when older sisters care for younger ones and the whole household helps itself, then the step into life is not a large one. Girls prepared in this way find in their husbands what they left behind with their parents.

"But amongst the educated classes the task is very complex. We have to take higher, finer, more delicate relations—and most particularly social ones—into consideration. Thus we have to educate our pupils with a view to appearance; it is necessary, it is inevitable, and might be quite good if one did not overstep the proper bounds; for in educating young girls for society, we tend to go too far and lose sight of their inner needs. This is the task most teachers accomplish only in part, if they do not actually fail in it.

"I worry about many of the things we teach our pupils at boarding school, as experience shows me how little use it will be to them in their future lives. How much of it is promptly cast aside, to be sunk in oblivion, as soon as a woman finds herself a wife and mother!

"Seeing that I have devoted myself to this profession, however, I cannot but have the pious wish that one day, with the aid of a faithful helpmeet, I might be able to inculcate in my pupils the things they need when they move into their own sphere of activity and independence; that I might be able to say to myself: in this respect their education is complete. Of course, our education actually continues one phase after another, if not by our own doing, then by virtue of circumstances, almost every year of our lives."

How true this was, Ottilie thought! What had she not learned in the course of last year's unforeseen passion! What trials awaited her, if not in the immediate future, then very soon!

The young man had not unintentionally mentioned a helpmeet, a wife; and for all his modesty he could not refrain from suggesting his intentions in an indirect way—indeed, various recent events and experiences had encouraged him to take a few steps towards his goal in the course of this visit.

The headmistress of the school was already getting on in years; for some time now she had been casting about amongst her colleagues for someone she could take into partnership with her. In the end she had proposed that the schoolmaster, in whom she rightly placed great trust, continue to manage the school with her, enjoying in effect the privileges of ownership, and finally come into possession of the school as heir and sole owner after her death. The main condition seemed to be that he find a suitable wife. Secretly, he had his eye and heart on Ottilie; and what doubts he had about this were partly outweighed by certain favorable turns of event. Now that Luciane had left the school, Ottilie could more easily return; there had been some rumors of her relationship to

Edward, but as with other such affairs, the matter was made light of, and it might even provide a reason for Ottilie's return. But no decision would have been made, no step taken, had not unexpected visitors once again given their own particular impulse. Indeed, the appearance of important people in any circle cannot fail to have results.

The count and baroness, who were often called upon to give an opinion on various boarding schools, since almost everyone is in need of advice about the education of their children, had decided to take a look at this one, of which they had heard so many good things. Now that they were married, they could perform the inspection together. But the baroness had other intentions besides. In the course of her last visit with Charlotte she had discussed with her in detail the whole problem of Edward and Ottilie. She insisted again and again that Ottilie should be sent away. She tried to give Charlotte, who still feared Edward's threats, the courage to do so. They spoke of various ways out, and in connection with the school the teacher's affection had been mentioned, and the baroness was all the more determined to undertake her projected visit.

Upon her arrival she made the schoolmaster's acquaintance; while they were inspecting the institution, they spoke about Ottilie. Even the count was glad to talk about her now that he had got to know her better during his recent visit. She had approached him, indeed she was attracted to him because his knowledgeable conversation made her feel that she could learn things she had not known before. And just as she had forgotten the world in her relationship with Edward, so the count's presence seemed suddenly to make the world desirable. Every attraction is mutual. The count was fond of Ottilie, whom he liked to think of as a daughter. In this respect, too, she was once again an irritation to the baroness, even more than before. Who knows what plots the baroness might have laid against her in times of greater passion! Now it was enough to remove this threat to wives by marrying her off.

And so, in a quiet but effective way, she cunningly suggested to the schoolmaster that he should plan a short trip to the manor and take prompt steps towards achieving his plans and desires, of which he made no secret to the lady.

Thus, with the principal's complete approval, he set out on his journey, nourishing in his heart of hearts the greatest hopes. He knew that Ottilie was not ill-disposed towards him; and if there was a certain difference in class between them, the spirit of the time would be inclined to gloss this over. In addition, the baroness had given him to understand that Ottilie would always remain poor. It was said that being related to a rich family was of no help to anyone; for even if they had the greatest of fortunes, one would have scruples about depriving of a considerable sum those who seemed to have a greater right to it because they were more closely related. And it is certainly strange that people very seldom take advantage of the great privilege they have to dispose of their belongings as they wish after their death by giving them to those they love best; it seems that, out of respect for tradition, they favor only those who would come into the fortune even if they had made no will.

In the course of the journey his heart made him regard Ottilie as an equal. The kindly way he was received raised his hopes. To be sure, Ottilie was not quite so open with him as she had been before; but she was also more grown up, more cultivated and, if you will, in general more communicative than he had ever known her. The ladies drew him into their confidence about many things relating to his field. But when he tried to approach his goal, a certain inner reluctance held him back.

On one occasion, however, Charlotte gave him an opportunity, saying to him in Ottilie's presence: "Now you have examined fairly well everything that is going on under my care, what do you think of Ottilie? I'm sure you can speak in her presence."

In his quietly perceptive way, the schoolmaster showed how he found Ottilie changed in certain very favorable ways: her freer demeanor, her greater fluency of speech, her increased understanding of the world, revealed more in her deeds than in her words; but he still thought it could be very useful for her to return to boarding school for a while and acquire in logical order and for all time what the world teaches only bit by bit and more to our confusion than to our satisfaction—indeed sometimes too late. He did not want to go on at length about this; Ottilie herself would know best what a coherent program she had been torn away from.

Ottilie could not deny it; but she could not admit what she felt upon hearing these words, for she was scarcely able to interpret it herself. Nothing in the world seemed incoherent when she thought about the man she loved, and she could not conceive how anything could cohere without him.

Charlotte's response to his suggestion was friendly, but tactically astute. Both she and Ottilie, she said, had long hoped for her return to the school. At this particular time the presence of such a dear friend and helper was indispensable to her; but she would not stand in the way later on, should Ottilie still wish to go back there long enough to end what she had begun and finish the course of studies that had been interrupted.

The schoolmaster gladly accepted this offer. Ottilie could say nothing against it, even though she shuddered at the thought. Charlotte, on the other hand, hoped to gain time; when Edward returned to find himself a happy father everything, she was convinced, would be resolved and one way or another Ottilie, too, would be taken care of.

After a serious conversation that gives the participants much food for thought, a certain silence usually sets in that looks very much like general embarrassment. They walked up and down the room, the school-master leafed through several books and finally came to the folio volume that had been left behind after Luciane's stay. Seeing that it contained nothing but pictures of monkeys, he closed it right away. This incident may, however, have given rise to a conversation whose traces can be found in Ottilie's notebooks.

FROM OTTILIE'S DIARY

How can anyone bear to draw such accurate pictures of those horrid monkeys? We debase ourselves enough if we look at them merely as animals; but it is really malicious to succumb to the temptation of trying to see in them people one knows.

You have to be somewhat perverse to enjoy looking at caricatures and cartoons. I owe it to our dear teacher that I was not plagued with the study of natural history; I never did like worms and beetles.

Recently he confessed that he felt the same way. "We should know nothing of nature but the living things that most immediately surround us. We are genuinely connected with trees that blossom, put forth leaves and bear fruit, with every bush we pass by, every blade of grass we tread on; they are our true companions. The birds that flit hither and yon amongst our branches and sing in our greenery belong to us; they have spoken to us from our childhood, and we learn to understand their language. We should ask ourselves whether any strange creature that has been torn from its natural habitat does not strike us as somewhat fearful, an impression dulled only by our being used to it. One has to lead a noisy, colorful life in order to be able to put up with having monkeys, parrots, blackamoors about one."

Sometimes, when I was overcome by curiosity and desire for such exotic things, I envied the traveler who can see such wonders in their living, everyday context. But he becomes a different person. You cannot walk beneath palm trees with impunity, and attitudes are sure to change in a country where elephants and tigers are at home.

Only those naturalists are to be respected who are capable of present-ing and describing the strangest and most exotic things in their local environment, in their own element with all that surrounds them. How much I would like to hear Humboldt some time!

A display case of biological specimens can take on the aspect of an Egyptian tomb, with the various animal and plant gods standing around embalmed. It is doubtless fitting for a caste of priests to contemplate it in mysterious semi-darkness; but it should not be introduced into gener-al education, especially since things closer to us and worthier of our respect are thus pushed into the background.

A teacher who can excite the sensibility by a single good deed, a single good poem, does more than one who makes us learn the forms and names of any number of lower natural phenomena; for the sole result of this—which we know anyway—is that the human form is the one that most perfectly and uniquely bears the divine likeness.

Let every man have the freedom to concern himself with what appeals to him, gives him pleasure, seems useful to him; but the proper study of mankind is man.

Chapter Eight

There are few people who know to concern themselves with the recent past. Either the present holds us in its forceful grip, or we lose ourselves in the past and seek to recall and restore what is gone forever in whatever way we can. Even in rich and noble families that owe much to their forebears, people are usually more mindful of their grandfather than of their father.

Our schoolmaster was moved to thoughts such as these on one of those lovely days when the departing winter creates the illusion of spring, while he was out walking through the expansive old manor garden, admiring the avenues of tall linden trees and the formal beds that Edward's father had created. They had flourished wonderfully well, just as their creator would have wished, but now that they were ready to be seen and enjoyed, nobody spoke of them anymore; hardly anyone went there, and everyone's attention and energy had turned in another direction, towards the free, open spaces.

On his return he remarked on this to Charlotte, who was not ill-disposed to hear it. "As life draws us on," she replied, "we think we are acting of our own free will, choosing our activities and amusements, but really, if we look more closely, we are simply obliged to follow the pitch, the inclination of our time."

"Indeed," said the schoolmaster; "and who can resist the current of his age? Time moves on, and in it attitudes, opinions, prejudices and passions move on too. If the son's early years happen to fall in a time of transition, one can be sure he will have nothing in common with his father. If the father lived in a period where people were anxious to acquire property and secure, limit and define it, and to assure their pleasures by cutting themselves off from the world, then the son will be eager to extend himself, to communicate, expand, and open up what had been closed."

"Whole epochs," Charlotte replied, "are like that father and son. We can hardly imagine the time when each little town had to have its own walls and moat, each noble homestead was built in the middle of a marsh and even modest manor-houses were accessible only by draw-

bridge. Even larger towns are removing their walls, the moats of prince-
ly castles are being filled in, cities are just great spots of land, and when
we see all this on our travels, we might almost think that universal peace
had been established and we were on the brink of the golden age. No
one feels comfortable now in a garden that does not resemble the open
countryside; nothing may create the impression of artifice or constraint;
we wish to breathe quite freely and unrestrictedly. Do you imagine, my
friend, that we could go back to our other, earlier way of life?"

"Why not?" answered the schoolmaster; "every mode of life has its
burdens, the restricted as much as the free. The latter presupposes su-
perfluity and only leads to wastefulness. Let us remain with your exam-
ple, which is striking enough. As soon as people are once more in need,
self-restriction is again the order of the day. Those who are forced to use
their land soon erect walls around their gardens again to protect their
produce. Thus a new outlook gradually comes into being. Utilitarian
purposes then hold sway, and even he who has considerable property
believes in the end that he must make use of it all. Believe me: it is
possible that your son will neglect all these gardens and retreat behind
his grandfather's solemn walls and tall lime trees."

Charlotte was secretly pleased to hear herself foretold a son, and thus
forgave the teacher his somewhat unpleasant prophecy about the fate of
her beautiful, beloved gardens. So she answered quite amiably, "We are
both not yet old enough to have experienced such contradictions several
times; but when I think back to my early youth and remember the com-
plaints I heard from older people, and when I consider states and cities
as well, then I can hardly gainsay your observation. But must we refrain
from hindering this natural process, can we not bring father and son,
parents and children to agree with one another? You have been kind
enough to predict that I will have a son; must he be in conflict with his
father of all people, and destroy what his parents have constructed in-
stead of completing and enhancing it by continuing in the same spirit?"

"There is a sensible way to achieve that," the schoolmaster replied,
"but it is seldom used. The father should make his son a co-proprietor,
have him help with the construction and planting and grant him the
same harmless freedoms he grants himself. One person's activities can
be woven in with another's, but not patched onto them. A young twig
can easily be grafted onto an old stem, but a full-grown branch cannot."

The teacher was pleased to have chanced to say something agreeable
to Charlotte and thus to have secured her favor at the very moment
when he saw himself forced to take leave of her. He had been away from
home far too long; but he had hesitated to go until he realized that he
had to wait for the birth of Charlotte's child before he could expect any
decision regarding Ottilie. He resigned himself to these circumstances,

then, and returned, with these hopes and prospects, to the school principal.

Charlotte's delivery was approaching. She kept more and more to her rooms. The women she had gathered around her were her only company. Ottilie took care of the housekeeping, scarcely daring to think about what she was doing. She was completely resigned; she was anxious to be of the greatest service possible to Charlotte, the baby, and Edward; but she did not see how this would be possible. Only her daily duties could save her from total despair.

A son had been successfully brought into the world, and the women were of the unanimous opinion that he was the living image of his father. But in her heart Ottilie was not convinced when she went to wish the mother happiness and greet the new arrival. Charlotte had sorely missed her husband during the preparations for her daughter's wedding; and now the father was not to be present at the birth of his son; he was not to decide upon the name the boy was to be given.

The first of all their friends to come by with congratulations was Mittler, who had already posted his spies to report right away on this event. He appeared, and in a very amiable mood too. He barely hid his triumph from Ottilie, and expressed it openly to Charlotte. He was the man to remove all worries and momentary hindrances. The christening should not be postponed for long. The old minister, one foot already in the grave, should link past and present with his blessing; the child should be called Otto; he could hardly have any other name than that of his father and his father's friend.

It took this man's whole relentless determination to counter the hundreds of reservations, arguments, hesitations, delays, vacillations, considerations, second and third thoughts, better or different opinions, since on such occasions as soon as one reservation is raised new ones keep cropping up, and, in trying to spare everyone's feelings, we always end up hurting someone's.

Mittler took over all the birth announcements and the invitations to the godparents; this was to be carried out at once, since he set great store by making the happy event, so significant in his view for the family itself, known to the wider world with its various ill-wishers and evil tongues. And of course the passionate events that had preceded it had not escaped the eye of the public, which believes in any event that everything that happens does so only to give it something to talk about.

The christening ceremony was to be solemn, but brief. They gathered together, and Mittler and Ottilie, as witnesses, were to hold the baby. The old minister, supported by the sexton, stepped slowly forward. The prayer had been said, Ottilie had taken the child in her arms, and as she was gazing lovingly down, she was greatly taken aback by the sight of his open eyes, for she thought she was looking into her own; such a likeness could not fail to amaze all who saw it. Mittler, who took the baby next, was likewise astonished to see in the child's features a striking resemblance, this time to the Captain, a resemblance the like of which he had never seen before.

The good old minister's weakness had prevented him from accompanying the christening with more than the customary liturgy. But Mittler, full of the occasion, recalled his former office—he had in general the habit of imagining in every instance how he would speak at this moment, what words he would utter. This time, since it was a gathering of friends alone surrounding him, he could restrain himself even less. So toward the end of the ceremony he began quite unabashedly to take the place of the old minister, making a lively speech about the expectations and duties of godparents. He went on in this vein all the longer since he thought he read Charlotte's approval in her contented expression.

That the good old minister would dearly have liked to sit down quite escaped the valiant speaker, who was even less aware of the fact that he was well on the way to causing a serious disaster; for having described in detail each person's relationship to the infant and thus caused sore trials for Ottilie's composure, he turned at last to the old man and said, "And you, worthy father, may now say with Simeon, 'Lord, now lettest thou thy servant depart in peace, for mine eyes have seen the salvation of this house.' "

Now he was about to come to a brilliant peroration, but soon he noticed that the minister, who was holding the baby, seemed at first to lean towards him, but then sank rapidly back. Only just prevented from falling, he was conducted to a chair, and despite all immediate aid, he had to be pronounced dead.

To see and imagine, not just in fantasy but with their own eyes, those awesome opposites birth and death, cradle and grave so directly connected, was a trying test for all present, especially since it had come so unexpectedly. Ottilie alone gazed with a sort of envy upon the departed minister, whose expression still kept its kind and friendly aspect. Her soul's life had been killed; why should her body be still preserved?

But if the unpleasant events of the day thus led her to reflect from time to time on transience, parting and loss, she was granted, as a comforting compensation, wondrous nightly visions that assured her of her beloved's existence and secured and animated her own. When she had lain down at night and was drifting in that sweet state between waking and sleeping, it seemed to her as if she were gazing into a bright, but softly lit room. Here she saw Edward quite clearly, not dressed as she had always seen him, but in soldier's garb, each time in a different pose, completely natural and in no way fanciful: standing, walking, reclining, riding. The figure, appearing in the finest detail, moved of its own volition before her eyes without her doing the slightest thing, without her willing it or making an effort of imagination. Sometimes she saw him surrounded in particular by something moving, darker than the light background; but she could scarcely distinguish the shadowy images that seemed to her at times like men, horses, trees and mountains. Usually she fell asleep over these visions, and when she awoke in the morning after a peaceful night she was refreshed and comforted; she felt convinced that Edward was still alive and that she was in the closest communication with him.

Chapter Nine

Spring had come—later, but more rapidly and joyously than usual. Now Ottilie found the fruit of her efforts in the garden; everything sprouted, leaved and blossomed at once; many plants that had been started in greenhouses and frames were now moved out into the open, and everything that needed to be taken care of was not just a labor of hope as before, but now was a pleasure and delight.

But she had to console the gardener for many a gap in the potted plants that had been made by Luciane in her recklessness, and many a spoilt symmetry in the tops of the trees. She consoled him by saying that it would all grow back again; but he was too deeply involved in his handicraft and too idealistic about it for this comfort to be of use to him. Just as the gardener should not be distracted by other hobbies and pastimes, so the steady course a plant takes towards its lasting or passing perfection should not be interrupted. Plants are like stubborn people: they will let you have anything if you approach them the right way. Quiet observation, steady consistency in doing the right thing at every season and every hour is demanded of no one more, perhaps, than of the gardener.

The good soul had these qualities in rich measure, which was why Ottilie was so glad to work with him; but he had been unable to use his talent with enjoyment for some time. For although he knew how to manage all aspects of fruit and vegetable gardening and could also meet the demands of old-fashioned ornamental gardening, and even though he could challenge nature itself in his management of the orangerie, flower bulbs, carnations or auriculas, it is generally the case that a person succeeds more with one thing than another. Thus he never really took to the newer specimen trees and fashionable flowers, and he had a kind of horror—which put him quite out of sorts—of the whole infinite field of botany that was just opening up with all those foreign names buzzing about in it. What the lords and ladies had begun to order last year he regarded as all the more useless trouble and waste when he saw many a costly plant die, and he was not on a very good footing with the commercial gardeners who, he thought, were not sufficiently honest in filling his orders.

After various kinds of experimentation he had made a sort of plan, which Ottilie supported all the more because it was based on the return of Edward, whose absence they felt in this and many other instances more keenly by the day.

As the plants began to root and sprout more and more, Ottilie felt herself increasingly bound to the gardens. Exactly a year ago she had come here as an insignificant stranger; how much she had gained since that time, and how much, alas, had she also lost since that time! She had never been so rich and so poor. These two sensations alternated from moment to moment, indeed they mingled so closely that she knew no other way out than to take up the nearest task at hand with devotion, indeed with passion. We can imagine how everything that had been especially dear to Edward most strongly claimed her attention; and why should she not hope that he himself would soon return, and that he would in person gratefully notice the loving services she had performed for him during his absence?

But she had a quite different task to perform for him as well. She had taken over the principal care of the baby, and because it had been decided not to give him to a nurse, but to feed him with milk and water, she was able to become his closest guardian. In this fair season the baby was to enjoy the open air; and so she preferred to take him out herself, carrying the sleeping innocent among the flowers and blossoms that were to rejoice so delightfully with him in his infancy, among the young shrubs and plants that seemed destined to grow taller with him. When she looked around her she could not fail to see what a rich and splendid heritage the child had been born into; for almost everything as far as the eye could see would one day be his. How devoutly was it to be wished in the view of all this that he should grow up in the presence of his father and mother, and confirm a renewed and happy union!

Ottilie sensed this with such innocence that she imagined it as something already decided, and scarcely gave a thought to herself at the idea. Beneath this clear sky, in this bright sunshine she suddenly realized that in order to be perfect her love must be completely selfless; and indeed, at times she thought she had attained this pinnacle already. She desired only her friend's well-being, she thought she was able to renounce him, even to go so far as never to see him again, if only she knew he was happy. But for her own part she was quite determined never to belong to another.

They had taken pains to make the autumn just as splendid as the spring. All of what are called summer flowers, all those that cannot stop blossoming in the fall and keep on growing boldly into the cold weather, asters in particular, had been sown in great numbers and now, planted everywhere, were to form a starry heaven covering the ground.

From Ottilie's Diary

When we read an interesting thought or hear a striking idea, we usually note it in our diary. But if we also took the trouble to write down original remarks, unusual opinions, brilliant flights of genius from our friends' letters, we would be greatly enriched. We keep letters without re-reading them; and in the end we destroy them for reasons of discretion, and so the loveliest and most spontaneous living expression disappears irretrievably for us as well as for others. I intend to make good this omission.

Now the year's tale begins all over again. Once more, thank goodness, we have reached its most charming chapter. Violets and lilies-of-the-valley are like inscriptions or vignettes accompanying it. It is always pleasing to open the book of life again at their page.

We scold the poor, particularly poor children, when they lie in the streets begging. Do we not notice that they start to busy themselves as soon as there is something to do? Scarcely has nature unfolded her loveliest treasures than the children are after them to start doing business; not a single child goes on begging, each one hands you a bouquet; the child has picked it before you awake from your slumbers, and the little petitioner gazes at you as appealingly as his offering. No one looks pitiful when they feel they have the right to ask for something.

Why is the year sometimes so short, sometimes so long? Why does it sometimes feel so short, and yet so long when we look back at it? The past year seems like that to me, and nowhere more strikingly than in the garden, where annuals and perennials are intermingled. And yet nothing is so transient that it does not leave a trace, something of its kind, behind it.

We can also take pleasure in the winter. We seem to spread ourselves more freely when the trees rise before us in ghostly transparency. They are nothing, but neither do they conceal anything. But once the buds and blossoms appear we become impatient for the full leafage to come out, the landscape to take shape and the tree to body forth its full form.

Everything that is perfect of its kind must transcend its kind, it must perforce become something else, something incomparable. In part of its song the nightingale is still a bird; but then it rises above its kind and seems to want every feathered creature to see what singing really is.

Life without love, without the presence of the one we love is just a "comédie à tiroir," a cheap, ill-made play. We pull out one drawer after another, put it back again and hasten on to the next. Everything there is that is good or meaningful seems only tenuously connected. We have to keep on beginning over again and wish we could end at every moment.

Chapter Ten

Charlotte, for her part, was happy and well. She took pleasure in the thriving baby boy; her eyes and heart were occupied hour after hour with his promising good looks. Through him she forged a new link with society and the estate. She became her former busy self; wherever she looked, she saw how much had been achieved in the past year, and felt pleased about it. Inexplicably moved, she went up to the moss hut with Ottilie and the baby and laid him on the little table as if on a household altar. Seeing two places still empty, she thought of former times, and felt new hope for herself and Ottilie.

Young women may look modestly about them at this or that young man, secretly wondering whether they would like him for a husband; but anyone in charge of a daughter or female ward looks farther afield. This was Charlotte's position at the moment, and she felt that a union between Ottilie and the Captain might not be impossible, for had they not once sat next to each other in the moss hut? She was not unaware that the Major's prospect of an advantageous marriage had not materialized.

Charlotte climbed higher, and Ottilie carried the baby. Charlotte gave herself up to various reflections. No doubt there is such a thing as shipwreck on dry land; to recover from it and re-establish oneself as quickly as possible is a fine and praiseworthy thing. Is not life, after all, a matter of profit and loss? Who has not made some outlay and seen his hopes dashed! How often do we take a particular path and then are led astray! How often are we distracted from a plan we have firmly intended to carry out, and drawn to an even grander one! A traveler, to his great annoyance, breaks a wheel and through this irritating accident makes the most charming new friends who change the course of his entire life. Fate grants us our wishes, but in its own way, to give us something better than we desired.

Such were Charlotte's thoughts as she climbed up to the new building on the hilltop, and here she found their truth confirmed. For the surroundings were much more beautiful than could have been imagined. Every little obstruction had been removed, and all the good features of the landscape and what time and nature had done to it could be seen plainly and in sharp outline. The green plantings were already showing leaves that were to fill out various gaps and connect the separate parts in a pleasing fashion.

The house itself was almost ready; the view, especially from the upper rooms, was most picturesque. The more one looked, the more delights one discovered. What effects the various times of day, the sun and the moon, must have up here! How wonderful it would be to stay here, and what a sudden urge to build and create welled up in Charlotte again now that all the rough work had been finished! All they needed was a cabinet maker, a paperer, a painter who knew how to use stencils and do delicate gilding, and the house would be fixed up in short order. A cellar and kitchen were soon fitted out; for at this distance from the manor house they had to have everything they needed right here. So the women and the baby lived up on the hill, and from this location, as if from a new focus, unexpected walks opened up for them. The weather being excellent, they took great pleasure and enjoyment from the fresh open air of this higher region.

Ottilie's favorite walk, sometimes alone, sometimes with the baby, went down along an easy footpath to the plane trees and led from there straight to the place where the boat they used to cross the lake was moored. Sometimes she enjoyed a trip on the water, though not with the baby, since Charlotte had been somewhat anxious about that. But she never failed to visit the gardener at the manor and to take a friendly interest in his care of the many seedlings that were now all thriving in the open.

During this pleasant period Charlotte was glad to receive the visit of an Englishman who had met Edward while traveling, and having seen him several times, was now curious to see the new gardens of which he had heard so much. He brought a recommendation from the count, and introduced at the same time a quiet, but very amiable young man as his traveling companion. As he went through the gardens with Charlotte and Ottilie, or with the gardeners and huntsmen, more often with his companion and at times by himself, it was obvious from his observations that he was a connoisseur and had, no doubt, constructed similar gardens himself. Although no longer young, he took a cheerful interest in everything that gives life grace and meaning.

In his company the women learned, for the first time, to appreciate their surroundings fully. His trained eye saw every effect afresh, and his pleasure was even greater because he had not known the area before and could hardly distinguish what they had created from what nature had provided.

It can properly be said that his observations expanded and enriched the gardens. From the very outset he realized what the struggling new plantings would look like in the future. He overlooked no spot where a beautiful effect might be brought out or added. Here he pointed out a spring which, if cleaned up, promised to add a decorative touch to a whole group of bushes, here a cavern which, if cleared and enlarged, would provide a welcome resting place, while they would only have to fell a few trees to have a view of the splendid cliffs rising behind them. He told the owners they were very lucky to have so much still to do, and begged them not to be too hasty with it, but to reserve for coming years the pleasure of creating and arranging.

Outside the times when the company met together, he was in no way obtrusive; for he spent most of the day capturing the picturesque view of the gardens with a portable camera obscura or sketching them to preserve for himself and others the happy products of his travels. He had done this for several years in all important places he had visited and had thus built up a wonderfully interesting collection. He showed the ladies a large portfolio which he carried around with him, and entertained them partly with the pictures, partly with his comments on them. They found it lovely to sit in this isolated spot and travel through the world, seeing coasts and harbors, mountains, lakes and rivers, cities, castles and many other historically important spots pass before their eyes.

Each of the two women had her own interest, Charlotte a more general one in what was historically notable, whereas Ottilie was primarily attracted by the places of which Edward had spoken frequently, where he had liked to stay and to which he had often returned; for we all find certain local features attractive, endearing or exciting in accordance with our character—because of their first impression on us, the associations they have for us, or just because we are used to them.

Thus she asked the Englishman what place he liked best and where he would make his home if he could choose freely. At this, he showed them more than one lovely spot and took his time telling them, in his strangely accented French, what had happened to him there to make him love and cherish it.

Yet in response to the question of where he usually lived and where he most liked to return, he spoke quite frankly, but unexpectedly:

"I've become used to being at home everywhere, and in the last analysis I find nothing more convenient than that others should build, garden, and do the domestic work for me. I have no great desire to go back to my own estate, in part for political reasons, but primarily because my son, for whom I originally built it up, to whom I hoped to bequeath it, and with whom I hoped to enjoy it, has no interest in any of it. Instead, like so many others, he has gone to India to make a better life, or rather to waste it there.

"Indeed, we spend far too much energy in life making preparations. Instead of setting out right away to make ourselves comfortable without spending lavishly, we extend ourselves increasingly, thus making our lives more and more uncomfortable. Who enjoys my buildings now, my park, my gardens? Not I, not even my relatives: strangers, visitors, curious passers-by, restless travelers.

"Even when we are very well off we are only ever half at home, especially in the country, where we miss much that we have grown used to in the city. The book we most urgently wish to read is not at hand, and the very things we have most need of have been left behind. We set up house, only to move out again, and even if we don't intend to, we are forced into it by relationships, passions, accidents, obligations or whatever."

The lord had no idea how much his remarks had affected the two friends. And how often do we not run this risk when venturing some generalization, even in company whose circumstances we know well. That even well-meaning people can make this kind of unintentionally wounding remark was nothing new to Charlotte; and she was in any event so conscious of how society functions that she did not feel any great pain, even when thoughtless persons carelessly forced her to take a closer look at something unpleasant. Ottilie on the other hand, who in her innocent youthfulness sensed things rather than saw them and was able or even bound to turn her eyes away from what she was not permitted or did not wish to see, was thrown into a most terrible state by these confidences. A delicate veil tore rudely before her eyes, and it seemed to her as if everything that had been done for the house and the estate, the gardens, the park and the whole surrounding landscape had actually been done in vain, since he who owned it all could not enjoy it, and was, like their present guest, forced by his nearest and dearest to roam the world in the most dangerous way. She had become used to listening and holding her peace, but this time she felt the most acute embarrassment, which was increased rather than lessened by their visitor's next remarks, with which he cheerfully persisted in his ponderous way.

"Now I think I am on the right track," he said, "since I regard myself as a permanent traveler, giving up many things in order to enjoy many others. I am used to change, in fact I have come to need it, just as we always expect a new stage set at the opera, since we have already seen so many. I know what to expect from the best and the worst inn; however good or bad it is, I never find what I am accustomed to. In the end it is all the same—whether we depend entirely on ingrained habits or on the most random accidents. At least I don't have the bother of losing or mislaying something, or of being unable to use my own familiar living room because repairs are being made, or that my favorite cup breaks and nothing tastes good to me in any other for a time—I am beyond all of that, and if the house starts burning down around my ears, then my servants just pack everything up and we drive off out of the courtyard and out of town. And with all these advantages, I haven't spent more at the end of a year, when I reckon everything up, than I would have spent at home."

In the course of this explanation Ottilie could only think of Edward traveling in difficulty and want on unpaved roads, lying in danger and need in the field, and from all this distress and hazard growing used to being homeless and friendless, to throwing everything away just so as not to be able to lose anything. Fortunately the group broke up for a while, and Ottilie had a chance to weep her troubles away in solitude. This realization had gripped her more powerfully than any dull pain, and she tried to make it even clearer, for when circumstances torture us, we often begin to torture ourselves.

Edward's life seemed to her so woeful, so pitiful, that she decided to do everything she could to bring about his reunion with Charlotte, whatever the cost, and to hide her pain and love for him in some lonely place where she could take refuge in some kind of useful activity.

Meanwhile the English lord's companion, a man of calm intellect and a close observer of others, had noticed the faux pas in their conversation and drawn his friend's attention to the similarity in the two sets of circumstances. The lord had been unaware of the family's situation; but his companion found nothing more fascinating in their travels than strange coincidences, natural or artificial, the clash of law and violence, common sense and reason, passion and prejudice, and he had learned before as well as after their arrival of what had happened and was happening in that household.

The lord was sorry to hear it, but it did not cause him embarrassment. He said one would have to say nothing at all in company if one wanted to avoid this sort of thing altogether; for not only significant remarks, but trivial ones as well could be just as distressing to the feelings of those present. "Let us make up for it tonight," said the Englishman, "and refrain from making general conversation. Let our friends hear some of those charming and profound tales and anecdotes with which our travels have enriched your portfolio and your memory!"

But even with the best intention the guests did not succeed this time in providing their friends with innocent entertainment. For once the nobleman's companion had stimulated their interest, and after various strange, remarkable, merry, touching and terrifying tales, he decided to conclude with an incident that, though strange, was in a lower key than the others. He had no idea how close to home it was for his listeners.

Curious Tale of the Childhood Sweethearts
Novella

Two young neighbors from prominent families, a boy and a girl, of just the right ages to make a fine couple some time in the future, were allowed to grow up in this pleasant prospect, and both sets of parents looked forward to a future union between them. But it soon became obvious that this plan was not to be realized, since a strange dislike grew up between the two fine creatures. Perhaps they were too alike. Both were self-possessed, strong-willed and firm-intentioned, individually loved and respected by their playmates, but always opponents when they were together; always constructive when alone, but mutually destructive when with each other, not competing towards a single goal but continually fighting over some project; thoroughly kind and lovable, but hostile, even vicious towards each other alone.

This strange relationship, evident in their childish games early on, became clearer as the years went by. And as boys like to play soldier, dividing themselves into groups to do battle with one another, so the bold and stubborn girl placed herself at the head of one army and fought against the other with such violence and ferocity that it would have been most shamefully put to flight had not her sole opponent held her firm, finally managing to disarm his fair enemy and take her captive. But even then she resisted so strongly that, to prevent his eyes from being scratched out while still not harming his opponent, he was obliged to tear off his silk neckerchief and bind her hands behind her back with it.

This she never forgave him, indeed she laid all kinds of secret plots and plans to harm him, with the result that their parents, who had been following these strange passions for some time, finally agreed to give up their dearest hopes and separate the two hostile children.

The boy soon distinguished himself in his new life. Whatever he was taught he learned easily. His patrons, as well as his own inner inclinations, destined him to be an officer. Wherever he went, he was liked and respected. His energetic character seemed motivated solely by the desire to promote the well-being of others, and without being clearly aware of it, he was inwardly quite glad to have lost the only opponent nature had created for him.

The girl, on the other hand, entered an entirely new phase. Her age, the growing influence of education, and more importantly a certain intuition drew her away from the violent games she had played with the boy. She felt that something was missing; there was nothing in her surroundings to excite her hatred. She had not yet found anyone she loved.

A young man, older than her former opponent and neighbor, much liked in society on account of his family, fortune and prominence, and much sought after by women, came to have a great affection for her. It was the first time a friend, a lover, an admirer had courted her. That he preferred her to many others who were older, more cultivated, more dazzling and who had higher social prospects than she had a most salutary effect on her. His constant, but not importunate attentions, his faithful support on various unpleasant occasions, his evident, but calm and hopeful cultivation of her parents (since of course she was still quite young): all this, coupled with the fact that their engagement was taken for granted, regarded as a fait accompli by everyone around them, spoke for him in her mind. She had so often been called his future wife that she finally regarded herself as such, and, when she exchanged rings with the man who had so long been called her husband-to-be, neither she nor anyone else assumed that the relationship needed to be tested any further.

The gradual development of their relationship was not hastened by the engagement. Both of them let things proceed at their own pace; they were glad to be together and to enjoy the pleasant season as the spring of a more serious life yet to come.

In the meanwhile her absent neighbor had completed his education in model fashion. Having risen to a well-earned rank in his chosen profession, he came on leave to visit his family. Quite naturally—yet how strange it seemed!—he met again his lovely young neighbor. In recent times she had nourished nothing but amiable feelings, thoughts of her family and her prospective marriage; she was in harmony with everything around her; she believed she was happy, and in a way she was. But now, for the first time in a long while, she was faced with something puzzling: she did not feel hatred, for she had become incapable of hate; her childhood hostility, which had in reality been only a subconscious recognition of the boy's inner worth, now manifested itself as happy amazement, pleasing contemplation and pleasurable admission, a half-willing, half-unwilling and nonetheless necessary attraction—and it was mutual. The long separation gave rise to still longer conversations. Even their childhood foolishness was the subject of many an amusing recollection on the part of these two who had since grown more reasonable, and it seemed as if that teasing enmity should at least be made up for by friendly attentions towards each other, as if that dramatic failure to recognize each other's good qualities had now to be transformed into express recognition.

On his part it was kept within proper, sensible bounds. His social standing, his position, his hopes and ambition were uppermost in his mind, and he gratefully accepted the friendship of the lovely bride-to-be as an additional satisfaction, without however relating it in any way to himself or feeling at all envious of her fiancé, with whom he was on the best of terms.

She saw it differently, however. She felt as if she had woken from a dream. Her fights with her young neighbor had been her first passion, and all that violence had just been a vehement, but as it were innate affection in the guise of resistance. In retrospect it seemed to her as if she had always loved him. She smiled at the thought of how she had taken up arms and attacked him; she thought she recalled the most pleasant of feelings when he had disarmed her; she imagined she had experienced the greatest bliss when he had tied her up; and everything she had done to hurt and annoy him now seemed to her an innocent means of attracting his attention. She cursed their separation, she deplored the sleep into which she had fallen, she condemned the dreamlike state that had dragged on so and had made her become engaged to such an insignificant man; she was transformed, doubly transformed, in prospect and in retrospect, so to speak.

If anyone had been able to share and discuss these feelings, which she kept quite to herself, he would not have reproached her: for once one saw the two together, her husband-to-be could of course not stand comparison with her neighbor. Where one could not withhold from the first a certain degree of trust, the second aroused one's utmost confidence; where one enjoyed the company of the first, one wished to have the second as a friend; and if one thought of higher sympathies and exceptional situations, one would probably have despaired of the first, while the second inspired one's greatest assurance. Women have a special native instinct for such matters, and have both cause and opportunity to develop it.

The more the lovely young woman, unbeknown to others, allowed such sentiments to grow within her, and the less anyone had occasion to say what advantages her future husband had, what circumstances and duty seemed to require and an inevitable necessity irrevocably to demand, so much the more did the lovely young creature favor her secret inclinations. While she was indissolubly bound on the one hand by society and family, her fiancé and her own promise, on the other hand the ambitious young neighbor made no secret of his attitudes, plans and prospects, behaving like a faithful but not even affectionate brother towards her. And now that he was actually contemplating leaving again shortly, it seemed as if her former childish sensibilities with all their insidious passion were again aroused, armed in this new phase of her existence with resentment and thus having a more tellingly disastrous effect. She decided to die in order to punish for his lack of interest the man she had once hated and now so passionately loved, and since she could not possess him, she would bind herself forever to his rueful imagination. He would, she thought, never be able to free himself from her dead image, he would never cease to reproach himself for not having sounded out, recognized and valued her feelings.

This strange delirium accompanied her everywhere. She disguised it by all kinds of externals, and if people thought she was behaving oddly, still no one was alert or perceptive enough to discover the real cause.

Meanwhile her friends and relatives had outdone themselves arranging various kinds of festivities. Hardly a day went by than something new and unexpected was put on. There was hardly a beautiful spot in nature that had not been decked out in preparation for throngs of happy guests. Our new arrival, too, wished to do his part before he left again, and invited the young couple with their immediate family to a river cruise. The party took place on a large, beautiful, handsomely decorated ship, one of those yachts that have a small ballroom and several other rooms, and seek to transfer to the water the comforts of dry land.

They drifted along the river to the sound of music; in the heat of the day the company had gathered in the lower rooms to enjoy games of skill and chance. The young host, unable to sit passively by, had taken the helm to relieve the old boatman who had dozed off at his side; and at this moment our waking friend needed all his caution, as he was approaching a spot where two islands narrowed the river bed and, spreading out their flat gravel shores now on this side, now on that, created a dangerous channel. The alert and careful helmsman was almost tempted to wake the captain, but he thought he could manage it himself and steered towards the narrows. At this moment his fair friend appeared on the upper deck with a wreath of flowers in her hair. She took it off and threw it to the helmsman. "Take this as a memento!" she called. "Don't bother me!" he called back, catching her wreath. "I need all my strength and attention." "I won't bother you anymore," she cried, "you won't see me again!" With these words she dashed to the front of the ship and leaped into the water. Several voices cried out: "Help, help! She's drowning!" He was in the most dreadful dilemma. What with all the noise, the old boatman woke up and tried to grasp the rudder, and the young man tried to hand it over; but there was no time to change command: the ship ran aground, and in that very moment, throwing off his heavier clothing, the young man plunged in and swam after his fair enemy.

Water is a hospitable element to anyone who is familiar with it and knows how to deal with it. It carried him, and the skillful swimmer never lost control. Soon he had reached his lovely friend whom the waters had torn from him; he took hold of her, managed to lift and carry her; they were both forcefully borne along by the current until the islands and flats were behind them and the river once more began to run broadly and calmly. Now he pulled himself together, recovering from the original emergency in which he had acted unconsciously and mechanically; raising his head and looking around, he paddled as best he could toward a nice flat bushy spot that ran conveniently out into the river. There he brought his lovely prize onto dry land; but he could find no breath of life in her. He was in despair, when suddenly he spied a well-trodden path running through the bushes. He put his precious burden on his shoulders, and soon noticed a solitary house. When he reached it he found good people there, a young couple. The accident, the emergency was soon explained. He thought for a moment; and they did what he then requested. A bright fire was made; woolen blankets were spread over a bed; furs, animal skins and everything else warm they had was quickly brought. The desire to save a life was all that mattered. Nothing was omitted to bring the beautiful, numbed, naked body back to life. Their efforts succeeded. She opened her eyes, and seeing her friend, flung her heavenly arms around his neck. She stayed thus for some time; a stream of tears poured from her eyes, completing her recovery. "Will you leave me," she cried out, "now that I have found you again in this way?" "Never," he cried, "never!"—quite unaware of what he was saying and doing. "Just take care of yourself," he added; "take care of yourself! Think of yourself for my sake and your own."

Now she thought of herself and noticed for the first time the state she was in. She felt no shame before her beloved, her savior; but she was glad to let him go and attend to himself; for everything about him was wet and dripping.

The young husband and wife conferred with each other. He offered the youth, she the beautiful maiden their wedding clothes, which were still hanging there complete and fit to clothe a couple from head to toe. In a short time the two adventurers were not just dressed, they were decked out in finery. They looked most charming, and stared at each other when they emerged, falling into each other's arms with violent and boundless passion, yet half laughing at the mummery. But the vigor of youth and the force of their love soon restored them, and if there had been music, they would have stepped up to dance.

To go from water to land, death to life, from the family to the wilderness, despair to delight, indifference to affection and passion, and all this in one moment—the mind could scarcely contain it all; it would burst or go mad. Only the heart can bear such a shattering sequence of events.

Completely absorbed in each other, it took a while before they could think of the worry and anxiety of those they had left behind, and they themselves could hardly contemplate without worry and anxiety the question of how they would confront them. "Shall we flee? Shall we hide?" the youth asked. "Let us stay together," she said, embracing him.

The farmer, who had heard their story of the stranded ship, hurried towards the shore without asking any more questions. The boat was just sailing in; with much difficulty it had been set afloat again. The company had sailed on in no particular direction hoping to find their lost friends again. So when they noticed the farmer shouting and waving and running to a good landing-place, they turned the ship towards the bank, and what a scene it was when they landed! The parents of the engaged couple hurried on shore first; the husband-to-be was almost out of his wits. Hardly had they heard that their beloved children had been saved than they saw them coming out from the bushes in their strange garb. Their parents did not recognize them until they had come quite close. "Who is this?" cried the mothers; "what is this?" cried the fathers. The rescued couple flung themselves down before them. "Your children," they cried, "at last united." "Forgive us!" cried the girl. "Give us your blessing!" cried the youth. "Give us your blessing," they cried together, as all present stood in dumb astonishment. "Your blessing!" their voices rang out a third time, and who could have refused them?

Chapter Eleven

The storyteller paused or had, rather, already finished, when he couldn't help noticing that Charlotte was very moved. She stood up, in fact, and left the room with a silent gesture of apology; for the story was familiar to her. It had actually happened to the Captain and a neighbor of his—not quite the way the Englishman had reported it, though its main outline was not distorted, just decorated and developed in more detail, as often happens with such stories when they have passed from one person to another and are filtered, finally, through the imagination of a tasteful and intelligent narrator. In most cases everything and nothing ends up the same.

Ottilie followed Charlotte, as the two visitors themselves requested, and now it was the lord's turn to remark that perhaps another mistake had been made, that they had perhaps related something known to or connected with the family. "We must try not to cause any more trouble," he continued. "In return for the pleasant and enjoyable time we have had here we seem to be striking an unlucky note with our hostesses; let us find a tactful way to take our leave."

"I must admit," replied his companion, "that there is one thing that keeps me here, something puzzling I would like to know more about before I leave. When we took the portable camera into the gardens yesterday, my lord, you were too busy choosing the most picturesque angle to notice what else was going on. You left the main path to get to a lonely spot on the lake which offered you a charming subject. Ottilie, who was with us, was reluctant to follow and asked if she could go there in the boat. I got in with her, and was delighted to see how skillful my lovely oarswoman was. I assured her that I had not been rocked so pleasantly over the waves since my stay in Switzerland, where the most charming girls had acted as ferrymen, but I could not help asking her why she had refused to take the side path; there had been a certain embarrassed anxiety about the way she avoided it. 'If you promise not to laugh at me,' she replied politely, 'I can tell you something of the reason, although even for me there is a mystery to it. I have never taken that side path without having an attack of the gooseflesh, which never happens to me anywhere else and which seems to have no explanation. So I prefer to avoid exposing myself to the sensation, especially as it is followed right afterwards by a headache on the left side, which is something I do sometimes suffer from.' We landed, Ottilie chatted with you, and I investigated the spot she had indicated from a distance. How surprised I was to see distinct traces of coal, which makes me think that by digging there we might perhaps find a considerable deposit below.

"Pardon me, my lord, I see you are smiling; I'm well aware that the only reason you look indulgently on my passion for these things you do not believe in is that you are a wise man and a friend of mine; but I cannot possibly leave here without experimenting with a pendulum on the charming young girl."

When talk turned to this subject, the lord invariably repeated his arguments against it, and his companion listened in all patience and modesty while still in the end persisting with his own opinion. He repeated, for his part, that it was precisely because the experiments did not work for everybody that the matter should not be dropped; rather, it should be studied more seriously and thoroughly, as many hidden connections and affinities amongst organic and inorganic objects, both within and between the two categories, might thus be revealed.

He had already spread out his equipment, gold rings, marcasites, and other metallic objects which he always had with him in a handsome case; and now he started experimenting with bits of metal hung on threads above others he had placed on the ground. "I won't blame you, my lord," he said, "for feeling a bit superior, as I can see by your face. Nothing is going to move for me now. But my experiment is only a pretext. When the ladies come back, I want to make them curious about the strange operations we are performing here."

The women returned. Charlotte saw immediately what was going on. "I've heard a good deal about these things," she said, "but I've never seen them in action. Now that you've set everything up so nicely, let me try if it works for me."

She took the thread in her hand, and being in deadly earnest about it, she held it steadily and serenely; but not the slightest movement could be seen. Then Ottilie was urged to try. She held the pendulum even more steadily, more naively and unselfconsciously over the metals below it. But at that moment the swinging pendulum was caught up as if by a powerful whirlpool, turning now to one side, now to the other according to the position of the metals beneath—now in circles, now in ellipses, or swinging back and forth in a straight line. It was enough to fulfill—to surpass even—the young man's every expectation.

The lord was somewhat surprised, but his companion was so filled with eagerness and delight that he could not stop, and kept on asking her to repeat and vary the experiments. Ottilie was glad enough to agree, until in the end she begged him politely to let her go, as she was beginning to have a headache again. Amazed, even delighted by this, he assured her enthusiastically that he would cure her of this trouble completely if she would entrust herself to his treatment. They hesitated a moment; but Charlotte, who quickly grasped what he was talking about, turned down his well-meaning proposal, since she was not inclined to permit on her premises something about which she had always had such strong apprehensions.

The visitors had gone and, despite the strange effect they had had, the ladies were left with the desire to see them again somewhere. Charlotte now took advantage of the fine weather to finish paying return calls in the neighborhood, which was hard to do, as the whole countryside had constantly come to visit, some people out of genuine interest, others purely out of custom. At home she was cheered by the sight of the baby; he was certainly deserving of every loving care. He seemed a miracle, a prodigy: handsome to behold, big, well-proportioned, strong and healthy; and what was more amazing was the dual resemblance that was growing more and more apparent. In features and figure the boy increasingly came to look like the Captain; his eyes became increasingly harder to distinguish from Ottilie's.

This strange connection and even more, perhaps, that happy feeling of tender affection a woman has for the child of a man she loves even when it is not her own, made Ottilie soon as good as a mother, or rather second mother, to the growing boy. If Charlotte had to go away, Ottilie remained alone with the baby and his nurse. Little Nan, jealous of the boy, on whom her mistress seemed to bestow her whole affection, had left in resentment some time ago and gone back to her parents. Ottilie continued to take the baby out in the fresh air and accustomed herself to taking longer and longer walks. She had the bottle with her so she could feed the child whenever necessary. Seldom did she fail to take a book with her too, and thus, walking and reading with the baby in her arms, she was the very picture of a charming *penserosa*.

Chapter Twelve

The main purpose of the campaign had been achieved and Edward had been decorated and honorably discharged. He went at once to his small estate, where he found a detailed report on his family, whom he had had closely observed without their being in any way aware of it. His peaceful refuge seemed most attractive; for during his absence he had ordered many improvements, rearrangements and renovations, so that what the garden and its surroundings lacked in expansiveness was made up for by the interior, more directly usable, parts of the house.

His active life having accustomed him to greater decisiveness, Edward now determined to take the steps he had long enough been planning.

First of all he summoned the Major. They were extremely pleased to see each other again. Early friendships, like blood relationships, have the great advantage that mistakes and misunderstandings of any kind never seriously damage them, and the old relationship is eventually restored.

Greeting him joyfully, Edward asked how his friend was and heard how fortune had favored him exactly as he had hoped. He then enquired, half jocularly, whether a romantic attachment were not developing. With pointed seriousness, his friend denied it.

"I can't deceive you, indeed it would not be proper to," continued Edward. "I must tell you straight away all my thoughts and plans. You know of my love for Ottilie and have long since realized that it was on account of her that I flung myself into battle. I won't deny that I hoped to end a life that had no meaning without her; but I must confess that I could never force myself to give up hope altogether. My happiness with her was so beautiful, so desirable, that I found it impossible to give it up completely. Many a comforting omen, many a positive sign had confirmed my belief, my delusion that Ottilie could be mine. A glass with our initials on it was tossed into the air at the foundation stone laying, but it did not break; someone caught it, and now I have it back. 'In just the same way,' I said to myself after so many doubtful hours in this lonesome spot, 'I will take the place of that glass and make myself a token whether we may be united or not. I will go and seek death, not as one who has taken leave of his senses, but as one who hopes to survive. Ottilie will be the prize for which I do battle; it will be she I hope to win, to conquer—behind every enemy line, in every entrenchment, in every beleaguered fortress. My wish to live will work a miracle—I intend to win Ottilie, not to lose her.' These feelings have guided me, they have stood me in good stead through every danger; but now here I am, and I feel as if I have attained my goal, conquered all obstacles, and nothing more can stand in my way. Ottilie is mine, and whatever stands between this thought and its realization I can only regard as utterly insignificant."

"With a few strokes you wipe out all the objections that could or should be made," the Major replied, "and yet I feel obliged to repeat them. I leave it to you to recall the full value of your relationship to your wife; you owe it to her, you owe it to yourself not to deceive yourself on this point. But how can I even think of the fact that you now have a son without also pointing out that you belong to each other forever, and that for the sake of the child you are honor bound to stay together, to share the responsibility for his upbringing and future welfare."

"Parents just delude themselves to think their presence so necessary for their children," answered Edward. "All living things find support and nourishment; and if a son, having lost his father early, does not have such a comfortable, well-favored youth, he may, for that very reason, gain an education for the world all the faster through the early recognition that he must consider others. It's not even a question of that: we have enough money to take care of several children, and it is by no means a duty or a benefit to heap so many advantages on a single head."

Just as the Major was about to give a brief account of Charlotte's virtue and Edward's long-standing relationship with her, Edward hastily interrupted: "I see now all too clearly that we acted foolishly. We always deceive ourselves if we try to realize youthful hopes and dreams in middle age; for every age of man has its own kind of happiness, its own hopes and expectations. What a shame when circumstances or self-delusion force us to grasp for what is past or still to come! We acted foolishly; but must we be stuck with it for life? Should we deny ourselves, out of some kind of scrupulousness, what the customs of our time do not forbid us? How often does a person rescind a plan or action, so why not do so in this particular instance? All is at stake, not just a single detail; not this or that condition of life, but the whole complex!"

The Major did not fail to point out, tactfully but emphatically, Edward's various relationships: with his wife, their families, society, his property; but he could not elicit the slightest positive response.

"All this, my friend," replied Edward, "passed through my mind in the confusion of battle when the earth was trembling with thundering hooves, when bullets whistled and companions fell right and left, my horse was injured, my cap torn by bullet-holes; I thought of it, too, by the quiet nightly fire under the starry vault of heaven. Then all my relationships came to mind; I thought them through with some emotion; I weighed them up, I came to terms with myself, repeatedly, and now for good.

"At such moments you, too, were in my thoughts (how can I conceal it?), you, too, were present; after all, have we not been the closest of friends for a long time? If there is anything I owe you, I am now in a position to pay you back with interest; if there is anything you owe me, you can now recompense me. I know you love Charlotte, and she deserves your love; I know she is not indifferent to you, and why should she not esteem you! Take her from my hand, unite me with Ottilie, and we will be the happiest people on earth!"

"For the very reason that you tempt me with such precious gifts," the Major replied, "I must be all the more cautious and firm. This suggestion, which in my heart I admire, makes things more difficult rather than simplifying them. You have spoken of yourself, but also of me, and just as you have spoken of fate, so you have also spoken of the reputation and honor of two men, irreproachable until now, who run the risk of appearing to society in a very strange light if they make this—to put it mildly—extraordinary bargain."

"The very fact that we've been irreproachable," Edward responded, "gives us the right to let ourselves be criticized for once. Those who have proved reliable all their lives make actions honorable that would seem dubious in others. As for me, I think these last trials I underwent, the difficult and dangerous deeds I did for others justify me in doing something for myself. As for you and Charlotte, let the future decide; but neither you nor anyone else can hold me back from my own plans. If I receive any help, I am willing to agree to anything; if I am left to my own devices or worse, if I am opposed, then regardless of anything else, I will take extreme steps."

The Major considered it his duty to block Edward's plans as long as possible; but he took the clever tack of pretending to give in and mentioning only the form and legal procedures by which the separation and remarriages were to be achieved. In the course of this, so many unpleasant, difficult and improper aspects came to light that Edward got extremely irritated.

"I see," he exclaimed finally, "that not only enemies, but friends, too, attack one's desires. My mind is firmly set on what I want, what I cannot do without; I intend to have it, and soon. I am well aware that such relationships cannot be dissolved and newly constituted without the collapse of much that is standing and much that wishes to remain. This sort of thing does not come to an end by reflection; all rights are equal in the eye of reason, and we can always find a counterweight for the lighter scale. And so, my friend, decide to act on my behalf and yours; decide for my sake and your own to unravel, untie and retie the knots! Don't let yourself be hampered by reflection of any sort; we have already caused the world to talk of us; it will talk of us again, and then, as with everything else that is no longer news, forget us and let us go our ways without bothering about us anymore."

The Major saw no other way out, and finally he had to admit that Edward was dealing with the matter once and for all as if it were obvious and inevitable, and was compelled to let him discuss in detail how it was to be arranged and to speak of the future in a cheerful, even jocular tone.

Growing serious and thoughtful again, Edward continued: "It would be criminal to deceive ourselves into leaving everything to the hopeful expectation that it will work out of its own accord and that fate will guide and favor us. We cannot possibly save ourselves or restore us all to peace that way; and how could I console myself, who in all innocence am to blame for everything! It was I who urged Charlotte to invite you into our house, and even Ottilie only joined us as a result of this move. We have no control over what came of it, but we do have the power to make it good again and to direct things so they serve our own well-being. Supposing you can turn your eyes away from the delightful prospects I am opening up for us, supposing you can impose sorry resignation on me and all of us, if you think it possible, if it might be possible;

and if we then plan to return to our original relationships, will we not be obliged to carry over into them much that is improper, awkward, and irritating without anything positive or happy coming of it? Would your own happy state be pleasant if you were prevented from seeing me and sharing my company? After all, considering what has happened it would always be embarrassing. In spite of our fortunes, Charlotte and I would be in a sorry state. And if, like other men of the world, you believe that years and distance deaden such emotions and erase such deeply graven lines, it is of those very years that I am speaking, which we do not wish to spend in want and distress, but in comfort and joy. And now to mention the most important thing: even if we could, at best, suffer through all this both psychologically and materially, what is to become of Ottilie, who would have to leave our house, do without our protection in society, and find her pitiful way in the cold and wicked world! Show me how Ottilie could be happy without me, without us all, and you will have given me an argument stronger than any other; and even if I cannot admit it or submit to it, I will be more than willing to consider this all again."

This was not an easy challenge, at least his friend could think of no adequate answer, and there was nothing left for him to do than to point out again and again how serious, how questionable, and in many ways how dangerous the whole plan was, and that at the very least they would have to consider very carefully how it was to be carried out. Edward submitted to this, but only on condition that his friend not leave him until they had reached complete agreement and undertaken the first steps.

Chapter Thirteen

Total strangers quite indifferent to each other reveal their inner selves once they have been living together for some time, and a certain degree of intimacy inevitably arises. Thus it was only to be expected that our two friends, living side by side and having to do with one another every hour of the day, had no secrets from each other. They recalled the memory of former times, and the Major did not conceal the fact that Charlotte had intended Ottilie for Edward upon his return from his travels, planning thereupon to marry him to the lovely child. Almost delirious over this revelation, Edward spoke openly of the mutual affection between Charlotte and the Major and, since it happened to suit his own convenience, elaborated vividly upon this theme.

The Major could neither quite admit nor deny it; but Edward just became even more set in his convictions. He thought of it all not just as a possibility, but as an actual fact. The parties concerned just had to agree on what they wanted; a divorce was certain to be obtained; early remarriage would follow, and then Edward and Ottilie would do some traveling.

Of all the pleasant things the imagination invents, there is perhaps nothing more charming than when lovers or a young married couple plan to enjoy their fresh new bond in a fresh new world and thus test and confirm a lasting covenant against changing situations. The Major and Charlotte, on the other hand, were to have complete authority to initiate and organize to everyone's mutual satisfaction all plans concerning property, money, and whatever material arrangements seemed desirable. But Edward based his greatest hope and saw his greatest advantage in the fact that, since the baby was to stay with his mother, the Major would educate the boy and guide and develop his talents as he saw fit. Thus it made sense that he had been christened Otto, the name they shared.

Edward had worked this all out with such finality that he could not wait a single day longer to start putting his plans into effect. On their way back to the estate they came to a small town where Edward had a house. Here he planned to wait for the Major's return. But he could not bring himself to stop there immediately, and he accompanied his friend through the township instead. They were both on horseback, and they rode along together deep in serious conversation.

Suddenly they saw in the distance the new house on the hill; they caught sight of its red tiles shining in the sun. An irrepressible longing took hold of Edward; everything had to be concluded this very evening. He would conceal himself in a nearby village; the Major would present the plan to Charlotte with some urgency, catching her off guard and forcing her by the unexpected proposal to reveal her true feelings. For Edward, who had projected his own desires onto Charlotte, was quite convinced that he was meeting her decided wishes, and because he himself could have no other desire, he hoped for her equally rapid acquiescence.

Full of joy, he saw the happy outcome before his mind's eye, and so that he could hear the news more rapidly from his hiding-place, some cannon shots were to be fired, and if night had fallen, rockets were to be let off.

The Major rode towards the manor. Charlotte was not there; but he was told that she was now living in the new house on the hill, though she was at the moment paying a call in the neighborhood and was not likely to be home early that day. He went back to the inn where he had stabled his horse.

Edward, meanwhile, driven on by uncontrollable impatience, crept out of his hiding-place towards his own gardens, taking solitary paths known only to hunters and fishermen. Towards evening he had reached the bushes near the lake, whose surface he now saw for the first time in all its purity and wholeness.

Ottilie had taken a walk to the lake that afternoon. She was carrying the baby and, as she often did, reading while she walked. So she came to the oak trees near the landing. The child had fallen asleep; she sat down, laid him down next to her and went on reading. The book was one of those that appeal to a sentimental mind and cannot be put down. She forgot the time of day, never thinking that she still had a long way back along the shore to the new house. She sat absorbed in her book, in herself, so lovely to behold that the trees and bushes round about should have been brought to life and given eyes to admire her and delight in her. And just at this moment a reddish glow from the sun sinking in the background fell upon her, gilding her cheek and shoulder.

Edward, who had managed to proceed so far unnoticed, pressed on even further, finding his park empty and the whole place abandoned. Finally he burst through the bushes near the oak trees, spied Ottilie, and she him; he rushed towards her and fell at her feet. After a long silence in which the two tried to compose themselves, he explained briefly how and why he had come. He had sent the Major to Charlotte; their fate was being decided, perhaps, at this very minute. He had never doubted her love, and she had surely never doubted his. He asked for her consent. She hesitated, he implored; he was about to take her in his arms as he had done in the past; she pointed to the baby boy.

Edward looked at him in astonishment. "Good Lord," he exclaimed, "if I had cause to doubt my wife or my friend, would not these features bear terrible witness against them? Isn't this the Major's face exactly? I've never seen such a likeness."

"Not at all," replied Ottilie, "everyone says the child looks like me." "Can it be?" said Edward, and at this moment the baby opened his eyes, two large, black, penetrating eyes, deep and friendly. The little boy looked so alertly at the world; he seemed to know the two who stood before him. Edward bent down to the child, he knelt once more before Ottilie. "It's you!" he cried, "those are your eyes. Oh! but just let me look into your own. Let me draw a veil over that unhappy hour which gave this little creature his existence. Shall I alarm your pure soul with the distressing thought that a husband and wife, estranged from each other, can desecrate a legal bond by their vivid fantasies? But yes, now that we have gone so far, now that my relation to Charlotte must be dissolved, now that you are to be mine, why should I not admit it? Why shouldn't I utter the harsh words: this child is the result of a double adultery! He separates me from my wife and my wife from me, even as he should have bound us together. Let him bear witness against me, let those splendid eyes tell yours that I belonged to you in the arms of another; and may you feel, Ottilie, really feel that I can atone for that mistake, that crime only in your arms!"

"Listen!" he cried, starting; he thought he had heard the shot that was to be the Major's signal. But it was a hunter shooting in the nearby hills. Silence followed; Edward was impatient.

Now Ottilie suddenly noticed that the sun had set behind the mountains. The last reflections glanced back from the windows of the summer-house. "You must go, Edward!" she cried. "We have done without each other for so long, we have endured for so long. Think what we both owe Charlotte. She must decide our fate; let us not anticipate her decision. I am yours, if she permits; if not, I must give you up. Let us wait, since you think it will be decided so soon. Go back to the village where the Major thinks you are still waiting. How many things can happen that may need to be explained! Is it probable that a mere cannon-shot should tell you the results of his negotiations? Perhaps he is looking for you this very minute. He has not met with Charlotte, that I know; he may have gone off to find her, since the servants know where she has gone. How many different possibilities there are! Leave me! She is due back now. She is waiting up there for me and the baby."

Ottilie spoke hurriedly. She conjured up all sorts of eventualities. She was happy to be with Edward, but felt that she had to make him leave. "I beg you, dearest, I implore you!" she said, "go back and wait for the Major." "I will obey your command," said Edward, gazing at her passionately and then clasping her tightly to him. She flung her arms around him and pressed him tenderly to her breast. Hope shot across the sky above their heads like a falling star. They imagined, they were convinced they belonged to each other; for the first time they exchanged kisses freely and unhesitatingly, separating only in the agony of necessity.

The sun had set, and twilight was already falling, filling the lake with its damp scent. Ottilie stood there with confused emotions; she looked over at the house on the hill and thought she saw Charlotte's white dress on the porch. The path around the lake was very long; she knew how anxious Charlotte would be to see the baby. She saw the plane trees on the other side; only a small space of water cut her off from the pathway leading up to the summer-house. Even as she catches sight of it, in thought she is already across. In the urgency of the moment the danger of venturing on the water with the baby quite disappears. She hurries to the boat, unaware of how her heart is beating, her feet are giving way beneath her and her senses failing.

She leaps into the boat, takes hold of the oar and pushes off. She has to push hard, and push again; the boat sways and drifts a little way out into the lake. On her left arm the baby, in her left hand the book, in her right hand the oar, she loses balance and topples into the boat. The oar slips out of her grasp to one side, and just as she tries to right herself, the child and the book slither off to the other, all of them into the water. She manages to grab hold of the baby's clothing; but her uncomfortable position prevents her from even getting up. With only her right hand free, she cannot turn and sit up. Finally she does manage; she pulls the child out of the water, but his eyes are closed and he has stopped breathing.

In an instant, her full presence of mind comes back, but her grief is all the greater. The boat is drifting out near the middle of the lake, the oar is floating far off, she can see nobody on the shore, and what use would it have been if she had! Cut off from everything, she drifts on the faithless unfathomable element.

She tries to give aid herself. She had heard so much about life-saving. She had even seen it done on the evening of her birthday. She undresses the child and dries him with her muslin dress. She opens her bodice and bares her bosom to the heavens for the first time; for the first time she presses a living being to her pure, naked breast, but, alas, living no more. The cold limbs of the pitiful creature chill her to the very heart. Endless tears stream from her eyes, giving the rigid little body a semblance of warmth and life. She does not give up: she wraps the child in her shawl and tries to make up for the lack of other aid in this deserted place by stroking, hugging and kissing him, breathing and weeping on him.

All in vain! Motionless the child lies in her arms, motionless the boat stands on the waters; but even here her beautiful soul does not leave her without recourse. She turns toward heaven. Kneeling, she sinks down into the boat and lifts the lifeless infant with both arms above her innocent breast, as white, and alas, as cold as marble, too. Tearfully she raises her eyes and calls upon help from whence a tender heart hopes to find the greatest fullness when it is everywhere absent.

And not in vain does she turn to the stars, which are now beginning to peep out one by one. A gentle breeze comes up and blows the boat towards the plane trees.

Chapter Fourteen

She ran up to the new building, summoned the doctor, gave him the child. With his habitual composure, he examined the fragile body stage by stage. Ottilie helped him in every way; she fetched and carried, concerned, but as if in another world; for the greatest misfortune, like the greatest good luck, changes the face of things; and she did not leave Charlotte's room, where all this was taking place, until the good man, every attempt exhausted, shook his head, answering her anxious questions at first with silence, then with a gentle "no." Hardly had she entered the living room than she fell face down, exhausted, on the carpet, unable to reach the sofa.

At this moment Charlotte's carriage was heard. In an urgent tone, the doctor begged those present to step back; he would go to her and prepare her. But she had already stepped into her room. She found Ottilie on the floor, and a house maid started towards her, crying and weeping. The doctor came in, and she learned the whole story at once. But how could she give up all hope at a single stroke! Experienced in these things, the wise and tactful man only begged her not to go to see the infant; he left the room, letting her think that he was making renewed attempts to revive the child. Charlotte sat down on the sofa, Ottilie was still stretched out on the ground, but with her lovely head resting on her friend's knee. The kind doctor paced back and forth; he appeared to be occupied with the baby, but in fact he was concerned about the women. So midnight came and the deathly silence grew deeper. Charlotte no longer deluded herself that the child could be revived; she asked to see him. He had been placed in a basket, wrapped in warm woolens; only his little face was visible; he lay there on the sofa beside her, calm and beautiful.

The accident had alarmed the whole village, and soon the news reached the inn. The Major had taken the usual path up to the manor; he went around the house and, stopping a servant who was fetching something from the annex, he questioned her closely and had the doctor sent out to him. The doctor, astonished at the arrival of his former patron, informed him of the present situation and took it upon himself to prepare Charlotte to see him. He went inside and began to speak with her, leading her from one thing to another until he finally conjured up the image of her friend, and his sympathy, of which she could be assured. He soon made the transition from his nearness in thought and spirit to the Major's actual presence. In short, she heard that her friend was at the door, knew everything and wished to be asked in.

The Major entered; Charlotte greeted him with a sad smile. He stood before her. She lifted the green silk coverlet over the little body, and in the dim glow of a candle he saw, not without an inward shudder, his own frozen image. Charlotte motioned to a chair, and so they sat opposite each other, silently, the whole night. Ottilie still lay peacefully on Charlotte's knees; she breathed gently; she slept, or seemed to sleep.

Morning came, the candle went out, and the two friends seemed to awaken from a heavy dream. Charlotte looked at the Major and said calmly: "Tell me, my friend, what fate brings you here to take part in this scene of sorrow?"

"This is not the time," the Major answered in the same soft voice as she—as if they had not wished to wake Ottilie—"this is not the time or place to hold back, to make long introductions or to approach things in a roundabout way. Your situation is so monstrous even the important matter that brought me here pales in significance."

He told her then, quite calmly and simply, the purpose of his visit, the reason why Edward had sent him and his own motivation, interest and intention in coming. He gave a most tactful and honest account of both reasons; Charlotte listened calmly and appeared neither shocked nor annoyed.

When the Major had finished, Charlotte answered very softly, so that he had to move his chair closer, "I have never been in a situation like this, but in similar ones I have always said: 'What will it look like tomorrow?' I am well aware that several people's fates are now in my hands; and there is no doubt what I should do; it can be briefly stated. I agree to the divorce. I should have agreed to it earlier; my hesitation, my resistance have caused the baby's death. Fate takes charge of certain things, and it is very stubborn. Reason and virtue, duty and all that is sacred oppose it in vain: things are bound to happen which seem justified to fate but not to us; and so it asserts itself, whatever course we take.

"But what am I saying! In fact, fate is trying to carry out my own wishes and intentions, which I have counteracted in my thoughtlessness. Didn't I always imagine Ottilie and Edward as a most charming match? Didn't I myself attempt to bring the two together? Weren't you yourself, my friend, an accomplice to these plans? And why couldn't I distinguish a man's stubbornness from true love? Why did I accept his proposal when I could have remained a friend to him and made him happy with another wife? And look at this poor unfortunate asleep here! I tremble to think of the moment when she will come back to consciousness from her death-like slumber. How can she live on, how can she console herself if she is unable to hope that her love can replace what she, as the tool of a mysterious fate, has taken from Edward? And through her affection, through the passion with which she loves him, she can give everything back to him. If love can endure all, it can do even more: it can restore all. There should be no thought of me at this time.

"Leave quietly, dear Major. Tell Edward that I agree to the divorce and that I leave it to you and Mittler to take care of everything, that I have no worries about my future and that I have no cause to be concerned in any way. I will sign any papers that are brought to me; but do not ask me to take an active part in it or participate in the thinking and planning."

The Major stood up. She gave him her hand over Ottilie's prostrate body. He pressed his lips to this dear hand. "And for myself, what may I hope?" he whispered softly.

"Do not ask me to answer that question yet," replied Charlotte. "We did not deserve to be made unhappy, but we do not yet deserve to be happy together."

The Major left, pitying Charlotte in his deepest heart, but unable to feel for the poor departed infant. A sacrifice of this kind seemed necessary for the happiness of them all. He thought of Charlotte with a child of his on her arm as the most perfect replacement for the loss she had caused Edward; he thought of his own son on his lap, a son who would more rightfully resemble him than the child who had died.

Such were the flattering hopes and thoughts passing through his mind on his way back to the inn when he met Edward, who, as there had been no fireworks or cannon-thunder to signal the success of his venture, had spent the whole night outdoors waiting for him. He had already heard of the accident, and he too, instead of pitying the poor dead creature, regarded what had happened, without quite admitting it to himself, as an act of fate that had removed at a stroke every obstacle to his happiness. So once Edward had been informed briefly of his wife's decision, it was easy for the Major to persuade him to return to the village and from there to the town where they would decide what should be done first.

After the Major had left her, Charlotte had been sitting lost in thought, but only for a few moments, when Ottilie sat up and looked at her friend with wide eyes. She lifted her head from Charlotte's lap, got up from the floor and stood before her.

"For the second time now," the lovely girl began with her irresistible seriousness and charm, "for the second time I have had the same experience. You once said to me that in a person's life things often repeat themselves, and always at significant moments. Now I find your observation was correct, and I am obliged to make a confession to you. Shortly after my mother's death, when I was a young child, I had moved my stool up close to you; you sat, as now, on the sofa; my head lay on your knees and I neither woke nor slept; I slumbered. I heard everything that was going on around me, especially everything that was said; and yet I was unable to move or speak, and even if I had wanted to I could not have given a sign that I was conscious. On that occasion you were talking about me with a friend of yours; you pitied my fate, left alone as an orphan in the world; you spoke of my dependency and of what an ill turn things might take if there were no lucky star to guide me. I understood it all clearly and took perhaps too literally your wishes and expectations for me. According to my own limited lights, I laid down rules for myself about these things; and I have lived within them for a long time: all my actions were in accordance with them when you loved and cared for me, when you took me into your house, and for some time afterward as well.

"But I have strayed from my path, I have broken my rules, I have even lost all sense of them. After this terrible event, you have once again made me see the position I am in, more pitiful now than before. Resting half-dazed on your lap I heard once again as if from another world your gentle voice at my ear; I heard what my prospects are; I

stand in dread of myself; but now, as once before, I have traced out a
new path for myself while in a trance-like state.

"I am determined, as I was before, and what I have determined to do
you shall learn immediately. I shall never be Edward's! God has opened
my eyes in a terrible way and made me see what a crime I have been
caught up in. I will repent; and let no one try to make me give up my
intentions! Dearest, beloved friend, make your decisions accordingly.
Ask the Major to come back; write to him that no steps are to be taken.
How anxious I was at not being able to move or stir when he was going.
I wanted to start up and cry out: Do not let him go in such wicked
expectations!"

Charlotte understood Ottilie's state of mind; but she hoped that with
time and by presenting things to her in the right way she might win her
over. But when she suggested that the future might bring hope and a
lessening of pain—"No!" cried Ottilie indignantly; "do not try to
change my mind or to act behind my back! The instant I hear you have
agreed to the divorce I will atone for my sin, my crime in the very same
lake!"

Chapter Fifteen

When friends, relatives, members of a single household, living happily
and peacefully together, devote more of their conversation than neces-
sary or appropriate to their current or future doings—when they re-
peatedly tell each other of their plans, projects and preoccupations and,
without actually accepting the others' advice, discuss life in general in a
way that suggests they are seeking it—then it happens that at important
times, when you would think that they needed other people's help and
support most, quite the contrary occurs: they withdraw into themselves,
acting for themselves in their own ways and, concealing the separate
paths they have taken, let their companions hear only of ends, results,
and achievements.

After so many strange and unhappy events a certain quiet seriousness
had settled upon the women, taking the form of affectionate restraint
and tact. Charlotte had had the child buried without great ceremony
in the chapel. He found a resting-place there as the first victim of an
impending fate.

Charlotte made her way back into life as far as possible, and she
found Ottilie was the first to need her support. She paid particular atten-
tion to her, but in an unobtrusive way. She knew how much the inno-
cent girl loved Edward; she had tried to learn what had happened just
before the accident and had pieced it together bit by bit, in part from
Ottilie herself, in part from correspondence with the Major.

Ottilie for her part made Charlotte's present life much easier. She was open, talkative even, but she never spoke of their present situation or of what had just happened. She had always been observant and noticing; she knew a good deal; and this now all became evident. She amused and distracted Charlotte, who still nourished the secret hope that a couple so dear to her might come together.

But Ottilie saw things differently. She had told Charlotte the secret basis of her way of life and had been released from her former restrictions and servitude. She felt that her repentance and the decision she had made relieved her of the burden of her wrongdoing, the accident. She no longer needed to put any constraints on herself; she had forgiven herself in her heart of hearts under the sole condition of total renunciation, and this condition was binding for all time.

Things went on in this way, and Charlotte came to realize how much the house and gardens, the lakes, cliffs and trees only served to renew their sense of tragedy daily. That they would have to move was only too evident, but how to do it was not so easy to work out.

Should the two women stay together? Edward's earlier wish seemed to demand it, his declarations and threats to make it necessary; but how could anyone fail to see that for all their good will, common sense and self-control the two women, living together, were in an embarrassing situation? Their conversations skirted the real issue. There were times, perhaps, when they only wanted to half understand, but more often an expression was misinterpreted, if not by the mind, then by the emotions. They were afraid to hurt each other, yet this very fear was their most vulnerable point and also their most hurtful.

If they were to move somewhere else and live separately, at least for a time, then the old question of where Ottilie should go came up again. That rich and noble family of which we heard before had attempted in vain to provide their promising only daughter with interesting and stimulating young companions. Charlotte had been asked to send Ottilie to them during the baroness' last visit and more recently by letter; now she brought the topic up once more. But Ottilie firmly refused to go into what is known as high society.

"Dear aunt," she said, "so that I won't appear stubborn and inflexible, let me tell you what I would otherwise be obliged to conceal. A person who has suffered uncommon misfortune, even if innocent, is marked in a terrible way. His presence inspires in all who meet him, all who set eyes on him, a kind of horror. Everyone claims to see his monstrous fate written on his face; everyone is curious and fearful at one and the same time. A house or a city where a monstrous deed has taken place remains terrifying to anyone who enters it. The light of day is not so bright there, and the stars seem to lose their shine.

"Excusable though it may be, how indiscreet people are towards such

unfortunates, how foolishly intrusive and clumsily kind! Forgive me for
speaking in this way; but I suffered terribly for that poor girl when
Luciane took her from the hidden rooms of the house she lived in, made
a fuss over her and forced her in her well-meaning way to take part in
games and dancing. When the poor thing, increasingly upset, took flight
and fell down in a faint in my arms while the assembled company,
aghast, was getting excited and really starting to be curious about the
unfortunate girl, I did not think a similar fate was to be mine; but my
sympathy, true and keen as it was, has not grown any less. Now I can
turn my compassion towards myself and take care not to be the cause of
such scenes."

"But, my dear child," replied Charlotte, "you cannot avoid being
seen. We don't have any convents in which to find a refuge from the
feelings you describe."

"Solitude is no sanctuary, dear aunt," replied Ottilie. "The most de-
sirable sanctuary is a place where we can be active. Atonement and
self-denial cannot shield us from an ominous fate if it is determined to
persecute us. If I am idly held up to the world, I find it repugnant and
frightening. But if I am happily working away, tirelessly doing my duty,
I don't mind who sees me, since I have no cause to fear being seen by
God."

"If I'm not very much mistaken," said Charlotte, "you're leaning
towards going back to boarding school."

"Yes," Ottilie answered, "I don't deny it. I think it must be a fine
calling, to teach others in the customary way when we ourselves have
been taught in the strangest. And doesn't history teach us that those
unfortunate sinners who withdrew into the wilderness in no way re-
mained hidden and protected there, as they had hoped? They were
called back into the world again to lead back onto the right path others
who had gone astray; and who could do so better than those who knew
already life's misleading detours? They were called to give help to the
unfortunate; and who could do so more readily than those beyond all
earthly misfortune?"

"What a strange calling you have chosen," replied Charlotte. "I won't
oppose it; do so, if you wish, but I hope it will be only for a short while."

"I'm really grateful," said Ottilie, "that you're willing to let me make
this experiment and gain this experience. Unless I flatter myself too
much, it will work out well. Once I am there, I shall remember how
many tests I took and how insignificant they were in comparison with
the test I faced later. How happy I will be to watch the young pupils'
difficulties, smile at their childish problems and gently show them the
way out of all their little errors. Happy people are not the right ones to
instruct those who are happy; it is human nature to demand more from
oneself and others than one has received. Only someone who is recover-

ing from misfortune can show himself and others how moderate good fortune can be a cause for delight."

"Let me raise one more objection to your plan," said Charlotte at last, after some hesitation, "an objection I think is the most important one. I am not thinking of you, but of someone else. You know the feelings of our good, sensible, earnest schoolmaster. If you take the path you propose you will grow dearer and more indispensable to him by the day. Since he already feels he cannot live without you, he will be unable to do his work without you in the future once he has become used to your help. You will start out by supporting him, only to spoil it for him in the end."

"Fate has not been kind to me," replied Ottilie, "and those who love me can expect to fare no better. Our friend is kind and intelligent, and so I hope he will come to regard himself simply as a friend; he will see in me a person singled out by fate, who can atone for a monstrous calamity perhaps only by dedicating herself to all that is holy and which alone, invisibly surrounding us, can protect us from the monstrous powers that threaten us."

Charlotte thought over in private all the dear child had said. From time to time she had enquired, ever so gently, whether there might be some hope of Ottilie's going back to Edward; but even the slightest suggestion, the faintest hopeful word, the smallest hint seemed to hurt Ottilie deeply. On one occasion, when there was no way of getting around it, she made her view on this quite plain.

"If your decision to give Edward up is so firm and irrevocable," responded Charlotte, "then you must beware of the danger of seeing him again. When we are separated from the one we love, the more passionate our feelings are, we can control them all the better by turning the whole force of our passion inward instead of outward; but how soon, how suddenly is our delusion revealed when once more the person we thought we had given up appears before us and we see that we cannot do without him. Do for now what you find most appropriate; put yourself to the test, change your present decision if you wish, but you must do so yourself, of your own free will. Do not let yourself be drawn back into your former life by chance or out of alarm; then you will feel unbearably divided. As I say, before you take this step, before you leave here and begin a new life, consider one more time whether you can really give Edward up forever. But once you have made up your mind, let us make an agreement that you will not have anything to do with him, not speak to him even if he should seek you out and put you under pressure to see him." Ottilie did not hesitate for a second, she gave Charlotte her word, as she had already given it to herself.

But Charlotte was still troubled by Edward's threat that he could renounce Ottilie only as long as she stayed with Charlotte. It was true that things had greatly changed since then and so much had happened that this threat, uttered in the heat of the moment, was doubtless no longer valid in the light of later events. Yet she did not wish in the slightest to risk taking any step that might wound him, and so she asked Mittler to try to find out Edward's present feelings.

Since the baby's death Mittler had come to see Charlotte several times, if only briefly. The accident, which made a reconciliation of husband and wife seem most unlikely, had affected him powerfully; but acting as ever on hope, he was secretly pleased by Ottilie's decision. He had faith in the passage of time and its soothing power and still believed he could bring Charlotte and Edward back together, seeing all these emotional turbulences only as tests of married love and faithfulness.

Charlotte had written to the Major right at the outset about Ottilie's first declaration of her intentions. She begged him urgently to persuade Edward not to take any further steps but to wait patiently and see if the dear child might not recover from her shock. She had told him, too, the main details of her later plans and inclinations, and now Mittler had the difficult task of preparing Edward for this change. But Mittler, knowing well that we can accept something that has taken place more readily than something only planned, persuaded Charlotte that the best thing would be to send Ottilie back to boarding school immediately.

So as soon as he had left, preparations were made for Ottilie's journey. She packed her things, but Charlotte could not help noticing that she made no move to take the beautiful chest or any of its contents. She said nothing, and let the girl silently do as she wish. The day of departure came; Charlotte's carriage would take Ottilie to a place they knew where she would spend the first night; on the second she would drive on to the school. Little Nan was to go with her and stay with her as her maid. The affectionate little girl had found her way back to Ottilie right after the baby's death and was by nature and inclination as devoted to her as she had ever been; in fact, she seemed with her amusing chatter to be trying to make up for the time she had missed and to serve her beloved mistress even more devotedly. She was quite beside herself now over her luck in being allowed to travel with Ottilie and see other parts, since she had never left her birthplace. She ran from the manor to the village telling her parents and relatives of her good fortune and saying her goodbyes. But as luck would have it, she happened to visit a friend who had the measles, and right away she showed signs of infection. The journey could not be postponed; Ottilie herself insisted on leaving; she knew the way from before, she knew the people who kept the inn where she would stay the night; Charlotte's coachman would be taking her there, and so there was no cause for concern.

Charlotte made no objection. Her mind, too, was running on plans for leaving this place; she only wanted to get the rooms Ottilie had been using ready for Edward, just as they had been before the Major had come to stay. Hope of bringing back happy times flares up in us at a moment's notice; and Charlotte had a right, in fact a need, to have such hopes as this.

Chapter Sixteen

When Mittler arrived to talk things over with Edward, he found him alone, his head resting on his right hand, his arm propped on the table. He seemed to be suffering a great deal. "Is your headache troubling you again?" Mittler asked. "It is troubling me," Edward replied, "but I cannot hate it, for it reminds me of Ottilie. Perhaps she is suffering now too, I think, leaning on her left arm, and suffering perhaps more than I. And why should I not bear it as she does? This pain has a healing power, I can almost say I welcome it; for it brings the image of her patience, and all her other virtues, all the more clearly, vividly, forcefully to mind; only in suffering do we sense most fully all the great qualities needed to bear it."

Finding his friend so resigned, Mittler did not hesitate to mention his errand, which he recounted stage by stage as the thought had originated with the women and as it had developed into a fully worked-out plan. Edward hardly said anything against it. From the little he said it appeared that he left everything to them; his headache seemed to have made him indifferent to everything.

Hardly was he alone than he began to pace up and down in his room. He was no longer aware of his headache; he was occupied with things outside himself. In the course of Mittler's narrative his fantasy had formed a vivid image of his dear Ottilie. He saw her alone, or as good as alone, on the familiar path, in the familiar inn whose rooms he had entered so often; he thought, he reflected—or rather he thought without reflecting; he only hoped and desired. He had to see her, speak to her. Why, for what purpose, what should come of it was not of moment. He did not resist, he was compelled to act.

He took his valet into his confidence and the man promptly found out the day and hour when Ottilie was to set out. The morning came; Edward rode off straight away, unaccompanied, to the place where Ottilie was to spend the night. He arrived there far too early; the astonished landlady received him with delight, since he had been the cause of a great piece of family fortune. He had witnessed the deeds of her son, who had been a brave soldier in battle, had praised them handsomely to the general, overcoming the objections of several people who had not wished him well, and procured the young man a medal. The landlady could not do enough to please him. She quickly cleared up as best she could in her dressing room, which was at the same time a coat closet and storeroom; but he announced to her the arrival of a lady who was to spend the night here, and had a little room provisionally set up for himself at the back behind the hall. The landlady thought all this mysterious, and it pleased her to do her patron a favor. Edward showed great interest and lent a helping hand throughout. And with what emotions did he spend the long, long hours till evening! He looked at the room around him where he was to set eyes on her; in its strange domesticity it seemed to him a heavenly abode. What plans he made, what decisions! Should he take her by surprise or prepare her beforehand? In the end the latter plan held sway; he sat down to write. This was the letter she was to receive:

EDWARD TO OTTILIE

"As you read this letter, dearest, I am close by. Do not start, do not be frightened; you have nothing to fear from me. I will not force myself upon you. You will not see me until you yourself give permission.

Think first of your position and of mine. How grateful I am that the step you are planning is not definitive; but it is a significant one nonetheless. Do not take it! Here, at this crossroad, as it were, reflect once more: Can you be mine, will you be mine? Oh, you would do us all a great favor, and me a munificent one.

Let me see you again, let me look on you again with joy. Let me ask this sweet question with my own lips, and answer it with your sweet self. Come to my breast, Ottilie, where you sometimes rested and where you will always belong!"

While he was writing he had the feeling that what he so much desired was near, that soon she would be there. She will come in through this door, she will read this letter, she whose vision I have so often conjured up will stand in reality before me. Will she still be the same? Will she look different, feel differently? He held the pen in his hand, he wanted to write down what he was thinking; but the carriage rolled into the courtyard. Hastily he added: "I hear you coming. Farewell—but only for a moment!"

He folded the letter and signed it; there was no time to seal it. He rushed into the room through which he hoped to reach the hallway, but suddenly he remembered that he had left his watch and signet on the table. She should not see these first; he hurried back and managed to remove them. From the entry he could hear the landlady approaching the room to show her guest in. He rushed towards the door to the little room, but it had swung shut. The key lay inside, where he had thrown it down when he hurried in; the lock had snapped closed and he was trapped. He pushed with all his might against the door; it did not yield. Oh how he wished he could have slipped through the crack like a ghost! In vain! He hid his face against the doorpost. Ottilie entered, the landlady stepped back when she caught sight of him. He could not stay hidden a single moment from Ottilie either. He turned towards her, and so the lovers stood looking at each other once again in the strangest way. She looked at him solemnly and calmly, stepping neither forward nor back, and as he moved to approach her, she stepped back a few paces to the table. He too stepped back. "Ottilie," he cried, "let me break this terrible silence! Are we no more than shadows standing opposite each other? But first of all, listen! it is an accident that you find me here right now. There is a letter there that was to prepare you. Read, I beg you, read it! and decide as you must."

She glanced down at the letter, thought a moment, then opened and read it. She read it without changing her expression, and laid it gently aside; then she pressed her hands together and raised them to her breast, bending forward a little and looking at her urgent supplicant with such a gaze that he was forced to give up all his desires and demands. This gesture broke his heart. He could not bear the sight of Ottilie in this posture. It looked for all the world as if she would fall to her knees if he persisted. In despair he hastened to the door, left her alone and sent the landlady in to her.

He paced up and down in the entryway. Night had fallen, and the room was silent. At last the landlady came out and took out the key. The good woman was moved and embarrassed; she did not know what to do. In the end, as she went away, she offered Edward the key, but he did not take it. She left the lamp there and went away.

Edward, in the darkest despair, fell upon Ottilie's doorstep weeping. Lovers can hardly ever have spent a more pitiful night so close together.

Day came; the coachman arrived; the landlady opened up and went into the room. Finding Ottilie asleep in her clothes, she went back and beckoned to Edward with a sympathetic smile. They both went in to the sleeping girl; but Edward could not bear to look at her. The landlady did not dare wake the sleeping child, and so she sat down across from her. At last Ottilie opened her lovely eyes and got up. She refused to have any breakfast. Now Edward came up to her. He begged her fervently to say just a word, to declare her wishes. His wishes were hers, he vowed; but she remained silent. Again he asked her, lovingly and urgently, if she would be his. How beautifully, her eyes cast down, she shook her head in gentle refusal! He asked if she wished to go to the boarding school. Indifferent, again she indicated 'no.' When he asked if he should bring her back to Charlotte, she assented with a serene nod. He hurried to the window and gave the driver orders; but quick as lightning she dashed from behind him out of the room, down the steps and into the carriage. The driver took the road towards the manor; Edward followed on horseback at some distance.

Chapter Seventeen

How very surprised Charlotte was when she saw Ottilie drive up and Edward burst into the courtyard at a gallop! She rushed to the door. Ottilie got out and came towards the house with Edward. She grasped the hands of the two spouses with some fervor, pressed them together, and hurried to her room. Edward flung his arms around Charlotte and dissolved in tears; unable to explain himself, he begged her to be patient with him and supportive and helpful to Ottilie. Hurrying to Ottilie's room, Charlotte was horrified to see upon entering that it had been totally cleared of furniture and only the bare walls remained. It seemed overlarge and uninviting. Everything had been taken away except for the little chest, which, as no one had known where to put it, had been left standing in the middle of the room. Ottilie lay on the ground, her head and arm draped over the chest. Charlotte went to her, asked what had happened, but received no answer.

Leaving her maid to bring Ottilie something to revive her, she hastened to Edward. She found him in the drawing room; but he, too, was uncommunicative. He threw himself down at her feet, bathed her hand in tears and fled to his room. When Charlotte got up to follow him, the valet appeared and told her what he could. The rest she could imagine. In her decisive way, she began to think what must be done. Ottilie's room was quickly set up again. Edward had found his just as he had left it, down to the last paper.

The three seemed to find themselves together again, but Ottilie persisted in her silence, and Edward could do nothing but ask his wife to show the patience he himself lacked. Charlotte sent messengers to Mittler and the Major. The former could not be found, but the latter was able to come. Edward poured out his heart to him, confessing every last detail, and so Charlotte found out what had happened, what had caused the strange change of plans and created so much disturbance.

She had an earnest talk with Edward, and could think of no other request than that the dear child not be put under any pressure for the moment. Edward was well aware what a fine person his wife was, how affectionate and reasonable; but his emotions had taken complete control of him. Charlotte gave him hope, promising to agree to the divorce. He did not trust her; he felt so sick that hope and faith deserted him by turns; he urged Charlotte to promise her hand to the Major; a kind of crazed depression had taken hold of him. To calm and restrain him,

Charlotte obeyed his request. She promised the Major her hand in the event that Ottilie should wish to marry Edward, but under the express condition that both men go on a journey together for a while. The Major had been commissioned by his patrons to do some business in another town, and Edward promised to go with him. In the course of making preparations they were comforted a little by the feeling that at least something was being done.

Meanwhile it was evident that Ottilie took neither food nor drink, and was still persisting in her silence. When they tried to encourage her, she got upset; and so they gave up. After all, is it not a common weakness to be reluctant to torture someone even for their own good? Charlotte thought through all possible solutions, and finally she had the idea of sending for the schoolmaster who had previously had such a good influence on Ottilie. He had written asking why she had not arrived, but they had not yet answered his letter.

So as not to take Ottilie by surprise, they spoke of this plan in her presence. She did not appear to agree; she deliberated; finally she seemed to have come to a decision, she hurried to her room and before evening sent the others the following letter.

Ottilie to Her Friends

"What need is there for me to say outright, dear friends, what is plain for all to see? I have strayed from my path, and I must find my way back again. A hostile and demonic power that has taken hold of me seems to prevent me from doing so, even if I had been able to find peace with myself once more.

It was my honest intention to renounce Edward, to separate from him. I hoped I would never meet him again. But it happened differently; without intending to, he found himself in my presence. Perhaps I interpreted too literally my promise not to communicate further with him. In accordance with my conscience and my feelings at the time, I did not speak, but remained silent before my friend, and now I have nothing more to say. Prompted by an inner impulse, it happened that I made a strict vow, one that might be burdensome if entered upon consciously. Let me keep to it as long as my heart demands it. Do not call in anyone from outside! Do not urge me to speak or to take more food and drink than I need. Help me through this time—be patient and considerate. I am young, and youth restores itself without prompting. Suffer me in your presence, make me happy in your love, instruct me through your conversation; but leave to me my innermost feelings!"

Because of a delay in the Major's business the men's trip, though long prepared for, did not take place. How pleased Edward was! Encouraged once more by Ottilie's letter and her comforting, hopeful words, and feeling justified in his staunch persistence, he suddenly declared that he would not go at all. "How foolish it is," he exclaimed, "to throw away rashly, deliberately the thing we most vitally need when we might be able to keep it, even though we risk its loss! And what for? Only that we may seem to have free will and choice. Often possessed by such foolish conceit, I have torn myself away from friends hours or even days too early, so as not to be forced to leave by the last inevitable deadline. But this time I will stay. Why should I go away? Hasn't she already been separated from me? It doesn't occur to me to take her hand or press her to my heart; I don't even dare to think of it, it makes me shudder. She has not gone away from me, but risen higher."

And so he stayed, as he wished and needed to. But nothing could be compared with the content he felt in her presence. And she too had the same feeling; she too could not break free of this blissful compulsion. As always they had an indescribable, almost magical power of attraction for each other. They lived under one roof; but even when they were not exactly thinking of each other and were occupied with other things, drawn back and forth by the doings of their friends, they still approached each other. If they chanced to be in the same room, it did not take long before they were standing or sitting beside each other. Only their immediate presence could put them completely at ease, and this presence was enough; not a glance, a word, a gesture, a touch was needed, just each other's company. Then they were not two people, but one person alone in complete unconscious contentment, at peace with self and world. Indeed, if one of the two had been held captive at one end of the house, the other would have moved, involuntarily, unintentionally, in that direction. Life was a puzzle to them, and only together could they find its solution.

Ottilie was quite calm and serene, and hence the friends were no longer concerned about her. She seldom left them, but she had contrived to take her meals alone. No one but little Nan waited on her.

Familiar experiences recur more often than we think, since our own nature is the main cause of them. Character, individuality, inclination, disposition, place, surroundings and habits—all form a whole where every individual floats, as it were, in an element or atmosphere comfortable for him alone. And so to our great astonishment we find people, so often accused of fickleness, unchanged after many years, and unchangeable, despite innumerable influences external and internal.

Thus in our friends' daily life everything moved almost in its accustomed way. Ottilie still showed her attentiveness through many a quiet little action, and the others behaved as usual. In this way the domestic circle was like a replica of their previous way of life, and they could be forgiven their delusion that all had remained the same.

The autumn days, in length the same as those of spring, called the company back into the house from outdoors at the same hour. The decorations of fruit and flowers typical of this season seemed to be the autumn of their first spring; the intervening time had been forgotten. For now the same flowers were blooming that had been planted in those first days; the fruits were ripening on the same trees they had seen flowering then.

The Major walked up and down; Mittler, too, often joined them. They came together regularly in the evenings. Edward usually read aloud, more vividly, with more feeling, better—more serenely, if you will—than before. It was as if, through happiness as much as emotion, he wanted to take away Ottilie's paralysis and unlock her silence again. He sat as before so that she could look at the book over his shoulder; he even became restless and distracted when she could not see it, even though he was not certain she was following his words with her eyes.

Gone was that unpleasant, embarrassing atmosphere of the time between. No one bore any grudges; every kind of bitterness had vanished. The Major played his violin to Charlotte's accompaniment, and Ottilie's piano playing joined as before with Edward's flute. So they drew nearer to Edward's birthday, which had not been celebrated the year before. This time it was to be observed without festivity in quiet companionableness. This was the agreement they had made with each other, in part expressly, in part tacitly. But the nearer the time came, the more Ottilie's solemnity, which they had sensed rather than actually noticed until now, increased. She often seemed to contemplate the flowers in the garden; she had signaled to the gardener that he should spare the summer flowers of every kind, and she lingered in particular near the asters which were blooming this year, as it happened, in countless masses.

Chapter Eighteen

The most important thing the friends noticed, though, as they watched in silence, was that Ottilie had unpacked the little chest for the first time, and had selected and cut out various fabrics, sufficient to make a single complete outfit. When she tried, with little Nan's help, to repack the rest, she could hardly do so; the chest was full to overflowing, even though part of the contents had been taken out. The envious young girl could not take her eyes off the things, especially since she saw that provision had been made for even the smallest accessory. Shoes, stockings, garters with embroidered mottoes, gloves and many other things still remained. She begged Ottilie to give her some of them. Ottilie refused, but, going straight to one of her dresser drawers, she let the child choose what she wished. Nan grabbed her booty awkwardly, running off with it straight away to show everyone else in the household her great fortune.

Finally Ottilie managed to pack everything back in carefully; then she opened a secret compartment in the lid. Here she kept little notes and letters from Edward, numerous dried flowers, souvenirs of their walks, a lock of his hair and all kinds of other objects. She added one more thing—her father's portrait—and locked the whole chest, hanging the delicate key around her neck again on a golden chain.

Meanwhile many hopes had arisen in her friends' hearts. Charlotte was convinced that Ottilie would begin to speak again on Edward's birthday; for she had recently shown a concealed activity, a kind of calm satisfaction with herself, a smile of the kind one has when keeping a virtuous and happy secret from one's loved ones. No one knew that Ottilie spent many an hour in a state of great weakness, from which she revived herself by sheer willpower during the times when she appeared in company.

Mittler had visited often during this time and had stayed longer than usual. The stubborn fellow knew only too well that there is a certain moment, and a certain moment alone, when the iron is hot. He interpreted Ottilie's silence and her refusal of food in his own favor. No step had yet been taken towards Edward and Charlotte's divorce; he hoped to steer the dear girl in some other useful direction; he listened, he yielded, he hinted and behaved himself tactically enough after his fashion.

But he always got carried away the moment he saw he had a chance to argue about topics he considered important. He tended to introspection, but when he was with others he related to them through action. If he once got talking when he was with friends, as we have already had frequent occasion to observe, his words poured out unthinkingly, hurting or healing, helping or harming as the case might happen to be.

The evening before Edward's birthday Charlotte and the Major were sitting together waiting for Edward, who had gone out riding. Mittler was pacing up and down the room. Ottilie had stayed in her bedroom laying out her finery for the next day and giving silent instructions to her little servant, who completely understood her and obeyed her unspoken commands.

Mittler had just embarked on one of his favorite topics. He liked to maintain that in the education of children, as also in the government of nations, nothing was more barbarous and inappropriate than prohibitions, restrictive laws and regulations. "Mankind is good by nature," he used to say, "and if you give a human being orders, he takes them up immediately, carrying them out and acting upon them. I for my own part prefer to be tolerant of faults and weaknesses in people I know until I can instill the opposite virtue, rather than getting rid of the fault and having nothing proper to put in its place. People are very willing to do what is good and useful when they have the opportunity; they do so in order to have something to do and spend no more time mulling it over than they do the silly pranks they play out of idleness and boredom.

"How it annoys me to hear pupils repeating the Ten Commandments in the classroom. The Fourth is quite a nice, sensible, positive Commandment. 'Thou shalt honor thy father and thy mother.' If children impress that properly upon their minds, they could practice it all day long. But as to the Fifth, what can we say to that? 'Thou shalt not kill.' As if anyone had the slightest desire to murder anyone else! You hate someone, you get angry, a hasty step and the result of it all—and much else besides—is that you come to the point where you happen to kill someone. But is it not barbarous to forbid children to kill and murder? If we were to say, 'Take care of the lives of others, remove what may harm them, save them even at your own peril; if you harm them, bear in mind that you are harming yourself'—those are commandments that have a place in educated, rational nations yet which are quite inadequately brought in as an appendix to the catechism.

"And as for the Sixth, I find it quite repugnant! What? Should we excite the curiosity of children about dangerous mysteries of which they have the merest inkling and stimulate their fancy to conjure up the wildest thoughts and ideas, thus forcing upon them what we would like to keep from them! It would be far better if such things were to be punished at will by a secret tribunal than that they be blabbered about in church and parish."

At that moment Ottilie came into the room. "'Thou shalt not commit adultery'," Mittler continued. "How crude, how indecent! Would it not sound quite different if we were to say, 'Thou shalt show respect for the marriage bond; when thou seest a husband and wife who love each other thou shalt take pleasure and delight in it as in the good fortune of a sunny day. If any cloud should fall upon their relationship, thou shalt essay to dispel it; thou shalt seek to make peace and reconcile them, to show them their worth to each other, and with supreme generosity work towards their welfare by making them see the joys of duty, most especially that which indissolubly unites man and wife?'"

Charlotte was in agony, and her embarrassment was all the more nerve-racking because she was convinced that Mittler had no idea what he was saying and where. Before she could interrupt him she saw Ottilie leaving the room with an altered expression.

"You will leave us the Seventh Commandment, I presume," Charlotte said with a forced laugh. "All the rest," replied Mittler, "if I can only save that one on which the others are based."

With a terrible cry little Nan burst into the room. "She's dying! My mistress is dying! Hurry! Hurry!"

When Ottilie had staggered back into her room, her finery lay spread out on several chairs all ready for the next morning, and little Nan, who was walking back and forth gazing at it admiringly, cried out, "Just look, dear mistress, it is a bridal dress quite worthy of you!"

At these words, Ottilie sinks down upon the sofa. Nan sees that her mistress has become pale and rigid; she runs to Charlotte, who comes at once. Their friend the house doctor arrives in haste; he thinks it simply a nervous collapse. He sends for some broth; Ottilie refuses it with a gesture of repugnance, and practically has convulsions as the cup is brought to her lips. With all the speed and gravity the occasion demands, he asks what Ottilie has eaten that day. Nan hesitates; he repeats his question; the girl confesses that Ottilie has eaten nothing.

Little Nan seems more nervous than is warranted. The doctor takes her into the next room, Charlotte follows, and the girl falls to her knees admitting that Ottilie has eaten virtually nothing for a long time. At Ottilie's request she has eaten all her meals for her; she said nothing about it, at the fervent urgings and threats of her mistress—and also, she adds in all innocence, because it tasted so very good.

The Major and Mittler arrived; they found Charlotte busy with the doctor. The pale angelic child was sitting, apparently conscious, in a corner of the sofa. They begged her to lie down; she refused, but indicated that the little chest should be brought in. She placed her feet on it and took up a comfortable, half-reclining position. She seemed to want to say good-bye, her gestures expressed the tenderest affection, love, apology and the fondest farewell to those standing by.

Dismounting, Edward heard what had happened, rushed into the room, knelt down by her side, clasped her hand and covered it with silent tears. He remained there a long time. Finally he cried, "Shall I never hear your voice again? Will you not come back to life with a single word for me? Very well, I will follow you; in the other life we will speak in other tongues!"

She pressed his hand fervently, turned on him a look full of love and life, and after a deep breath, an angelic, silent movement of her lips, she cried, all lovely and delicate, summoning up her strength, "Promise me you will live!" But at that very moment she sank back. "I promise!" he called to her, but he was only calling it after her; she had already passed away.

After a tearful night the duty of burying the dear body fell to Charlotte. The Major and Mittler assisted her. Edward's condition was pitiful to see. As soon as he could pull himself out of his despair and reflect a little, he insisted that Ottilie should not be taken away from the house; she was to be looked after and cared for as if she were still living; for she was not dead—she could not be dead. They did as he wished, at least no one did what he had expressly forbidden. He did not ask to see her.

Yet another shock, another cause for worry concerned the friends. Little Nan, having been roundly scolded by the doctor, forced to confess by means of threats, and heaped with reproaches once she had done so, had taken flight. After a long search she was found again, but she seemed to be out of her mind. Her parents took her into their care. The best treatment appeared useless; she had to be locked up, as she kept threatening to run away.

Bit by bit Edward was torn from his terrible despair, but only to his greater misfortune; for now he realized, now it was clear to him that he had lost the light of his life forever. They tried to persuade him that Ottilie, buried in the chapel, would still be amongst the living and would not lack a quiet, pleasant home. It was difficult to obtain his consent, and only on condition that she be carried in an open coffin and lie under the vault covered by a glass case with an ever-burning lamp beside it did he agree at last and seem to have accepted it all.

Her lovely body was dressed in the clothes she had prepared for herself; on her head was placed a wreath of asters, which shone in sympathy like sorrowing stars. All the gardens were robbed of their flowers to decorate the bier, the church, the chapel. They lay desolate as if winter had already obliterated all joy from the flower beds. In the earliest hours of the morning she was carried out of the house in the open coffin, and the dawning sun flushed once more her angelic face. Those present thronged around the pallbearers; no one wished to go ahead, no one to follow behind, everyone wanted to be near her, to enjoy her presence one last time. Boys, men, and women, no one was unmoved. The girls, who felt their loss most keenly, were inconsolable.

Little Nan was not there. She had been kept at home, or rather, she had not been told the day and hour of the funeral. She was kept under supervision in a room facing the garden at her parents' house. But once she heard the bells ringing she knew at once what was happening, and since her guardian had left her to see the procession, she escaped through the window into a corridor and from there, since she found all the doors closed, into the upper attic.

The procession was just weaving its way along the neat, leaf-strewn path through the village. Little Nan saw her mistress distinctly below her, more vivid, more perfect, more beautiful than all who were following the procession. Ethereal, as if borne along on clouds or waves, she seemed to motion to her servant; confused, swaying, swooning, Nan fell.

With a terrible cry on all sides, the crowd parted. The pushing and shoving forced the pallbearers to set down the coffin. The girl lay quite close to it; she appeared to have shattered every leg and limb. She was picked up, and laid, by chance or by special design, upon Ottilie's body, indeed she seemed to be trying to reach her beloved mistress with her last breath of life. But hardly had her trembling limbs touched Ottilie's garments, her powerless fingers reached Ottilie's folded hands, than the girl sprang up, raised her arms and eyes to heaven, then fell down on her knees before the coffin and gazed up at her mistress in a reverent trance.

Finally she leaped up as if inspired and cried out with sacred joy: "Yes, she has forgiven me! What no mortal, what I myself could not forgive God has forgiven me through her gaze, her gesture, her lips. Now she is resting gently and peacefully; but you saw how she raised herself up and blessed me with unfolded hands, and looked upon me kindly! You all heard her, you are my witnesses, saying to me: 'You are forgiven!' Now I am no longer a murderess amongst you, she has forgiven me, God has forgiven me, and no one can reproach me anymore."

The people crowded around; they marveled, listened, and looked again and again, and scarcely a soul knew what should be done. "Bear her to rest now," said the girl; "she has done her part, suffered her lot, and can live among us no more." The bier moved on, Nan following at the head of the procession, and they reached the church and chapel.

Now Ottilie's coffin stood there enclosed in a strong oak case, at her head the coffin of the baby, at her feet the little chest. A woman had been found to watch for the first while over the body, which lay there lovely to behold under the glass cover. But little Nan refused to let anyone deprive her of this task; she wished to remain alone, without any companionship, and diligently tend the lamp, which had been lit for the first time. She begged so eagerly and persistently that her request was granted, to prevent her growing more disturbed, which everyone feared.

But she was not alone for long; for just as night was falling and the wavering lamp took over and shed a brighter light, the architect entered the chapel. Its walls with their pious decorations appeared to him more ancient and fraught with meaning than he could ever have believed.

Little Nan sat at one side of the coffin. She did not recognize him at first; but silently she pointed to her deceased mistress. And so he stood at the other side, all youthful strength and grace, sunk in his own thoughts, motionless, pensive, his arms lowered, wringing his folded hands for pity, his head and eyes turned towards the departed Ottilie.

Once before he had stood this way before Belisarius. Involuntarily he fell into the same pose; but how natural it was now! Here too something invaluable and fine had fallen from grandeur; and if in the one case it had been a man's valor, intelligence, power, and fortune that had been mourned as irretrievably lost—qualities essential to nations and princes in their decisive hours that had been, not valued, but repudiated and rejected; so in this case such very different quiet virtues, called forth so recently by nature from her capacious depths, had been wiped out so soon by her indifferent hand—rare, lovely, charming virtues whose kindly influence the needy world welcomes always with delight and satisfaction and mourns with sorrow and longing.

The young man was silent, and so was the girl for a time; but when she saw the tears keep welling up in his eyes, when she saw how he seemed to be dissolved in sorrow, she spoke to him with such passion and sincerity, kindliness and certainty that, astonished at her flow of words, he took hold of himself and saw in his mind's eye his lovely friend as a living power in a higher region. He dried his tears, his sorrow lessened, and, kneeling down, he took his leave of Ottilie, gave little Nan his hand in fond farewell, and left that very night without seeing anyone else.

The doctor had spent the night in the church without Nan's knowledge, and found her cheerful and comforted the next morning. He had been prepared for great confusion; he expected that she would speak of conversations with Ottilie during the night and other such apparitions, but she was natural, calm and totally self-possessed. She had a clear and very accurate memory of everything that had happened, and nothing she said strayed from truth and reality, with the exception of the events at the funeral, which she recounted joyfully over and over: How Ottilie had raised herself up, blessed her, forgiven her, and granted her peace of mind forever.

Ottilie's continuing beautiful state, more sleep- than death-like, attracted many visitors. Those who lived nearby wished to see her once again, and all were eager to hear little Nan tell her incredible tale; many came to make fun of it, most of them to cast doubt on it, and a few to give credence to it.

Any need that goes unsatisfied turns us to faith. Little Nan, shattered in the eyes of the world, had been made whole at the touch of the hallowed body; why should not others experience the same in this place? At first anxious mothers brought children suffering from some malady, and thought they saw improvement right away. People's confidence increased, and in the end there was no one old or weak who had not sought comfort and relief here. The crowd of visitors grew, and soon it was necessary to close the chapel, indeed the church as well except for the hours when services were held.

Edward did not venture to visit his departed Ottilie. He lived unawares, he seemed to have no more tears, to be capable of no more sorrow. With every passing day he took less part in conversation, had less food and drink. He still seemed to find some comfort in his glass, which had, to be sure, been no truthful prophet to him. He still liked to contemplate the intertwined initials, and his grave and serious face seemed to suggest that even now he hoped to be united with Ottilie. And as every circumstance and happenstance seems to favor and lift up a man who is happy, so the pettiest incidents often come together to hurt and injure one who is unhappy.

One day, as Edward raised his beloved glass to his lips, he set it down again in horror; it was the same and not the same; he could not see a small mark he knew. When questioned, the valet was forced to admit that the original glass had recently been broken and replaced by a similar one, also from Edward's childhood. Edward could feel no anger; reality had sealed his fate, and how could a glass affect him? But it weighed heavily upon him all the same. Drink seemed repugnant to him from now on; he appeared to refrain deliberately from eating or participating in conversation.

But from time to time a restlessness came over him. He asked once more for something to eat, he began to speak again. "Oh, how unhappy I am," he said one time to the Major, who seldom left his side, "all my achievements have been a falsehood, an imitation! What to her was bliss has become anguish to me; and yet, for the sake of that bliss I must accept this anguish. I must follow her along her path; but my nature and my promise hold me back. It is a terrible duty to imitate the inimitable. How very much I am aware, old friend, that genius is needed for everything, even for martyrdom."

With Edward in this sorry state, what need is there to tell of the trouble taken by his wife, friends, doctor, relatives as they struggled for a time to help him? In the end he was found dead. Mittler was the first to make the sad discovery. He called the doctor and noted with his usual precision and composure the circumstances in which the deceased had been found. Charlotte hastened in; she suspected suicide; she was about to accuse herself and them all of unforgivable negligence. But the doctor pointed out physical, and Mittler ethical reasons to convince her that this was not the case. Death had quite clearly taken Edward by surprise. He had taken a quiet moment to spread out before him objects that had belonged to Ottilie from a case and a portfolio, things he usually kept carefully hidden: a lock of hair, flowers plucked in happier times, all the notes she had sent him, starting with the very first which his wife had handed him by such ominous chance. He could not have wished to reveal all this in the event of accidental discovery. And so this heart, which had so recently been touched by infinite emotion, lay in imperturbable peace. And since he had passed away thinking of his saint, he might rightfully be called blessed. Charlotte gave him a place beside Ottilie and decreed that no one else should be buried in that vault. On this condition she made generous donations to church and school, the minister and the teacher.

So the lovers rest side by side. Peace hovers above their resting place, smiling angels in their likeness look down at them from the vault, and what a charming moment it will be when in time to come the two awake together.

NOVELLA

Translated by Victor Lange

Novella

The heavy mist of an autumn morning veiled the spacious courts of the Prince's castle; but gradually, through the rising haze, the hunting party could more or less clearly be discerned, moving about on horseback and on foot. One could distinguish the hurried activities of those near by: stirrups were lengthened or shortened, guns and ammunition were handed up, game bags were arranged, while the dogs, impatiently straining at their leashes, threatened to drag their handlers along with them. Here and there, too, a horse pranced, driven by its own fiery nature or excited by the spur of its rider, who, even in the half light of dawn, could not resist showing off. All were waiting for the Prince, who tarried too long in taking leave of his young wife.

Married only a short while before, they already knew the happiness of congenial dispositions; both were active and energetic, each liked to share the interests and pursuits of the other. The Prince's father had lived to see the time when it became common conviction that all members of the commonwealth should pass their days in equal industry and, each in his own way, produce, earn, and enjoy.

How far this had been realized could be observed during these very days, when the main market was about to be held, an event which might almost be considered a fair. The day before, the Prince had led his wife on horseback through the busy display of wares and had shown her how here the products of the mountain region and those of the plains were exchanged to mutual profit; with all this bustle before them he could demonstrate to her the industriousness of his people.

Although during these days the Prince conferred almost exclusively with his advisers about such pressing matters and worked especially closely with his Minister of Finance, his Huntmaster too would have his right: upon his pleading and in this favorable autumn weather the temptation to go on a long-postponed hunt was irresistible. It would be a rare and special occasion for the household itself, as well as for the many strangers who had come to the fair.

The Princess reluctantly stayed at home; it had been planned to push far into the mountains in order to stir up the peaceful animals in those distant forests with an unexpected foray.

In parting, her husband suggested that she should go on a ride with Friedrich, the Prince's uncle. "I shall leave you our Honorio too," he said, "as equerry and page. He will attend to everything." Saying this as he descended the stairs, he gave the necessary orders to a handsome youth and soon left with guests and train.

The Princess, who had waved her handkerchief to her husband as long as he was still in the courtyard, now retired to the rooms at the back of the castle which commanded a free view towards the mountains, so much the lovelier as the castle itself stood on a height above the river, and on all sides afforded splendid and varied prospects. She found the fine telescope still in the position in which it had been left on the previous evening, when they had entertained themselves by looking across the rich hilly country to the height of the forest and the tall ruins of the ancient family castle, which stood out conspicuously in the evening light. At that hour the great masses of light and shadow conveyed most vividly the grandeur of this impressive and venerable building. This morning, the sharp glass strikingly revealed the fall colors of those many kinds of trees which had struggled up between the stones, unhindered and undisturbed through many long years. But the Princess now tipped the telescope in the direction of a barren, stony area, across which the hunting party could be expected to pass. She waited patiently for the moment when they were to come into view, and was not disappointed: for with the help of the powerful magnifying instrument, her eyes could distinctly recognize the Prince and his chief equerry. Indeed, she waved once again with her handkerchief, as she noticed, or rather thought she noticed, that they halted for a moment and looked back toward the castle.

Friedrich, the Prince's uncle, was announced and came in, attended by an artist who carried a large portfolio under his arm. "Dear Cousin," said the vigorous old gentleman, "we have brought you some views of the old castle. They were sketched from various points and show how those strong battlements have, throughout many long years, resisted time and the elements; you will see how here and there the walls had to yield, and have crashed down in ruins. As a matter of fact, we only needed to make this wilderness accessible; it takes little more to surprise and delight any visitor."

As the old Prince pointed out the various drawings he continued, "Here, as you advance along the narrow path through the outer ring to the fortress proper, one of the most massive rocks of the whole mountain rises before you. A tower has been built upon it, yet no one would be able to say where nature ends and art and craftsmanship begin. Farther on you notice adjoining sidewalls and dungeons, steeply terraced. But I am not quite accurate; this ancient summit is in reality almost completely surrounded by a forest. For one hundred and fifty years, no axe has sounded here, and everywhere huge trees have grown. Wherever you keep close to the walls, the trunks and roots of the smooth maple, the rough oak, and the slender pine will make it difficult for you to move. You must twist your way round them and carefully plot your foot paths. See how well our artist has expressed the character of all this, with how much accuracy he has drawn the various kinds of trunks and roots, twisting among the masonry, and the huge boughs thrusting through the openings in the walls. It is a wilderness unlike any other, a unique place, where you can see traces of the long-vanished power of man in tenacious struggle with the ever-living, ever-working power of nature."

He put another sketch before her and continued: "What do you say to the castle yard? The collapse of the old gate tower has made it inaccessible and no one had entered it for countless years. We tried to reach it from the side, and finally provided a convenient but hidden way by breaking through walls and blasting vaults. Once we were inside, there was no need for further clearing. Here you will notice a flat rock smoothed by nature; in some places enormous trees found a chance to strike roots. They have grown slowly but vigorously, and now their branches reach up into the galleries on which the knights used to walk; indeed, they even penetrate through doors and windows into the arched halls. We shall not drive them away—they have become the masters, and may remain so. By clearing away deep piles of dried leaves we found the most extraordinary place, perfectly leveled, the like of which may perhaps not be found anywhere else in the world.

"On the steps leading up to the main tower—it is quite remarkable and must be seen—a maple tree has taken root, and has grown so big that you can hardly get past it to ascend the highest tower from which you can enjoy an unlimited view. Yet up there, too, you are pleasantly in the shade: the same tree rises wonderfully high into the air and spreads over the whole area.

"Let us be grateful to this able artist who, in these sketches, conveys everything to us so admirably, as if we were actually on the spot. He has spent the best hours of the day and of the season on them, and has for weeks actually lived there. In this corner we have set up a small but pleasant dwelling for him and the warder we assigned to him. You cannot believe, my dear, what a wonderful view into the country, the castle and the ruins he has created for himself there. But now, having sketched everything so neatly and expressively, he will finish his drawings down here at his ease. We intend to decorate our garden hall with these pictures, and no one shall look at them so near to our civilized flower beds, arbors, and shady walks without wishing in contrast to contemplate up there all the evidence of the old and the new, the stubborn, inflexible and indestructible, but also the fresh, pliant and irresistible."

Honorio entered and announced that the horses were ready; the Princess turned to the uncle: "Why don't we ride up, and actually look at what you have shown me in these sketches. Ever since I have been here, I have heard about this project, and I am now all the more eager to see with my own eyes what seemed impossible in all accounts of it, and remains even now a little improbable in the pictures."

"Not yet, my dear," replied the Prince. "You saw in these pictures what eventually it can and will become; for the present many things are as yet only begun, and a work of art requires completion if it is not to be put to shame by nature."

"Well then, let us at least ride towards it, if only to the lower parts. Today I feel like being where I can look far out into the world."

"As you will," replied the Prince.

"But let us go through the town," continued the lady, "across the great market square with its countless booths that have made it look like a little city, or an army camp. It is as if the wants and occupations of all the families in the land were there spread out, focused in this one spot, and brought into the light of day. If you observe carefully, you can see there everything man produces and needs. For a moment you imagine that money is not necessary, that all business could be conducted by barter, and of course, basically, that is true enough. The Prince started me on this trend of thought last night, and now I have become doubly aware that here, where mountains and plain meet, both can clearly indicate their needs and their wishes. The highlander can process the timber of his forests in a thousand different shapes, and mold his iron for all kinds of uses, and the others from below come to meet him with a variety of products in which, often enough, you can hardly discover the original material or immediately recognize the purpose."

"I know," said the Prince, "that my nephew devotes much of his attention to these problems. What matters most at this particular season is that more should be received than spent. To achieve this is, after all, the sum total of all national economy, as well as of the smallest household. Still, forgive me, my dear, I have never liked to ride through a market or fair: one is hindered and delayed at every step, and then the memory of that monstrous disaster always flares up in my mind. It burned itself, as it were, into my eyes. I was present on one occasion where just such a mass of goods was destroyed by flames. I had scarcely—"

"We must not waste these bright hours of daylight," interrupted the Princess, since the Prince had on several occasions frightened her with a minute description of the catastrophe. On one of his journeys, he had gone to bed in the best inn on the market place, which was just then swarming with the noise and bustle of a fair. He had been exceedingly tired, and suddenly in the dead of night, was awakened by screams, and by flames billowing towards his lodging.

The Princess hastened to mount her favorite horse, and led her half-reluctant, half-eager companion, instead of through the rear gate up the mountain, by the front gate down the hill. For who would not have enjoyed riding at her side and following her wherever she led? Even Honorio had willingly forgone the very great pleasure of a hunt in order to devote himself to her.

As anticipated, they could ride across the market place only step by step. But with her singular charm the Princess made any delay entertaining by her spirited comments. "I seem to be repeating yesterday's lesson," she said, "since we are unavoidably slowed down." The crowd pressed so closely around them that they could continue only at the slowest pace. The people liked to see the young princess, and by their pleased smiles indicated their satisfaction that the first lady of the land should also be the loveliest and the most graceful.

It was a motley crowd: mountain people, who lived quietly among their rocks, firs and spruces, lowlanders from the hills, plains and fields, and small-town tradesmen—all were assembled here. The Princess looked at the people for a while, then turned to her companions, and told them how she was struck by the fact that wherever they came from, these country people used far more material for their clothes than necessary, more cloth and linen, more ribbons for trimming. "It really seems as if the women could not be bedecked enough and the men not puffed out enough to please themselves."

"Let us allow them that," replied the uncle. "Spend their extra money where they will, the people are happy doing it, and happiest when they spend it on dressing up." The Princess nodded in agreement.

They had finally reached an open space which led to the outskirts of the town. There at the end of the line of booths and stalls they noticed a fairly large wooden structure, from which there came a sudden earsplitting roar. It was feeding time for the wild animals which were exhibited there. They heard the powerful voice of the lion, more natural in the forest or desert; the horses shuddered and neighed, and everybody felt the terrible force with which the king of the wilderness drew attention to himself amid the innocent pursuits of a civilized community. As they approached the building they could not miss seeing huge, garish posters representing those exotic animals in the crudest and most violent colors. In these pictures, by which the peaceful citizen was to be irresistibly tempted, a tremendous, fierce tiger attacked a Negro, and was about to tear him to pieces; a lion stood in solemn majesty, as if he could find no prey worthy of him; compared to these two powerful animals, the others, equally striking and uncommon, attracted less attention.

"Let us stop here on our way back," said the Princess, "and look at these rare creatures." "It is a strange thing," replied the Prince, "that people want forever to be excited by something terrible. In his cage, I am sure, the tiger lies perfectly calm, but here it has to pounce wildly upon a Negro, so that we should believe the same thing may be seen inside. Is there not enough murder and violent death in the world, enough burning and destruction? Must the ballad singers repeat it at every corner? People want to be frightened, so that they may afterwards feel all the more vividly how pleasant and delightful it is to breathe freely."

But no matter how many anxious thoughts these fearful pictures pro-duced in their minds, all were swept aside as the group passed through the gate and entered a most cheerful scene. The river along which they rode was narrow here and could take only light boats, but as it grew was eventually to enrich the life of distant lands. The group moved on through well-tended fruit and pleasure gardens, coming gradually into the open and more thickly settled countryside. They passed through an occasional thicket or small wood and were delighted by a view here and there of charming villages. Soon they entered a sloping meadow valley, recently mowed for the second time, smooth as velvet, watered by a stream that rushed towards them from a spring higher up. The woods were left behind and after a steep climb they reached a higher and even more open spot. Some distance ahead, beyond clumps of trees, the old castle, the goal of their journey, rose like wooded peaks. One could not reach the place without occasionally turning around, and behind them to the left, through a clearing, they saw the Prince's castle bathed in the light of the morning sun. The upper part of the town lay half hidden in a light mist of smoke, and down farther to the right they recognized the lower town and a few bends of the river with its meadows and mills. On the other side there extended a wide and fertile stretch of land.

Having satisfied themselves with so magnificent a view, or rather, as often happens when we look out from a high place, doubly eager to find an even wider view, they rode along a broad, stony stretch until they saw before them the green-crowned summit of the castle ruins, a few old trees at its foot. They passed through these, and soon found themselves at the steepest, least accessible side. Giant rocks lay there untouched by change since the beginning of time, solid, towering high. What had fallen among them was irregularly piled up in huge slabs and broken pieces—as if to bar even the boldest from any attempt to scale it. But the sheerest and most precipitous incline seems to challenge youth, and to try to master and conquer is for them the greatest delight. The Prin-cess was ready to make an attempt, Honorio was at hand, and the Prince, a little more concerned with comfort, but unwilling to appear weak, agreed. The horses were left there under the trees, and the party hoped to reach the point where an enormous projecting rock offered a level place from which they would have a view not only as vast as that of a bird's eye, but at the same time most picturesque.

The sun, nearly at its height, lent its clearest light; the Prince's residence with all its ramified buildings, wings, cupolas and towers stood our magnificently. The upper town spread before them, even the lower could now easily be seen; indeed, through the telescope they could distinguish the individual booths on the market square. Honorio was in the habit of always carrying this useful instrument on his rides. You could look up and down the river and follow on one side the terraced land and on the other the slowly rising, rolling, and fertile slopes. There were innumerable villages—as a matter of fact, it had long been a subject of contention, how many one might be able to count from up here.

A serene stillness lay over the wide expanse—as it so often does at noon when, as the ancients said, Pan is asleep and all nature holds her breath, lest he be awakened.

"It is not the first time," said the Princess, "that standing on such a high and commanding spot, I realize how simple and peaceful nature can look, and how it gives you the impression that there is nothing disagreeable in the whole world; but when you return to the dwellings of men, whether they be rich or poor, comfortable or cramped, there is always something to fight or quarrel about, to settle or to straighten out."

Honorio, who had meanwhile looked through his telescope towards the town, suddenly called out, "Look, look, there is a fire in the market square!" They could see a little smoke, but the daylight dimmed the brightness of the flames. "The fire is spreading!" cried Honorio, still looking through the instrument. The Princess could now see the conflagration with the naked eye. From time to time a red flame shot up and smoke rose.

"Let us turn back," said the Prince. "I don't like this; I have always been afraid of having to go through such a disaster again."

When they had reached the foot of the castle where the horses had been left, the Princess said to the old Prince: "You ride ahead, quickly, and take the groom along; leave Honorio with me, we will follow." The uncle accepted this reasonable and prudent suggestion, and rode, as fast as the ground permitted, down the rough, stony slope.

When the Princess mounted her horse, Honorio said: "Do ride slowly, Your Highness, all fire equipment in the town and in the castle is in the best order; not even such an extraordinary and unexpected emergency will cause confusion. But here where we are, the ground is bad, there are small stones and stubbly grass, and it is not safe to ride too fast; anyhow, by the time we reach the town, the fire will be extinguished." The Princess did not believe that; she saw the smoke spreading and even thought she had noticed a shooting flame and heard an explosion. She remembered all the terrifying pictures which her uncle's oft-repeated story of the fire that he had once witnessed had so vividly impressed upon her.

That catastrophe, in its striking suddenness, had been frightful enough to leave behind it for life a horror of its recurrence. At night a furious fire had seized booth after booth on the wide and crowded market square, long before the people sleeping in and near these buildings could have been shaken out of their deep dreams. The old Prince, a stranger in the town, had just fallen asleep after a weary journey. He had leapt to the window and seen everything fearfully illuminated; flames darting in all directions, from right and left, rolled towards him. The houses on the square, reddened by the reflection, seemed to glow, about to burst into flames at any moment. Below him the fire raged relentlessly; boards cracked, beams crackled, canvas flew up and the dusky, tattered burning ends wafted about in the air as if evil spirits in their own element, forever changing shape, were engaged in a wild dance, consuming themselves, only here and there emerging from the glowing heat. Everybody screamed and howled, and tried to save what they could; servants and their masters made every effort to drag away bales that the fire had already seized, and to tear away from the burning scaffolding this or that in order to throw into boxes what they would in the end have to leave to the flames. How many of them wished for only a moment's respite from the crackling fire, and as they looked about for a chance of a breathing spell, all their belongings were swallowed by the flames. What lay still in darkness on one side was smoldering on the other. A few determined, stubborn people grimly resisted the enemy and managed to save some of their belongings, though at a loss of eyebrows and hair. All these scenes of mad confusion now rose again before the Princess's mind; the clear view of the morning was overclouded, her eyes darkened; wood and field had assumed a look of strangeness and anguish.

As they entered the peaceful valley, hardly aware of its refreshing coolness, they had gone only a few paces beyond the source of the brook when the Princess noticed far down in the thicket something strange. She recognized it immediately as the tiger, coming towards them as she had seen him in the poster only a short time ago. This sight, together with the picture that had just been in her mind, gave her the strangest feeling. "Get away! Princess!" cried Honorio, "get away!" She turned her horse towards the steep hill from which they had just come. The young man drew his pistol and, approaching the animal, fired when he seemed near enough. But he missed, the tiger sprang to the side, the horse was startled, and the provoked beast pursued his course straight towards the Princess. She rode as fast as her horse would go, up the steep, rocky slope, forgetting for a moment that so delicate a creature, unused to such exertion, might not be able to stand it for long. Driven on by the Princess in her terror, it did overexert itself, stumbling again and again on the loose gravel, and finally fell exhausted to the ground after one last violent effort. The lady, resolute and skillful, was instantly on her feet; the horse, too, rose. The tiger came nearer, though not rapidly—the uneven ground, the sharp stones, seemed to hinder his progress. Honorio rode immediately behind him, and slowed down as he came alongside the beast. This seemed to give him new strength and, at the same moment, both reached the place where the Princess stood by her horse. Honorio bent down and with his second pistol shot the animal through the head. It fell, and as it lay stretched out in full length it seemed to reveal the might and terror of which now only the physical form was left. Honorio had leapt from his horse and knelt on the tiger, restraining its last movements and holding his drawn hunting knife in his hand. He was a handsome sight as he sprang forward, very much as the Princess had seen him before in ring and lance tournaments. Just so in the riding course would his bullet, as he darted by, hit the brow of the Turk's-head on the pole, right under the turban. Just so, elegantly prancing up, would he pick the Moor's-head off the ground with his naked saber. He was dexterous and lucky in all such arts, and this now stood him in good stead.

"Do kill him," said the Princess. "I am afraid he will hurt you with his claws."

"No," replied the young man, "he is dead enough and I do not want to spoil this skin which next winter shall shine on your sleigh."

"Don't speak lightly. A moment like this calls forth our most solemn feelings."

"I was never more solemn in my life," said Honorio. "But for that very reason, I think only of what is most joyful—I look at this tiger's skin as it accompanies you in your pleasures."

"It would always remind me of this terrible moment," she replied.

"Still, it is a less pretentious sign of triumph," replied the young man, his cheeks glowing, "than the weapons of slain enemies displayed in proud procession before the victor."

"I shall always remember your courage and skill when I see it," replied the Princess, "and I need not add that you can depend on my gratitude and the Prince's lifelong favor. But rise, the animal is dead, let us see what should be done next. Do rise now." "Since I am already kneeling before you," replied Honorio, "which I know I dare not do under any other circumstance, let me beg you to assure me at this moment of your favor and grace. I have often asked the Prince for permission to travel. Surely he who is fortunate enough to sit at your table, whom you honor with the privilege of entertaining your company, should have seen something of the world. Travelers come to us from all parts, and when the conversation turns to some city, some important place anywhere in the world, the question is certain to be asked of us whether we have been there. None are credited with any wisdom except those who have seen such sights; it is as if we had to inform ourselves mainly for the benefit of others."

"Do rise," insisted the Princess, "I should not like to ask a favor or make a request of my husband which I know would go against his convictions; but I am sure that it would be easy to remove the cause for his keeping you here. He wanted to see you develop into an independent, self-reliant nobleman, to do yourself and him credit abroad one day, as you have done hitherto at court. I should think that today's courageous act will be as good a recommendation as any young man could hope to have for his travels."

The Princess did not have time to notice that sadness, rather than pleasure, crossed his face. Nor did Honorio have an opportunity to express his feelings, for a woman with a boy at her hand came running up the hill in great haste, straight towards the two. Honorio collected himself and rose. The woman, crying loudly, threw herself on the body of the tiger. This action, as well as her gaudy and strange, yet neat, costume, left no doubt that she was the owner and keeper of the animal. The boy had dark eyes and jet black hair, and held a flute in his hand. He knelt next to his mother, deeply moved and, like her, cried, though a little less violently.

The intense outbursts of this woman's passion were like a stream plunging from one rock to the next. She used a sort of natural language, brief and abrupt, yet at the same time compelling and pathetic. It would be impossible to translate it into our kind of speech; its general meaning was this: "They have murdered you, poor creature, murdered you needlessly! You were tame and would certainly have lain down to wait for us. Your feet were tender and your claws had lost their power. You missed the hot sun that would have given them strength. You were the most beautiful among your kind. Whoever saw such a regal tiger magnificently stretched out in sleep as you now lie here, dead, never to rise again! When you awoke early in the morning and opened your jaws and showed your red tongue, it almost seemed as if you were smiling. And even though you roared, you still took your feed—almost playfully— from the hands of a woman, from the fingers of a child. For how long now have we accompanied you on your journeys, how long has your company meant everything to us. In truth, for us, out of the eater came forth meat, and out of the strong came forth sweetness. It will be so no more! Woe! Woe!"

She had not finished her lamentations, when a group of riders came galloping along the side of the castle mountain. They were soon recognized as the hunting party, the Prince himself in the lead. They had pursued their game in the hills beyond, and had noticed the clouds of smoke. Racing across valleys and ravines as if in fierce chase, they had taken the most direct way towards that awful sign. As they rode along the rocky slope, they stopped short and seemed startled by the un-expected sight of the group which stood out prominently in the wide empty space. After the first recognition they were silent, then, recover-ing their presence of mind, what was not obvious was explained in a few words. There stood the Prince, contemplating this strange and unheard-of incident, about him a circle of riders and those who had followed him hurriedly on foot. It was clear what had to be done next, and the Prince was busy giving the necessary orders when suddenly a man forced his way into the circle. He was tall and dressed in the same curiously gaudy manner as the woman and the child. The whole family now joined in sorrow and dismay. The man composed himself and, standing at a re-spectful distance from the Prince, said, "This is no time for lamentation. My Lord, the lion, too, is loose; he is coming this way towards the mountains; but, pray, spare him, have mercy, so that he may not die like this poor beast."

"The lion?" asked the Prince, "have you found his track?"

"Yes, sir! One of the peasants down there who had quite needlessly taken refuge in a tree directed me up this way, a little farther to the left. But I saw this crowd of people and horses, and came here to get more information and perhaps help."

"Very well, then," ordered the Prince, "let the hunting party move up in this direction. Load your guns and proceed cautiously; it does not matter if you drive him into the deep woods. But I am afraid that in the end we may not be able to spare your lion. Why were you careless enough to let the animals escape?"

"When the fire broke out," replied the man, "we remained quiet and watchful; it spread fast, but at some distance from us; we had water enough to protect ourselves, but an explosion threw the fire in our direc-tion, indeed, beyond us. We were suddenly too rushed, and now we are ruined.'

The Prince was still busy giving orders; but for a moment everything seemed to halt as a man came running down from the old castle—it was the warder who was in charge of the artist's workshop and who lived there and supervised the workmen. He was out of breath, but managed to report briefly that the lion was lying perfectly quiet in the sun behind the upper ring-wall at the foot of a century-old beech tree. He seemed almost annoyed as he concluded—"Why did I take my gun into town yesterday to have it cleaned? If I had had it with me, he would never have got up again. His skin would have belonged to me, and I would have boasted about it all my life, and rightly, too."

The Prince, whose military experience stood him in good stead and who was used to finding himself in a situation where unavoidable danger threatened from several sides, said to the man, "What guarantee can you give me that if we spare your lion, he might not cause a good deal of harm among the people?"

"This woman and child," answered the father hastily, "are willing to keep him tame and quiet until I can bring up a cage, and we can carry him back harmless and unharmed."

At that moment the boy put his flute to his lips—an instrument that used to be called the soft or sweet flute. It was short-stemmed like a pipe, and anyone who played it well could produce the most delicious tones. Meanwhile the Prince inquired of the warder how the lion had come up. "By the narrow path, which is walled in on both sides and which has always been and will always be the only real road of access. Two footpaths that used to lead up have been so obstructed that there is now only that one way by which one can reach the magic castle which the place is to become through Prince Friedrich's taste and talent."

After some reflection, while looking at the child who had continued to play softly as if preluding, the Prince turned to Honorio and said, "You have done much today; now complete the day's work. Guard that narrow road; keep your rifles ready, but do not shoot unless the animal cannot be driven back in any other way. If necessary, make a fire which will frighten him if he should want to come down. The man and woman must assume responsibility for everything else." Honorio hurried to execute the orders.

The child continued to play, not really a tune, but an irregular sequence of tones, and, possibly for that reason, it was especially moving. Everyone seemed enchanted by these melodious passages, when the father began to speak in a curiously dignified and exalted manner.

"God has given wisdom to the Prince and also the knowledge to recognize that all God's works are wise, each in its own way. Behold the rock, standing fast and motionless, defying the weather and the sunshine. Primeval trees crown its summit, and thus enhanced, it commands a wide view; but if any part of it should fall, it would not remain what it was: it will crumble in many pieces and cover the slope of the mountain. But they will not stay there, either; they will tumble on down, the brook will receive them and carry them to the river. They cannot resist, they are no longer stubborn and rough; smooth and rounded they travel even faster from river to river and on to the ocean where giants march and dwarfs abound in the depths.

"But who shall praise the glory of the Lord, Whom the stars praise through all Eternity? Why look afar? Behold the bee, how it gathers busily late in the fall, building its house true and level, architect and workman at once. See the ant, it knows its way and loses it not. It builds its dwelling of grass and earth and pine needles. It piles it high and arches it in; but its work has been in vain—the horse stamps and scrapes it to pieces; look, he has trodden down those delicate beams and scattered the planks, impatiently he snorts and cannot rest; for the Lord has made the horse the comrade of the wind and the companion of the storm, that he may carry man where he wills, and woman where she desires. But in the forest of palms there appeared the lion; proudly he roams the desert ruling over all animals and nothing can resist him. Yet man knows how to tame him, and the fiercest of living creatures has reverence for the image of God, in which, too, the angels are made, who serve the Lord and His servants. For in the den of lions Daniel was not afraid; he remained steadfast and faithful, and the wild roaring did not interrupt his song of praise."

These words were spoken with a kind of natural enthusiasm and accompanied here and there by the child's sweet music. When the father had ended, the boy began to sing with much skill in a clear, melodious voice. The father in turn took the flute and accompanied the child as he sang:

> From the dens, in this direction,
> Prophet's song of praise I hear;
> Angels lend him their protection,
> What has the good man to fear?

> Lion, lioness, agazing,
> Mildly pressing round him came;
> Yea, that humble, holy praising,
> It hath made them tame.

The father continued playing the flute, while the mother occasionally joined in as second voice.

The effect was especially striking when the child began to rearrange the lines of the song in a different sequence and thereby produced, not a new meaning but a far greater intensity of feeling.

> Angel-host around doth hover,
> Us in heavenly tones to cheer;
> In the dens our head doth cover,—
> What has the poor child to fear?

> For that humble, holy praising
> Will permit no evil nigh:
> Angels hover, watching, gazing;
> Who so safe as I?

All three now joined with force and conviction.

For th' Eternal rules above us,
Lands and oceans rules His will;
Lions even as lambs shall love us,
And the proudest waves be still.

Whetted sword to scabbard cleaving,
Faith and Hope victorious see:
Strong who, loving and believing,
Prays, O Lord, to Thee.

The others were silent and listened intently. Only when the music ceased could one observe the impression it had made. They all seemed calmed and each was moved in his own way. The Prince, as if only now fully aware of the danger that had threatened earlier, looked at his wife who, holding his arm, covered her eyes with an embroidered handkerchief. She was relieved that the oppressive feeling with which her heart had been filled only a few minutes before had now gone from her. Complete silence reigned over the crowd—they appeared to have forgotten the terror of the fire below and of the lion above them who might arise at any moment.

The Prince stirred the group with a sign to bring the horses. He turned to the woman and said, "Do you really think that you can calm the lion when you find him, by your song, the singing of this child, and the music of this flute? And that you can take him back to his cage, harmless and unharmed?" They assured him that this was so. The warder was given to them as a guide. The Prince and a few of his attendants left hurriedly while the Princess, accompanied by the rest, followed more leisurely. Mother and son and the warder, who had meanwhile armed himself with a rifle, proceeded to climb towards the mountain.

Before they entered the narrow pass which gave them access to the castle, they found the hunters busy heaping up dry brushwood to light a fire if it were required. "There is no need for that," said the woman. "All will go well and peacefully."

Farther on, sitting on a part of the wall, they found Honorio on guard, his double-barreled rifle in his lap, as if prepared for any eventuality. He hardly seemed to notice the approaching group, but sat, lost in deep thought, looking about absently. The woman asked him not to allow the fire to be lit, but Honorio appeared not to pay any attention to her words. She spoke again, more urgently, and said: "Young man, you have slain my tiger—but I do not bear you any ill will. Now spare my lion and I will bless you."

Honorio looked straight ahead at the setting sun. "You are looking towards the west," continued the woman, "and you are right—there is much to do there. Hurry, do not delay, you will conquer. But first of all conquer yourself!" At this he seemed to smile; the woman went on her way and only turned once more to look back on him. The sun cast a glowing light over his face—she thought that she had never seen a more beautiful youth.

"If your child," said the warder, "can, as you are convinced, entice the lion and pacify him with his flute and his singing, we shall get hold of him very easily. He lies close to the broken walls through which we have made a passageway into the castle yard since the main gate is blocked by rubble. When the child leads him inside, I can close the opening without much trouble. And at the right moment the boy can slip away by one of the small winding staircases in the corner. We must hide, but I shall place myself so that I can have a bullet ready if the child should need help."

"All these precautions are unnecessary; God and our own skill, our faith and fortune are our best aid." "That may be," replied the warder, "but I know my duties. Let me lead you first by a rather difficult path to the top of the wall, immediately opposite the opening I have mentioned. Let the lad then descend into the arena and lead away the animal if it will follow him." This was done. Warder and mother saw from their hiding place above how the child descended the winding stairs, showed himself in the open space of the courtyard and disappeared again in the dark opening on the other side. They could hear the tone of his flute, which gradually grew fainter, and at last ceased altogether. The pause was ominous enough; the old hunter, accustomed to every kind of peril, felt the oppressive suspense in this extraordinary incident. He would have preferred to engage the dangerous beast himself. But the mother, cheerful and assured, and bending over to listen, did not betray the slightest apprehension.

At last the flute could be heard again, the child, his eyes bright and pleased, emerged from the dark cavern, and behind him the lion, walking slowly and, as it seemed, with some difficulty. Now and then the animal tried to lie down, but the boy led him in a half circle through the autumn-tinged trees. Eventually, in the last rays of the sun pouring in through a break in the ruined walls, he sat down as if transfigured. Once again he began his soothing song which we cannot refrain from repeating:

From the dens, in this direction,
Prophet's song of praise I hear;
Angels lend him their protection,
What has the good man to fear?

Lion, lioness, agazing,
Mildly pressing round him came;

Yea, that humble, holy praising,
It hath made them tame.

Meanwhile the lion had lain down close to the child and lifted his heavy right paw into his lap. The boy, as he sang, stroked it and soon noticed that a sharp thorn had caught between the balls of the animal's foot. He carefully extracted it, and with a smile took the silken handkerchief from his neck to bind up the forbidding foot of the huge beast. His mother was overjoyed and, bending back with her arms outstretched, would have shouted and clapped her hands as she was accustomed, had not a rough grip of the warder reminded her that the danger was not yet over.

The child sang on triumphantly, having first introduced the tune with a few notes on the flute.

For th' Eternal rules above us,
Lands and oceans rules His will;
Lions even as lambs shall love us,
And the proudest waves be still.

Whetted sword to scabbard cleaving,
Faith and Hope victorious see:
Strong who, loving and believing,
Prays, O Lord, to Thee.

Were it possible to imagine that the features of so fierce a monster, the tyrant of the forest and the despot of the animal kingdom, could display an expression of friendliness, of grateful contentment, it might have been witnessed on this occasion. The child, with his exalted look, seemed now like a mighty victorious conqueror. The lion, on the other hand, was not so much vanquished—for his strength though concealed was still in him—as tamed and surrendered to his own peaceful will. The child fluted and sang on, transposing the lines in his fashion and adding to them:

And so blessed angel bringeth
To good children help in need;
Fetters o'er the cruel flingeth,
Worthy act with wings doth speed.

So have tamed, and firmly iron'd
To a poor child's feeble knee,
Him, the forest's lordly tyrant,
Pious Thought and Melody.

Notes

The Sorrows of Young Werther

P. 9, Batteux, Wood, de Piles, Winckelmann, Sulzer, Heyne. Theoreticians of art and literature whose works were current in the late eighteenth century. Charles Batteux (1713–1780) was author of the highly influential *Cours de belles lettres ou Principes de la littérature* (5 vols., 1747–50). Robert Wood's (1716–1771) *Essay on the Original Genius and Writings of Homer* appeared in 1768. Roger de Piles (1635–1709) published treatises on painting which were still much discussed in the eighteenth century. Johanm Joachim Winckelmann (1717–1768), the founder of the modern discipline of art history, published his *Gedanken über die Nachahmung der griechischen Werke (Thoughts on the Imitation of Greek Works)* to great acclaim in 1755. Johann Georg Sulzer (1720–1779) systematized Enlightenment theory of the arts in his *Allgemeine Theorie der Schönen Künste (General Theory of the Fine Arts)*, the first volume of which appeared in 1771. Christian Gottlob Heyne (1729–1812) reformed the study of classical Gottlob Heyne (1729–1812) reformed the study of classical philology and his lectures at the University of Göttingen were widely known.

P. 19, Klopstock. Friedrich Gottlieb Klopstock (1724–1803) was the leading sentimental poet of the eighteenth century, best known for his *Odes* and for his Christian epic *Messias*. The poem alluded to here is undoubtedly his ode "Die Frühlingsfeier" ("Celebration of Spring"), first published in 1759 and reprinted in the 1771 edition of the poet's *Odes*.

P. 23, Lavater. Johann Caspar Lavater (1741–1801) was best known for his highly emotional sermons, a collection of which from the year 1773 is alluded to here. Goethe entertained a long and important relationship with Lavater and collaborated with him in the latter's physiognomic studies. (See also *Poetry and Truth*, vols. 4 and 5 of this series.)

P. 26, Ossian. Legendary Celtic bard of the third century. In 1765 the Scotsman James Macphearson (1736–1796) published *The Works of Ossian*, one of the most influential forgeries of the eighteenth century. Goethe as well as his mentor Johann Gottfried Herder (1744–1803) were initially convinced of the authenticity of the work.

P. 57, Kennicot, Semler, Michaelis. Benjamin Kennikot (1718–83), Johann Salamo Semler (1725–91), and Johann David Michaelis (1717–1791) were all critical theologians who, along with many others in the eighteenth century, endeavored to establish the varying degrees of authenticity of the books of the Bible. Their names allude here to the rational theology of the age.

P. 87, Emilia Galotti. Tragedy by Gotthold Ephraim Lessing (1729–1781) which appeared in 1772. See "Afterword."

Elective Affinities

P. 188, Artemesia. Middle Eastern (Carian) queen of the fourth century B. C., wife of Mausoleus. The *mausoleum* which she had built in memory of her deceased husband was counted among the seven wonders of the ancient world.

P. 189, widow of Ephesus. Allusion to a story that appears in La Fontaine's *Contes et nouvelles en vers* (1665–1685), in which the widow of Ephesus quickly abandons her intention to starve to death in the tomb of her husband, giving herself there to a soldier. The widow of Ephesus represents, then, quite the opposite from the faithful Artemesia.

P. 196, van Dyck's "Belisarius." Antonis van Dyck (1599–1641), Flemish painter. Belisarius was a Roman general of the sixth century, vanquisher of the Vandals and Ostragoths. By order of the emperor Justinian, he was blinded and is so represented in the etching referred to here.

P. 197, the well-known painting by Poussin: Ahasuerus and Esther. Nicolas Poussin (1594–1665), French painter. The story of Ahasuerus and Esther is related in the Book of Esther in the Old Testament. There it is told how Esther twice faints in the presence of the king Ahasuerus before she manages to reveal to him that she belongs to the Jewish people. The painting shows one such scene.

P. 197, Terburg's "Paternal Admonition'. . . Wille's splendid engraving. Gerard Terborch (1608–1681), Dutch genre painter. Johann Georg Wille (1715–1808), German engraver.

P. 257, the Ten Commandments. Mittler's numbering of the Commandments here refers to the Protestant catechism.

Afterword

It is difficult today to realize that Goethe's *The Sorrows of Young Werther*—still the most popular of his works—represents an act of artistic audacity. First published in 1774 (a second version, which our text follows, appeared in 1787), it boldly transformed the conventions of the sentimental epistolary novel and in doing so elaborated a new form of novelistic discourse. Its major generic predecessors, Richardson's *Clarissa* (1747) and Rousseau's *Julie ou La Nouvelle Héloïse* (1761), are compendious books, disquisitional even in their emotionality. Both resemble slightly a moral tract. The compact *Werther*, however, unfolds its fictional world without tendentious moralizing and achieves in the shaping of its letters a lyrical intensity previously unknown in narrative prose. Whereas the earlier novels are built around intricate plot structures, Goethe's juxtaposes discrete, mutually resonant moments, a structural principle which he called, in the visual vocabulary he always favored, 'mirroring' (*Spiegelung*). The traditional epistolary novel is dramatic; its letters are conceived with a view toward possible responses and consequences. What Werther writes to the distant Wilhelm, by contrast, plays no role in furthering the action; even the few letters addressed to Charlotte, among them the protagonist's last, do not seek to elicit an answer. The writing takes place in what might be called a pragmatic vacuum. Its function is not to communicate something to someone, but rather to make imaginatively accessible the tonality of a unique subjective experience. *Werther* is the first European novel in which subjectivity *per se* acquires aesthetic concretization.

This radical generic innovation emerged from an intense period of creative labor. In his autobiography *Poetry and Truth*, Goethe claims to have written the novel in four weeks (see vol. 4 of this series, p. 431), a figure which, although certainly too small, suggests that the older poet remembered the compositional process as a consuming one. We do know that the novel was begun in early February, 1774, and in May of the same year was sent to the publisher. During this period Goethe worked through (much as one 'works through' something in psychoanalysis) a complex of experiences which had occurred for the most part a year and a half earlier during the poet's service as a practicing attorney at the Imperial Court in Wetzlar. Those experiences are essentially two: Goethe's passion for a woman named Charlotte Buff who was engaged to, and soon married, an official called Johann Kestner with whom Goethe had a friendship; and the poet's identification with a young suicide, the writer Carl Wilhelm Jerusalem, also caught in the anguish of an amorous triangle. Imaginatively repeating these events eighteen months after their occurence, Goethe achieves for his novel a unique blend of immediacy and distance. Intimately sensed desires and anxieties are cast in an aesthetic structure so rigorous that the novel can dispense with the legitimation of official moral discourse.

Few contemporary readers were adequate to the combination of empathy and reflective distance *Werther* demanded. Such enlightened literati as Lessing were disturbed by the novel's moral reticence, but affirmative identification with the protagonist on the part of youth was sometimes disastrously total. The same split is discernible within the fiction. On the one hand the novel has its superficial moralizers, incapable of grasping the complexity of psychic conflict; one thinks especially of Albert's remarks on suicide as reported in the important letter of August 12, 1771. On the other hand, Werther, who narcissistically projects himself into books as well as the destinies of other individuals, provides the prototype of an uncritical, identificatory type of reading. The crisis of understanding and comprehension, which the reception of the novel reveals, is a phenomenon internal to the fiction itself. *The Sorrows of Young Werther* articulates a subjective experience which is both entirely compelling (leading, for instance, to acts of psychic identification) *and* opposed to the prevailing moral code. The name which our culture has since given to that experience is romantic love.

Two major shifts in the life of Western Europe during the last third of the eighteenth century engender this new form of eros. First of all, the social sphere of intimate relations becomes functionally differentiated within the society as a whole. Whom one loves and marries is decided independently of such non-amorous considerations as economic gain and the formation of family alliances; or at least these matters are not at the forefront of awareness. The subjective correlate of this is that one no longer desires in the beloved such general qualities as virtue or public esteem; love no longer borrows its values from other functional spheres. Rather, what one loves in the beloved is the particularity of that person, his or her absolute difference from everyone else. This is why, when Werther attempts to describe Charotte to Wilhelm, the predicates he reaches for are so unsatisfying; what ultimately enchants him is not some ideal she embodies, but her unique, and inexpressible, individuality. The second cultural change which brings forth the phenomenon of romantic love is the crystallization of that social structure which today is referred to as the nuclear family: the family unit reduced to parents and children. It is within this structure that childhood, conceived as a domain of experience *sui generis*, emerges. And this sphere, in turn, assumes enormous importance in the formation of psychological identity: childhood becomes a kind of emotional cocoon in which the subject's patterns of affection and aversion, the orientation and nuances of his desire, first come into being. The dominant figure of this phase is, of course, the mother, who assumes the role of primary educator and caretaker within the new family structure. To love romantically is therefore always to act out what Freud called the family romance (*Familienroman*, literally: family novel), the plot of which binds the male subject's desire to the figure of the mother and at the same time requires that he renounce that desire. This is precisely the contradiction Werther suffers through in his impossible and yet inescapable love for Charlotte.

One of the most magnificent letters in the novel, that of June 16, 1771, recounts the sudden formation of this love. Entering the house where Charlotte reigns as virtual mother to her siblings, Werther beholds a spectacle, the epiphany of his desire's radiant object: at the center of the image is Charlotte herself, in virginal white except for the pink colored ribbons at her arms and breast (one of these will become a fetish for Werther); surrounding her are six of her siblings, all expressing with outstretched hands their childish demand; finally, linking the two components of the image, the gift of nourishment in its most basic form, the bread of life. This scene lends Werther's love for Charlotte its unique character. The paradigm of his passion is the child's longing for the nourishing maternal presence. Indeed, even the erotically most charged letter of the novel, that evoking the image of the bird at Charlotte's lips, is focussed on the oral register and the experience of feeding. It is no accident that throughout the novel Werther identifies so strongly with the children, for his desire draws its pathos from early childhood phantasies. He confesses as much himself to Wilhelm on one occasion, writing that he relates to his "heart" as if it were a sick child needing spoiling.

Beyond this anchorage in childhood, Werther's love for Charlotte is correlated with two other domains, literature and nature. Thus, the memory of a particular poem by Klopstock triggers the flood of feeling that overcomes Werther in the climactic scene of the letter of June 16. And just as this remembered poem, an ode in celebration of Spring, has as its theme the presence of the divine in nature, Werther's own experience of nature throughout the first phase of his love is jubilantly pantheistic. One might say that for Werther love, literature and nature become all-consuming experiences; they absorb him into an imaginary world in which the constraints of social obligation seem completely erased. This is one of the novel's most fascinating and innovative features, its exploration of emotional experiences which shatter the contours of the responsible self. *The Sorrows of Young Werther* is built around a series of ecstatic transgressions that carry the protagonist beyond the limits of the social. This is why the letters often tend toward the lyrical; such extremity of experience can only be conveyed in a discourse that pushes expression outside the sayable.

The extrasocial, extralinguistic region into which Werther ventures affords him the experience of an unconditioned oneness, a state without difference and alterity which might be termed the romantic absolute. The most salient feature of this absolute is its extreme ambiguity. Unmoored to any set of stable social norms, it shifts abruptly from a positive, euphoric value to a bleakly disphoric one. Thus, the letter of May 10, 1771, describes an experience in which Werther, lying in the grass, feels himself taken up within the eternal life that animates all of nature. By the 18th of August, however, nature is sensed (no less ecstatically) as the abyss of an infinite grave, as a monster which second by second consumes itself. Werther's joyous sense of at once containing within himself and being contained within the cosmos yields to a desire to annihilate himself by plunging into something he experiences as chaos, a kind of active nothingness. In the same way, the idyllic scenery of his Wahlheim retreat transforms itself into the image of a surging flood. The literary world of the novel is no less polarized: whereas Klopstockian praise of the divine presence suffused throughout nature provides the impetus to Werther's and Charlotte's first moment of intimacy, their last, openly transgressive embrace issues from the unending lament of the Ossian poems and their monotonous evocation of absence. Even Charlotte vacillates for Werther between radically opposed imaginary values, much as the memory of her eyes appears to him now as radiance, now as gaping blackness. It is in this sense that Werther is the first romantic hero in European literature: in art, love and nature, he seeks an absolute which—precisely because it exists outside any system of differentiation—appears to the subject both as Being itself, divine presence, and as Nothingness, the radical absence of divinity.

Because it is the absolute which, in all its ambiguity, the romantic subject *desires*, the position that subject takes vis-à-vis the differentiated world of society is necessarily that of the transgressor. Certainly this is the case with Werther, whose love for Charlotte is marked from the beginning by the fact that, by law, she is forbidden him. But in addition to the obviously Oedipal situation in which he finds himself, it can be said that for Werther all social regulations, from norms of appropriately 'adult' behavior to conventionalized religious beliefs, are essentially negative: proscriptive and punitive. A forceful example of this is provided by the scenes which open Part Two of the novel and which involve Werther's employment at court. In these scenes the protagonist suffers the negativity of the social in two of its aspects, first as the pedantry of bureaucratic power and then as the exclusionary force of class distinction. Both these aspects reappear in the figure of Albert, who is on the one hand a dutiful bureaucrat, tediously moderate in everything, and on the other the sovereign husband whose right it is to forbid contact between Werther and Charlotte. The social problem this novel articulates is one which violently affects the protagonist in every dimension of his experience. Perhaps one could say it is the problem of socialization as such; that is: of the traumatic and tenuous inscription of the child (Werther's ideal till the end) into the social order.

In addition to Werther, the novel knows three other transgressor figures whose stories function as reduced modls of the hero's own. There is the clerk dismissed from the office of Charlotte's father because of his amorous interest in Charlotte and now wandering the heath, madly searching for flowers for his beloved; there is the young peasant whose love for his widowed mistress is blocked by her deceitful brother, eliciting a desparately violent act of revenge; and finally there is the girl who, betrayed by the lover for whom she had sacrificed everything, takes her own life. Like Werther, all these figures experience a desire, which, however natural it appears, is nevertheless socially unacceptable; all three suffer an enforced separation from the beloved object as soon as they bring their illicit desire to expression; and all three end by throwing themselves (or being cast) into a form of radical otherness: madness, crime, suicide. The destinies of these three unfortunates prefigure for Werther the possible outcomes of his own dilemma. The romantic subject can choose no other end than a mode of total exclusion from the social. As this becomes clear to Werther, he begins to identify his passion with that of Christ, an identification which, it should be mentioned, is suggested in the novel's title. But this must not be construed as a religious act. On the contrary, it is Christ's moment of doubt on the Cross, His sense that the Father has turned away from Him, which Werther reenacts. Werther's imitation of Christ testifies only to the absence of any religious belief he might share with a community. No clergyman, the novel's last sentence notes, accompanies him to his grave.

From the beginning Werther's desire aimed for an experience inaccessible to common parlance, unthinkable in the categories of common sense. His suicide, the most radical form of excommunication, is the culmination of this tendency. It is an act fundamentally different from the self-willed death of Emilia Galotti, the heroine of the drama by Lessing which Werther apparently reads in before taking his own life. Emilia's death occurs for the sake of a moral idea: after all she commits suicide in order to save her virtue from the debauchery of the Prince's court. Her death generates a meaning, a tragic meaning, that can become a jointly held cultural value. Werther, by contrast, dies for the sake of an imaginary construct which has reality only in his assertion of it. In other words, his feverish dream of an eternal love to Charlotte within the space of a reintegrated family bears the purely subjective significance of phantasy. The brilliant audacity of *The Sorrows of Young Werther* is to accord this significance an independent legitimacy within its fictional universe. The novel refuses every explanatory solution, be it psychological or moral. Not even the "editor's" intervention near the end of the work provides a final and, as it were, official judgment regarding the unhappy sequence of events. On the contrary, what the reader senses most acutely in this juxtaposition of objective narrative with the personal utterances of the protagonist is the sheer and utter incommensurability of the two modes of discourse; they know no common measure. If, as I mentioned at the outset, Goethe's is the first novel which aesthetically renders subjectivity *per se*, then it accomplishes this by lending Werther's speech the status of an enigma. Werther is the first romantic subject to the degree that he cannot be fully understood. However empathetic our response to his experience, he remains for us ineluctably strange.

Thirty-five years separate the publication of *Werther* (1774) from that of Goethe's third novel, *Elective Affinities* (1809). During this period the poet had conducted a remarkably active and various career at the ducal court in Weimar, he had done scientific work of staggering merit and, of course, become an internationally famous author. He had witnessed the turmoil of the French Revolution and the Napoleonic Wars and recognized that these events had ushered in a new political epoch. The ambitious cultural program of classicism, which he had promulgated in collaboration with Friedrich Schiller, had essentially collapsed and the Romantics, who in many ways had developed aspects of Goethe's early work, were beginning to exhibit political, philosophical and aesthetic tendencies he found questionable. Schiller himself was dead, a loss which doubtless affected Goethe profoundly. However, despite the tremendous experiential distance which separates the two novels, it is interesting to note that, at least as regards its thematic material, *Elective Affinities* represents a return to *Werther*. The contours of repetition stand out starkly if we compare the two works with the novel composed between them. Whereas *Wilhelm Meister's Apprenticeship* (1795, see vol. 9 of this series) centers on the uplifting narrative of cultivation or *Bildung*, *Werther* and *Elective Affinities* both tell a story of tragic love. One could also say that Goethe's prototypical *Bildungsroman* narrates the successful (even if delayed and precarious) constitution of a family, but *Werther* and *Elective Affinities* unfold plots involving familial crises. Both are organized around *failed* love: a desire which, rather than issuing in a new family, threatens the disintegration of an existing family structure.

Despite their thematic similarity, *Werther* and *Elective Affinities* press novelistic discourse in very different directions. The earlier work is structured around a single character, the other figures in the story serving essentially as functions of that character's interior life. *Elective Affinities* is concerned not with what happens within a single character, but rather with what occurs between several. And it is only out of this 'between,' this interplay of relationships, that the 'interiority' of a character's life comes into being; psychology is grounded in the dynamics of interpersonal arrays. This feature of the novel's structure is highlighted by the metaphor of the title. To see the destinies of Edward, Charlotte, Ottilie and the Captain in terms of the chemical phenomenon the Swede Bergmann had designated in 1775 as an 'elective affinity' is to cast their lives as a regulated series of dissolutions and recombinations within a group. Beneath the threshold of their conscious awareness, the characters behave according to a syntax as relentless and impersonal as the laws of chemistry. And it is with an almost scientific detachment and rigor that the novel sets its elements into play in order to discern their laws of combination. *Elective Affinities*—this too is suggested by the title metaphor—is an experimental novel.

What this strikingly modern fictional experiment submits to analysis is the force of modernity itself. This force—the text calls it the "monstrous rights" of the present—presides over the child's conception during Edward's and Charlotte's act of imaginary adultery, perhaps the moment of sheerest tragic error in the novel. But the signs of a relentless movement of time, at once erasing inherited order and bringing forth the new, are legible throughout the work. Even our monuments to the dead (and that is to say our cultural and personal memory) are susceptible to time's ravage, Ottilie notes at one point in her remarkable diary. This dolorous truth certainly holds within the narrative: Goethe's bold fictional experiment traces the lineaments of change at all levels of the characters' lives. Their intricate landscaping projects, for instance, reveal not merely a shift in gardening fashion, but rather an historical transformation in the very way nature is apprehended. Nature is remade in the course of the novel into an object of aesthetic contemplation, an image produced in order to be taken in by carefully positioned spectators. The same historicity of nature is legible in the old gardener's relationship to his own daily practice: a new botany and a new form of catalogue sales have created a world in which he can no longer find his way. One might say that *Elective Affinities* anticipates what will only occur in the latter part of the nineteenth century when the coming of photography completes the recasting of nature as image. Hence the dark figure of the English lord, who, together with a travelling companion devoted to the latest scientific sensation, wanders the world in search of appealing visual prospects to be captured, and rendered transportable, with the aid of his *camera obscura*.

The novel's fascination with the force of modernization is nowhere more in evidence than in the figure of the Captain, this planner, surveyor and mapmaker who, in every domain of his busy activity, replaces inherited traditions with rationalized procedures. He is the very embodiment of technical, or applied knowledge. Everywhere he introduces method where previously the randomness of mood and occasion reigned. This is the reason he criticizes Charlotte's arrangement of the paths and resting places in her portion of the park and the same concern for rational construction guides his reorganization of Edward's papers, his institutionalization of alms-giving in the village, his summoning of a surgeon to deal with emergencies. It is also the Captain who initiates the group's endeavors in self-education, its not entirely successful attempt to keep pace with the proliferation of scientific knowledge. The changes which, with the Captain's arrival, begin to sweep across Edward's and Charlotte's estate are carried by currents of innovation that course through the world at large; their seemingly timeless idyll is in fact in the grip of massive social and cultural change. Contrary to its reputation as a hermetic work impervious to contemporary reality, *Elective Affinities* is in fact a profoundly historical novel.

Even the novel's adjunct figures are bearers of emergent cultural forms. Mittler, whose name means precisely the 'mediation' he systematically fails to accomplish, has given up a traditional symbolic office for a kind of family counselling based on psychological and legal knowledge. The consequences of this change come to jarringly tragicomic expression in the baptism scene, in which the loquacious Mittler displaces the elderly minister. Instead of securing the child's position in life, his words literally cause the death of the frail clergyman, much as his disquisition on the psychological ramifications of the commandment forbidding adultery later precipitates Ottilie's end. Less dramatic, but no less penetrating are the changes wrought by the young assistant teacher, who sets into practice the ideas of the new pedagogical discipline that since Rousseau and Pestalozzi had firmly established itself in Germany. His supervisor prepares young ladies for *le monde*, the theatrical space of aristocratic life in which they present their learned repertoire of charms and talents; her prize student is the devilish and thoroughly aristocratic Luciane. The young teacher, however, is unconcerned with cultivating conventionally valued appearances. Rather, he seeks to convey an organic understanding that cleaves to the growth of his pupils' abilities and his attention is therefore always directed toward their inner life, the hidden movements of their joys and trepidations. His discipline is subtler, but not essentially different than the magnetic manipulations of the Lord's travelling companion. Indeed, in the juxtaposition of these two figures the novel discloses the darker side of what might be called the modern science (interpretive or experimental) of the soul.

It is significant that both the teaching assistant and the travelling companion focus their efforts on Ottilie. Much as the Captain embodies the emergent type of the civil servant whose status and influence are based on training and knowledge, Ottilie too exhibits a new shape of personal identity. She is the image of a new feminine ideal. The power of this ideal is revealed in the fact that she exerts a commanding presence that is independent of any worldly support. An orphan, she is without property or inherited social position and of course she possesses none of the flashy skills of her antipode Luciane. But she nevertheless elicits the devotion of several of the male characters and Luciane is astute in sensing that Ottilie threatens her own merely conventional preeminence. In the novel's aristocratic milieu, the quiet girl represents a radically new kind of beloved object. What the men admire and desire in Ottilie has little to do with beauty and nothing at all with the accoutrements of social position. To love Ottilie, as not only Edward but also the teacher and the architect do, is to love a mysterious inwardness, a depth of soul that seems to shine forth from her dark eyes.

As Ottilie's domesticity and her silent attention to the needs of others indicate, the paradigm of this inwardness is once again the figure of the mother. This links her to Werther's beloved Charlotte, whose eye color, of course, she shares. But there is a fundamental difference between the two figures: whereas the earlier novel presents Charlotte from the beginning as a complete and essentially unquestioned image, *Elective Affinities* lays bare the labor of construction which fashions Ottilie into a maternal ideal. Ottilie's mysterious subjectivity arises out of the discourse of others. Thus, her first sense of herself as an orphan whose task in life is only to serve derives from the words Charlotte speaks over her as she lies half conscious on her guardian's lap. Her education, as we have seen, is shaped by the young teacher, who sees his pedagogical goal as the production of "mothers." The architect, who emerges as the novel's major male figure when Edward and the Captain are absent, only radicalizes the procedure. His casting of Ottilie as the Virgin Mary in his ultimate *tableau vivant* and then his rendering of her in the angelic faces of his chapel paintings transform her maternal aura into the object of an aestheticized cult, the pattern for which Goethe probably drew from the Romantic painting of the time. Sitting in the finished chapel, Ottilie feels herself absorbed into the painted figures above her, as if her very being were that of an image. And indeed, in the tragic scene of the child's drowning she seems to freeze into a stone Niobe weeping over her lost child.

Of course, in addition to the teacher's pedagogy and the architect's art, it is Edward's desire which most decisively shapes Ottilie into a maternal image. This desire is relentlessly childish. His first wife was older than he, a sort of mother, it is remarked at one point, and his marriage to Charlotte represents the return to a youthful passion. That his love for Ottilie (like Werther's for Charlotte) derives from childhood phantasies is cunningly revealed in the motif of the plane trees which Edward, as a young boy, saves when his father orders them uprooted. They suggest a wish he preserves in secret, outside the sphere of paternal order. And the image that emerges as the object of that forbidden wish is the figure of the ideal mother, the Virgin who knows no other male than her son and whose love for the son is therefore total. This is the image that Ottilie comes ever more to embody in the course of the narrative. By significant accident her birthday falls on the very day Edward transplanted the plane trees, as if she were born out of his sequestered wish. Edward's remark that man is a true Narcissus thus betrays the innermost tendency of his love. The doubly indefinite girl (she is an orphan *and* she hovers at the threshold between childhood and sexual maturity) functions as the screen of his insistent projections; her devotion to him is the mirror in which he finds the image of his own full self, much as the child discovers its identity in the mother's loving gaze. A cluster of symmetries deployed across the narrative stresses this essentially narcissistic character of Edward's and Ottilie's relationship: the perfect fit of their music making, the parallelism of their headaches, the merging of their handwriting. Edward even composes letters to himself 'from' Ottilie, showing thereby that he loves her *as* the imaginary product of his own discourse.

Edward's urgent narcissism, however, does not dominate the entire plot as Werther's does in the earlier novel; rather, it participates in an overriding pattern of relationships that engages the other characters as well. Thus, with Ottilie's arrival at the estate and the completion of the experimental set, the four friends commence the chemical minuet suggested by the novel's title. An initial pairing binds Edward to the Captain and Charlotte to Ottilie, each pair absorbed in a distinct set of activities and each accorded a separate spatial domain within the novel's meticulously structured topography. But soon the bond of shared interests yields to the pull of desire and a new constellation emerges. Edward comes to love in his profoundly childish way the child-mother Ottilie, and Charlotte, measured and reasonable to a fault, discovers her affective affinity to the thoroughly dutiful Captain. The characters execute their dance with uncanny precision, each couple's steps the symmetrical complement of the other's. Indeed, perhaps the most striking feature of the novel is its extraordinary *formalization*; even the characters' names—the two *Otto*'s, Charl*otte*, and *Ott*ilie—are variations on a single anagrammatic nucleus. Not until Flaubert and James will the European novel know such rigorous composition, such deliberate artistry. Impassively constructed, *Elective Affinities* is an utterly singular formation within the landscape of European Romanticism.

This precision of aesthetic arrangement, this algebraic coolness, lends the novel its psychological complexity and acumen. Multiply determined by a network of echoes and correspondences stretching across the entire text, the characters' every action resonates with a significance of which they are thoroughly unaware. Each occasion is an anniversary recalling earlier events and even the different objects which in succession occupy the narrative focus—the fateful rowboat, for instance, or Ottilie's birthday chest—are taken up in a play of reiteration and variation. An additional dimension of meaning is achieved through the dense fabric of allusions which Goethe has woven into the narrative and which heightens the reader's impression that the story conforms to a choreography far more powerful than the characters' conscious resolve. Neither enlightened sophistication in matters of the heart nor adherence to moral principles is capable of averting the disaster toward which the narrative relentlessly drifts. Thus, beneath the placid surface of modern love Goethe's novelistic experiment discloses an unconscious, archaic scene. Where human misfortune follows from the implacable workings of a law inscribed in the very nature of things, the Greeks identified something they thought of as necessity or fate, and it is this power which haunts the world of *Elective Affinities*. The point was well understood by one of the work's first and most insightful readers, the philosopher K. W. F. Solger, who characterized the novel in a penetrating review as a modern counterpart to Attic tragedy. Perhaps this aspect of the novel most compels our attention. In a world that is thoroughly contemporary, a world in which, for example, nature has been rendered an object of technical and aesthetic mastery and social life has been entirely privatized, *Elective Affinities* rediscovers tragic necessity. Modernity, in the unique definition this novel gives the term, is the recrudescence of myth in the present.

Goethe once remarked that *Elective Affinities* was his "best book"; it may also be his saddest. Like the mystery play *Pandora* (see vol. 8 of this series), which originated during the same period, it attests to what the poet himself called a sense of "infinite loss." Indeed, across the novel's anagrammatic play of crossed love a single word is reiterated: *tot* (dead), and this word is inflected in the name and destiny of that love's issue, the infant Otto. No reader can escape the feeling that death everywhere hovers at the edges of the novelistic world. The mythical resonances make this clear. Mittler, the maladroit mediator, is a Hermes figure, an emissary to the underworld, and the plane trees, in which Edward sees the blossoming of his desire, stand according to archaic tradition at the entrance to Hades. Even the story of successful love and rebirth told by the English lord only adds to the catalogue of loss. As Charlotte recognizes, the novella inverts the truth: the heroine, who was the Captain's youthful beloved, in fact did not survive her suicidal plunge. The characters themselves fervently misapprehend their tragic entanglement, deny the fateful logic of their desire. This inability to acknowledge their own complicity reaches its extreme when Edward and the Captain attempt to make sense of the child's horrible drowning, interpreting it as a "sacrifice" which would remove the last obstacle to their wishes. Only Ottilie, in the knowledge that no meaning can supplement the child's loss, refuses to accept the sacrificial interpretation. In the end, Ottilie's refusal—the novel's single transcendent ethical gesture—assumes the form of utter passivity, a radical abstention that removes her from the realm of speech and life. The novel itself is faithful to Ottilie's tragic insight. It abjures the sort of aesthetic euphemism vis-à-vis loss which, for instance, Charlotte's renovation of the churchyard and the architect's decoration of the chapel exemplify. The fairy-tale surmise of the novel's last sentence sadly evokes a happy ending which will never happen. The incomparable beauty of *Elective Affinities*—and perhaps this is beauty's modern form—is deeply touched by mourning.

The text which completes this volume, the *Novella*, was first published in 1828 in the fifteenth volume of Goethe's authenticated edition of his collected works, the so-called *Ausgabe letzter Hand*. Though it reaches back to an artistic conception formed as early as 1797, the narrative is in fact the product of a late summer's and autumn's work in 1826. It is the product, then, of a near-octogenarian and it exhibits the characteristic marks of the old Goethe's style (*Altersstil*). These are: on the one hand, a remarkable instinct for what may be called the abstractive detail, the object or gesture which seems to encapsulate an entire thematic complex; and, on the other hand, an extraordinarily self-conscious formal virtuosity, an unrivalled capacity to cite, combine and transform the multiple languages of literary tradition. This latter feature is manifest in the work's title. Goethe rejected a suggestion by Eckermann, the diligent recorder of his conversations, to call the work *A Novella* because the indefinite article would suggest the text was only one instance among many rather than a reflection on the form itself. In the same conversation, Goethe formulated a generic definition of the novella as a short prose narrative organized around a single "unheard-of event" (*unerhörte Begebenheit*). This formulation, which has been the source of tangled critical debates, merely accentuates what had been the salient feature of the genre since its beginnings with Boccaccio and Cervantes. As its name indicates, the novella had always been directed toward the new, that is: the case (*casus*) without precedent which is therefore not yet subsumed by law or canonical narrative; the "unheard-of" case. The stress on the question of form in the title signals, then, that what stands to issue in this text is the question of the novella form itself:

How can the new be told? How can art become the site where the new emerges? The narrative answers that this is possible when art succeeds in bringing the old into the present, maintaining and transforming it simultaneously.

It is revealing that the first conception of the work took shape in the late 1790's. This was the time when virtually all of German intelligentsia was laboring to come to terms with that radically unheard-of event, the French Revolution. The same period witnessed a revival of the novella genre, which was to become one of the principal forms of the Romantics and which maintained its prestige into the twentieth century. Goethe himself contributed immensely to the genre's revival with his *Conversations of German Refugees* (1795), a work that directly addresses the political turmoil of the revolutionary period (see vol. 10 of this series). Of course, the original conception foresaw an epic poem written in hexameters in the manner of *Hermann and Dorothea* (1797), another of Goethe's attempts to master aesthetically the historical turbulence of the time (see vol. 8 of this series). At the advice of Schiller and Wilhelm von Humboldt, however, he abandoned the project on the grounds that the dynamics of the story were incompatible with the epic's slow narrative pace. Nevertheless, when the story (which in the first sketches carried the title *The Hunt*) thirty years later found adequate formal expression as a novella, the revolutionary theme remained vital. A reference in the second paragraph ("The Prince's father had lived to see the time. . .") locates the novella's action a generation after the Revolution. Likewise, the uncle's traumatic memory of the great urban fire he experienced years before can be read as alluding to the social and political virulence of the 90's. The outbreak of fire unleashing the novella's unheard-of event signifies, then, a second historical explosion of the new, the return of revolutionary ferment. And the narration, in its slightly delayed turn to a peaceful end, suggests that the way to manage this emergence of the new and to integrate it productively into the flow of time is through *humane authority*. This principle is embodied in the Prince, whose rule is grounded in tradition, but whose primary governmental concern is for the common wealth and welfare of his subjects. Goethe's response to the French Revolution—and we must recall here his position in the Grand Duchy of Saxe-Weimar—was a conciliatory conservatism.

The miraculous turn of the novella's conclusion adds an interesting twist to this pliant conservatism. It indicates that the source from which authority draws the paradigm of humane conciliation is art. Confronted with the elemental forces of change which the fire has unleashed—the natural energy (however debilitated by captivity) of the tiger and lion— the Prince rejects the gesture of violence, the intransigent and ill-motivated reaction of Honario, whose name refers to the traditional aristocratic code of martial honor. Instead, he listens to—and hears and understands—the voice of art as represented in the family of the animal keepers. These three figures—father, mother and youthful son—enter the novella's aristocratic milieu as if from a world long lost. At this point the narrative boldly modulates its tone: the poised and measured prose of the preparatory sections yields to a foreign speech across which the emergence of poetry itself is unfolded. First we hear, albeit through the filter of translation, the "natural language" of maternal lament. Next follows the forcefully prophetic speech of the father, richly interwoven with quotations from the Old Testament. The sequence culminates in the poetry of the child, a lyrical movement in perpetual transformation which combines utter simplicity of expression with consummate artistry. The site where the final sequence occurs is the ancient castle ruin, where the antagonism of elemental, natural force and civilization is visibly enacted. Guided by the spirit of Daniel which his song calls to life, the child enters this impromptu lion's den and with the magic flute of his art tames (not vanquishes) the glorious and terrifying beast. The narrative achieves its final miraculous reconciliation, in other words, by drawing into the present the primordial source of the Occidental literary, ethical and religious traditions. It is through this simultaneous preservation and transformation of tradition that the *Novella* renders—or brings about—its unheard-of event.

D. E. W.